BEING NETTA WILDE

HAZEL WARD

1

IT SHOULD HAVE BEEN A GOOD DAY

It was her birthday. Fifty today. It should have been a good day. Liza and Will were staying for the weekend. The first time in ages. She would finish early, make a nice dinner and try to connect with them like normal mothers did.

She bought a huge meringue for dessert, and cakes for the whole office on the way in. There were cards and some presents on her desk — bath oils and creams, chocolates, and a scarf. They weren't really to her taste but it was a nice thought. She knew her colleagues wouldn't have made the effort for the other managers. She was the popular one. And why not? She worked hard enough for it.

No one really knew how difficult it was for her to be Annette Grey, Head of Regulation at Mason and Partners, Property and Construction Consultants. No one understood just how much energy she expelled being the outgoing, assured person she presented to them every day, without fail.

It had been almost two years since the divorce. Since her family discarded her. Two years of soul searching and always finding herself at fault. Two years of humiliating atonement, begging for scraps of forgiveness that never quite came. Not a day passed when she didn't feel herself clinging on, at the edge of a deep, dark hole. A vortex of self-doubt and loathing. Not one day. No. No one knew the effort it took for her to just leave the flat some mornings. It was completely invisible to her colleagues, and that was how she preferred it. But today was her birthday. She felt brighter. Not exactly happy but optimistic. It was going to be a good day.

Actually, it was a good day. Until Malcolm Jefferson called her into his office to tell her they were having a management restructure and she was going to be made redundant. Once again, she was obsolete. Surplus to requirements.

'I shouldn't really be telling you this right now, and I must ask you to keep it to yourself. You know we're supposed to go through the appropriate procedures, but I wanted you to know as soon as possible, Annette. I'm sorry it had to be today. I was going to wait until next week but head office has brought the start of the consultation process forward to Monday. I had no choice.'

She was felled. Speechless. She watched his mouth moving up and down, not quite taking in what he was saying, and unsure how to respond. What were the right words? She'd started her department from scratch and built it into one of the best teams in the organisation and now they were cutting her out and giving it to someone else, in another part of the country, to manage.

She didn't know how she'd got through the hours until home time. They were endless. Her focus was all over the place. She couldn't concentrate on anything and she couldn't face anyone. When her team suggested taking her for a lunchtime birthday drink, she made an excuse about having to finish a report so she could leave early to prepare for the children's visit. But she was still there when they called to her to have a great weekend as they left. She waited until she was sure they'd all gone, then she left too.

Unsurprisingly, the evening was a disaster. On the way out of the office, she saw Jefferson making a beeline for her and was so intent on avoiding him that she caught the meringue in the revolving doors, squashing it beyond recognition. She made steak and mushroom pie, the children's old favourite but, in typical teenage fashion, no one had thought to tell her they'd become vegetarians. Liza had been so vocal about the poor cows that she felt too guilty to eat it herself. The pie was binned. They ate potatoes, carrots and peas, followed by meringue snow.

The news about her job was too raw for her to share so she internalised it, as she always did. The children couldn't see her anguish. Only the distance placed between them. She tried to show them how happy she was to have them there, she really did, but it was as if all her joy had been extinguished. There was a tension in her demeanour that was impossible to shake loose from and they felt it. She could see her agitation transferring over to them.

On Saturday morning, she caught glimpses of them muttering secretively to each other and constantly messaging. Their father probably. Mum's off on one again, no doubt.

'Shall we go out for lunch? We can get you some proper veggie food.' She wanted it to sound light-hearted but, as usual, it just sounded as if she was trying too hard. She couldn't bear the thought of another awkward meal with nothing to break the silence but the occasional sounds of the neighbours arguing or, worse still, doing happy stuff.

'There's a nice Mexican restaurant in the high street. Do you still like Mexican?'

She saw the look they gave each other.

Will gulped. He always did that when he was embarrassed. 'Actually Mum, we're going to be heading back home. Grandma and Grandpa have come up to see us before they go away. They're going to Portugal for the summer. Sorry.'

'No, it's fine. Honestly. Absolutely fine. I'll drive you back.' She attempted a casual smile but coming as it did, through gritted teeth, it looked practically menacing.

'Erm, no it's all right. Dad's already on his way. He won't be long.'

They'd hardly had time to get their things together before Colin was buzzing to come up. He could have waited in the car and just messaged them, but no. He had to come up, didn't he? He had to come up and register his self-satisfaction with her. Just to underscore the fact that she was, as always, a waste of space.

She stayed in the lounge while Liza went to meet him at the door. They'd already said their goodbyes, so they could have just gone straight out, but he insisted on coming in, gloating and full of faux concern. 'Sorry, but you know what my parents are like. I didn't even know they were going away but, I gather Mum's been nagging Dad for ages. I think he just gave in and booked something. And then they showed up demanding to see the kids before they went off.'

His eyes moved skywards in a ridiculously overplayed gesture. All that was missing was an exaggerated comedy wink and elbow nudge. The children looked embarrassed for him. They bundled him down the hall and out of the flat, leaving her alone again.

She stood behind the front door for a while, listening to

their laughter and chatter fading away. When it was gone, she sank into a chair on the balcony and watched the families and dog walkers in the park that her flat overlooked. She was a useless mother but at least she'd been good at her job. A high earner who could provide for her family financially. Or so she'd thought. Who was going to support them now? Certainly not their father. Colin, the deluded artist who'd sold nothing in the last twelve years.

She had to recover from this and get a grip. She must stop wallowing in self-pity and think about getting another job. But it was no good. She was stuck in a mire of misery that she couldn't drag herself out of. She'd devoted nearly half of her life to Mason and Partners. She'd given them everything, and it meant nothing. Life as she knew it, was over.

If the weekend was wretched, Monday was even worse. Jefferson asked if they could 'check in' to see how she was coping with the news. She loathed his clumsy empathy — management by numbers. It made her even more irritated, if that were possible.

'I'm fine Malcolm. I don't take it personally.' She was aware that she was snapping like a little attack dog nipping at his well-heeled ankles.

'I know. You've always been very strong Annette. My best —'

'I just don't understand. Why me?'

He couldn't meet her eyes and was, instead, looking over her left shoulder. He seemed to be searching for something to say but all he could manage was an acknowledgement that it was unfair.

'I'm sorry. The company needs to lose some of its higher paid management tier.'

'And so you chose me.'

'It was out of my hands. There are others, across the other regions,' he said. As if that were any kind of consolation.

Then, the thing that she'd been dreading happening, happened. She heard herself whimpering. Digging into her reserves, she made it stop but there was worse to come. She became aware that her hands were trembling and then, her whole body shook. This time, there was nothing she could do to make it go away. She cried out as a sudden, sharp pain tore through her chest sending Jefferson running into the main office in a blind panic yelling for someone — anyone — to help.

The first aider was called, then 999. She was covered in a blanket like some frail pensioner and wheeled through the office to a waiting ambulance. She couldn't have been any more mortified.

It was just a reaction to stress apparently. She was perfectly healthy otherwise. The doctor suggested she took a few days off to recover. She refused. She needed to be at work now more than ever. Jefferson disagreed. He put her on sick leave, for the sake of her well-being, and wouldn't be swayed. She needed a bit of time to think things through, he told her. A bit of 'me-time'.

She only went back into the office for her redundancy consultation interviews. She wasn't there when Jefferson announced the changes to her department, after which 'me-time' was extended to three months of gardening leave.

She wouldn't be there for her official leaving day. She

didn't want to be. The thought of having to attend a farewell party and pretend to be cheery would have sent her body back into stressful spasms. She crept back in to the office under cover of darkness one evening to empty her desk and pick up her things. She left her pass and equipment with the security guard and stole away from Mason and Partners, not daring to look back.

2

'ME-TIME' AND THE TAMPON GIRL

She did her best to fill the void that was 'me-time'. Yet another misunderstanding on Malcolm Jefferson's part. The last person she needed to spend time with was herself.

Neither did she want to spend it with her family. The children hadn't contacted her since that dreadful weekend and, for once, she was grateful for it. Colin had emailed her though, to say they'd been invited to spend a few weeks in Portugal with his parents. Naturally, they needed the money for flights and extra spends. She dutifully transferred the requested amount into his account. Just as she always did, secretly glad of the respite it would buy her.

She ignored calls from her parents and instead sent them messages that things were manic and she'd be in touch soon. Anything to get out of speaking to them because, if she did that, she'd have to tell them that she had no job. And then, she'd have to field questions about what she was going to do to change that. So, she rewrote her CV, sent out job applications, tidied and re-tidied the flat, and spent hours on the balcony gazing at the park, until the unbearableness of her isolation drove her out to shop for things that she had no intention of buying. Whatever she did, nothing could fill the deficit in her life that she usually filled with work.

After two weeks, her sanity was saved by an old colleague who'd retired a couple of years back. They weren't close. She'd mastered the art of professional friendliness but she'd long ago forgotten how to be good at proper relationships. Paula was an expert though. She'd managed HR at Masons so perhaps it came with the territory. Since retirement, she'd kept in touch with Annette on and off. The off being more down to Annette than Paula.

Apparently, she'd heard the news through the grapevine and suggested catching up over coffee. Nowadays, she volunteered at a foodbank and asked Annette to meet her there first. It was at a church on an estate Annette normally avoided if she could. It was a run-down kind of place. Not where you generally went to for socialising. But Paula had been insistent and Annette was desperate for any kind of occupation. Besides, since Paula already knew her terrible secret, there was no need for pretence which might do her some good.

She parked on the road outside the church and waited for fifteen minutes before texting Paula to announce her arrival. Although she felt quite safe, she was reluctant to leave the car. She was a fish out of water and she knew, all too well, what happened to fishes out of water. They floundered. She did not want to flounder. A reply came back:

'Sorry, busy. Come round to the hall — behind church'.

Her body sank down into the seat. She closed her eyes and sighed. Going inside hadn't been in the plan. She'd hoped for a quick hello in the car, followed by a friendly chat in a nice, guilt-free café. Getting up close and personal to charity was something to be avoided. It made her uneasy. Well, face-to-face charity anyway. She did plenty of giving through the safe anonymity of direct debit. She could even manage donating a bag of old clothes, but seeing real people in difficult circumstances flustered her. She imagined herself through their eyes, a middle class, condescending do-gooder, and it brought her out in a cold sweat. So, although she knew it was wrong, she avoided it wherever possible. But there was no way around it this time. She had to button herself up, go in and hope to hell that she didn't flounder.

The church was old. Victorian Gothic. Once it had probably nestled quite nicely among back-to-back and terraced houses of the same vintage but they'd long been replaced by tower blocks and small squat boxes which themselves were ripe for regeneration. The busy road had left its mark on the church's red brick walls which were now sooty brown, and the graveyard was littered with fast-food cartons and empty drink cans and bottles.

She followed the path around the side of the church to a small car park at the back. At the far end was a more modern, square building. Its wide windows were decorated with brightly painted pictures of smiley faced characters. Placed at angles around the paintings were welcome notices in five or six different languages, none of which she knew. At least, she guessed they were welcome notices.

The entrance was through a set of double doors. On one of them was a notice:

FOODBANK
    Open Tuesday and Friday
    11.00 am – 3.00 pm.

                    .   .   .

She looked at her watch. Another thirty minutes until closing time.

As soon as she stepped through the entrance, she heard raised voices. Ahead of her was another set of doors, this one propped wide open, presumably to allow a steady flow through to the main hall. But right now the space was blocked by four people standing slap bang in the middle of it. One of them was shouting at the others. Annette had walked straight into an argument.

She hesitated to hastily replan her approach. It was impossible to get past them without finding herself in the thick of it, but backing away might be seen as insensitive or, if nothing else, would draw attention to her. On the other side of the quartet a small crowd had gathered. She wasn't sure if they were trying to leave too, or were just interested. Either way, none of them seemed to be going anywhere.

In the centre of the row was a girl, who was shouting: 'I just want some fucking tampons.'

She was about Will's age, maybe a little older, and was small with short black hair that accentuated her elfin features. Her face was sharp, lacking any form of softness. Everything about her — cheekbones, elbows, knees — seemed to jut out at acute angles. She wore a thin T-shirt and tight jeans which emphasised the narrowness of her hips and the meagreness of her legs. Worse, they left no hiding place for the crimson stain in her crotch.

'You need a voucher,' one of the volunteers said.

'I don't have time to get a fucking voucher. I just need tampons. That's all.'

A stout, pleasant-looking woman in her mid-sixties emerged from the crowd. It was Paula. Softer around the edges and with hair whiter than Annette remembered, but it was still Paula. She held a small packet out to the girl. 'Here. The toilet's over there.'

The girl snatched the parcel and made for the toilet, pushing past Annette and knocking her sideways. As she passed, the girl glowered at Annette. Her eyes were blood-shot and her face was streaked with mascara, but there was a 'fuck you' defiance in her contemptuous glare that completely shook Annette. Her composure was crumbling. It was too much. She had to get out.

She hovered in the car park watching the coming and going of people through the double doors. Some glanced shiftily in her direction as they passed. She must look odd, she supposed, standing here in her expensive clothes, for no obvious reason. This is where smokers had the edge. Able to look busy doing nothing and still remain inconspicuous and unthreatening.

One of the double doors swung open. The tampon girl emerged. She'd cleaned her face up and was wearing a long cardigan that came down to her thighs. It was much too large for her but, fastened up, it covered the tell-tale stain. Her hands seemed tiny poking through the baggy sleeves which were rolled back several times, making it look as if she had a large ring doughnut dangling above each of her bony wrists. Annette was sure it was the cardie Paula had been wearing.

Maybe it was the sight of her in that oversized thing, her face, set like an angry child still raw from the fight. She didn't know, but something made Annette reach in to her purse and pull out twenty pounds.

'Please. Have this.'

The girl shook her head. 'Nah, you're all right.'

'But I saw you inside-'

'I said no!'

She slapped Annette's arm away, and stormed off. The blow, though only light, loosened Annette's grip and the money fell from her hand and floated to the ground. The wind carried it a few feet away, tripping over puddles from the morning showers. She stepped on the soggy note, scooped it up and returned it to her purse. There were several bystanders observing her now.

'I'll have it if she don't want it,' someone said, and the others laughed. She'd become a side show. She was ashamed and angry with herself and she wished to God that Paula would get a move on.

'We get them sometimes,' Paula explained over coffee. 'It's hard to say no but, if you let everyone off the voucher, we'd have nothing left to give the legitimate ones.'

'But you gave her some anyway,' said Annette.

'Well, you saw the state she was in. I gave her what I could. Personal hygiene donations are a bit hit and miss.'

'I don't know how you can do it Paula. It must be … difficult.'

'It can be hard sometimes, but it's worse for the people who have to use it. Anyway, it's good for me. It makes me feel relevant somehow. That's why I asked you to meet me here. I thought you might be missing a bit of relevance in your life.'

Annette couldn't think of a way to reply to that without sounding pathetic so she examined the inside of her coffee cup.

'I've been there too, you know. Come and help. You'll see,' said Paula.

'I couldn't. I'm not good in those situations. I'm not like you, I don't have what it takes.'

'Annette, you're one of the most considerate people I know. You'd be absolutely fine.'

'But I'm not though.'

Paula's brow folded. Her head moved a fraction from side to side, more twitch than shake. Enough for Annette to see her protestations were being dismissed.

'The Annette I remember was someone who went out of her way to help people.'

Annette returned her gaze to the coffee cup. Usually she kept all these personal doubts inside but something had happened in these last few weeks to dislodge them from that secret space in which they were compacted. Now, they were swimming around inside her, anchorless.

'It's easy to do that from the safety of a nice comfortable office, with people you've known for years. People who are like you.'

'You're being too hard on yourself,' said Paula.

'No, I'm not. I'm being honest. That person you knew was a professional manager. That's all. I was kind because I needed to be to get things done. Outside of work, I don't interact well with others. Those people are alien to me. I can't connect with them. I don't mean to sound snobbish about it. I mean, I certainly don't look down on them. Far from it. If anything, I feel inferior in their presence. I just don't think I could cope with all that judgement.'

'They're just people like you and me. No one's going to judge you. Frankly, they don't have time for it.'

It only that were true. She'd seen the look on that girl's face. And those people laughing at her. What were they doing if they weren't judging her?

'I'm sorry Paula. I can't.'

'You're being made redundant,' said Paula. 'It's natural to have doubts about yourself. That sort of thing knocks you sideways. When I retired, I thought I'd be fine but I wasn't. Within weeks I was desperate for some purpose. I was completely down in the dumps until my neighbour suggested helping out at the foodbank where he volunteered. I won't deny it was hard to adjust to it when I first started helping out but they were very patient with me. Don't imagine it's all doom and gloom. All them and us. Whatever you think a foodbank is, I can guarantee you'll be wrong. It's a real community, and I don't just mean the volunteer team. Think about it. It would give you something to lift you out of yourself until you get another job.'

Back home, she felt a pressing need to speak to her children. She rang Liza, 'How are you darling?'

'All right. What's wrong?' said Liza.

'Nothing. I just wanted to check in. See how you are.'

Check in? For God's sake, had she turned into Jefferson? Were things that bad?

'I'm okay. Are you? You sound a bit funny.'

'I'm fine. I just felt like a chat.'

'Oh! My friends are here. They're helping me pack. We're flying out tomorrow. Remember? Another time, yeah?'

'Yes, sorry. I didn't mean to bother you. I'll try Will.'

She heard the sound of giggling as Liza called out to Will to ask if he was available for a check-in, and cringed.

'He's just on his way out for a run,' she said, still giggling. 'He'll call later.'

And then Liza was gone. Will wouldn't call and she knew it. They never did. Only when they wanted something.

. . .

She spent the next week doing her best to block out the foodbank by keeping busy. Whatever she did, she couldn't get it out of her head. She tried to think about finding work but lacked her usual sense of urgency. She drafted emails that remained unsent, agreed appointments with agencies then couldn't make herself go and cancelled. Any self-confidence she had was waning. She was unravelling and for once she couldn't stop it. She needed something.

Paula was right, she needed to feel relevant again. She'd felt useful when the children were small and she was the centre of their world, before everything went wrong. Even when they rejected her, in keeping them afloat materially, she had something to anchor her. And without fail, there'd always been her job. That had been a constant.

None of these were any good to her now. She craved a new purpose. But a foodbank? Was that really the answer? Was it really something she could cope with right now? And that girl. What if there were more like her? Besides, she hadn't been entirely honest with Paula about her reasons for saying no. In truth she hadn't been entirely honest with herself. Yes, she'd been worried about those people judging her but there were others who were far harsher critics, herself included. She would be the one dissecting her behaviour, poring over each and every reaction to the slightest thing and looking for missteps to beat herself up with. Equally though, she would judge herself as badly for not doing it. She was her own worst enemy. Well, perhaps not the worst. She could always rely on her family to bring her down further. Colin especially. What would he say? She had a pretty good idea that he wouldn't be congratulating her on finding some relevance. Still, he'd be in Portugal for another couple of weeks. So, if she decided to give it a go, he'd be none the wiser.

That was it then. She'd made the decision, without actually making the decision. She picked up the phone and called Paula. Just for a few weeks. Until her gardening leave ran out. If she could stand it that long.

3

A LOVELY MAN

This time she drove around the back of the church to park. As before, she was reluctant to get out of the car. It had all happened so quickly that now she was beginning to regret her decision. The call to Paula had only been yesterday and she'd expected her to say think it over for a few days, or come next week.

Instead she said: 'That's great, come along tomorrow at ten and we'll get you started.'

So, here Annette was, sitting in her nice comfortable car on a drizzly Friday morning and waiting for the courage to miraculously sweep her up and transport her through those double doors. The trouble was it didn't want to come. She kept thinking about the last time she'd been here. That girl and those people laughing at her in the car park. What was she doing here?

She'd all but made up her mind to go home when she saw Paula striding purposefully towards her. Reluctantly, she dragged herself out to meet her.

'You're here, well done. Shall we go inside and meet

your new co-workers? We're just getting everything ready to open.'

Co-workers. Paula always did know how to say the right thing. Annette followed as she took her around the room and introduced her to a blur of faces, many of whom she forgot as soon as she moved on to the next one.

An hour later, the interior doors were propped open and the front unlocked. A queue had already formed outside.

'These are the ones who've run out of food. They probably haven't had breakfast yet,' said Neil.

She'd been assigned to him to learn the ropes. Before opening, he'd explained the procedures and walked her up and down the shelves of stock to show her what went where.

They spent the morning bagging up parcels and taking them to the meeters and greeters who sat with the clients. This was how they eased new volunteers in, she guessed. They got them to do the straightforward stuff so they didn't offend anybody with their self-conscious, trying-too-hard-to-be-relaxed, affectations. She would have happily done that all day. Out of harm's way with minimal contact with the clientele, some of whom made her feel distinctly on edge.

Every now and then the sound of raised voices breached the relative safety of the back of the room where the stock was kept. Much as she tried to appear unaffected by it, she couldn't stop herself from slyly checking the direction of its source. Neil seemed quite oblivious to it. He just carried on talking, pointing out this and that, with no hint of concern.

Sadly, after a few hours, Neil said it was time for her to observe him meeting and greeting. If delivering the parcels to the greeting area had been daunting, it was nothing compared to the prospect of actually speaking to people. As soon as that thought entered her head, she could tell her face had frozen rigid. It was as if a juggernaut was heading towards her and all she could do was widen her eyes and open her mouth to let out a silent scream.

Undoubtedly sensing her panic, Neil gave her a warm smile. 'Don't worry. You won't need to say anything. I'll do the talking.'

'Sorry. Yes, of course. How silly of me,' she said, anxious not to sound too relieved.

She sat at his side as he met customers face to face. He listened to their stories, helped them decide what groceries they needed most and gave advice on other support agencies. As she observed him and the other helpers, she realised very quickly that her preconception of what a volunteer was had been way out. They were not, as she'd assumed, mostly retired like Paula. They were people of all ages and situations.

Of all of them, the one person she could least have imagined she would find there was Neil. He was a good-looking man. No older than late thirties, slim with a faded golden tan and what looked to be a permanent stubble. She could tell by the trace of dark hair on his shaved head that he was beginning to recede. His toned, muscular arms suggested a lot of time spent at the gym. Although he didn't say it outright, his conversation with clients led her to believe he was unemployed. He had tattoos, lots of them, covering his arms. It had been a long time since she'd been in the company of anyone with tattoos, except for Janice at work who got herself a small rose on the back of her shoulder to mark her fortieth birthday. That was nothing compared to this.

If his appearance suggested someone who thought a lot of himself, his manner indicated the opposite. He was incredibly polite and respectful but not in a superficial way. It was a natural and easy-going kindness that didn't overstep the mark. He was what her mother would call a lovely man. People relaxed around him, in contrast to herself. She could see them stiffening as soon as they laid eyes on her. Neil seemed to know instinctively how to behave around them so that somehow, even if they were just scraping by, his clients left with their dignity intact, walking taller and feeling more human. She marvelled at how he managed to do that with so little effort.

Their first client was Kayley, a single mum with two small children and an older one at school. 'This one should be there an all but he's a bit poorly. Aren't yer, bab?' She ruffled the hair of a sickly looking boy with a runny nose. He was so much smaller than Annette's children were at that age. He didn't look old enough to be at school.

'He gets free dinners so I could do with him being there really but they sent him home yesterday. So, Mum's got to magic up some dinner from somewhere else, hasn't she?' She pulled him up on her lap and wiped his nose then turned to Neil. 'I've got two quid to last me until next Tuesday so if you've got any idea how to stretch this parcel out, go for it.'

'Pasta and rice are good for filling them up,' he said. 'They'll make your tinned fish and meat go further too. So will lentils. The chickpeas are a good swap if you run out of meat or fish. We don't have any fresh meat but if you can get some cheap sausages, you can chop them up or roll the sausage meat into meatballs. When we're done, go over to the café and get a sandwich and a drink. That'll keep him happy for a bit.' He scribbled something on a piece of paper. 'Give them this Kayley. It'll get you an extra bag of cakes for the kids. They're all homemade by us and off the record, so they don't come off your voucher.'

'Thanks Neil. You're a sweetheart,' she said, her face cracking into a broad grin. She turned to Annette. 'You checking he's doing it properly, are yer?'

The heat shot through Annette's cheeks. She imagined her face, a bright red beacon. 'Oh no. Actually, he's training me up.'

'Oh, right.' Kayley looked surprised, 'Well, you can't go wrong learning from him. He's one of the best.'

Neil gave the same note to the next clients, Andy and Faye, a gaunt couple who looked as if they hadn't had a decent meal in months. Annette wondered if they'd been feeding their children over themselves. She wanted to ask Neil what he thought, but it didn't feel right. He seemed to know them quite well. After they'd gone, he explained that their eldest daughter attended the school his partner taught at.

Halfway through the day, someone brought them a coffee and biscuit. The idea of eating the biscuit made her feel ridiculously guilty so she ended up giving it to a little girl who'd come in with her dad. She sipped on her drink and thought about the day she'd come to meet Paula and how she'd been afraid of floundering if she stepped inside this building. The morning had been difficult but not as hard as she'd expected it to be. Meeting Andy, Faye and Kayley had been the lowest points for her. She'd felt embarrassed to be witness to their poverty, as if she was somehow prying. Both times she'd nearly crumbled but had managed to hold it together. But it was the plight of an elderly man called Bert that did for her. His wife had recently died and his benefits had somehow gone astray while under review. With no savings to speak of, Bert had eaten everything left in his cupboards. Too ashamed to ask for help, he was existing on bread and a bit of fish paste rather than default on his bills, until his neighbour noticed something was wrong. She gave him a hot meal and helped him to get his benefits sorted.

He was so distressed he could hardly speak and his neighbour had to do the talking for him. 'They said they'd get it sorted but you know what they're like at those places. In one ear and out the other. Anyway, he's got this voucher now…' Her voice trailed off as she watched Bert's head drop. 'Doesn't think he should be 'ere. I keep telling him it's not his fault but, yer know.'

She took his hand. 'You're a daft old sod Bert. It's not your fault. You shouldn't have to be 'ere but you've got just as much right as all these others. What would Marie say if she knew you'd been starving yourself?' She turned to Neil and Annette and half-whispered: 'That's his late wife.'

To open him up, Neil coaxed Bert into a conversation about football. It helped that they were both Birmingham City fans. Annette sat quietly in her chair, afraid to look too closely for fear of letting go of her emotions and equally afraid to look away in case she appeared uncaring. Floundering. She was floundering. She'd congratulated herself too early. Disgusted with her unjustified sensitivity, she swallowed down the lump in her throat with such force that it came out as a loud gulp.

Neil glanced in her direction. 'Annette, do you mind organising some tea?' he said, with no hint of judgement in his voice.

'Yes, no problem. How do you like your tea, Bert?' The action of rising from the chair loosened the pressure and by the time she returned she had a grip on herself again.

Of course, they weren't all like Bert. Many customers seemed to take it in their stride. Some hung around for a chat with people they knew. Some sat happily in the café after they collected their parcels while their children played in the corner play area. Unfortunately, there were others who were not quite so agreeable. One or two were quite brusque. Some just met her polite smile with a cold, hard stare and some were downright rude and aggressive. For the most part though, she was surprised to discover a knitted-together community that she really hadn't expected to be there. She was even surprised to find that it hadn't been as horrible as she'd thought it would be. Enjoyable would be too much of a stretch but grounding, yes. Definitely grounding.

Three o'clock came around unbelievably quickly. The doors were locked and everyone gathered in the makeshift café that they'd directed people to earlier. Mostly it served up drinks and biscuits, sandwiches and homemade cakes, free of charge. By the end of the day, everything had been given away.

As they sat and chatted, each of the volunteers pulled out packed lunches. Annette hadn't eaten since breakfast and she hadn't brought anything with her. Foolishly, she'd assumed she'd be able to buy something from somewhere.

'I forgot to tell you to bring something to eat, didn't I?' said Paula. 'Here. You can share mine. I always make too much.'

'Oh no, really. I'm not hungry.' She'd been sitting quietly at the edge of the group, hoping no one had noticed, but her stomach was already whining.

'Nonsense. Here.' Paula offered her a sandwich.

'Try one of these mini quiches, Annette,' said Neil, 'I'm testing out different fillings. Chris is sick of them, so I thought I'd get a few willing tasters here. These are Mediterranean veg.' He placed a big plastic tub on the table.

She bit into one of the quiches. The pastry was soft, crumbly and buttery. The filling creamy and light. 'It's delicious.'

The others helped themselves and emptied the container.

'I'm getting mixed herbs, tomato, red peppers and a hint of feta,' said George, a retired postman who was also Paula's neighbour. 'Seriously mate, it's very good. If Chris is fed up with them, keep bringing them in. I'll help you to get rid of them.'

'Do you enjoy cooking?' she asked Neil.

'Yeah, I love it. It gives me a real buzz. It's my therapy. That, and this place.'

'What did you think? Honestly,' said Paula as they walked to their cars.

'It was challenging,' said Annette.

'Is that it? Honestly?'

'Honestly, it was challenging, and terrifying and, at times, hard to get through.'

'Well, I suppose I asked for honesty, didn't I? Will you come again?' said Paula.

'Does it get any easier? Will I ever get used to it?' said Annette.

'No and no. But it's better than sitting at home feeling sorry for yourself.'

She was right. It certainly put a fresh perspective on Annette's personal difficulties and actually, some of the day had been quite pleasant. Besides, she had three months of gardening leave to use up before she could get another job. Three months of excruciatingly tedious 'me time'.

'I'll give it a couple of weeks. I'll see you on Tuesday,' she said.

'Good for you. Can I make a suggestion for the next time? Perhaps leave the office clothes behind and wear something a little less formal. It makes some of our clients rather nervous.'

Paula's advice had caused her some consternation but did explain the unease she seemed to instil in some of the clients. Apparently, she looked like an official. Not the best look when you're mixing with people who generally feel they've had a rough deal from officialdom.

She spent the weekend before her second visit deliberating over her clothes. She had work clothes and weekend clothes. She'd always considered her weekend clothes to be her casual uniform. They weren't necessarily what others might consider casual but they would have to do. She wasn't going to rush out and buy new clothes for something she'd only be doing for a few weeks — three months at the most. The following Tuesday, she went back to the foodbank in a linen shirtdress and flat sandals and received a nod of approval from Paula.

Over the next few weeks Annette grew more accustomed to the foodbank and its clients. She still found it hard to sit through some of their stories without feeling overwhelmed but, by and large, she managed to keep her emotions in check.

It gradually dawned on her that the frequent raised voices were not necessarily a threat. Some people just spoke more loudly than she was used to in the cosseted, over-polite circles she usually moved in. She soon noticed that she no longer had an overwhelming sense of dread on foodbank days. And then she found she was impatient for Tuesdays and Fridays to come around.

Presumably, the clients were becoming used to her too. Now that she dressed less like a civil servant on a placement study, they stopped to chat with her rather than shoot off as soon as they had their parcels. Even though it was usually mundane stuff, it was a nice experience. Occasionally, it also gave some of them licence to be quite rude to her, something she would normally recoil from. Strangely though, she found the rudeness weirdly comforting, because it meant she'd been accepted. Once she'd got over the embarrassment, it was something to share and laugh about in the post-closure get togethers which she always enjoyed.

She liked the way everyone sat round the table sharing bits of food and bits of their lives. She felt at home. No one quizzed her on why she wasn't looking for work. No one criticised her. They just took her for who she was. She was beginning to think of them as friends. Not colleagues, or team members. Proper friends. And yes, she had found some relevance. More than that, she was starting to notice a change in herself. Nothing major. Little things. She was more relaxed, less panicky and smiling more. She was actually finding things to smile about which, in itself, was quite a shift.

In particular, she was growing closer to Paula and Neil. In all the years she'd known Paula, she'd only really seen her as a fellow worker. Someone to keep at arm's length. Only now was she discovering what a warm and decent person Paula was.

As for Neil, she clicked with him immediately. It was as if he'd looked into her on that first day and saw just how thin-skinned she really was. Paper thin, in fact. It was as if he'd seen all of that and concluded that it was his job to take care of her. So he did, in his characteristic sensitive way. Asking for nothing in return. She soon couldn't imagine either of them not being a part of her life, and she couldn't imagine not being part of life at the foodbank.

4

MR PALMER'S PARTY

Neil wasn't joking when he called cooking his therapy. When they got to know each other better, he explained why, 'I'm a recovering addict. I've been clean for about eight years now but I seem to have become addicted to cooking. It drives Chris up the wall but it keeps me sane.'

Another thing to get her head around. To say she was taken aback was a gross understatement.

Then, as if that wasn't enough, he added, 'Also, I've been inside. I've got a criminal record. Petty crime, from when I was using. It's all long behind me, but I wanted you to know. I wanted to be up front with you. So you know what you're dealing with.'

He was watching her closely, probably looking for signs of distaste. It wasn't as if she'd been a stranger to drugs at uni. They'd smoked weed, popped the occasional pill. Even shoplifted for kicks. But she was a different person now. Colin had seen to that. Still, it would be hypocritical of her to be outraged. She wondered how many other people he'd had this conversation with and what their responses had been. She did her best not to let her expression be one of surprise. Possibly, she overdid it because she realised that she was now scowling.

He looked worried. 'I've shocked you.'

She cleared her throat. 'Well, yes. I suppose you could say I'm a bit shocked but only because I've led quite a sheltered life, for such a long time, that it never occurred to me. So, you don't do either of those things now?'

He shook his head. 'Completely clean in both respects. If I ever did fall, not that I would, Chris is there to put me back on the straight and narrow.'

'Thank you for telling me,' she said. 'I hope my response doesn't stop us being friends? I'm still learning how to take all these new situations in my stride. I'm like a tortoise poking my head out at the world after a long hibernation. I'm afraid it makes me a bit slow and clumsy in my reactions.'

He laughed. Not in nasty way but in that way that left her in no doubt she was in on the joke. 'Annette you are priceless. I think I'm in love with you. We're having a party on Saturday afternoon. Come. Paula will be there. And some of the others. Naturally, I'll be cooking.'

The door was open when she got there. She clutched a bottle of wine with both hands, not sure what to do. It felt rude to walk straight in. Then again, it would be absurd to ring the bell.

'You here for Mr Palmer's party?'

The question jolted her out of her deliberations. Two boys, in their mid-teens, stood behind her each carrying a couple of big metal boxes. Was she here for Mr Palmer's party? Neil's surname was Prentice.

'Er, yes, I think so. Does Neil Prentice live here too?'

'Yeah, yeah. Cool. Just go in. He's in there somewhere.'

From the front, the place was a medium sized, neat terrace. Inside, it was a Tardis of a house. The three main ground-floor rooms had been knocked through into one and an extension added to the back. The entire space was painted white, offset by bright modern and African art. At the back of the room were open patio doors, surrounded by floor-to-ceiling windows that drew in the bright August sunlight and made the walls gleam. Aside from two sofas, some chairs placed on the outer edges, and four very large speakers, there was no furniture.

The modern kitchen was separated from the rest of the room by a long marble counter, piled high with food. Opposite the food counter, the two boys who'd shown her in were setting up some decks and other equipment. There were clusters of people everywhere, some spilling out into the back garden. Children careered around them, weaving in and out, amazingly, without bumping into anybody.

In front of the windowed back wall stood a tall, broad man with grey flecked, dreadlocks that fell past his shoulders. His skin was the colour of burnt umber. He seemed to be enclosed by the bright light from the windows to his rear, as if an aura was emanating from him. She had never seen anyone so god-like. His voice was deep and rich and his pronounced Brummie accent served only to enhance it. She felt she could just dive right in and lose herself in that voice. The congregation of people surrounding him must have felt the same since they were all listening intently to his story. When he finished, there was an outburst of laughter. One or two even clapped.

Next to him was a pretty woman, a little younger than

him, her hair styled into a short, natural Afro. She was similar in size to Annette. Not quite as tall, but taller than average. Although beside him, she was diminutive. But there was something about the way she held herself that made her statuesque. Annette couldn't take her eyes off either of them. They were mesmerising. A golden couple.

'Stunning, isn't he?' Neil appeared beside her. 'Come on, I'll introduce you.'

He grabbed hold of her and drove her forward towards this colossus, kissing and hugging guests as he went, promising to come back and talk to them later. 'Annette, this is Chris.'

The big man looked down at her and held out his hand, 'So, I get to meet my rival at last. Annette, it's good to meet you. I really have heard so much about you.'

She shook hands with him, 'Really? I'm so sorry. How boring for you?'

'No, honestly I'm joking. I'm glad he's found someone else to cook for. Since he's taken it up again, I've put on half a stone. Look at this.' He lifted his shirt to reveal his belly overlap.

'You should go to the gym more. That might help,' said Neil.

'Too much marking to do, and you know I need my beauty sleep.'

Neil gave him a pained look. It must have been a private joke between them. 'He's a physics teacher,' he said. 'Just been made head of department.'

'Oh, congratulations. Is that the reason for the party?'

'Chris doesn't need a reason for a party,' said Neil.

'You know you love it,' said Chris.

Neil shoved his hands in his pockets. 'Yeah, I do.' The two men caught each other's eye and laughed. Neil put his arm around the woman next to Chris. 'And this is the other lady in my life. Say hello to our friend Corrine.'

Corrine was good company. When Neil and Chris were hauled away by the other guests, she took care of Annette. Giving her a tasting course on some of the more exotic dishes on offer and supplying her with rum punch.

Annette scanned the mounds of food. 'It must have taken Neil days to prepare all of this.'

'Well, he has been going at it for a while,' said Corrine. 'But it's not all him. It's Chris's aunties and his mum. You can't come to one of these parties empty-handed you know. It's a cardinal sin.'

'Oh right.' Annette thought about the meagre bottle of wine she'd brought and, straight away, felt inadequate. 'What did you bring?' She hardly dared ask.

'Oh, I've long been a sinner,' said Corrine. 'I didn't bring anything. I'm a single mum on benefits. Every penny counts for me. I'll probably take some of this home. The leftovers will feed us for a week.'

'You don't use a foodbank?'

'Not now my benefits are sorted. But I have done. When it comes to my kids, I ain't too proud to beg. Hey, wasn't that a song?'

Annette nodded. 'The Temptations.' She was suddenly transported back to her childhood. Her dad loved that sort of stuff. He used to play it all the time. Even now, she could still recall a lot of those old Motown hits.

'You like soul music?' said Corrine.

'Yes, I used to. I've not had much time for music lately.'

'Oh no, don't say that. You should always have time for music. It lifts you up.'

Right on cue, the boy DJs, who, it turned out, were pupils at Chris's school, put the music on. From then on conversation was impossible. Just standing still was difficult. It was so loud, everything bounced.

Two children ran over to Corrine and tugged at her dress. 'Mummy, come and dance.'

Corrine raised her voice to make herself heard. 'Just a minute, can't you see I'm talking to someone? Let's have some manners please. This is Annette. Introduce yourselves nicely.'

The children giggled. The boy made a show of taking a huge breath and shouted at the top of his voice: 'Hel-lo, I'm Kendrick.'

'Well, how do you do Kendrick?' said Annette loudly. 'How old are you?'

'Eight.'

His sister said something but it was drowned out by the music.

'Goodness girl, do you think we'll be able to hear that little squeak over all this noise? You've got to get some air into your lungs and shout just like Kendrick,' said Corrine.

'Like this, look.' Kendrick puffed his chest out.

The little girl giggled again, then breathed in until her cheeks puffed out. The sound that came out of her mouth was more gasp than shout. 'My name is Shani, and I'm six. Come on.'

They pulled Annette and Corrine into the middle of the room to find a space among the dancers. Paula joined them from the garden, along with George and his wife. There were people of all ages doing their thing. Young, old and somewhere in between. It felt like the whole house was moving to the beat.

The dancing, the children and the throbbing room took her back to when Will was small and Liza was still a baby. She would play him music like this. Or sometimes, all that sixties stuff her parents used to listen to. He loved it so much. They'd jump up and down until they were so worn out all they could do was roll around on the floor.

She held Shani's hand, bobbed about clumsily, and felt nothing but utter joy.

5

ANNETTE COMES CLEAN

The adrenaline from the party was like rocket fuel that kept her going for ages afterwards. She'd danced until her feet were numb. She'd been introduced to more people than she could remember and they'd all treated her as if they'd known her for years. She was on a natural high immediately afterwards.

Convinced she was stronger and a little more able to withstand the knocks, she made up her mind that it was time to tell her family she would soon be unemployed. She'd start with her parents and work her way up to Colin and the children.

Once she'd set her mind to it, she would have liked to go straight over to her parents' house and tell them but she thought the better of it. Best to take a few days to plan her strategy and make sure she was fully prepared. It was Friday. The children were back from Portugal now and she knew they sometimes visited their grandparents at weekends. She wasn't ready to face them with the news, so she'd go on Monday morning. Then, if it went badly, she'd have the foodbank the following day to help her get over it.

She sent her father a message to ask if they were around on that day for a visit. Straight away, the query came back as to why she wasn't at work. Bollocks. She hadn't considered that. She tapped out: '*I'll explain when I see you,*' then deleted it without sending. That would only set them off worrying. Her mother would be in pieces by Monday. If she could last that long. More likely, they'd ring her as soon as they got the message. Then she'd have to answer it and tell them there and then. Instead she wrote: '*Day off,*' and sent it. It felt wrong lying to them but what else could she do? All things considered, it was for the best.

Sunday went on forever. Sunday night seemed endless. She woke every hour to find herself rehearsing the little speech she'd been working on. By six o'clock she gave up. She got out of bed and tried to distract herself with morning TV. Finally, the time came to leave. She was in the process of gathering her things together when her mobile rang. She didn't recognise the number but answered it anyway.

'Annette, it's Corrine. I hope you don't mind me calling. Neil gave me your number.'

Her first thoughts were that something terrible had happened, 'Is everything all right? Are Neil and Chris all right?'

'Yes, they're fine. Sorry, I know this is a real cheek but I didn't know who else to ask. The thing is, I've got a job interview and the kids were supposed to be going to their dad's today but he's let me down and now I'm stuck. I've got no one to look after them.'

'Oh right, I see. Well, that's a problem that can easily be solved. Shall I come over to you? I can be there in half an hour.'

'Actually, I'm outside. Honestly, that's not as weird as it sounds. Carl, their dad, lives near here and I was on my way there when I got his message. I was so flustered I called Neil. I forgot they were still on holiday. He told me to head towards here. He thought you wouldn't mind. I'm really, really sorry.'

Corrine looked much more flustered than the cheerful, easy going person she'd met at the party. 'I don't know how to thank you for this. I really want this job. It sounds so good. It's at a college, close to the kids' school so I could pick them up from the after-school club straight after I finish. It's perfect. I just need to get to the interview and then wow them with my amazing personality, and make them think it doesn't matter that I haven't had a job for the last three years.'

'Are you nervous?'

'Terrified. I'm so rusty. It's been seven years since my last interview, and that was one old guy. This is a panel of three.'

'Well, the thing to do when they ask for examples of what you've done to demonstrate a competency is to remember all of your experience. Not just paid work. That way, if you have gaps in your paid employment, you can fill them with the other stuff.'

'Right, okay. Like when I've done admin stuff for the kids' clubs, or when I helped my brother with his business?'

'Yes, exactly. It shows you have a broad range of experience, and you're flexible and well-rounded. That's important to an employer. Oh, and when you go in there, shake each one of them by the hand. Smile and keep the eye contact. Tell them you're pleased to meet them, but don't stare. That's just scary.'

'Hey, you know lots about this stuff.'

'Well, I've interviewed lots of people over the years. Also, when we worked together, Paula and I used to do a lot of staff career coaching. Mentoring. That sort of thing. The other advice we used to give was to try to look relaxed but sit up straight, and make sure you share your attention with each interviewer. Don't just focus on one person.'

'Okay. Thanks Annette, I'd better get going.'

'Do you have enough time to get back home to change?'

Corrine's face fell. 'I have changed. I don't have anything else. Oh my God, it's inappropriate isn't it? I look as though I'm on a night out.'

Annette could have slapped herself. What a clumsy mistake to make. How stupid of her. And now poor Corrine was going to spend the whole interview worrying about her appearance. She was bound to mess it up. She had to fix things. 'I might be able to help.'

They went into her bedroom and she slid open the mirrored doors of her walk-in wardrobe. On one side, arranged in shades of grey and black, were her suits. On the other side, shirts and tops, again neatly organised into colour blocks. 'You're about the same size as me. I'm sure we can find something.'

They opted for a light grey skirt suit and a candy pink shirt which was by far the brightest thing in the wardrobe. Annette had been cajoled into buying it by a colour specialist who'd come into Masons to coach them on dressing to make the most of themselves. It had always made her feel too conspicuous so she rarely wore it, but it suited Corrine's skin tones perfectly.

'You look fantastic,' she said.

Corrine admired herself in the mirrored doors. 'I do look pretty smart, don't I? I've got a good feeling about this interview.'

Annette dropped her off at the college so that she didn't have to rely on the bus to get her there on time. With the kids in the car, she carried on to buy some child-friendly food and drink, paper, pens and paints.

Afterwards, they went to the park by the flat. In the children's play area, Kendrick and Shani joined in with the other kids making the most of the last few days of the summer holidays. As they walked back to the flat, they sang Shani's favourite song, 'The Wheels on the Bus' and even Kendrick who said it was stupid, gave in and sang along.

They could hear her landline ringing through the door but, by the time she opened it, the caller had rung off. Then her mobile started up. It was her parents' number. She put her hand over her eyes, and sighed. Sod it. She'd forgotten to tell them she wasn't coming.

'Do you want me to answer it?' said Kendrick, his expression much too serious for an eight-year-old.

'No, it's okay. I know who it is. I'll call them back in a minute.' She was smiling at him but his face remained tense. 'Let's get something to eat first. You must be starving. I am.' He relaxed and smiled at her. She made some lunch and left them eating while she composed herself and made the call.

Her dad answered. 'Where on earth are you? You were supposed to have been here at ten. We've been worried sick about you.'

'Sorry Dad. I had an emergency and completely forgot to call you.'

'What kind of emergency? Has something happened?'

She could hear her mother in the background. 'What emergency? Are the kids all right?'

'Are the kids all right?' he echoed.

'Yes, they're fine Dad. It was a friend of mine. She had an interview and her babysitter let her down. She didn't have anyone else, so I'm looking after her children.' There was silence on the other end of the line. 'It's the holidays you see. Otherwise they would have been in school and it wouldn't have been a problem.'

'Everyone's fine. She just had to look after a friend's children. Her friend had an interview, apparently.'

It sounded as though he was holding the phone away. She could picture the scene in her parents' living room right now.

'What friend, what children?' Her mother's voice wasn't much further away. She was probably standing over him. Poised to snatch the phone off him.

'I don't know. Someone from work I expect,' he said.

'No Dad. Not from work. This is a new friend. She's … new.'

'She says it's a new friend.'

'What new friend? Give it to me.' There was a rustling as her mother wrestled the phone from her father. 'Annette?'

'Hello Mum. I'm sorry I forgot to let you know I wasn't coming. It was all a bit of a last-minute rush and it completely slipped my mind.'

'Well, at least we know where we stand in the pecking order now, don't we? We've been out of our minds with worry.'

'Yes, Dad said.'

'He's been pacing the room up and down for the last hour. And now we find you've been looking after some new friend's children without giving us a minute's thought.'

'I'm really sorry,' said Annette.

'If only you'd given your own children that much attention. You might not be in the situation you're in now.' Her mum had worked herself up into outrage. As always when that happened, she was more concerned about expressing her anger than the impact her words might have.

'Mum, you know I had to go out to work,' said Annette, trying not to let it get to her.

'I'm not saying it's your fault for having to work so hard. Although I would never have stood for your father shirking his responsibilities in the way some people have. But what I can't believe. What I can't believe, Annette, is that you've taken a day off work to look after someone else's children when you should be using the time to be with your own family.'

'Well that's just it. I haven't taken the day off work, Mum. I've been off work for nearly two months now. I'm being made redundant.' There, she'd said it. She waited for the backlash. She didn't need to wait long.

'You've been, you've been. Oh my good God. Speak to your father. I can't take it in. Arthur, she says she's been made redundant. Two months ago. Take this. Speak to her.'

Her dad came back on the phone, 'What's this? Is that right? You've been made redundant?'

'Yes Dad. Well technically, I'm on extended leave for another month. But yes, I've been made redundant. Usual reasons. Structure changes. You know how it works.'

'How awful for you love, I'm sorry. I know how much you put into that company. They must be mad letting you go.'

'Well then they must be mad. I'm sorry I didn't tell you earlier. I just found it hard to talk about, but I'm getting over it now.'

'You'll be back on the ladder in no time. Got any interviews lined up?'

'No. I did have, but I wasn't ready. I'm doing some volunteering instead. At a foodbank.'

'A foodbank?' He sounded surprised. She couldn't blame him. She'd surprised herself.

'She's never having to go to a foodbank, is she?' said her mother.

'No,' said her dad, 'She's volunteering at one. She's not ready yet to look for a new job.'

'Well she'll have to make herself ready,' said her mother. 'Who else is going to pay the bills?'

'Tell Mum I'm all right for a while for money. I'm getting a good pay off,' she said.

'I'll try love. Have you told Colin and the kids?'

'Not yet. I thought I'd tell you first.'

Her dad sighed. 'Best of two evils was it? You're going to have to face the music and tell them you know? It's no use sticking your head in the sand and hoping no one will notice.'

'I know. I need to work myself up to it first.'

There was a long pause.

'Well someone has to tell them. Do you want me to do it?'

'Oh Dad, would you?'

'I'll call Colin. I don't suppose he'll be very happy about it.'

'No Dad, I don't suppose he will be.'

Corrine was in a much better mood when she got back. 'I think it went well. They were nice. Really friendly. I took your advice and filled in with stuff I'd done outside of work and they seemed fine with it. One of the ladies that interviewed me complimented me on my great outfit when she showed me out.'

'Keep it. If you get the job, you'll need it. If you're not

successful this time, it'll do for your next interview. I've got plenty and I don't really need them now.'

'If you're sure? Thank you so much, for everything. You're a good friend.'

A good friend. Was she? She didn't know. She'd forgotten what it was to be a good friend. Until recently, just being a normal friend was a deeply buried mystery.

Shani sat on Corrine's lap. 'I painted a picture of you in your new clothes, Mummy. You look so pretty. And here's one of Auntie Net.'

Corrine studied the pictures. 'They're lovely, baby. But Auntie Net doesn't look very happy. Couldn't you have given her a nice smile? She has such a sweet smile.'

'That's because I made it just after she spoke to her mummy and daddy on the phone and they made her sad.'

Annette blushed. She thought she'd hidden it well but clearly, she hadn't. Either that or Shani was a six-year-old mystic. Her first instinct was to do as she always did. Put on her disguise and bluff it out but she felt unusually safe with Corrine and ended up telling her everything. More in fact than she'd intended to.

When she finished it was Corrine's turn to hand out the advice, 'Sometimes your parents have very particular ideas about how you should behave. They seem to think just because they brought you up, they have the right to tell you how to live, long after they should. Mine were very strict but we were really close. They were so angry when I moved in with Carl, they didn't speak to me for two years. That was hard. Going from speaking to them every day to nothing. Not even a Christmas or birthday card. They weren't even there when Kendrick was born. I was gutted. But, being the pig-headed individual that I am, I refused to give in. In the end, they caved in and came to see us. When he saw his beautiful little grandson, my dad cried.'

Kendrick rolled his eyes. He must have heard the story before. Corrine rolled hers back at him mockingly. 'Then, they were almost as angry when me and Carl split up. So, what can you do? You just have to live your life the way you think is best and let everyone else catch up. Do what you want to do, Net. Your family will come around to it. If you don't mind me saying so, it sounds as if it will do them all a bit of good. Especially your ex and your kids.'

The talk with Corrine helped. It was good to share and get some perspective. As soon as she'd said goodbye to her parents, the usual knot between her shoulders had reappeared, along with a feeling in her stomach. As if she were on the verge of vomiting. She knew why. It was because she was waiting for Colin to call and tell her what a thoughtless, heartless, useless piece of crap she was. If only she could be more like Corrine and refuse to give in. What she wouldn't give to be that kind of pig-headed individual again.

She dropped them off home and told Corrine she'd be happy to babysit another time. She'd had such a good time with the children.

The flat seemed even more empty than usual when she got back. She cleared away the pens and paints and cast her mind back to when Will and Liza were that age. She was already working full time by then so it was Colin who got to do most of the fun things with them. She tried to remember what they were like, before things started to go downhill, but she couldn't. Perhaps the rot had already begun to set in by then and she hadn't noticed.

The phone rang. Of course, it was Colin. 'Is it true?'

'Is what true?'

'About you being made redundant?'

'Yes.'

'Two months ago?'

'Yes. Well, technically, next month.'

'And you didn't think it important enough to tell us?'

'I've been a bit preoccupied.'

'With a foodbank by all accounts. A bloody foodbank. I mean, Jesus Christ, Annette. What is wrong with you? You don't even have the decency to tell the people who depend on you that you've lost your job and instead of looking for another one, you're fannying about at a bloody foodbank.'

'Yes, that's right. That's it exactly.'

She put the phone down before he could say anything else. For a moment, her lungs felt airless and she was light-headed. A frisson of nervous excitement ran through her, making her tingle. This was new territory for her. She'd never done that before. Been so blasé. It felt rather good. Anyway, Corrine was right. It might do them some good if she did what she wanted for a change.

When he rang back, she let it ring out and she deleted his voicemail messages without listening to them.

6

HELLO NETTA WILDE

The first time she saw Colin Grey was Manchester, 1987, at a student party she'd been dragged along to by Claire and Sasha. She was still Netta then. Normally they wouldn't have gone anywhere near a party like that but they were broke and they'd heard there'd be lots of free booze. And she needed to get drunk.

It had been a really shit party. Full of accountants or rather soon-to-be accountants. Accountants in waiting so to speak. She had nothing personally against accountants but that didn't mean she wanted to socialise with them. The rumour about the drink had been true though. The kitchen table was so loaded with alcohol it looked like it might cave in at any minute.

They each lifted a wine bottle off it and it still didn't look any lighter. Some guy said something to her about gate-crashers. She just gave him one of her looks and she could swear she saw him visibly shrink back and wither.

'Come on,' said Sasha. 'Let's find the music and see if they've got anything worth dancing to.'

The room was sweaty and heavy with the smell of cigarettes and body odour. It seemed like everyone from the accountancy faculty was here, and few of them knew the value of a good anti-perspirant.

They pushed and shoved their way to the stereo. It was being manned by an unexceptional pair sifting through the music on offer.

'Got any Clash?' Netta said.

'I don't think so,' said one of the DJs.

'Sex Pistols?'

His mate picked through the records. 'Doesn't look like it.'

'X-Ray Spex? Joy Division?'

'Er no, sorry. Just newer stuff.'

She let out a shh noise through her teeth, to show her disgust.

'I think there's some Cure. And some Smiths,' he said, defensive. He was obviously doing his best to look cool about it, but Netta had seen him slyly slip 'Never Gonna Give You Up,' back in between the other singles and it made it all the easier for her to dismiss him.

'They'll do. Stick 'em on, and anything else you've got like that.'

'I'm not the DJ.'

'Don't care. Do it anyway.'

He shrugged and changed the record. There was an outburst of cheering as the opening notes of 'Close to Me' filled the room.

Netta and her friends found a space and made it their own by edging everyone else out with their arms as they moved. She elbowed someone who was dancing too close. If you could call it dancing. It was him, the Rick Astley fan.

'Have you seen them?' he said.

'Who?'

He pointed to her T-shirt. 'The Clash, have you seen them?'

'Course.' She hadn't. She was way too young, but she wasn't going to tell him that.

'Cool.'

'How is that cool?'

'Well, you know. It's The Clash.'

'You like 'em, do you?'

'Yeah, course. Doesn't everybody?'

'I fucking hope not.'

She turned away from him. Claire caught her eye and pulled a face. Sasha did one too. All three of them had to shoegaze so that he couldn't see them cracking up.

'Do you want to get a drink?' he said, after a while. She waved the wine bottle in the air without looking at him, and carried on dancing. 'Right, sorry. I'm not very good at this am I?'

Something about the slightly pathetic way he said that made her feel just a tiny bit guilty. With a sideways glance, she took him in properly. Tallish, slim, but not skinny. Nice eyes. Kind of soulful. Bit of a straight dresser though and, fuck! That hair! It could have been cloned from Rick Astley's. All right, so he definitely wasn't her type but she didn't have to squash him completely. For once, she could be nice and let him down gently. She smiled and said a friendly, 'Ha,' to let him know she didn't really think he was a creepy-looking dickhead. That should do it.

She saw Doogie come in and scan the room. Probably looking for her. It wouldn't be long before he saw her. They didn't exactly blend in with the crowd. She could tell he was pissed off. No way would he be somewhere like this if he didn't have to be.

He clocked her and came over. He stopped in front of her, ignoring everyone else, and kissed her full on.

She tightened her lips, refusing to enjoy it. 'Finished?'

He looked at her aghast and held out his arms in a 'what have I done now?' kind of way.

'Don't ever kiss me again, you pile of shit.'

'Come on Netta. Don't be so fucking melodramatic. She's a friend, that's all. I swear.'

'Fuck off, Doogie. I'm not interested.'

He blew air loudly out of his nostrils. 'I've told you before, there's nothing to be jealous about.'

'I'm not jealous, but my time's too precious to waste on wankers like you. Go fuck yourself.'

'You'll miss me when I'm gone. Last chance, babe. You know you're gonna regret this.'

She lifted a single finger to his face.

'Right then, I'm going.' He gave Rick Astley a dismissive look. 'Don't even try mate. You couldn't handle her.'

She sneered back at him. 'Fuck off, Fuckwit.'

Doogie went to say something, then stopped himself. He put his hand around the back of her neck and wrenched her in. In spite of everything, his nearness made her sick with excitement. 'See you around, Net. It was fucking amazing, while it lasted.'

'Was it?' She tugged herself free and stared him out.

He sucked his teeth. 'Like I said, you'll regret it.' He sauntered off to the kitchen.

She took a glug from the wine bottle, wanting to wash away that last kiss and the feel of him on her lips. 'The fuck I will,' she muttered, more to herself than anyone.

An hour later, Claire went to check the coast was clear. 'He's in the other room, eating some Sloane's face off,' she said. 'We've done our time here, let's go.'

'Where are you going?' asked Rick Astley.

He asked Netta, but Sasha answered. 'A club. Hacienda probably. Haven't decided yet.'

'Yeah, we've had enough too. All right if we come with you?'

Netta was about to tell them no, absolutely not, when Claire said: 'Do what you like. Makes no difference to us.'

They made their way along Oxford Road singing a medley of Smiths songs. The party was a disaster but it had allowed them to get pissed for nothing. As they'd left, Netta had stolen some flowers from someone's front garden. She hung them from her back pocket and was swirling her arms and hips around in the style of Morrisey. She knew tomorrow she'd wake up feeling bad and not just because of the drink. She was glad to see the back of Doogie. She didn't know how she'd lasted so long with him. It would hurt for a while but she'd get over it.

Rick Astley was watching her. He had a really stupid grin on his face. 'I'm Colin by the way.'

'Yeah? What course you doing?'

He gulped and looked at his feet. 'Accounting and Finance. You?'

'English.'

He wrinkled his nose. It made him look quite cute, 'I think I've seen you around campus a few times. It's Netta isn't it?'

'Yeah, that's me.'

'Well hello Netta Wilde. Pleased to meet you.' He said it in a phoney American accent.

She was so busy thinking what a weirdo he was that it didn't occur to her to ask how he knew her surname.

7

SAINT ANNETTE AND THE JOB CLUB CO-OPERATIVE.

Not long after her interview, Corrine came into the food-bank and threw her arms around Annette. 'I got the job. Thank you. I don't think I could have done it without you.' She'd caused quite a stir. Everyone, including the regular customers who'd been trying for months, maybe years to get something, was interested to know how she did it. It was as if getting a job was some fabled myth that they'd only heard about in fairy tales.

After that some of them started asking Annette for advice when they had an interview coming up. She gave it gladly. It was just the standard stuff that she'd told Corrine and she had no idea if it would help, but giving it made her feel that little bit less of a bad person.

An idea had been formulating in her head. Although Corrine had been the trigger, it was Barry that swung it. Barry was a regular. He had four kids, one of them still a baby, and his benefits often didn't stretch through to the next week. He'd been made redundant eighteen months earlier, completely out the blue, and had been to more interviews than he could remember, until his confidence was shot. He'd got through to a face-to-face interview for a new company setting up a call centre. He'd never worked in one before but, he told her, he was willing to try anything.

'Do you have a decent suit?' Yes, he did. 'Good. The first thing to do is to make a good visible impression so make sure you wear it with a well-ironed shirt and polished shoes.' He nodded, taking it all in. 'The other thing to remember, is that this is a job that will require you to speak clearly and confidently. Do you think you'll be able to manage that in the interview?'

He looked downcast. 'I'm not sure. I'm a bit of a mumbler when I get nervous. If you'd asked me a year ago, I'd have said yes but these days, I don't know. It's not doing the job. It's the interview.'

'Well, you might not realise it Barry, but you have a really nice voice. It's very warm and it has a good pitch, which is just the kind of voice that people trust. That probably got you past the phone interview, so you're doing well so far.'

'Oh, right.' He seemed genuinely surprised.

She carried on: 'This may sound a bit silly, but can you picture someone who is confident, charming and approachable. Maybe somebody you admire? Not overly confident, but the kind of person who'd be good in an interview?'

He nodded.

'Think of the qualities that makes that person the way they are. Think of the way they behave.'

'Er, okay,' he said.

'Now imagine yourself as that person. It doesn't matter that it's not you. Just be like that person for the interview. Practise at home if you can.'

He looked sceptical.

'I did say it might sound a bit silly but believe me, it does work,' she said. 'I used to do it all the time. I was always a nervous wreck before I went up for a promotion but I had one suit that I saved for interviews and important meetings. When I put it on, I also put on this other persona. Like an alter ego. It worked for me. Try it out at home and see what you think.'

'Sharon'll think I've gone mad,' he said.

'You don't have to put the suit on. Especially with four kids in the house. Just try and relax into your alter ego. Not over the top though, Barry. Essentially, he's just a more confident, relaxed you, but every bit as polite and friendly.'

'You really think I've got a nice voice?'

'It's so lovely and mellow, I could drink it.'

He shook his head. 'I never knew. No one's ever told me that before.'

She sent him off with the same general advice she'd given Corrine, hoping that the person he admired was not some megalomaniac egotistical world leader, or anyone like that.

She didn't see Barry for nearly two weeks. She hoped he was staying away because he had enough money to live on and not because he was embarrassed that he'd failed again.

When he did return, it was with his wife and the younger children. They waited in the queue for Annette despite someone else being free, then he handed her his voucher. 'I hope this is the last time we'll be coming, Annette.' His face cracked into a big smile. 'I got the job.'

There was a loud cheer from everyone in the room. Barry's wife handed her a piece of folded paper. 'We just wanted to thank you. He's been so low lately. It means such a lot to him to be in work again. This is for you. It's not much, but it's heartfelt.'

Annette looked at the paper. On the front was a child's drawing of a smiley faced family with four children. Written inside were the words:

'*To Annette*
Thank you for making Daddy happy again.'

'We're going to have to call you Saint Annette, at this rate,' said Paula after Barry had gone. 'Seriously, it was a good thing you did.'

'I've had this idea,' said Annette. 'I'm not sure if it will work but I think we might be able to support others like Corrine and Barry. The advice I've been giving them is mostly just the sort of coaching we used to do at Masons. I wonder if we could offer it as an extra service. Free of charge. Perhaps we could use one of the spare rooms off the hall. We could do practice interviews too. If people wanted it.'

'That's a great idea,' said Paula. 'We could help with CVs as well. I've still got some of my old coaching manuals at home. I'll have to dig them out. It's been a few years for me and it's surprising how quickly you forget these things.'

'Also, I thought we could put together some clothes. Suits, shirts, tops. That kind of thing. The sort we could loan out for interviews. In case our clients don't have some-thing suitable to wear. I have lots of work clothes that I can donate. Although, they'll only fit ladies of the same size. If they can manage it, we can ask for a small donation to cover the cleaning costs.'

'I think I still have some too. I like the idea but I'm not

sure we'll cover cleaning costs with donations,' said Paula.
'Most of them struggle as it is. But we won't let that stop us.
Let's take it one step at a time.'

'Chris and I might have a couple of decent old suits we
could pass on,' said Neil.

Some of the other volunteers thought they might have
something too.

'Do you want me to knock up some posters to stick on
the wall? I'll have them done and printed in no time,' volunteered George. 'What do you want me to call it?'

'I hadn't thought that far,' said Annette.

'How about the Job Club Co-operative,' suggested
Paula.

'That's good,' said George. 'Like the early co-operative
movement. Everyone working together for mutual benefit.'

'That's perfect,' said Annette. Yes, that was it precisely.
Everyone got something from it.

'We'll need to do some research on how to set up something like this,' said Paula. 'Come over for Sunday lunch.
Afterwards, we'll trawl the internet and see what we can
find.'

'Isn't the internet amazing?' said Paula. 'Do you remember
how hard it used to be to find information like this? I know I
sound like a real old timer, but it never ceases to astonish
me. Tap in a few words, press a button and all this comes
up. Absolutely amazing.'

Neither of them had guessed there would be so much
advice on starting up a job club just hanging around in the
cloud, waiting for them to pick it up. Within minutes they
had all the guidance they needed.

It seemed there were job clubs of all sorts out there.

They varied in the services they offered, the structure they took and the frequency in which they met. The next step for Annette and Paula was to work out what they wanted this particular job club to look and feel like.

The first thing they agreed on was that it would be fairly basic in the service it offered. They weren't trying to mimic what the experts already did much better than they could. They would offer three things — interview advice, the loan of interview clothes and informal CV appraisal.

The club would be an annexe to the foodbank, subject to the vicar's permission. So, it would be open on the same days and would be run by the two of them. Other volunteers could be drafted in if they had some relevant experience and wanted to help but, on no account, should it leave the foodbank short of manpower.

Concerned that if they made it too formal it would turn people off, they chose to keep it informal but would offer appointments where necessary. Clothes would be loaned out for a week. They were undecided on what to do about the cost of cleaning. From their research, it appeared that it was possible to apply for funding for job clubs but after some consideration, they decided not to do that in the first instance. They had no idea if this thing was going to take off. It could close after a few weeks. They would wash what could be washed themselves and look elsewhere for help with dry cleaning.

As well as agreeing to letting them have a room, the vicar gave them a temporary reprieve on the cleaning problem. He said the church would be able to grant a £50 bursary out of its local charity fund. It would help for a short while at least, until they sorted something out. One or two of the volunteers pointed out that, for their own self-esteem, some customers might actually prefer to give them something. So, they agreed to accept discretionary donations while making it clear they were not compulsory or expected.

After that, it didn't take long to set up. They picked a suitable room, a couple of clothing rails were purchased and posters were put up around the hall and on the double doors. They put together some advice sheets to hand out and George printed off twenty of them, to start.

Almost as soon as it opened, the Job Club Co-operative saw a consistent trickle of customers through its door. Some dropped by out of curiosity. Others, just in case an interview came their way. Some turned up because they'd got through to an interview and wanted as much help as they could. If nothing else, they could at least say they'd done their absolute best to get the job.

THE NEMESIS THAT WASN'T

At first there were a few things to iron out. The intention behind the job club was a well-meaning one but the absence of proper rigour left it in danger of folding before it had a chance to get off the ground. The main issue was their lack of foresight. Or rather, their naivety. As George put it, they had failed to take into account one important element: human nature.

The prospect of returning a well-cut suit or a smart dress proved too much for some clients, especially those who weren't foodbank regulars. They lost half of their collection within a matter of weeks. Neil was forced to organise a posse of volunteers to track down the absent items. They managed to retrieve some of them by shaming the culprits into handing them over on the doorstep and only occasionally did they have to wrestle them out of the offender's hands.

After that, they tightened up on checking the clients' credentials to make sure they had their real addresses. Most were happy to work within the new rules. They were, after all, used to much more meticulous fact checking and besides, they saw this as a community project that they all had a stake in. When someone walked out of the club with a hanger full of clothes, pats on the back and shouts of good luck from the volunteers and the clients became the habitual thing to do. It must have given them a real shot in the arm knowing that so many were rooting for them.

Paula, began to stick the thank you messages and cards on the wall. She thought it would provide a confidence boost to others when they saw them. The successes were pretty small in terms of getting people work, but there were enough of them to provide a lift. Some landed a job after several interviews, so they became regulars for a while.

From conversations with clients they found they weren't only using the advice when looking for work. Some were also using it in other types of interviews like benefit consultations, and were finding they had more confidence to ask questions.

The takeaway advice sheets proved popular and George had to print more off, in greater numbers. They started to see non-foodbank clients who'd heard about them by word of mouth.

The extent of its popularity was unexpected. It wasn't as if they couldn't get this advice from the Jobcentres. Their websites were packed with useful information and the volunteers that signed on testified that the advisors were, by and large, very good and did their best to give very similar, if not better, advice.

'Maybe it's the personal aspect,' said Ash, one of the younger volunteers who was looking for work himself. 'Nice as they are, it's still a bit official. You know? And the clothes help too. You don't get that at the Jobcentre. Yeah, I think the clothes help a lot.'

'We need more clothes,' said Annette. 'But where do we

get them from? We could try the charity shops but that would cost money, and we don't have any.'

'Masons,' said Paula. 'We have lots of former colleagues who might be able to provide some work clothes they don't wear anymore, and they come in all shapes, sizes and genders. Let's contact Malcolm Jefferson.'

Malcolm Jefferson. Annette felt herself visibly shudder. The name alone brought back bad memories that she'd tried so hard to forget. She did her best to think of something to say but all she could manage was, 'Erm.' She knew it made sense but she couldn't, she just couldn't, think about Malcolm Jefferson without recalling her shame and despair the day he told her she was no longer an essential cog in the wheels of Mason and Partners

As always, Paula guessed what was going on in her head. 'We still keep in touch from time to time. Shall I call him? We could go and see him together.'

'Okay. Together,' she said.

But when the day came, Netta had to face him alone.

'I'm really sorry. I just feel so awful, I can't get out of bed. I think it's the flu. Do you want me to postpone it?'

'No, don't trouble yourself Paula, I'll go on my own.'

'Are you sure you'll be all right?'

'Yes, of course, I'll be fine. It's not as if I haven't been there before. Just take care of yourself. I'll pop by later to see how you are. I'll be fine. Absolutely fine.' Who was she trying to convince? She put the phone down and scrunched her body into a tight ball.

She took the same journey in that used to be her regular commute. She recalled that morning of her birthday. It had been a lovely summer day. She'd come in early to buy fresh cakes and that bloody meringue, not realising she was about to experience a seismic shift in her life.

The year had just tipped into October. Aside from a few bare branches on the tree-lined streets, nothing had altered outside. All was the same and yet everything was different.

The butterflies in her stomach had been with her all morning but they got worse as she approached the building, and the ringing in her ears was making her increasingly unsteady. How ironic, she thought, to be handing out advice about combatting nervousness when here I am on the verge of crapping myself. If my friends could see me now. She'd worn her 'alter ego' suit and given herself a good talking to in the mirror that morning, but none of it mattered one bit. In spite of the pep talk, in spite of her alleged confidence, in spite of everything, she had a strong compulsion to turn around and run away. 'Oh Barry, I've let you down.' She closed her eyes. As if Barry could hear her. As if anyone could hear her.

'Annette? I thought it was you. Come in, Malcolm's expecting you. It's so nice to see you again.' It was Janice, Jefferson's PA. Janice with her respectably frivolous tattooed shoulder. 'That was lucky, I'd just popped down to let reception know you were coming and spotted you. I thought you'd changed your mind for a minute.'

'Oh no, I … er … thought I'd left something in the car. My phone. It turns out I have it right here. It's nice to see you too, Janice.'

It was too late to run now. She'd been caught and reeled in by Janice who was steering her into the lift and onwards towards Malcolm Jefferson, the smarmiest of smarmy reptiles it had ever been her misfortune to come across.

Janice insisted on taking her via the circuitous route, past her old team. They greeted her like the prodigal manager. Everyone wanted to know how she was doing and what she was up to now. They all wanted to tell her how much they missed her. Back when she'd worked there, she would have found this sort of thing acutely embarrassing. That was then. Now she allowed herself a degree of self-satisfaction and let herself get swept up in the tidal wave of excitement that carried her all the way to Malcolm Jefferson's office.

'You look so well,' he kept saying. 'Ten years younger. Honestly, you look great. What's all this about you and Paula Lewis doing some charity work? Tell me all about it.'

That word charity. It still made her inwardly flinch, as if someone had just scraped their nails along a blackboard. And did he have to make it sound so smug? She was itching to slap him down with a haughty retort but she fought it. Like it or not, she needed Malcolm Jefferson. 'We help out at a foodbank and we've just opened up a new venture called the Job Club Co-operative. That's what I've come to talk to you about.'

He sat back in his chair. 'Fire away.'

And so she did. She told him about the idea, its successes and its shortcomings. The more she talked about it, the more enthused she became. Jefferson listened without interrupting and by the time she finished, he was sitting up, his elbows on the desk and leaning so far in, their heads were almost touching.

'And that's it really, Malcolm. We need help, and we thought our old colleagues at Masons might want to help us.'

He rubbed his hands together. 'Right. Well, let's get started then. How about if we arrange for you and Paula to come in and talk to us about it? We'll rope in as many as we can to come and listen to you and take it from there. I'm

sure you'll get some interest if you talk about it the way
you've just done to me.'

No one could have been more amazed by Jefferson's
response than Annette. No one could have been less amazed
by it than Paula. 'I know he can be a bit grating but his
heart's in the right place.'

'So, what you're saying is, I shouldn't judge a book by its
covers?'

'Am I?' She laughed.

Jefferson was true to his word. The next day, Janice
called to arrange their talk and the following week they were
back at Mason and Partners. They brought Ash with them
to talk about his experience of job hunting while living on
benefits. Although he didn't claim benefits, Neil came along
for moral support. It went down well. When Ash spoke,
some of the audience were visibly moved. Annette's former
team offered to organise the clothing collection and delivery.
All they had to do now was wait.

Neil gave her a ride home and she invited him up to the
flat.

'Nice place. Great view,' he said.

'Yes, I suppose it is.'

'I didn't realise you'd been quite so high up at Masons.'

She busied herself making coffee. 'Not that high really.'

'Sounded it to me, from what your team mates were
saying.'

'Being high up's no good to you when they give you the
chop. You just have further to fall. Although, it did give me a
redundancy package that means I don't have to rush into
another job, if I'm careful. I'm grateful for that much.'

'Talking of money.' He handed her an envelope

containing a bundle of twenty-pound notes. 'It's a hundred quid.'

'Where has this come from?'

'I finally put the cooking to some practical use. I've been baking. A couple of the kids at Chris's school have been selling them in the break times. Their parents use the food-bank. And Corrine sold some at the college. It's to help with the cleaning bills. I wanted to do my bit. I can't really give the advice you give but I wanted to do something.'

'My God, this is wonderful. Thank you. You must have cooked yourself into the ground to make this much.'

'Nah, I enjoy it.'

'Have you ever thought about doing it professionally?' she said. 'You're so good at it, I'm sure you'd find something.' He didn't speak and Annette felt she'd said too much. 'I'm sorry, I'm prying. It's none of my business.'

'No, you're not. I don't mind. Actually, I have worked in a professional kitchen before, but I couldn't take the pressure. I mean, the people were great but the pace you have to work at. The hours. The structure. All of it. It was too much. I used to get panic attacks all the time and then I'd hate myself for being such a lightweight. That's when I got into drugs, and you know where that took me. I'm sure I'll find something I can do that doesn't kill me, one of these days. Chris doesn't mind. He understands. He doesn't push too hard. He just keeps telling me, baby steps. I'm lucky to have him.'

'You're both lucky. I've never seen two people who care so much for each other. It's uplifting to be around. Can I say that without embarrassing you?'

He laughed. 'You just did.'

'Oh, how rude of me. Even more surprising is that I said it without embarrassing myself. A few months ago, that

would have been a definite no-no. I'd have just looked
quietly on with envy. You're good for me Neil Prentice. You
all are.'

'I think you're good for me too, Annette Grey. I'm glad
to have you as a friend.'

He put his arms around her and she rested her head on
his shoulder. There was a feeling in her gut that she didn't
recognise at first, and then it came to her. It was content-
ment and just a touch of astonishment that she, Annette
Grey, had some proper friends. Her eyes were leaking water.
She pulled herself off his damp sweatshirt. 'Sorry, it's been a
bit of an eventful few weeks.'

He kissed her forehead. 'That's okay. What else are
friends for?'

'I think we're going to need more rails,' said Ash.

Malcolm Jefferson had turned up in one of Masons'
vans. 'We brought a couple with us,' he said. 'But they are
beginning to bow.'

Adele and Hayley, two of the managers from Annette's
old department, had come with him.

'We asked people to bring everything cleaned, ironed
and on hangers so we didn't mess them up,' said Hayley.
'Some people didn't quite get the message and brought stuff
that wasn't really interview suitable. We were going to give
them to a charity shop, but Malcolm thought we should
bring them, in case they might be of use to some of your
foodbank customers. It's all good quality stuff. We made it
clear that we didn't want any rubbish and we've checked
every single item.'

'We've got some boxes of shoes and handbags as well,'
said Adele.

Paula clapped her hands together. 'This is wonderful. Just wonderful.'

Ash and Hayley went to the nearest discount store to buy another two rails. In all, they now had six rails of interview clothing in varying sizes. They placed the unsuitable items on tables by the café with a notice telling people to help themselves.

The Masons team stayed for a couple of hours, helping to set things up and talking to some of the job club clients. When it was time for them to go, Malcolm Jefferson came to say goodbye. 'This is a nice place. Friendly,' he said. 'Not what I was expecting at all.'

'What were you expecting?' Annette asked, already knowing that if she'd been his shoes, she would probably have said the same.

He frowned. 'I don't know really. Not this I suppose. One more thing Annette, some of your old colleagues — me included — thought we'd like to carry on helping out. We wondered if you'd allow us to come and help with the advice and coaching. If you agree, we can sort it out on a rota basis so we can be released from work.'

Annette's heart sank. Not having to spend any more time with Malcolm Jefferson had been one of the few good things to have come out of the redundancy. Now here he was telling her he wanted to be around on a regular basis. 'Malcolm, that's very generous of you, but please don't feel in any way obliged to.'

'Oh no, we'd like to. I'd like to. Especially now I've seen the place. It's not until you come to somewhere like this that you realise there's more to life than work and your own four walls.' He let out a sigh that sounded so forlorn she felt quite moved.

'I'll have to ask the rest of the volunteers,' she said.

'We'll wait to hear then.' He went to leave. As he reached the door, he stopped. 'I know you've not always thought the best of me Annette, and maybe my attempts to put people at ease are a bit clumsy, but I do care. I hope you know that much about me.'

'Of course I do.'

He looked satisfied. 'Then we'll await your instructions, Madame Grey.' He gave her a salute and went.

She forced her face into a smile but underneath she was ashamed. She'd lied to Malcolm. The truth was, no, she had never known that. In all the time she'd worked with him she'd never once considered that he cared for anyone other than himself. She'd always seen him as the idiot with no social skills, the unfeeling corporate man who pattered out platitudes by the book whenever confronted with sticky situations.

Paula came over and sat with her. 'I hear they want to come back and help.'

'Yes,' she said distractedly. She was still thinking about what Malcolm had said.

'Would that be a problem for you?'

'Er no. I don't think so.' Paula was looking at her. Waiting for some qualification, no doubt. 'It's just. It's just that, well, I've never really been that keen on Malcolm.'

'You know, it was Malcolm who told me about your redundancy. He asked me to keep an eye on you. He was very worried about you at the time.'

She hadn't been expecting that. She'd always assumed it was one of Paula's old team that told her and it being Malcolm had never crossed her mind. That he'd taken the trouble to contact Paula because he was worried about her was even more surprising. She thought about the day he told her she was being made redundant. He didn't need to tell her on that day. He could have followed procedure. He should have followed procedure, but he chose to tell her. Probably because he thought it was the decent thing to do.

Decency. She considered the word. She'd never before thought about Malcolm Jefferson as a decent person. It seemed she'd been wrong.

9

THE RETURN OF TAMPON GIRL

Alan the vicar had been understanding about the clothing and agreed to let them move to a bigger room that they could use solely for the purpose of the job club. The new room had grilles on the windows so they were able to leave everything there, set up and ready to go. It saved them a lot of time and freed up Annette and Paula's spare bedrooms which had been taken over by the clothes and accessories for all but two days a week.

The lack of bedroom space had been particularly irksome to Liza and Will, for some reason, on the few occasions they agreed to spend some time at Annette's. She didn't know why. She'd expected them to be pleased that it gave them an excuse not to stay overnight. Even when she told them everything was back to normal, they didn't exactly rush round and beg to stay.

After Paula's revelation about Malcolm, it seemed churlish to try to stop him coming back. Annette gave them her full backing and he and the other volunteers from Masons became part of the team. Although they came for the job club, on quieter days they helped out in the foodbank. There were four of them who came regularly. One a day on a fortnightly basis. Malcolm, Adele, Hayley and Simon who had taken over from Paula when she retired. They tried to keep to set days, so that people who wanted to see them again knew when to expect them. Occasionally Malcolm would do an extra day, or he'd pop in when he was passing to see how they were getting on.

The Masons volunteers did more than provide good advice. They also set up foodbank collection points around their office, and brought donations of food and hygiene items with them every week. Adele came up with an idea to help with the cost of cleaning. She left a collection tin on the reception desk at Masons for people to drop in their spare change. Although not large amounts, the money provided a welcome boost to their cleaning fund.

Having an extra pair of hands in the job club meant that she and Paula didn't need to stretch themselves quite so thinly. It was helpful too, learning new techniques from those with more on-the-ground experience. She'd been out of work for a few months now and Paula much longer. It was easy to forget how quickly things moved on in the business world.

Malcolm was a revelation. For all his awkwardness around her, he had no problem getting on with other people. Especially the men. They seemed particularly appreciative of his tactful honesty. It was a competence of his that had, until now, passed her by completely. His charms were not entirely lost on some of the foodbank's female customers either. Several of the middle-aged ladies displayed a visible flush when he spoke to them, and there was a noticeable increase in lipstick application on 'Malcolm days'. He appeared to have found his niche.

With some of the clients, he offered himself up as a

referee and, on occasion, passed on information about companies that he knew to be recruiting. One morning, he brought a flip chart and easel with him and stood it outside the job club room. In large capitals, he wrote:

THESE COMPANIES HAVE VACANCIES THIS WEEK
PELHAM TOOLS - SKILLED STAFF
FOSTERS – WAREHOUSE STAFF
GRAHAM KNIGHT – CALL CENTRE STAFF
ASK INSIDE FOR MORE DETAILS

A small gathering assembled around the board and within minutes there was an orderly queue waiting for more information.

'I've just asked some local business people to let me know if they've got any vacancies coming up,' he said, matter of factly. 'We're doing them a favour as much as they're doing us one. I thought the flip chart might help to bring the jobs to people's attention. We can update it every time we come.'

Well, just goes to show how little you know, Annette reminded herself. Note to self. Never, ever jump to conclusions about someone before getting to know them. And that means you, Annette Grey.

Word was beginning to spread about the job club. This was in part due to Alan who had talked about it in his church network. They began to receive visitors from other parishes who were interested in doing something similar. Annette and Paula were being called on to give talks and help other job club co-ops set up. They tried to do this on the days when they weren't needed at the foodbank. Life was getting busy.

Annette was helping a lady choose an outfit when, out of the corner of her eye, she caught sight of someone walking towards the waiting area. She'd only seen her that one time but she doubted very much that she'd ever forget that face. It was the girl who'd caused a commotion the afternoon that she'd met Paula here for the first time. The one who was so desperate for tampons. Their eyes met for a moment, then the girl turned away and slumped down on a chair. Annette turned her attention back to her customer. The woman chose a dress and jacket and, after further words of encouragement and good wishes, she left.

Annette went back to the table she'd been working from and waited. The girl had sunk even further down into the chair. She was scrolling through her phone, oblivious to the goings on around her. The other helpers were busy and Annette was the only one free. She wondered whether to say something. Maybe cough or call out, 'next', but that wasn't the way they did things around here. It wasn't the way she did things now. She waited a little longer, but there was still no sign that this young woman had an interest in anything but her screen. It was pointless waiting for her to look up. She'd have to make the first move. She walked over to the small figure slowly sliding down the seat. 'Hello, I'm Annette. Can I help you?'

The girl looked her up and down, then let out a long, exaggerated sigh. 'I got an interview.'

'Right, and you've come here for some advice?'

'I need clothes. I don't have anything to wear.'

'Okay, let's take a few details and go from there.' She led her over to a table, 'What's your name?'

'Kelly.'

'And your surname, Kelly?'

'Payne.'

'And your address?'

The girl sat up straight, her green eyes narrowed into slits. She reminded Annette of a cat, ready to pounce on an unsuspecting mouse. 'What do you need my address for?'

'Well, if we're going to lend you some clothes, we need to know where you live. In case for some reason you're not able to return them and we have to come and collect them.'

'You mean in case I pinch 'em. You think I'm a thief?' Her voice grew louder and she was beginning to attract attention.

One of the other clients, a middle-aged man, called over to her. 'Calm down girl, this ain't the officials. These people are doing their best, ye know. They're all right. Show some respect, ennit?'

Kelly's eyes widened. She cocked her head to one side and glared at the man.

'It's nothing personal Kelly,' said Annette. 'We do this with everybody but since you ask, a few people haven't returned clothing which makes it difficult for us to support others. You seem like an honest person to me so I'm sure you'll understand that, for everybody's sake, we have to have your address and some proof that you actually live there.'

'I don't have any proof on me. It's not like I carry this stuff about, is it?'

'Well perhaps you could come back later with some and then we can see if we have anything suitable. You're welcome to ask for advice about the interview now though if you'd like to.'

'Nah, you're all right. I'll come back.' She got up as if to go, then changed her mind. 'Do you remember me?'

'Yes.'

'Yeah, I remember you too.'

She pulled a hood over her head and went. Annette wasn't sure if that last statement was an acknowledgement or a threat. Time was, that would have had her frozen in terror. Today it only caused her some discomfort. Enough to make her scan the car park when she left that afternoon, and lock the doors as soon as she got in the car. All the same, she didn't expect to see Kelly Payne again.

She was wrong, however. Kelly Payne returned the next time the foodbank was open. She threw some official letters on the table. 'This good enough for you?'

Annette picked up the letters and checked them over. 'Thank you. Yes, they're fine.' She filled out the details on a form.

'So, do I get some clothes then?'

'Is that all you want?'

'Yeah.'

'You don't need any advice on the interview? You feel fully prepared?'

'I don't need anything else. I just need some decent clothes to get me through it.' There it was again, that angry impatience, just like the last time, and the time before that, *I just want some fucking tampons*. 'Don't worry, I'll bring them back. Like I said, I'm not a thief.'

She was not going to get any further with this one. She knew it. She had to accept that some people did not want her help. Most were perfectly capable of getting through an interview without any interference from her. This girl was different though. There was so much indignation in her, she wondered if it were possible to disguise it enough, not only to get her a job but also to actually keep it. She doubted it very much.

'Well?' Kelly was tapping her fingers on the table.

'When's your interview?'

'Monday.'

'And what's the job?'

'Call centre. It's a new one opening up on Broad Street.'

Jesus, was every job in this bloody city in a call centre?

'Well then, let's find you something to wear.'

They didn't have much in her size but, with the help of a belt that pulled in the waist, they managed to find a dress to go under the only jacket that didn't swamp her. Luckily too, they found a decent pair of shoes to go with them.

'The loan is for one week. No need to clean them. We do that when you return them. Could you just sign to say you accept the terms and conditions?' She grabbed an advice printout and handed it to Kelly with her receipt. 'Might be worth having a read before your interview. Good luck.'

Kelly brought everything back, hung tidily on the hangers, the following week. When Annette asked how she got on she just shrugged. 'Won't know 'til next week. Not expecting anything though. It was obvious they didn't like the look of me as soon as I walked in.'

'How do you know that?' asked Annette

'I just did. I'm not an idiot. See yer.'

Annette watched Kelly go. Her tiny frame gave her an air of vulnerability regardless of that hard-edged exterior. Annette wondered who was taking care of her. Who was making sure she was safe in this spiteful world, and who was there to mop up her tears? She stopped herself, annoyed by her own hypocrisy. Who was mopping up her children's tears? Certainly not her.

When she got home that evening, she called them. Liza was in high spirits. 'My art teacher says I'm on course for top grades in my GCSEs.'

'That's great. Well done, darling.'

'Dad's happy. Thinks I'm a chip off the old block. I'm thinking of doing art when I go to uni.'

'Really? Well I'm sure Dad will love that. Two artists in the family. How wonderful.' She made herself sound pleased. She knew she should be happy for Liza's sake. Why was it then that all she could think of was two starving artists that she'd have to support?

As if reading her mind Liza said: 'So you'd better hurry up and get another job, otherwise we'll all be in the shit.'

'Liza! What kind of language is that?'

Liza laughed and so did she. It hadn't really shocked her but pretending to be outraged served its purpose. It deflected the conversation away from her getting another job and, better still, it allowed them to share an all too rare mother-daughter moment. It felt as if they would both put the phone down in a good mood.

Annette hadn't seen her come in. She'd been deep in conversation with a woman who'd worked for the same company for twenty-five years. It had gone into administration and she'd been left with nothing until her benefits came through.

The woman was close to tears. 'I know it sounds silly but it's as if I'm going through a bereavement. I just don't know how I'm going to get over it.'

Annette saw herself in this woman who she'd never met before, but who'd managed to put into a few succinct words the feelings she'd been struggling with for the past few months. 'If you ever need someone to talk to, you know where I am.' Then she looked up and there was Kelly, itchy and impatient. The woman left, promising to keep in touch.

Kelly came over to Annette. 'I didn't get it.'

'I'm sorry to hear that,' said Annette. 'Did they say why? Did they give you any feedback?'

'Yeah. What was it now? Oh yeah.' Kelly held her hands out wide, as if astounded. 'Apparently, my temperament isn't really suited to client interaction.'

'I see.'

They watched each other for a few seconds until Kelly starting giggling. She was immediately transformed. Her colourless complexion became luminous and her eyes gleamed. She was quite enchanting. Annette's unease drifted away and her face creased.

'I suppose I could do with some help,' said Kelly.

'I'll do my best,' said Annette. 'It can't be all me though. You need to help yourself too.'

Kelly gave her a sideways look, as if summing her up. 'I'll consider myself told off then, shall I? So, is this the start of a beautiful friendship, milady?'

'We'll see. You may be a bit too much for me to handle.'

'Oh, I doubt it. I reckon you could look after yourself, if it came down to it.'

After two interview coaching sessions, there was little else that Annette could do for Kelly. When she turned up for a third session, they tidied up her CV. Not that there was much to work with. Her school and employment records were pitifully sparse and she gave away very little about herself. By the end of those three sessions, the only new facts that Annette was able to extricate was that Kelly was nine-teen and lived with her boyfriend, Craig.

Annette thought she'd made it clear that there was no

need to come back until she had an actual interview but Kelly came back again the following week.

'Hi. Do you have another interview already?'

Kelly shrugged. 'Nah. Just thought I'd pop in. See if you needed any help.'

'Oh! That's very nice of you,' said Annette.

Kelly shrugged again. 'Got nothing better to do.'

'Okay,' said Annette, biding her time while she was thinking what to say. 'Well, we're pretty much okay here in the job club but they might need some packers in the foodbank.'

Kelly sniffed. 'Yeah, all right. Might as well.'

When she took Kelly to meet George, he looked sceptical. That was probably because he was one of the volunteers she'd been arguing with, that time she'd come in asking for tampons.

'You think you've got what it takes to be a volunteer?' he said.

She huffed. 'Have to be special, do yer?'

'No. But you do have to be patient and polite.'

She held up her hands. 'Well, being as I'm shit at both of them things, that's me out.'

George stared at her poker faced. 'Is that your idea of a joke?'

'Yeah,' she said. 'And, for the record, you're not exactly polite yerself mate.'

He sniffed. 'All right. Point taken. We'll give you a chance. But stay away from the customers for now. When you've proved yourself, we'll consider you helping out in the café.'

'Whoo,' she said.

George folded his arms and sniffed again.

She rolled her eyes. 'Sorry.'

Annette didn't see much of Kelly for the rest of that day until they closed up. She was already in the café when Kelly came in, behind the other packers. Kelly held back and watched them pulling chairs around some pushed-together tables.

George called over to her. 'Come on Kelly, grab a chair. Don't be shy.'

Annette patted the seat next to her. 'This one's free.'

Kelly came over and sat down without saying a word. She gripped the edges of the seat, her eyes darting from one person to another. She was observing, just as Annette had done on her first day. She was weighing up these new people and this new situation. By the looks of it, it was as foreign to Kelly as it had been to her on that first day.

Annette held out her lunch box. 'Sandwich?'

Kelly looked as if she hadn't understood her, then glanced at the lunchbox. 'Cheers. I'm fucking starving.'

'Tea or coffee, Kelly?' said Paula.

'Tea. No sugar,' said Kelly. Then, as an afterthought, she added, 'Thanks.'

Paula put the mug down, along with a plate containing a couple of sandwiches. 'From me and George,' she said. 'If you come again on Friday, remember to bring something with you.'

'Do you want a mini quiche, Kelly?' said Neil.

'Eh?' she said.

'A mini quiche.'

She narrowed her eyes. 'What's it got in it?'

'Cheese, eggs, bacon,' he said.

'Go on then.'

Kelly came back on the next foodbank day. This time she

was allowed to take the parcels out to the meeters and greeters. Annette noticed that occasionally she'd stop and chat with one or two of the clients. She seemed to know them. In fact, she seemed a lot more relaxed with the clients than the volunteers.

At the end of the day, when they sat down in the café, she pulled out a bag of crisps.

'Is that your lunch?' said Neil.

'Yeah.' It was almost a question. As if she was surprised that he'd asked.

Neil shook his head. 'Bloody hell. Here, have one of these. It's a bit healthier.'

'What is it?'

'It's a chicken salad roll. Organic, free range chicken,' he said, a hint of exasperation in his voice.

'All right, keep it down.' She took one of his rolls and took out the salad leaves before biting into it.

Neil laughed. 'Is it fair to say you've got a limited palate, Kel?'

'Fuck off,' she said, swallowing down a mouthful of roll.

As the weeks rolled by, Kelly became an established member of the team and she and Neil settled into a lunchtime pattern. She pulled out a bag of crisps or similar and he gave her a plateful of something decent to eat. He seemed determined to get some healthy food into her and maybe widen her culinary tastes at the same time, and she seemed to play along with it. Annette guessed he secretly enjoyed feeding Kelly. She also wondered what Kelly ate the rest of the week. By the look of her, not a lot.

Some days Kelly would come in and be fine, but there were others when she'd turn up in the foulest mood. They dealt with her mood swings, by sending her off to do bag packing and letting her get on with it.

'She's got a cob on,' said George, one morning. 'We've sent her to the back, out of harm's way.'

Generally, the volunteers took her tantrums in their stride but on one particular day when she was being especially irritating, George voiced what they were probably all thinking. 'Oi moody miss. Get yourself off to Cob Corner and give us all a rest will you?'

Kelly rounded on him. 'What the fuck is that supposed to mean?'

'You heard, you bolshy little sod. Go and work in the back and sort that miserable face out before you scare the customers away.'

The entire room experienced a tumbleweed moment as Kelly glared at him, hands on hips. George was the only person who seemed oblivious to it. He waited until he'd handed over a parcel and said goodbye to his customer, then turned to look at her. 'You still here?' He pointed towards the shelves of food behind them. 'Cob Corner.'

Kelly snorted. She appeared to be weighing up her options. 'You're a cheeky old fucker. You know that, don't yer?'

George shrugged. 'Been called worse. You going, or staying? Because if you're staying you better put a smile on that face of yours.' Kelly's lips twitched into menacing sneer. 'That's better,' he said, with a look that said it wasn't really. 'You look almost human now.'

'Fuck you, George.' She flounced off to the back of the room and stayed there, in a sulk, for the rest of the day.

On the next foodbank day, Kelly didn't show up. Neither did she make an appearance on the following day. They all assumed she'd taken the huff and wasn't coming back. Some of them admitted they were secretly relieved. But their relief was short-lived. The next week, she strolled through the doors as though nothing had happened. Annette was pleased to see her. Even though they had nothing in common, she still liked Kelly and, on her good days, Kelly seemed to like her too.

While the incident with George wasn't exactly a watershed moment, Kelly did seem to be making an effort to be less touchy which was just as well since, during her absence, there had been discussions about whether the place was better without her. Annette considered whether she should say something to her. A friendly warning. As it was, she didn't need to. Neil beat her to it.

It had been silly really, Kelly had been arguing with a client who, it had to be said, was borderline obnoxious but her reaction to him only made his behaviour worse. Annette could see she was about to blow a fuse so she offered to take over. To her shock, Kelly turned on her, her face in hers. 'What, you think I can't look after myself, or you worried I might offend twat face here? He's a dick and he deserves everything he gets, and you know nothing about me.'

Instinctively Annette backed away. That seemed to rile Kelly all the more. 'Fucking condescending cow. Fucking middle-class posho doing your bit for charity. You think these people care about you? They wouldn't give a toss if you dropped down dead tomorrow, so long as they got their fucking food parcel.' She stormed out through the double doors leaving the shocked volunteers and customers reeling in her wake.

'Well somebody's upset,' said George.

Neil went after her but she was nowhere to be seen. Annette was frozen to the spot, swallowing air, trying to remain in control.

'What about my fucking food parcel?' said twat face, bringing her back to life.

She grabbed his few remaining items, threw them into the bag, and practically tossed it at him. He snatched it off her with a look of contempt. Perhaps Kelly was right. Perhaps she was nothing to these people. Just some middle-class nob who was trying to fool herself she was doing something worthwhile.

Paula put her arm around her. 'She didn't mean it. She's just upset about something. It's the way she deals with things she can't really handle. You know that, don't you?'

'Yes, yes, of course,' said Annette. It cut into her, all the same. She went through the rest of the day with her professional face on. It was a bit over the top but better that than show what she was really thinking.

Kelly turned up, looking shamefaced, just as they were locking up. 'Sorry,' she mumbled, to no one in particular.

'It's Net you should be apologising to,' said Neil. 'What you said to her was disgraceful.'

'It's okay, Neil,' said Annette. 'Really.'

'No, it's not.' His voice was low but angry. 'Kelly, you can't go around talking to people like that. If you can't treat people with decency and respect then we don't want you here.'

Kelly's eyes were red. She looked worn out. 'I said I was sorry. That twat just got to me.'

'Not good enough,' he said. 'We do not get angry with clients. No matter how bad they are. And we do not have a go at each other. Is that clear?' She nodded. 'Do you want to carry on here?' She nodded again. 'I'll speak to the others and see if they'll let you back in. I don't know if they will though. You crossed a line today. If you want to keep on coming you've got to behave yourself. Last chance. Now, go home and I'll call you later, yeah?'

Kelly's whisper was barely audible. 'Okay.'

Annette felt so sorry for her. 'Come on, Kelly. I'll drop you off home.'

They made the journey back to Kelly's flat in silence. Annette stopped the car at the corner of her road.

Kelly stayed in her seat. 'Net, I didn't mean those things I said to you. I just lost it. Sorry. Things are just a bit shit for me right now and I took it out on you. I don't know why I do that — take it out on the people I care about.'

'It's all right. I do understand. In a non-condescending way, obviously.' Kelly gave a weak little laugh. 'Do you want to talk about the shit things?'

Kelly swallowed something down. 'Nah, you're all right. I know I'm a bitch but please don't hate me, Net. I couldn't stand that.'

10

MUM AND DAD PAY A VISIT

'We just wanted to let you know we're spending Christmas in Cornwall this year.' Even over the phone, Colin sounded smug.

'Cornwall?' Annette knew she'd heard him right. It was the disbelief that made her ask.

'Yes, Cornwall. Mum and Dad have rented a house so we're going with them. The whole family will be there. The kids are really looking forward to it. We're going on Wednesday to help with the preparations and we'll be back a few days after new year.'

'But that's only a couple of days away. I won't be able to see them before you go.' She wanted to say, 'what about me?' but she was aware of just how needy that would sound and, anyway, it would play right into his hands. Another point scored in his 'let's annihilate Annette' game.

'Well.' He paused, pretending to think. Pretending he gave a damn. 'I suppose they could come over to yours for a couple of hours after school tomorrow. It's their last day. They finish at one.'

Tomorrow was Tuesday. A foodbank day. It was also the

day she'd arranged to meet with several of the new job clubs to talk about forming a network. If she'd had more notice, she could have rescheduled it but it was too late now. She knew what his reaction was going to be, but she had no choice. 'I'm rather busy tomorrow, Colin. Can't they come in the evening and stay overnight?'

'Busy? Looking after the poor, I suppose. Sorry Annette, we can't all be at your beck and call. We're heading off early so they need to be here on Wednesday morning. Why don't you come over when you've finished your busy day? If you can fit us in?'

'I'm sure I can. I'll be there at six.'

Cornwall. How could they? They didn't even ask if she minded not seeing them, didn't even consider her enough to give more than two days' notice. Yet they must have been planning the trip for a while.

She spent the rest of the day picking away at things. What was it about her that made them so callous towards her? What had she done to them to make them dislike her so much? Her eyes and head ached. Every inch of her wanted to give in and break down but she refused to let it happen. She held herself in, like she always did on these occasions. She might have learned to relax a bit more now but sometimes it was necessary to go back to firmly established habits and be the old, indestructible Annette. Yes, sometimes it was best to build yourself a fortress and stay there until the hurt went away.

She went to bed early, exhausted by the effort of holding it all in but, as usual, sleep wouldn't come. She tossed and fidgeted for hours until she was sick of lying there, and got up to make herself a hot, milky drink.

As the fridge door swung shut, she caught sight of Shani's painting of her taped on to it. The angry eyebrows and downturned mouth — that was her all right. That child had a talent, if not for art then certainly for seeing into people's hearts. She pulled on a thick coat and went out onto the balcony.

The starched white grass below was visible under the moon's clear glow and there was a sharpness to the air that cut into her nostrils. With any luck it would snow and, if it was really bad, they wouldn't be able to go to Cornwall. 'Don't be silly. They'll go and you'll be here on your own. Get used to it.' She tutted. 'Still angry, I see. It's very unbecoming you know, and it really won't get you what you want.' In spite of herself, she smiled. That was something her gran used to say to her when she was young. 'I think you could have been right all along, Gran. No more anger. I'm done with it. Merry Christmas one and all.'

She drew the hot chocolate to her lips and let it slide silkily down her throat to heat her up her from the inside. Perhaps now she would sleep.

The job club had been quiet for a week. No one was interested in interviewing this close to Christmas. But Tuesday was hectic. Although the meeting had been worthwhile, it took Paula and Annette away from the foodbank for a couple of hours on a day when it was busier than ever. Perhaps because it was almost Christmas and people found themselves even more strapped for cash than usual.

Neil had made an enormous amount of mince pies and was handing them out to anyone that wanted them. 'If you've got a freezer, put them in and they'll be fine for Christmas. I'll be bringing in some more festive treats on Friday if anyone's around.'

An elderly lady gave him a kiss which then started a

Mexican wave style of kisses around the room for all the volunteers. Just as Malcolm Jefferson came striding through the doors, an overexcited woman grabbed him and landed her lips square on his.

'And a very happy Christmas to you too, Melanie. Looks like my timing was perfect.' He returned the compliment with a peck on her cheek and moved around to the other side of the counter. 'All hands to the pump, is it?' he said, rolling up his sleeves and calling out for the next customer.

He'd been told he wasn't needed for the job club but he came anyway. He brought with him the other Masons employees and Ash, the foodbank volunteer who'd spoken so movingly about his own experiences to people he now called team mates. Malcolm had been so impressed with him that day, and then more so through his ongoing contact with him at the club, that he'd offered him a job as soon as something came up.

One of the smaller rooms had been turned into Santa's grotto. The idea had been Ash's, himself a father. He organised donations of selection packs and children's gifts at Masons and their business partners, as did Chris and Corrine at their places of work. The volunteers had all arrived especially early that morning to decorate the room. Kelly who had been on her best behaviour since being allowed back into the fold, and Emily, one of the regular clients, had taken on the role of Santa's elves and were distracting the disorderly chain of excited children with games and Christmas songs. Meanwhile George, heavily disguised in a Santa suit, patiently listened to each child's Christmas list and gave them a small present and a pack of chocolate goodies. Although there were one or two upsets, by and large, every one of them left the grotto happy.

Amid the chaos, Annette noticed her parents near the

double doors clutching each other's hand and nervously scanning the room — out of place and ill at ease. She waved and saw their relief when they spotted her. She swept them up and guided them around the different queues, into the empty job club and settled them down with a cup of tea and a mince pie.

'This is a surprise,' she said, not sure what else to say.

'Well, if we waited for you to come and see us, we'd be waiting a very long time, wouldn't we?' Her mother had her high and mighty face on. Annette felt like a naughty teenager who'd just been found out for playing truant.

'Sorry. I've been really busy.'

'Yes, we can see that,' sniffed her mother.

Her father surveyed the racks of clothes.

'This is our Job Club Co-operative,' Annette explained. 'We give people interview coaching and lend them something to wear if they need it.'

'I see. Good idea,' he said. 'Is it always that busy out there?'

'Well it's always busy but it's especially so today. The run up to Christmas. People have even less spare cash, and they rarely have spare cash at the best of times.'

'Yes, I suppose so,' said her father. 'It must be awful to be in that sort of situation. Thank goodness we were never that unlucky.'

'Well, we put money by for a rainy day. Just in case,' said her mother.

'It's not quite the same thing Mum. Our customers haven't been in a position to put money by. And if they did once, then it's all been used up on necessities well before they're forced to come here.'

'Annette's right love. We might have had to be careful,

but we never really went without did, we? I mean, I never lost my job once,' said her dad.

Her mother heaved her chest up. 'Well, I should hope not. You had a job for life with the Civil Service.'

Her dad nodded agreement. 'That's right love. We can't all be that lucky, can we?'

'Actually, not all of our customers are unemployed,' said Annette. 'Some are working and on low wages. Some are pensioners who have to rely on pension top ups and something happens that means they have to choose between food and paying a bill.'

Her dad cleared his throat. 'I don't think we realised that. Did we, love?'

Her mum shook her head.

'Anyway, how did you find me?' Annette was sure she hadn't given them the address.

'Colin told us the area. I think one of the kids saw something when they were over at your flat, then Dad did a bit of research.' Her mother's lip curled when she said Colin's name, so that it came out like a snarl. Whether she meant it to or not, it perfectly matched her feelings towards him.

She'd made it quite plain to Annette that she despised Colin Grey. As far as she was concerned, he was a self-opinionated, self-centred waste of space who had systematically leeched off her daughter for years. That was bad enough, but what was even more aggravating was that she couldn't tell him that. For the sake of her grandchildren, she had to pretend that she actually liked him.

It was this personal outrage that fuelled her loathing further so that it seemed to simmer like a boiling cauldron underneath the surface, permanently ready to overspill. She took every opportunity to remind her daughter of her indignation so much so that in the past Annette had found

herself defending Colin. Lately however, she was beginning
to think her mother may have a point, even if she couldn't
bring herself to openly admit that to her.

Not that her mum saved her disdain solely for Colin.
She often told Annette that, in her view, most of her troubles had been brought on by her willingness to be his door-
mat. If she had only stood up to him from day one, things
would have been very different. Unfortunately, it wasn't
quite that simple but then, her mother didn't know that. She
didn't realise how hard it was to say no to Colin.

Much like his wife, her father was not exactly Colin's
number one fan either but he had a milder temperament
than her and generally provided a more circumspect view.
He was a placater who always tried to see things on both
sides and keep everyone happy.

'You know they're going to Cornwall tomorrow, don't
you love?' he said.

'Yes, I'm going to see them this evening.'

'You do know he's doing this on purpose?' said her
mother. 'It's because you won't look for another job. That's
why he's doing it.'

'Mum, I'm sure that's not the case.'

'I think your mum's right, love,' said her dad. 'Daft as it
might sound, I think he's doing this to try to bring you to
your senses. It's just the odd hints that slip out every now
and then, and he's got the kids wrapped around his little
finger. They daren't speak to you in case they offend him.
When did they tell you that they were going away?'

She shuffled in her seat. 'Yesterday.' It came out like a
croak.

'I knew it Arthur,' said her mother. 'We only found out
on Sunday, when we went over to see them. Dad told them

there and then that if they didn't tell you straight away, he'd do it himself.'

There was a flicker of anger in her dad's eyes. Unusual for him. 'I'm sorry love, I should have called you then, but we thought it was best it came from them.'

'It's okay Dad. Don't worry,' she said, more composed now.

'All the same, I wish I'd called you. Have you started looking for a job yet?'

'No. I've been too caught up in all of this.' She gestured towards the main hall.

Her mother stiffened, 'Charity's all very well Annette, but it doesn't pay the bills. Whether we like it or not, you've got two homes to support.'

'I'm not ready to go back to work yet. I'm managing, with my redundancy money and my savings.'

'How long is that going to last you? That family of yours has expensive tastes.'

'Mum, I'm not going back yet, and that's that. I have important work to do here. The family will just have to learn to do without a few luxuries.'

'Important work? Anyone would think she was a bloody missionary. Arthur, talk some sense into her.'

Annette and her mother both looked at her dad who was visibly squirming under the spotlight. 'The thing is sweetheart, this decision of yours affects us too. The children have stopped coming over to visit us. I mean, they seemed pleased enough to see us when we went over there but they used to pop in sometimes, after school and weekends. That sort of thing. And well, we miss them and we're a little bit worried about them.'

'I'm sure they're fine Dad, they've been very busy with

their mock exams so I expect that's why they haven't been to see you. I'll mention it to them when I see them later.'

'Fat lot you'd know. It's not as if you see them very often is it?' said her mother.

'Come on now Geraldine love, that's not going to get us anywhere,' said her dad. 'We've put our case to Annette and there's nothing more we can say. She's obviously very attached to this place, and I can see why. It looks like she's doing a good job here. She's had a hard time of it lately. Let's give her the chance to get herself back on her feet, eh?'

Annette's mum put the mug down on the table, probably with more force than she'd intended. 'Well, if you want my advice, which of course you won't, don't take too long over it. And, never mind everyone else. Keep an eye on those children of yours before he turns them completely against us all.'

Her father stood up and put his arm on her mum's shoulder. 'We'd better get off and let you get back on with things. We're going to Auntie Janet's for Christmas. You're welcome to come. She'd love to see you.'

'Thanks Dad but I'll be fine.'

'I don't like to think of you on your own at Christmas,' he said.

'Oh, I won't be alone.'

Her mother looked hopeful. 'Anything we should know about?'

She knew what her mum was implying. Wishing for. In truth she didn't know what she was going to do. She had some vague idea about helping out at a centre for the homeless but that was all it was. Frankly, the only thing worse than spending Christmas alone would be spending it trapped at Auntie Janet's with her parents. Naturally she couldn't tell them that. She'd have to try and sidestep the question. 'No, nothing like that. I'll pop over and see you on Christmas Eve.'

'Nice mince pies by the way,' said her father. 'Did you make them?'

'No, my friend Neil did.' She pointed him out to them as they made their exit through the main room.

Her mother's interest was piqued again. 'Your friend? He looks nice.'

Neil came over to say hello. He insisted on giving them a pack of mince pies and stayed with Annette to wave them off. 'Was that me she was referring to?' Her mum had been louder than she'd realised.

'Oh yes. I think it was the mince pies that swung it.'

'She's obviously a very discerning woman. What are you doing for Christmas, by the way?'

The roads on the way into Moseley were a nightmare. There was the usual rush hour traffic from people going home from work. Added to that were the Christmas shoppers heading out of town and the Christmas revellers partying in the local bars and restaurants. Result? Traffic chaos. By the time she'd crawled the few miles from her flat to the house she was forty minutes late and cursing herself for not coming straight from the foodbank. No doubt Colin would have something to say about her tardiness.

She turned into the leafy street and parked up outside the spacious semi that used to be her home. In no rush for her verbal beating, she stayed a while in the car to gather herself together and prepare.

Through the lounge window she could see Liza on the couch, watching TV and talking on her phone. On the wall above her was one of Colin's God-awful paintings. The house was littered with them. Well, he had to put them somewhere. No one else wanted them.

She got out of the car and hovered in the street, trying to catch Liza's eye. But Liza was still talking, her eyes staring at the TV. From this spot, she could see the inside of the lounge in greater detail. In the corner of the room was a tall, thin Christmas tree, very artfully arranged with sparkling white lights. No sign of the tacky baubles that the kids used to love when they were little. It was a fake tree. Real ones were far too unpredictable for Colin's liking. There were a few Christmas-related ornaments placed in the window and on the large mantelpiece over the fireplace. Again, nothing cheap or gaudy.

That the curtains were wide open and the lights on, both upstairs and down, was probably deliberate. Everything Colin did was deliberate. He was announcing to the world that he had taste, that he was an artist. He was probably staging his own little announcement to her too. *So what, if I can't be bothered to close my curtains? I'm that fun, unconstrained kind of guy who doesn't care what people think of me.* Ironic, considering the opposite was true.

The only room she could see that was in darkness was his studio at the side of the house. It had been a garage when they first moved in. The plan had always been to convert it to an extra room. She'd envisaged an extra sitting room. Somewhere the kids could bring their friends. Colin had other ideas. As usual, he got what he wanted.

She'd always hated his studio. Not least because it cost so much to build. The whole of her 2008 bonus, to be exact. A whole year of pushing herself to be the top of her game, of pretending to be 'hungry for it' like a performing seal waiting for a fish to be thrown its way. A whole year, for that shitty room.

In fact, it was possible to map out that house in terms of her annual bonuses and in terms of her work performance. The new kitchen was 2006. The bathroom makeover, 2007. The second bathroom and the bedroom over the studio was 2009 and 2010. That was an expensive one but she didn't mind it so much. At least it got Liza a bigger room. The one that really pissed her off was his last project in 2015, completed just a few months before he said they didn't want her there anymore. It was their bedroom.

Liza's head turned her way as she walked up the path. She waved but there was still no recognition. There was a wreath on the door. A classy one, naturally. No tat in this house, thank you. She rang the doorbell. The door keys were still on her keyring but she hadn't used them in over two years.

Will opened the door. 'Hey Mum. Merry Christmas.'

'Merry Christmas.' She stepped into the warm, bright hall. 'It looks nice and Christmassy in here,' she lied.

She heard Liza saying. 'Gotta go. My mum's here. Yeah, right. Message you later.' She came out into the hall. 'Hi.'

'Hello darling. Happy Christmas,' said Annette.

'Do you want a coffee?' said Will.

They went into the kitchen. It had had another makeover since she last saw it. The old pantry had been knocked out to make the room bigger. Not that it was small before. The cupboards had been changed. Someone had spent a lot of cash on this room and she knew who it was. She resisted the urge to comment on it to Liza and Will but it irked her nevertheless that she was funding yet another of Colin's unnecessary whims. Will was making her a cappuccino on Colin's new coffee machine. She must have paid for that too.

It occurred to her that Colin was missing. 'Is your dad not here?'

'No. He's gone out,' said Liza. 'He had to pick something up before the trip.'

There was something about the way she said that. Annette couldn't put her finger on it. Maybe it was because she looked away when she said it. It didn't feel natural. The nonchalance was too forced. On the plus side, Colin wasn't at home. Christmas had come early in that respect.

'Sorry we're not going to be here,' said Will. 'It's just that Grandma's not well and we thought it would be nice for her.' He gulped and looked at his feet.

That woman, always turning up like a bad penny. Amazing how often she'd suddenly fallen ill when she wanted something. It wasn't hard to guess where Colin had learned his manipulation skills from. No doubt the two of them had cooked it up together. No doubt the entire Grey family had closed ranks to support poor, hard done by Colin. Just as they always did.

'Don't worry about me, I'm spending Christmas with friends. I'll be fine.'

'Oh!' They seemed almost disappointed. They must have been hoping she would have a miserable time.

She qualified it: 'I know it won't be the same as spending it with you but we can have a call on Christmas morning. If you're not too busy.'

Liza's smile was triumphant but Will's reaction was more subdued. Then, as if a further test was required, Liza asked: 'What friends?'

'Oh, you don't know them. They're friends I met through the foodbank.' It was obvious they didn't believe her. Normally she would have spared them the details but this irritated her. 'I'm going with Paula, who I used to work with, to Neil and Chris's house to stay on Christmas Eve. Chris has a big family and I think they'll be coming over for a get-together that night. Neil's going to cook Christmas dinner for the four of us, and three other friends. I'm not sure what's happening on Boxing Day. I think another friend, Corrine, will be coming over at some point. And there might be another party to go to. If I'm up to it.'

They looked taken aback. She guessed it was because all this socialising sounded nothing like the mother they knew. She folded her arms and put on an earnest expression. 'But I'll miss you both terribly. Obviously.'

She stayed for an hour then left before Colin came back.

On the drive home, she reflected on the last hour. The children were a little restrained, but that was nothing new. They were often that way around her. In fact, anything but restraint was a rare but welcome occurrence. But her parents' warnings had lodged themselves in her head. She played back the things that they'd said, or hadn't said, looking for signs of purposeful vengeance being meted out by her ex-husband. There was nothing obvious as far as she could tell but then, as her mother had so bluntly put it, how would she know? One thing she did know was that Colin was too clever for the obvious. His was a well-practised, subtle technique that left you wondering whether something had really just happened, or if you'd imagined it all along.

11

AN EPIPHANY OF SORTS

She woke up on Christmas Eve with the same feeling of dread that resurfaced every year. Normally it was because of the worry that in twenty-four hours she would spend the entire day treading on eggshells, afraid that the wrong word or the wrong look could ruin it for everyone.

After she'd moved out, Christmas was the one day when she was allowed back in to the inner sanctum of the family. It was the only time they took pity on her and let her spend it with them. Although the honour wasn't hers alone. There was normally at least one set of grandparents there, which didn't make it any easier.

This was her first Christmas without them. She would not have to arrange her face into a fixed smile and keep it there, on show, in case someone accused her of not enjoying herself. She didn't have to pretend to be anything tomorrow. So why then the familiar pangs? Because in spite of the gut-wrenching, sometimes vomit-inducing anguish she subjected herself to on these occasions, the thought of them being somewhere else, enjoying themselves without her, was agonising.

She was losing them. Her parents were right. She'd been trying not to think about it since Tuesday but Liza's expression, when she thought that she'd be spending Christmas alone, was nothing short of delight. Everyone said that Liza looked like her, but right then, she was pure Colin.

Putting it to the back of her mind had been fairly easy until now because she'd been so occupied. For the two days following her visit on Tuesday everyone descended on Neil's house for a final baking push, ready for the last foodbank before Christmas. This time he'd made an array of things and help was needed to ice cakes, and bag up mince pies and cookies.

'This must have cost you a fortune,' said Paula.

'Not really,' said Neil. 'I kept some of the money back that I raised for the job club dry cleaning and Chris's mum has been having regular collections at her church. So, it's pretty much all covered. She and the aunties have made some rum cakes too.'

Those two days may have been busy but Friday at the foodbank had been borderline pandemonium. Luckily the team had been bolstered again by the Masons volunteers and Alan the vicar and his wife. The Masons team brought sherry and mince pies with them to offer out to customers and helpers. She recognised them as ones they had every year at the company's Christmas party. This, along with the presence of the church choir belting out carols, put everyone in a good mood and people seemed reluctant to leave.

There were queues for the food parcels, queues for Neil's free baking, and small groups idly chatting or singing along with the choir. The local schools had already broken up so there were more children around and Santa's grotto was in a state of siege. Maybe it was the comfortable warmth of the atmosphere, or perhaps the sherry. No one seemed to mind the squeeze and everyone was full of seasonal goodwill.

Afterwards, the volunteers decamped to a nearby pub that specialised in Thai food for their own Christmas celebration. The drinks flowed, the food was excellent, and everyone was in a great mood. There were so many of them they filled two large tables. Annette realised she liked every single person in the party. There was not one of them who made her uncomfortable, and that included Malcolm, who she now counted as a friend. She'd been wrong about him. How many others, she wondered, had she been wrong about over the years?

The atmosphere brought to mind her student days in Manchester. She had so many friends back then. They often used to go out in a big group. Mostly to the pubs and student bars. That was how she'd met Doogie. One of his friends knew Sasha. Not that they'd needed any introduction. The Sex Pistols were on the jukebox in some grotty old pub at the time. She was throwing herself around, pogo style, with Sasha and Claire when she noticed him staring at her from the other side of the room. His face was a picture. A mixture of wonder and amusement. The sight of him stopped her in her tracks. He was the most beautiful creature she'd ever seen. She smiled at him. He came over to her and, before he could speak, she just kissed him. She couldn't help herself.

Doogie. What would he make of her now? If he'd walked into the pub at that moment would he even know her? And even if he recognised the form and shape of what was once Netta Wilde, what would he think of the person she'd become? She pushed it to the back of her mind. It didn't matter what Doogie might think. Or what Colin thought for that matter. She was here with her friends and she was enjoying herself. That was enough.

In the taxi home that night, Paula asked her if she was looking forward to Christmas and she said yes without thinking. The day's events and the evening party had given her this wonderful feeling of well-being that she thought would last forever. It did last through Saturday as she did her last-minute shopping and settled down to wrap presents in the evening. But it was the morning of Christmas Eve now. The flat was cheerless and there was nothing to distract her. She'd woken with that customary suggestion of impending doom, and she'd promised to visit her parents today so it could only get worse. She'd arranged to go over for lunch, before picking up Paula. It gave her an exit strategy if things got too tense.

When her mother opened the door, the sound of 'Frosty the Snowman' floated along the hall like a reassuring aroma. The Ronettes, if she wasn't mistaken. Her dad was playing his Phil Spector Christmas album. That was the thing about Arthur Wilde. He may be one of the mildest mannered and, yes, boring, men on the planet but come Christmas a meta-morphosis took place. Okay, he still liked his comfy cardie and slippers. Two whiskies and he was out for the count. But once he'd got those CDs out, he'd be dancing around the house like a man possessed by the Yuletide spirit and you knew, without a doubt, Christmas had arrived in the Wilde household.

Her mum gave her an exasperated look, but Annette could tell she loved it too. 'Honestly, he's been playing them non-stop since Wednesday. He'll wear them out.'

'I doubt that very much, love,' said her father. 'I've had

them for twenty years now and they're still going strong. Merry Christmas Nettie, my darling.'

'Come in,' said her mother, 'I've made your favourite. Steak and mushroom pie.'

The scene of her birthday meal with all its associated baggage immediately sprang to mind.

'You do still like it don't you?' Her mother's expression changed to unease.

'I love it Mum. I haven't had it in ages.'

'Did you see the children before they went away?' asked her mum, her fork hovering over her lunch plate.

'Yes,' said Annette.

'Well?'

'It was a bit strained. Colin wasn't there though so I can't really say whether it's his influence or just, you know, the way they feel about me at the moment.'

'He doesn't have to be there to brainwash them. You of all people should know that.'

Her dad put down his knife and fork. 'Your mum didn't mean that to come out the way it did, sweetheart.'

'Yes, I did Arthur. Stop trying to soften my words,' said her mum.

Her dad grimaced, 'Come on Gee. It's Christmas. Let's not worry about it today.'

'It's all right Dad,' said Annette. 'For what it's worth I think there was something not quite right about their behaviour but there's not much I can do about it at the moment.'

The acknowledgement seemed to please her mother. 'What will you do then?'

'I don't know yet Mum, but I'll think of something. Don't let it worry you. It'll only spoil your Christmas.'

Her dad switched the CD over to *White Christmas*. 'Annette's right. She'll think of something. She's very resourceful. Tell us about Friday. It was a foodbank day wasn't it? Was it as busy as Tuesday?'

'Oh, busier.'

She proceeded to tell them about everything that had happened on Friday. They seemed genuinely interested. Even her mother asked questions and laughed out loud when she told them about Father Christmas being mobbed by over-zealous children.

'I've brought you some more of Neil's mince pies, as you enjoyed them so much.'

'You sure he's just a friend?' said her mum.

'Yes Mum. He has a partner. A husband.'

'Oh, I see. That's a shame.'

Annette and her dad exchanged smirks.

'Lovely pie, Mum,' she said. 'I'd forgotten how good it tasted.'

'You know, that place has a good effect on you,' said her dad as he walked with her to the car. 'You've a lovely glow about you. It's nice to see. Have a very happy Christmas Nettie.'

He skipped back up the path singing 'Santa Claus is Coming to Town.'

She watched him go, filled with nostalgia for Christmases past. Maybe everybody thought their childhood Christmases were special. She couldn't say, but she knew hers were. That was probably one of the reasons her adult Christmases always fell a bit flat. She could never recreate that cosiness and they always felt a bit cold and joyless. Especially when everything else deteriorated. Getting through a normal day was hard enough but Christmas, with all that hype and the relentless pressure to appear happy, killed it dead.

She set off for Paula's house. The tension in her stomach had already loosened. It hadn't been as bad as she'd expected it to be. In fact, it had been rather nice.

Paula lived alone and had no children but she'd decorated her house as if she did. 'I used to do it for my nephews and nieces and my godchildren. Now I do it for their kids but, if I'm really honest, I do it as much for myself as them. I don't see why I should miss out on all the fun just because I live on my own.'

The contrast with Annette's own flat, devoid of any decoration except for a few Christmas cards, was stark. She vowed to make more of an effort next year.

If Paula's house glittered, Neil and Chris's positively dazzled. In the corner of the room was a huge tree, festooned with trimmings and lights, under which sat a mountain of presents. They'd seen the tree before, when they'd helped with the cooking but the room had been unfinished. Now that is was complete, it looked spectacular.

They got stuck in to setting out the buffet ready for the guests while Chris and Neil filled up the drinks table.

'Best leave that side empty.' Chris gestured to the counter. 'It'll soon get filled up.'

And it did. As each group of guests came in, they brought with them a dish of food or a bottle of something. Soon the place was full of people dressed in their party clothes. The children crowded around the tree looking for a gift with their name on it. The women commandeered the sofas and the chairs, and the men congregated in the back of the room.

In the middle of all of this were Chris and Neil, exuding happiness. They completed each other in a way she'd never seen before. It was a million miles away from her relationship with Colin, even at its best, and she envied them for it.

Chris's dad called Neil over to help him with the stereo. The soft background music switched to Darlene Love belting out 'Marshmallow World.' It was the same album she'd heard at her parents' house, and that she'd heard every Christmas as a girl. She recalled that afternoon, her dad, tripping along the garden path in his moccasins, and realised how much she loved his seasonal transformation from quiet and unassuming father and husband to suburban bon vivant.

'My dad loves this stuff,' said Chris. 'Can't get enough of it.'

'Mine too. He insists on playing it over and over, every Christmas,' she said.

He laughed. 'Yeah, same with mine. Must be something about the age. I used to hate it, but it's recently started to grow on me.'

They gazed at the cluster of elderly men singing their hearts out.

'I know what you mean,' she said. 'It wouldn't be Christmas without it. Is Neil's family coming over?'

He shook his head. 'He lost touch with them in his wilderness years. Before I knew him. They didn't really get on and I think the way he was made it worse.'

'The drugs?'

'You'd think so, wouldn't you? But actually, I don't think they could get their heads round him being gay. That was the worst thing for him. I mean he cleaned himself up but he couldn't make himself straight. I think it just became easier for him to let them go, you know? It still gets to him though. Especially at times like this. Luckily, my family love him, so he has a ready-made one. And, you may have noticed, he collects friends. They become his family too.'

She hadn't noticed.

He smiled, 'I don't mean that in a bad way. He genuinely loves you and Corrine, and Paula. You're his surrogate family. His side of this lot. You make him happy and that makes me happy.' He put his arm around her and kissed the top of her head, 'I love you too, little surrogate sister-in-law.'

She reached up and kissed his cheek. 'Thank you. It's been a long time since I've said this to anyone, but I love you both too.'

There, she'd said it and, whilst it was mildly embarrassing to admit her feelings, the sky hadn't fallen in and Chris looked perfectly comfortable with it.

'Wow,' he said. 'Praise indeed.'

'How did you and Neil meet?'

'At a rehab drop-in centre where I volunteer. He walked in. No, let me rephrase that. He burst in. Really cocky. Like he owned the place. But you could tell that wasn't the person underneath. He was hard work at first. Always acting like he didn't care about anything when he was actually so full of self-disgust, he couldn't believe anyone would like him, let alone love him. I knew he was worth hanging on for though. It took a while but, one by one, the layers peeled away and he saw himself for the adorable, sweet guy he is. Then he let me in.'

That explained why she felt such an affinity with Neil. They were two peas in a pod. Except that she was still at the self-loathing stage and she didn't have someone like Chris to rescue her. She didn't have someone to tell her she was worth it. All she'd had in a long time was Colin and all she got from him was how fucking useless she was at everything.

'He still lacks confidence though,' said Chris. 'You know what a brilliant cook he is, Net. He's scared to take the next step and do it for a living again. I'm hopeful that one day he'll be strong enough. I think that would make him feel like he's achieved something.'

They were interrupted by the sound of a tinkling piano that had been borrowed from one of the aunties especially for the evening.

'I hope you like singing,' he said.

Phil Spector was switched off and the entire party gathered around elderly Auntie May, who was sitting in front of the piano running her twig-like fingers up and down the scales. She was in her eighties, the oldest of the aunties and uncles. Petite, and so delicate she looked as though a sudden draught would sweep her up and carry her off into the night. She began with 'Oh Come All Ye Faithful' then, 'Silent Night' and everyone sang and clapped in time to her tinny warble. Whether you were religious or not, the mood was catching and Annette found she was singing and clapping along with everyone else.

At eleven o'clock, the music stopped. Winter coats were thrown on. Small children were scooped up and everyone bustled out the door, some still singing.

'Midnight Mass,' said Neil. 'You don't have to come if you don't want to.'

'I've never been to one. I'd like to see what it's like,' said Annette. 'I didn't know you were religious.'

He picked up one of the nephews and sat him on his shoulders, 'I'm not but that doesn't matter. It's nice being there. I dunno, maybe it's the tradition or the fact that I'm surrounded by this. I love it. I love all of it.'

She walked with Paula and Connie, Chris's mum, and listened to them talking about the importance of family without commenting. Since hers so often felt so foreign to her, she didn't feel qualified to have an opinion. Still, it made her think of her own children. Throughout the evening she'd been trying to think of a Christmas that she'd spent with them when she didn't feel on edge, but she couldn't. She really was an awful mother. It was no wonder they chose to stay with Colin. Hardly surprising that visiting her was more obligation than choice. They were fifteen and seventeen. Not long now before they became adults. Time was running out and her opportunity to make amends was fast diminishing. Will was going off to university next year and he hadn't even discussed it with her. She was virtually a stranger to them. No more than some distant relative, five times removed. The sort you only went to see when you were desperate for something — like money. But it was no more than she deserved. Wasn't it?

Her deliberations were cut short by Connie gesturing to Chris and Neil walking ahead of them, each with a child on their shoulders. 'I hope someday they'll have kids. It's my dream you know?'

'It's possible,' said Paula. 'More difficult, but possible. There are processes. If that doesn't bother you?'

'Lord no. I don't mind how they get them. Test tube, adoption. I don't care. They'd be wonderful parents.' Connie laughed at herself. 'Listen to me. You'd think I have enough grandchildren, wouldn't you? But look how they are with kids. They would make such a lovely family.'

'You're right. They would,' said Annette. 'They're both very special.'

She wished she'd been special too. She wished she'd been the sort of person who would have made a wonderful parent. She wished she'd been a half-decent one. But she was none of those things. She knew it and, as always, it tortured her.

Halfway through the sermon, she felt something inside her let go. Not snap exactly, but loosen. It was as if all those things that had been dragging her down, that she'd been bottling up for so long, were flowing from her.

She began to sob. Other members of the congregation looked over at her. They didn't seem to mind at all. They even looked pleased.

Neil held her hand 'It affected me like that the first time I came,' he whispered. 'Just let it go. You'll feel better for it.'

For once, she had no desire to suppress it. She relinquished control and let it all come out. The wretchedness, the misery, the grief. All were washed away.

After the service, people came up and hugged her. First the aunties and uncles, then people she'd never met. 'God bless you sister,' they said, one after the other.

They probably think I've found God, she thought. She hadn't. She was still a non-believer. But she had experienced an epiphany of sorts and she felt different. Cleansed.

12

CHRISTMAS BUT NOT AS YOU KNOW IT

There was a weightlessness about her now. A sense of freedom that she hadn't experienced in a long time. She didn't know how long it would last but it felt wrong to sleep through it. She lay in the bed next to Paula's, in one of Neil and Chris's guest bedrooms. They'd been talking for the last hour. It seemed neither of them were in a hurry for the night to end.

'Our presents would be left at the end of the bed in pillowcases,' said Paula. 'There was always a little tin of toffees in there, with pictures of puppies or kittens on the lid. Do you remember those? We'd wake up in the middle of the night and have a secret rummage for them, take one out then leave the tin under our pillows until morning. As soon as we woke up, we'd have the second one.'

'I used to get a new pair of slippers every year,' said Annette. 'God, the excitement of those slippers and wondering what they'd be like this time round. That was as thrilling to me as any of the other presents. You could smell the newness on them when you opened the box. The feeling of putting them on, first thing on Christmas morning, my gran staying over and being there to open the presents with us, and Dad with his Christmas tunes. That was Christmas to me.'

'This is nice,' said Paula. 'I feel as if I've been transported back in time. I'm in the bedroom I shared with my sisters, waiting for my parents to go to sleep so that we can open the toffees.'

They giggled into their pillows like schoolgirls.

'We should get some sleep,' said Paula. 'Perhaps there'll be pillowcases with presents in the morning.'

There were no pillowcases, and no new slippers waiting for them, but Annette still woke up that morning with a sense of hope. Overnight the axis of her existence had shifted. For once that didn't frighten her. Intuitively she knew that whatever happened going forward, it would be good.

They had a leisurely breakfast before clearing away the debris from the night before. They would save present opening for later, when the other guests arrived – Sean from two doors down who lived alone, and Calvin, one of Chris's pupils, with his mum Sarah who attended the rehab centre where Chris volunteered.

Doreen and Joe, their next-door neighbours called on them mid-morning, before their daughter came to pick them up. Chris dug out the Phil Spector album and put it on just for them.

Annette's phone rang. It was her dad. 'You must have a sixth sense for this old music,' she said to him.

'Just wanted to see how you were doing. Sounds like you're having a good time.'

'Yes I am. You'd have loved it here last night Dad. All

your favourite tunes. Chris's dad is as big a fan as you. He had all the uncles singing along to them. I could just imagine you, right in the middle of it, joining in.'

'You know me too well, sweetheart. Sounds right up my street. Mum wants to say hello. Have a lovely day.' He passed the phone over.

'Annette? Judging by Dad's happy face you must be having a nice time? He's been very worried about you, you know.'

'Yes, I'm having a great time. Mum, do you remember the Christmas slippers?'

'The what?'

'Every year. I used to have a new pair of slippers. My Christmas slippers.'

'Oh yes, I do. Whatever made you bring that up?'

'Paula and I were talking about our childhood Christmases last night and I remembered the slippers. I really loved the slippers.'

'Yes, you did. We used to try so hard to get you a completely different pair every year. We had to keep a list to make sure we didn't duplicate. Are you sure you're all right love?'

'Yes Mum. More than all right. In fact, I'm feeling really happy.'

'My goodness, your dad will be pleased.'

As her mother put the phone down, she could hear her saying: 'This'll cheer you up.'

It was time she rang her own children and was just about to, when her phone went again. She hoped it might be Liza or Will, but it wasn't. She hid her disappointment as she answered it. 'Good morning. Merry Christmas.'

'Yeah, merry Christmas. Sorry to call you, Net. I just. I just –'

'Kelly, what's the matter. Has something happened?'

'It's Craig. We had a big row last night and now he's gone to his mum's for Christmas and left me here on my own. I just needed to speak to someone that's all. Sorry.'

'That's okay. Do you want me to come over?' The others were watching her, concerned. Neil was mouthing at her to invite Kelly over. 'Why don't I come and pick you up? You can come over here and join us.'

'No, I couldn't. I can't just turn up uninvited.'

'You are invited. Neil and Chris would love it if you came.'

'Yeah, I bet.'

Neil took the phone. 'Kelly, this is your official invite. Now get yourself ready. Net'll be over to pick you up. You're coming here to spend the rest of the day with us and, if you don't mind the sofa, you can stay over.'

Annette had never been inside Kelly's flat before. She'd dropped her off outside, but had never been invited in. It was in a purpose-built, six-storey block that had seen better days. The lift smelt of disinfectant with an underlying hint of urine in the background. On the way up to the flat she read some of the graffiti on its walls. *'Jerome Robbins u crak munster,'* and *'Patti Bird pulls pennis like she pulls pints,'* were the most original and intriguing. Even if they did lose points for spelling inaccuracies.

The flat was sparse. A big wide screen TV stood precariously on a lopsided unit. There was a PlayStation on the floor in front of it. A threadbare sofa was the only seating to grace the room and, aside from a tatty coffee table loaded up with empty lager cans, that was it. She tried to not to look around. She didn't want Kelly to think she was judging her, but Kelly was no fool.

'I know it's a shithole. It's Craig's flat not mine, but he don't look after it and I'm fucked if I'm gonna run round cleaning up after him.'

'Good for you. You're not his cleaner.'

'Yeah well, right now, I'm not his anything. The last thing he said to me was not to be here when he got back.'

'Well then, let's get you out of here, Cinderella. Your carriage awaits.'

They sat in the car for a while so that Kelly could relay the full details of the fight they'd had the night before because Craig had spent all day out and came home drunk and lairy. She told her how she'd had to be rescued from him by the neighbours and how, when she crept back into the flat that morning, he told her he was going to his mum's and didn't want to see her again. It took some time for all of this to be retold so, when they got back, two of the other guests, Calvin and Sarah, had already arrived.

Calvin was playing computer games with Chris. His mother Sarah, a gaunt washed-out woman with skin like crepe paper and wispy blonde hair sat watching them. There but not fully there. She was the exact opposite of her son, a lively boy of about fifteen. There were no obvious similarities between them except their self-evident care for one another. She looked as if she'd been on the verge of drowning and the one thing that stopped her going under was this boy with his restless eyes that couldn't quite hide a watchfulness. Eyes that followed his mother everywhere, looking out for her whenever she left his side. You could tell too, that Calvin liked Chris. Annette imagined he was a popular teacher at school. The sort that didn't have to try too hard to gain the respect of his pupils.

Sean, from two doors down, came shortly after they arrived. He'd only moved into his house eight months ago but he was an old friend of Chris's. Sean was mid-forties at most. The sides of his head were shaved high and on the top was a mop of slicked back, brown hair. He had a full beard, some piercings, and tattoos. More than Neil. He wasn't a particularly tall man and this was accentuated by the fact that he was standing next to Chris who was pointing each one of them out to him by way of introduction. He flashed a smile and two gold teeth at her. The lines around his eyes suggested he smiled a lot and the relaxed aura about him gave the impression he found it easy to do so. He wore jeans and a checked shirt open over a T-shirt that caught her eye. It was old and faded but it was definitely The Damned. Sean might have looked like he was a hipster but there was more than a touch of punk about him. A very charming punk. 'I think I've seen you ladies before,' he said to Annette and Paula. 'Weren't you at Chris's party here in the summer?'

'We were,' said Paula. 'I thought you looked familiar.'

'I'm obviously not very memorable. I don't think you remember speaking to me,' he said to Annette.

It was true. She couldn't remember seeing him there.

'It's all right. I think you'd had a few by the time I turned up and it was only a couple of words. I was asking the lady you were with about the rum punch.'

Annette thought for a moment. Somewhere from the deep recesses a memory popped up of a man that could have been Sean, talking to Corrine. 'Yes, I do remember now. I'm afraid I'd had a bit too much of the rum punch myself by that time so it's all a bit blurry.'

He laughed. 'Yeah, I don't remember too much after I'd

had a few glasses. I just remember that lady encouraging me to try it.'

'Was that Corrine?' said Chris. 'From what I remember she was trying to get everyone as drunk on that stuff as she was.'

Dinner took all afternoon to eat. They were in no rush, and allowed themselves to savour Neil's cooking. He really was good at it.

Calvin and Kelly got on well. She could talk his language and had similar frames of reference so the two became allies in this group of oldies. She told him she had a brother his age and asked if they liked the same things. She'd never mentioned her family before. Annette was deliberating on whether to delve further, but Paula got in first. 'Have you got any other brothers or sisters?'

'I've got another brother as well, and a half-sister. She's only little though.'

'Are your mum and dad separated then Kelly?' said Paula.

'Nah, my mum's dead. Cancer. My dad remarried. Can't stand her.'

There was a silence, finally broken by Calvin, 'Man, your mum's dead? That's bad. Do you miss her? I would really miss her.' He glanced over at Sarah who lowered her eyes.

'Yeah, sometimes,' said Kelly. 'It was a long time ago. I've got used to it now.'

'How old were you when it happened?' said Annette.

'Twelve. A long time ago.'

Not that long ago, thought Annette.

Neil got up from his chair. 'Right who's for Christmas

pud? Kel, come and give me a hand.'

She moaned. 'I don't like Christmas pudding.'

'You'll like mine. If not, there's always mince pies.'

Kelly grunted. 'Don't take this the wrong way Neil, but I'm a bit bloody sick of your mince pies. I'll try the Christmas pud.'

Chris let out a belly laugh. 'Now you know how I feel.'

By the time they flopped down on the couches to rest their stomachs it was dark outside. There were presents for them all to open, including Kelly.

'We swapped the labels on a couple of ours while you were picking her up. Didn't think you'd mind,' whispered Paula.

When the wrapping paper was cleared away, someone suggested playing charades. It didn't go down too well with the young people but, once they got the hang of it, they seemed to be having a good time.

'Someone's phone's ringing,' said Sean.

'Oh, that's mine.' Annette ran over and answered it, just in time.

'Mum?'

'Will!' Shit, she'd forgotten to ring them.

'Yeah, hi. We just thought we'd give you a call to see how you are.'

'Yes, hi darling. Yes, sorry. Things got a bit hectic here and I didn't have time to ring you this morning. Sorry. Have you had a good Christmas?'

'Yeah, great, yeah. Thanks for the presents by the way. They were great. Sounds like you're having a party.'

There were shrieks and hoots in the background. Above it all was Kelly's outraged voice. 'You have got to be fucking kidding me. No way was that Lord of the Rings.'

'Who was that?' said Will.

'Just a friend. Her name's Kelly. We're playing charades. You know how heated that can get.'

'She sounds young.'

'Yes, she is. Well she's a little bit older than you. That's Calvin you can hear now. He and his mum have come to dinner as well. He's fifteen.'

'Same age as Liza.'

'Yes, I suppose so. Is she there?'

Liza came on. 'Enjoying your Christmas then, are you?' It sounded like an accusation.

'Yes, thank you darling. Are you?'

'It's all right. A bit quiet.'

'Not too boring I hope?'

There was a pause. She was plainly considering her answer carefully. 'No, it's great.'

The charades erupted into hysterics again, Calvin was complaining that he'd never heard of 'Gone with the Wind' and Kelly was backing him up. Annette considered going upstairs to the quiet of the bedroom, then thought the better of it. Why should she hide the fact that she was having a good time?

'It's very noisy there. What's going on?' said Liza.

'Charades. We've got a couple of young people here that seem to be struggling with the concept.' She raised her eyebrows at Kelly and Calvin, setting off an explosion of whooping and jeering.

'I thought it was all old people there.'

'Not exactly. It's a mixture.'

'How young?'

'Around the same age as you and Will. Slightly older

than Will.'

'Didn't take you long to replace us then?'

She slammed the phone down. Annette felt sick. She'd done it again. Liza and Will were over two hundred miles away and yet she'd still managed to hurt them. Whatever she did, she never seemed to get it right.

Craig turned up not long after lunch on Boxing Day.

Calvin and Sarah had slept in the other spare room. Sean was back and was reacquainted with Corrine whose children were spending the day with their dad. Kelly and Calvin had just started the washing up when the doorbell rang.

'Kelly, it's for you,' called Chris.

She tossed the tea towel aside and rushed out. They watched her talking to him from the front window.

'I know him,' said Sarah. 'He's a right little shit. Thinks he's God's gift. She can do a lot better.'

'You're not wrong, Sare,' said Chris. 'How did he know where she was?'

'She's been messaging someone all morning, Sir,' said Calvin.

Kelly turned to come in and they all shot back to their seats.

'It's Craig,' she said. 'He's come to say sorry. He wants me to go back home with him.'

'Are you going?' asked Annette. It was a rhetorical question. Kelly's body language had already given away the answer.

'Yeah. I'm gonna give him another chance.'

Annette helped her carry her things out to the car. Kelly could have managed on her own but Annette wanted a closer look at Craig. He was older than she'd imagined. Easily ten years Kelly's senior. That explained why she seemed so much older than her actual years. Then again, he was like a big kid. So maybe not.

'This is Annette,' Kelly told him.

He looked her up and down, as if working out how much he'd get for her. She disliked him already.

'All right?'

'Yes, thank you. You?'

He grunted, as if she'd said something funny, then jumped in the car and told Kelly to hurry up.

She gave Annette a hug. 'Take no notice of him. He's a dickhead. I'll see you soon, yeah?'

13

THE HALF-BIRTHDAY

Generally, she didn't much like Sundays. When she still lived with the family, those were the difficult days. The days when she had no work to hide behind. On Saturdays, there were classes or clubs to take the children to. Shopping to do. Occasionally, even an extra day in the office to meet a big deadline. Sundays though. They were days when they did things together. Or, at least, that was the theory. In practice, it was her doing her best not to act like an outsider within her own kith and kin.

After they'd thrown her out, Sundays were nothing days. Empty and pointless, long drawn-out affairs, the highlight of which was the evening when it was over, and she could occupy herself preparing for work. These days it was still her least favourite day but, in the last few months, she'd occasionally found things to fill it. So it didn't drag quite so much. However, this particular Sunday was different. She'd already planned how she was going to spend it.

Yesterday, she'd been in the middle of the supermarket, when the sudden realisation of the date hit her. She'd glanced at her phone to check the time — she hadn't worn a watch in months — when she noticed. It made her stop short, half way along the post-Christmas sale aisle. She stared blankly at the cut-price cakes, puddings, and panettones, finally settling on a box of Belgian chocolates. Focussing on its bright yellow sticker allowed her to concentrate while the other shoppers absent-mindedly swerved their trollies around her. In less than twenty-four hours, it would be exactly six months from the day that Malcolm had given her the news she was to be made redundant. Exactly six months from one of the worst birthdays of her life. In less than a full day she would be, precisely, fifty and a half.

Was it really only half a year? Six months, twenty-six weeks, one hundred and eighty-two and a half days. It didn't matter which way you looked at it, the time had flown. Yes, the birthday had been horrendous but things had improved, far more than she could have imagined back in July. Surely that was cause for celebration? It was, after all, her half birthday. 'Right.' She grabbed the chocolates from the shelf and took herself off to find a nice bottle of Prosecco which, she decided, was a good place to start.

And so, it was Sunday morning. She was breakfasting on warmed croissants and Bucks Fizz, and opening a single card placed against a small gift-wrapped box on her coffee table. She'd chosen the words carefully last night, so it was no surprise that they fitted her mood:

'*To Annette*
Have a great day.
Keep moving forward.
Annette x'

Flakes of warm, buttery pastry fell onto her chest as she ate. And again, with the next bite. She brushed them off and licked her lips. There was something very satisfying about messy eating. Harder to do when you're with someone. Unless it's somebody that really loves you and doesn't care that you have debris stuck to your face, and food dandruff down your front. On your own, you can make a real pig of yourself and no one cares. The last time she'd had a breakfast like this was the morning after her wedding. Her first day as Annette Grey. But she wasn't going to let that spoil her enjoyment of it.

Next, she opened the box. A pot of face cream. It was about time she became a woman who moisturised on a regular basis. It was about time she began to care for herself. *Self-love and self-respect go hand in hand*. It was something Corrine had said to her on Boxing Day, when she told her about Liza being upset and about how she loathed herself for not realising that they might interpret her spending Christmas with Kelly and Calvin the wrong way. *Self-love and self-respect go hand in hand*. She desperately wanted some self-respect. Some self-love wouldn't go amiss either.

The cream was an inexpensive brand. There was no way she could justify paying a lot for it. Not after what she'd seen in the last six months. Besides, she couldn't afford it now. Since she'd been placed on gardening leave, she'd been spending as little as possible on herself to try to eke out what was left of her salary, but the last of it was spent on Christmas. Now she was living off her redundancy money. Today's little food luxuries were a one off, and she was going to make the most of them.

She sank into a hot bath and pampered herself with oils and lotions bought for her on previous birthdays by colleagues, unaware they would sit at the back of her cupboard, untouched until now. She put on the new moisturiser then placed it on the dressing table as a reminder of her new regime. Next, she laid out a pair of jeans and a T-shirt on the bed.

The jeans had caught her eye in the supermarket yesterday. They fitted well, so she bought two pairs. One blue and one in that faded washed-out colour, somewhere between black and grey. She hadn't bought new clothes in over a year and, caught up in the excitement, chose four T-shirts to complete her new uniform. Now, she stood hesitantly over these alien garments. It was hard to remember when she'd last worn jeans. When the children were small? At any rate, she couldn't go on wearing her old weekend casuals forever. She hated them anyway. They reminded her too much of that stiff, beige frump, Annette Grey. She didn't want to be that person any longer. She wasn't that person any longer. Jeans suited her life now. 'Get on with it. What are you afraid of?' She tutted, pulled the jeans on and studied herself in the mirror. Not too bad. They'd do.

It was 7th January. She hadn't spoken to the children since Christmas Day. She'd sent them both the usual message on New Year's Eve but only Will replied. Ordinarily she would have called them by now but she was conducting an experiment to see who would break first. It was part of a new undertaking she'd been mulling over since New Year's Day, after another party. This time at Chris's sister's house.

The closeness of that family group and the natural warmth that emanated from it, threw her own familial situation into sharp relief. Of course, it was all her own fault. She was a terrible mother, and a pretty poor daughter too. There could be no doubt about that. And, just in case she ever did forget it, Colin and her mother very helpfully gave her enough reminders. But, if the last six months had taught her anything, it was that it was never too late to change. Her eyes had been opened wide, on so many levels, and she was already in a state of evolution. She wasn't sure what she was evolving into and whether it would eventually reunite her with her family but she was certain of one thing. She didn't particularly like the person she was evolving from. Surely then, any change had to be good?

The buzzer went as she was wrestling with these thoughts. It was Kelly, her voice breaking over the intercom. Her tear stained face and eyes, red with anger and too much crying, confirmed what Annette had already guessed. Something bad had happened.

Kelly threw herself on the sofa. 'I don't know who the fuck he thinks he is, treating me like this. He thinks I can't see what he's up to, but I've got eyes. I can see the fuckin' obvious. I know, for one, he's pinched a tenner out of my purse and I know who he's spent it on. He must think I'm a fucking idiot.'

Annette placed a mug of tea in front of her. 'Is this Craig?'

'The bastard's seeing someone else.'

'Are you sure?'

She nodded. 'Yeah, his ex. She told me. He's gone back to her. Well, he's still living with me, but he's fucking us both. At least, he would, if I let him near me.'

Unable to think of an appropriate response, Annette reached out and took her hand. It felt cold and lifeless. Kelly's thin jacket was a useless barrier against the winter chill. She wanted to wrap her up in soft, warm woollens and keep her safe. Safe from what? From the weather? Or from Craig, and men like him?

Craig. What a repulsive toad he was. She recalled the way he'd looked at her on Boxing Day. Assessing how much she was worth. She could have forgiven him that, even though it turned her stomach, if he'd been good to Kelly. But it was the way he treated her. Or, to be exact, the way Kelly said he treated her, that made Annette despise him. What was it about these men and their sense of entitlement? She was at a loss as to why Kelly stayed with him. But then, who was she to judge? What did she know about men? Or relationships, come to that?

'I've given him an ultimatum, me or her,' she said.

'If he chooses you, can you trust him?'

'Dunno. We'll see. If he does me over again though, that's it, I'm walking. No question.'

She picked up the mug, as if to signal the end of the discussion so Annette changed the subject. 'Have you eaten today?'

'Yeah, yeah, I had some breakfast.'

She was lying, Annette could tell. 'Well how about some comfort food then?'

She took a pyramid of stacked profiteroles from the fridge.

'Nice,' said Kelly. 'You expecting visitors, or were you gonna eat all that yourself?'

'All for me. Shameful isn't it?'

Kelly's eyes flashed around the room and settled, first on the half-finished glass and then on the card. 'Oh my God, is it your birthday?'

'No, but it's a sort of, celebration. It's my half birthday. My actual birthday was such a horrible day, I thought I'd treat myself today.'

'Good idea. Like the jeans and tee by the way. Make you look younger.'

Annette blushed. 'Thanks. Time for some changes, I thought.'

Kelly studied her. 'Don't change too much, Net. I like you the way you are.'

'Oh, okay.' Straight away, she felt ridiculous. Her response had been awkward and silly, but she was still unaccustomed enough to compliments to be taken by surprise when they happened. She gathered herself. 'You don't know the whole me. There are parts that definitely need to go.'

'Hmm.' Kelly screwed up her face. 'Nah, sorry Net, can't see it. Right, I'll just help you with these, then I'll go.'

They finished off the Prosecco and profiteroles, but neither was in a rush to say goodbye. Before long it was lunch time, so they shared cheese, cold meats and dips with a glass each of chilled Sauvignon Blanc.

'So, this is how you poshos live is it? I think I like it.'

Annette smiled. She probably was a posho as far as Kelly was concerned. 'It's something I used to enjoy doing, but it doesn't happen very often these days.'

Kelly threw a slice of bresaola into her mouth. Two months ago, she wouldn't have touched it. Annette wasn't the only one changing.

It was mid-afternoon when Kelly left, and the wine was finished. Annette had planned a day of quiet introspection but the visit knocked her off balance and the drink tired her out. What she really needed right then, was a nice lie down.

She was woken by the sound of her phone ringing. By the time she got out of bed, the caller had hung up. Parched and desperate for coffee, she filled the kettle.

She heard the message beep over the sound of water coming to boil. It was from Liza:

'Call me urgently.'

Even the writing sounded angry. She noticed four

similar messages sent in the last two hours. Each one was more and more fractious. So, Liza had broken first. She settled herself down and called.

'About time, where have you been? I've been trying to get hold of you for hours.' Liza sounded as testy as her messages.

Annette moved forward to the edge of the sofa. 'Sorry darling, I didn't notice your messages. I've been a bit tied up. What's the matter?'

'There's a school trip to Canada. I've told them I'll go but I need £2,000. Can you transfer it?'

Money. She might have known. 'Well, no Liza, I'm sorry.'

'What do you mean, no?'

'I don't have that kind of money to spare now that I'm not working.'

'But it's only £2,000.' She could have been asking for a bar of chocolate, or a new dress.

'That's a lot of money, Liza. I'm sorry, but you're going to have to miss this one.'

'I can't. I've already told them I'm going.'

'Well, I'm sure they'll understand. Unless perhaps, your dad can pay for it?'

Colin was there in the background. 'Is that your mum? Finally called back, has she?'

'Yes, she says you've got to pay for it.'

'Don't be ridiculous, she knows I've got no money.'

'Dad says don't be ridiculous. You're the one that's loaded.'

Annette held her breath and did a mental count to ten. 'Liza, I have never been loaded and I'm definitely not now. I'm sorry darling. There's nothing I can do this time.'

'Then why don't you get a job for Christ's sake? Why

don't you do something useful, instead of lounging around on your arse all day? I mean, what is the point of you if you can't even give me a measly two grand for a school trip?'

'Liza, I'm not—' Too late, the phone went dead. She'd been cut off. Again!

She sat back. Frozen. So, they could still harm her at will. The surface scars may have healed but the cuts were still there deep within. Nagging sores that refused to go away. Keeping her in her place. Knocking her back whenever she tried to move on. Her chest tightened. She felt a hard lump in her windpipe blocking the airwaves. She took deep breaths, in, out, in, out, until her hands stopped shaking. In, out, in, out, until she was sure the tears weren't going to come. In, out, in, out, until her resolve was steadied. No. She would not call back begging forgiveness and bearing gifts. Not this time. Not anymore. She swallowed down her coffee.

The phone beeped again. Another message:

'I can't believe you could be so mean to me. You're the worst mother in the world.'

A second came through:

'I never want to speak to you again. EVER!!!'

She was crushed and all at once the nice things that had happened earlier meant nothing. What *was* the point of her if she couldn't provide for her family? Perhaps, she really was the worst. She caught herself before she fell into that all too familiar well of self-disgust. She must not let herself get dragged back. She had to find a way of reconnecting with Liza and Will without dropping into that same old trap of assuaging her guilt with money.

She went out onto the balcony. It had been a lovely winter's day. The early frost had given way to clear blue skies and she hadn't set foot outside the flat. It was too late now. The flimsy winter sun had all but faded and it would be dark soon. Instead, she would sit and watch what was left of it going down over the lake in the park.

It was quite a nice setting really. Not that she'd noticed when she first bought the place. Back then she just wanted somewhere quick and reasonably close to the children with enough space for them to stay over. Although as it turned out, they didn't do that too often. So, the location itself had been more luck than judgement. All the same, she appreciated it now.

She liked to watch the weeping willows, hypnotically skimming the water and, depending on her mood, either the families playing on the grass, or the solitary dog walkers. Lonely people, with only their pets for company. This morning she'd been in the mood for families. Now, she searched for the dog walkers. This time last year she saw them as kindred spirits but lately, she was ashamed to admit, they made her feel slightly superior because she had friends now. Sometimes, that was a good feeling to have.

The phone rang again. She steeled herself for another round of verbal abuse but it wasn't Liza this time. It was Paula.

'Annette, how are you?'

'Good, good. I'm good.'

'I'm not disturbing you?' said Paula.

'No, not at all. I was just watching the sun go down on my balcony. Not one of my most productive moments.'

'Sounds delightful. I hear today is a special day.'

'Kelly! Honestly Paula, it's a bit silly really. I just thought it was a good excuse to treat myself. It's not really a special day.'

'Nonsense. Kelly's let everyone know and we're all agreed that we're taking you out for a meal tonight. It's no use trying to wriggle out of it. All you need to do is turn up. Oh, and Kelly says you're to come as you are. Apparently, she wants us to see your new look.'

'Okay, you've talked me into it,' said Annette. A night out with friends would do her good.

'Anywhere in particular you'd like to go?'

She thought for a minute. Yes, there was somewhere in particular. Somewhere she could do with help getting back to. 'There's a place I used to go to a lot. I haven't been for a long time but it's still there. It's called the Rajdoot.'

14

THEY CHOSE THE RAJDOOT

They chose the Rajdoot to tell her. The place where they'd celebrated birthdays, anniversaries, and all of her promotions. They chose that special place, to tell her they wanted a divorce.

'It's what we all want Annette,' said Colin.

She gawped at him, incredulous. Not quite believing what she'd just heard. Her head jerked nervously towards the other side of the table, to Liza and Will. Surely, they didn't want it too? Surely not? Surely, they didn't want to force her out, to banish her?

'Is this true?' she asked them.

Liza and Will sat, red-faced and silent, their eyes fixed on their chicken kormas.

'Come on Annette. Play fair. Can't you see how uncomfortable you're making them? This is exactly the problem I've been talking about. You have no idea how difficult you make things for us. You're impossible to live with.'

She gasped, surprising the occupants of the next table. 'That's not true. It's not true is it?'

She turned to her children once more. Again, they

refused to raise their heads. Liza screwed her eyes shut. Will was concentrating on mixing rice with curry sauce. Steering it into a neat, flat circle on his plate.

Colin glanced around at the people in the surrounding tables who were pretending to be disinterested. 'For God's sake. Don't make this any harder than it has to be. If you must have the truth, I'll tell you. All three of us can't stand your moods any longer. We've put up with them long enough. We've discussed it and we've come to the conclusion we'd be far happier without you. And you'd be a lot less miserable living on your own.'

She thought at that moment she would die. She felt her heart stop for a few seconds, then flutter back into life. A sickly phoenix rising from scarcely stoked ashes. And then nothing. Numbness. Stasis. Meanwhile, he was prattling on about soonest being best, a thinly disguised smile on his smug face. He was enjoying this, she could tell. He was in his element. She wanted so much to hit him right then. To pick up his vindaloo and throw it over him while it was still steaming hot. She imagined the momentary satisfaction of watching him screaming in pain. Frantically scratching around for the water jug to cool his burning skin and emptying it onto his face to soothe his smarting eyes. Yes, she wanted that so much, but she couldn't do it. It wasn't her style. Her style was one of quiet acceptance, when all the time a violent storm raged inside.

She sat, rigid. Completely still, when really, she was floating above herself, and all around them. But still, she couldn't see into her children's eyes. Instead, she saw herself begin to fold, to scrunch her body in tight, as if it were vacuum packed, in order to subdue the anger and malice seething beneath her surface. Her lips pinched and pulled themselves into a tiny, red ball. As if the pain weren't enough, she chewed the inside of her cheeks until the taste of blood filled her mouth.

'We'll give you some space to think it over,' he said.

They got up and left her there. Alone with her pent-up fury and, of course, with the bill. The final slap in the face.

From her window seat she watched them hurrying along the street. The children kept glancing back. She thought they were saying something, but she couldn't be sure. Colin put his arms around them and they became a single, solid, six-legged unit all moving on without her until they disappeared around the corner and she knew they wouldn't be coming back.

She buried her face in her hands and noticed it was wet. She didn't know how long she'd been crying. No wonder they'd rushed out, and no wonder they'd been looking back at her. They were embarrassed. She scanned the other tables. All eyes seemed to be on her. Peering furtively over menus. Whispering covertly behind hands that barely concealed their purpose. The room suddenly felt hot and small. Her lungs grew tinier and tinier until all she could do was pant. She had to get out before she suffocated.

She delved both hands into her bag and rummaged around for her purse. Faster and faster she searched. *Where is it? It has to be in here. It has to be.* She was panicking now, throwing things out onto the table, until at last she found it. She pulled out some money and tossed it down. Then she gathered up her possessions, piled them back in and stood, so abruptly that her chair fell backwards, alarming the waiters and customers alike. Someone was calling her name, asking her if she was all right. She couldn't stop. She ran to the door, wrenched it open, and fled.

She trudged aimlessly around the streets for hours. Her misery was a heavy weight and each step a huge effort. She found herself in a park and collapsed onto a bench. The warm summer breeze brushed against her damp skin and made her shiver. It was quite late now. The park was empty. She looked out onto the dark green space ahead and up at the vast sky, the colour of a fresh bruise.

A small grunt tried to push its way out of her. She closed her mouth and swallowed it down. Undeterred it pressed itself up through the back of her throat, coming out of her nose like suppressed laughter and causing a mild explosion to spill out of her nostrils. She wiped it away on the remnants of a soggy tissue and turned her thoughts back to them. Her family. The grasping gang of three. The club to which she did not belong. She imagined them planning it together while she was at work. How could she not have seen it coming? What was she doing, not to see the signs? The cruelty of it ran through her head on an endless loop. She hated them then. Almost as much as she hated herself for feeling that way about her own children. It was her fault they didn't want her. She'd worked so hard to give them everything. Everything except the one thing they needed from her. She'd failed them.

She looked up to the sky again and howled, until her tears were empty and they became nothing but dried up tics and convulsions. When she could weep no more, she sank back down and listened to the rise and fall of her breath until she regained control. She knew then what she must do. They didn't want her, and there was no point hiding from it. She would go home and pack.

15

RETURNING TO THE RAJDOOT

She'd never understood why, of all the possible places to tell her, they chose the Rajdoot. She'd replayed that summer's night in 2015 over and over and the question still bothered her. The thing, the terrible thing, that happened to her that night — the realisation that they didn't want her — was an open wound that she still carried.

She'd lost count of the number of times she'd walked past the restaurant, turning her face away at the last minute because she couldn't bear to relive the memory. Because she thought she might be recognised. Because they might be in there. Having a good time. Gloating over what they'd done. So, the decision to go to the Rajdoot again was not taken lightly. She knew all of her strength and resolve would be called upon to go in there, to order a meal, act like she was enjoying herself and pretend that the last time she'd been there, had not broken her into a thousand tiny pieces. She knew all of this, but she needed to do it. It was time. First though, she had to cross the threshold, and that was proving difficult.

She'd been standing across the street for twenty minutes

watching the diners inside. Her friends were nowhere to be seen. It might have helped if they were. She was already twenty minutes late so they must be in there. Probably at the back somewhere. There were a couple of empty window tables but they always saved them for the regulars. It would take less than a minute to walk over and go through the door, but her feet refused to move. If it hadn't been for Neil stepping outside, she might have stayed there all night. He pressed the phone to his ear and a couple of seconds later, hers rang. He heard it before she did. He looked at her, puzzled for a moment, then strolled over, as if nothing at all was odd, and put his arm under hers. 'Come on missus, we're all starving.'

At first, she felt an involuntary resistance but his gentle firmness melted her and she let him take her into the Rajdoot.

It hadn't changed at all. It looked exactly the same as that last time. Modern, but not contemporary, with fake leather seating that made embarrassing noises if you moved too quickly. She recognised some faces. Ex-neighbours, Adam and Jude. They watched her being guided to the back by Neil. Him holding her hand with the all the tenderness of a lover and she, following with the meek blindness of one. They probably thought he was her boyfriend. Jude's eyes moved downwards as Annette scanned them. She'd never liked her. Or him for that matter. Let them think what they want. What did she care? She felt a degree of satisfaction at that new idea. Yes, what did it matter to her what they thought?

'Here she is, the half-birthday girl,' said Paula. 'I was beginning to think I'd got the wrong restaurant.'

'Sorry everyone, it was just harder to get here than I thought it would be,' she said.

Paula squeezed her hand. 'You're here now. That's all that matters. You look great. Kelly was right. Have a glass of wine and relax. This is your special day.'

Her special day. How embarrassing and idiotic she was. There was an outbreak of laughter. Her shoulders loosened, her body relaxed and then, she was laughing too. 'Yes, here's to my special day. May there be many more.'

The glasses clinked and everyone cheered. Corrine handed her a menu. 'We're all ready to order when you are.'

Annette gave it a fleeting look but she already knew what she wanted. She'd been waiting for it for more than two years. 'I'll have onion bhaji to start please. Then a vegetable Balti with chickpeas, extra spinach and mushrooms, and no potatoes.'

The waiter was new. New to her, anyway. He would check if the chef could make that up, as it wasn't on the menu. Within minutes a short, round man in chef's whites came bustling out of the kitchen, his arms wide open and his face beaming. He clasped his hands around hers. 'Mrs Grey! I knew it would be you. As soon as I saw that order, I knew it would be you. Welcome back, welcome back.'

'Hello Mr Shah,' she said. 'It's nice to see you again. You have a good memory. It's been over two years.'

'Two years, has it really? Even if it was five, how could I forget one of my favourite customers. And these are your colleagues?'

'No Mr Shah, they're my friends.'

'I see. Welcome to you all.'

Kelly held up her glass. 'Cheers mate. We're having a little party. Celebrating Annette's half-birthday, as it happens.'

Mr Shah raised his eyebrows. 'A half-birthday you say?'

'We missed her actual birthday you see Mr Shah,' said

Paula. 'So we thought we'd make the most of her half-birthday.'

'A double celebration then. A half-birthday and a return to my restaurant.' He called the waiter over and told him to bring two bottles of Champagne. 'On the house. And now Mrs Grey, I'm going to cook you the best Balti you've had in the last two years, and then you won't leave it so long next time.'

'You're popular,' said Chris.

'Oh, he's just being nice. He's a very kind man.' She thought back to the last time she was here. The concerned voice asking if she was all right. She was sure it had been Mr Shah. Yes, he was a very kind man. She looked down and checked her hands. No, they were not trembling. Her eyes were dry. She was going to be all right.

Neil broke her chain of thought. 'So, you used to come here a lot then?'

'Yes, I used to come here regularly with my family until …' They were all looking at her now, hanging on her every word. She took in some air. 'Until they told me they wanted a divorce. I mean, it was my husband who wanted the divorce, but it was he and the children that wanted me to move out.' Corrine whistled through her teeth. 'Actually, it was here they told me. That was the last time I came here.'

'Fuck,' said Kelly, 'that's —'

From the corner of her eye, she could see Paula shaking her head at Kelly. Corrine laid her hand on her arm. She patted Corrine's hand. 'It's okay. I'm okay. Coming here again was always going to be a struggle, but I wanted to do it. I'm so glad I've managed it. Thanks to you, and Mr Shah's Champagne.'

They all raised their glasses in a toast to exorcising demons and to friendship, and the conversation drifted along easily. They ordered more wine while Paula and Annette entertained them with stories about their former lives at Mason and Partners.

She'd just finished telling them about the Christmas party in which a longstanding feud between two department heads spilled over into a drink-fuelled ruckus that ended in fisticuffs, when Kelly cut in.

'Net, there's a guy over there who can't take his eyes off you. Told you that new look did something for you.'

'Actually, don't look over,' said Paula. 'I know I only met him a few times but I think it might be your ex.'

'What does he look like?' said Annette.

'Around six feet, shoulder length, light brown hair.'

'Nice eyes,' said Corrine.

'Bit of a paunch though,' said Neil. 'Hasn't been to the gym for a while.'

Midway between a large mouthful of wine, Annette snorted into her glass, 'If it is Colin, he's never been to the gym in his life. It's not the sort of thing artists do, apparently.'

'He's coming over,' said Kelly.

Colin stood a few feet away from the table. 'Annette. This is a surprise. I had no idea you still frequented this place. What a shame you didn't tell us you were coming.' He nodded to a previously empty table at the front, now occupied by three people. Liza, Will and a middle-aged woman with long blonde hair and a close-fitting T-shirt barely containing her. It was a band T-shirt. The Clash. He had to have bought that for her. No doubt about it.

'Didn't realise she needed anyone's permission,' said Kelly loudly, and with some menace.

The sound of her voice startled the occupants of the

window table. Will and Liza both turned sharply towards them.

Colin took no notice. 'Annette, could we talk outside?'

'She's busy,' said Kelly.

Only then did he acknowledge her existence. 'It won't take long.'

Annette got up and grabbed the back of her chair, reluctant to let go. It wasn't that she was drunk, although hadn't had this much alcohol in a long while. It was more that she was afraid if she went outside, past Adam and Jude, past the table with her children and that unknown woman, she might not return. 'Neil, if I'm not back in ten minutes, will you come out and get me?'

'Yep, no problem darling.'

Colin glanced at Neil then swaggered off towards the door. She followed him out.

They stopped at his table. Annette gave a little wave. She felt awkward, like she'd been caught trespassing on hallowed ground. 'Hello everyone.'

'Hey Mum,' said Will.

'Hi. Hello Liza.'

Liza let out a wordless humph and turned her head away in a dramatic demonstration of disgust. Annette recalled the earlier message, *I never want to speak to you again. EVER!!!* Naturally, this latest action was a deliberate attempt to humiliate her, to make her repent. Well, today was not her day for repentance. The woman watched Annette and said nothing.

'Mum and I are just going outside for a chat. We won't be long, as she's in a hurry to get back to her friends.'

She noticed the emphasis he'd put on the word hurry as if it were somehow abhorrent. She said nothing. What could she say? It was true. She didn't want to spend a minute longer than she had to with the man who'd ruined her life.

He held the door open for her and closed it behind them. 'Interesting friends.'

She waited for his mouth to curl in that way of his. That unpleasant, scornful way that told her, without needing to say it, that she'd made bad choices and this was another thing she couldn't get right. And yet, although he had meant it disparagingly, he was right. They were interesting. That was indisputable.

'What did you want to talk to me about Colin?'

'Liza. She's very upset because you've refused to pay for her trip.'

'I'm sure she'll get over it.'

He looked surprised by her answer, or perhaps by the firmness with which she'd said it. 'That was rather crass. This is our daughter's happiness we're talking about here and you've just dismissed it with a heartless and flippant remark. I know you're not really around enough to be close to her like I am, so you won't understand the peer pressure she's subjected to. All of her friends come from wealthy families. That sort of trip is nothing to them and they expect her to be the same. She'll be an outcast if she doesn't go.'

Her insides lurched. The thought of Liza, an outcast in an ocean of privileged princesses, made her feel sick. She must not give in. She must not give in. 'I think that's a bit of an exaggeration, Colin. Don't you?'

'And how would you know? How many times have you seen her in the last six months? How much time have you given over to actually talk to her to find out about her life?'

'My door's always open to the children. I've lost count of the number of times I've asked them to come over but they're just not interested.' She sensed that she was beginning to wobble, she had to rein it in and regain control. She breathed in and let it out with a heavy sigh. 'In any case, I don't have the money now that I'm not working.'

'It's been nearly six months since you left Masons. Surely there have been opportunities for you to find another job?'

'That has nothing to do with it and, actually, it's only been three months. I was on paid gardening leave for the first three months.' Why did everyone keep forgetting that?

He ignored her clarification. 'Yes, it has. If you took your responsibilities to your children seriously, you'd be out there earning money right now, instead of hanging around with unsavoury young women like that one in there. She can't be much older than Will. Yet you prefer her company to his. Are you ever going to be a proper mother to them? I mean, do I have to spell it out to you? Your behaviour is making your children unhappy. Can I be any clearer?'

She flinched. How dare he? After everything. How dare he?

Before either of them could say any more, the door opened and it was Neil. 'Ten minutes are up, Net. Everything okay?'

She looked at Colin. 'Yes, it's fine. Thanks Neil. Let's go back inside.'

She stopped at the family's table. 'Neil, these are my children Will and Liza and, I'm sorry, I don't think we've met?'

The woman looked at her as if she was nothing. 'I'm Arianne. Colin's friend.'

Of course she was.

'Are you going to pay for my trip?' said Liza.

'No Liza, I'm not. I've already told you that I can't afford it.'

'Then I have nothing to say to you, or your friend.' She

began to cry. Annette took a step towards her. 'Stay away from me. I don't want you near me. I want Dad.'

Colin wrapped his arm around her. 'I'm sorry darling. I tried but she just won't budge.'

Annette felt herself go limp. Neil whispered into her ear: 'I think it's best if we leave them to it.' He took hold of her and led her back to their table. She slumped down into the chair. Someone put a glass of wine into her hand.

'Mr Shah was worried you weren't coming back for your special Balti,' said Paula. 'He's been back and forth twice already.'

Mr Shah appeared almost immediately with the dish. 'Especially for you Mrs Grey. I hope you like it.'

She took a mouthful while he stood over her expectantly. It was as good as she'd remembered. 'It's absolutely delicious. Thank you so much. For everything.' He patted her shoulder and went back into the kitchen.

'She's a bit of a drama queen,' said Kelly, nodding in Liza's direction.

'Oh, that's rich coming from you,' said Corrine.

The tension was gone. The conversation continued as if Annette had never left her seat, and another bottle of wine was ordered.

'Hey Mum.' Will stood over her, his hands in his pockets, his eyes wandering between Annette and the floor. 'We're going. I just wanted to, you know, say goodbye.'

Chris grabbed a chair for him and he sat down at her side.

'Thank you darling. That means a lot to me.' She felt lifted but then she saw him peeking over at Kelly and guessed that his visit was as much out of curiosity as anything else. She introduced him one by one to her friends, and saw his disappointment when Kelly showed little interest.

'Sorry about Liza. She doesn't mean it. She's just a bit stressed, that's all.'

'I'd love to see you. Both of you. You're welcome to come over to the flat anytime. It would be so nice if you visited sometime.'

'Yeah sure, when the exams are over. It's just a bit mental right now, with the build up to my A levels.'

He was looking for an escape route. She provided him with one. 'Of course. Whenever you're not too busy.'

16

BAD DREAMS AND A GOLEM

They insisted on seeing her home. She told them she could have made it on her own, but they said it was unlikely. She had to agree, she was a bit worse for wear. So she gave in.

As they walked to the taxi, Corrine looped arms with her. 'You did the right thing.'

'Did I? I'm not so sure. It felt right at the time but when she started crying.'

'How many times has she done that before?'

'Oh, loads. She can turn it on and off whenever she needs to but it doesn't stop me thinking this time it might be real.'

'I know. None of us wants to see our kids upset, but sometimes you have to tell them the hard truth. That can hurt, but they get over it. Trust me. It will all work out just fine.'

She waved them off when they reached the flat, in spite of their insistence that one of them should go up with her to make sure she got in safely. The front door was easy enough. A couple were going in just as she reached it and they held the lift open for her. They got out on the third floor. The doors closed but nothing happened. A few minutes went by and she was still waiting for her floor to appear. It took a few minutes more to realise she'd forgotten to press any buttons. She pushed one. The doors opened and there was the couple standing by their front door, watching her.

'Everything all right?' called the man, just as the lift closed again.

She quickly found the number one and pressed it before it reopened.

Her door keys were nowhere to be found and she was having trouble manoeuvring her way around the inside of her bag. At that precise moment, the most logical course of action seemed to be to empty it out onto the floor. She scrambled around the untidy pile at her feet. Still no keys. She shook the bag out again. Nothing came out, but she could have sworn she heard something jangling. She held it to her ear and gave it another shake. 'Definitely in there,' she said. But it was one o'clock in the morning. Her neighbours were in bed, and there was no one there to confirm her suspicions. She turned the bag inside out. 'You moron!' She'd forgotten the zip pocket at the back. There they were.

After one or two attempts, she managed to get the key into the hole and open the door. She did a little celebratory dance, just for the hell of it, then bent down to pick up her things. The blood rushed to her head. Straight away, she felt woozy. Standing up very slowly, she put her foot behind the pile, and pushed it into her hall.

Normally she knew her limits. She wasn't a big drinker. Two glasses were more than enough. She liked alcohol, but not the effect it had on her. She couldn't cope with the lack of self-control, being someone who needed to keep herself in check on a permanent basis. Usually, when she veered too close to the edge of containment, she'd switch to tonic water and let everyone think she was on G and T, but tonight she had wanted to give herself up to it. She wanted to lose herself in the comfort of wine, and laughter, and friendship. She wanted the night to go on forever, and now look at her. Barely able to make it to bed in one piece, and doing silly dances in the communal hallway.

It must have been Will that triggered her to carry on drinking. She could just about take Liza, with her tantrums, but she'd always imagined he'd found her a little less tiresome. Tonight, he proved her wrong. He hadn't really come over because he wanted to talk to her. It was Kelly he was interested in. The look on his face when she invited him here said it all. And, in spite of everything she'd promised herself, she bailed him out. 'Stupid, stupid fool. What did you expect?'

Her phone beeped, still on the floor in the hallway. She lowered herself down, as slowly as she could manage. It was a message from Neil:

'We're back. You get in okay?'

She tapped out:

'Yes, just fine.'

'We had a great night. Hope you did too?'

After several attempts she managed to type:

'The best. Thank you. Goodnight.'

'Sweet dreams xx'

Corrine was right. It would all work out fine. She had her friends to help her through the hard times. She lay down on the floor and fell asleep.

It was her birthday. She knew that because she was walking

into the office with cakes and a huge meringue, and there were cards and some presents on her desk. More bath oils and creams to add to her collection. Some chocolates, and a scarf which wasn't really her taste but it was a nice thought. Her team were there to welcome her. Janice was saying how great it was to see her and how much she liked her new image. She looked down at herself. How odd! She was still wearing the jeans and T-shirt. Where were her work clothes? She began to search for them under her desk, in her drawers, the cupboards.

'What are you looking for?' asked Janice.

'My work clothes, my suit.'

'You don't need them, Annette. You're fine as you are.'

'No, no. I do, I do. They're my uniform you see. I can't do this without them.'

Just then Malcolm Jefferson opened the door. 'Annette, you're here. Could I have a word?'

She shook her head. She knew what was coming next and she didn't want to hear it all over again. She was walking backwards towards the exit, but her colleagues stood in the way.

'It's for the best, Annette,' said Janice.

'But I don't want to.'

'It will all work out just fine.'

'No Janice, you don't understand. My family. They need me.'

It was no use. Janice and Malcolm each had an arm and they were dragging her into his office and pushing her down into a chair.

'I shouldn't really be telling you this right now, and I must ask you to keep it to yourself. You know we're supposed to go through the appropriate procedures, but I wanted you to know as soon as possible.'

She put her hands over her ears and screwed her eyes up tight but still she could hear him.

'The thing is Annette, we've been considering this for a long time now. We're finding you increasingly hard to live with.'

What? This wasn't the redundancy speech. It was the divorce speech. She opened her eyes. Malcolm had turned into Colin. Janice had gone. Replaced by Liza and Will. Sitting in the corner, like a golem, was the mysterious blonde woman from the restaurant. Looking right through her, as if she was nothing.

Colin continued his speech: 'We think it would be better for all if you moved out. You and I haven't been compatible for a long time, but now it's affecting Liza and Will. They find your insular behaviour disturbing. I think we need to make a clean break of it and divorce. The children will stay in the house with me. It would be too much to expect them to move and you've clearly demonstrated, countless times, you're not fit to take care of them. Obviously, I'm not in a position to contribute financially, but your salary will more than cover the upkeep of two homes. That's the least you can do for your children, don't you think?'

'But I love you all, I do,' said Annette.

'Then pay for my trip,' said Liza. 'Or I'll be, like, an outcast.'

'I don't have the money,' she wailed.

'You're the worst mother in the world,' screamed her daughter.

Annette started shaking. Next came a searing pain in her chest. She called out to Will to help her.

He shrugged. 'Sorry Mum, it's all a bit mental right now.'

'I think soonest is best, Annette. We'll give you some space to think it over,' said Colin.

They walked out, leaving her alone with the golem. She banged her head down on the table and pleaded, 'Come back, don't leave me here, I can't bear it.' She banged her head again and, this time, it woke her up.

It was somewhere between night and day. The sky was blue-black. The moon, a translucent white disc, made the frosted ground below the balcony shimmer, as if scattered with fairy dust. She snuggled her hands deep into the pockets of the coat she'd fallen asleep in. It was so soothing, just to be here, standing quietly in the stillness. She watched her breath leaking from her nose and mouth and dwindling into the ether, becoming at one with the universe. Everything seemed right. She'd been agitated by the dream but all that stuff was history. It could only hurt her now if she let it, and she wouldn't. She was done with the past. From now on, she would only look backwards when it suited her. From now on, she would look forward.

17

THE RECKONING

So, she was fifty and a half, and one day. She lay in bed with a pillow over her head feeling every year, hour, minute of it, if not older. That was another reason why she rarely drank. She'd forgotten that. Gingerly lifting a corner, she sneaked a look at the bedside clock. Ten-thirty. Thank goodness it was Monday and she had nowhere in particular to go. Tentatively, she sat up, stepped out of the bed and went into the kitchen. She hung on to the drainer and filled a large glass with water, drank it down in one go and poured herself another. Then she lowered herself onto the sofa in the hope that her stomach would settle. A wave of saliva rushed to the top of her mouth and she made it to the bathroom with only seconds to spare before violently heaving, until there was nothing left for her to expel. She lay down on the floor and cooled her clammy skin on the cold tiles. The last time she'd been that drunk was at university. It was quite common then but she didn't recall it having such a debilitating effect on her in those days. She pulled off her clothes, crawled into the shower and let the hot water purge her.

Afterwards, she felt mildly better. Perhaps she could

manage a black coffee and two paracetamols. The caffeine might be just what she needed to get her back on her feet. Crossing the hall, she saw the contents of her bag in a heap on the floor. On the top of it was her phone — dead.

Images of the night before flashed through her mind. Liza's refusal to speak to her. Will's obvious reluctance to visit. Colin doing his best to shame her into handing out more money, and that woman, the golem, with her platinum hair cascading loosely past her shoulders and her Clash T-shirt. The exact same one she'd had years ago. Although admittedly, she'd never been able to fill it out like Oriel, or Ariel, or Alan, or whatever her name was. Why on earth would he have bought her that? The number of times Colin complained about her wearing it after they were married.

She plugged the phone into the charger. When its battery came back to life, she saw she had two missed calls from Colin and a message from Neil. Ignoring the calls, she sent a quick reply to Neil to say she was recuperating from her night out but otherwise she was fine.

She began to think about her financial situation. She hadn't been lying to Liza. She really couldn't afford to pay for her trip. She'd been unemployed for nearly three months. The redundancy package had been good and she had savings but they wouldn't last long if she remained unemployed. She had to do something. There were three options that she'd been thinking about since Christmas. Getting another job, selling the flat and buying somewhere cheaper, and reducing her maintenance payments. It was time to make some decisions.

The prospect of going back into paid employment was considered. It didn't have to be in the corporate world. There were other jobs, like working for a charity instance. Financially, it made sense to return to work. But no. She couldn't do it. She wasn't ready. Whether she'd ever be ready was another question but she would have to, at some point, when the money was gone. For now, she ruled it out. The other two solutions would give her more time. That was what she needed right now. Although they weren't going to be without their issues. She had no idea how they would turn out but, instinctively, she knew they'd be difficult for her. She decided to tackle them in order and work her way up to the most unpleasant.

Since she had no interest in the housing market, she didn't have a clue about how much her flat was worth. She'd only had it for about two years but with the help of an inheritance from her late grandmother, she'd paid off the mortgage already.

Ada Wilde had been a woman who appreciated nice things, but she was not someone who frittered money away. Even so, her extensive savings came as a surprise to her relatives. Everyone assumed she lived frugally because she had to, but the reality was more complicated. In truth, she was a woman out of her time, although if asked, it would have been difficult to place which time she belonged to. In some ways she was stuck in the past, never quite losing that make do and mend mentality, but in others she was way ahead of her era.

After the war, Alf Wilde returned to his wife and baby son, conceived during a rare two days of leave and, as Ada liked to tell it, decided he didn't like the look of them and promptly left. As it happened, she wasn't that keen on him either, so she wasn't all that bothered. But what she was, was very bloody annoyed. She'd worked in the munitions factory until she became pregnant. She'd been bombed out and half-starved through rationing. She'd be buggered if she was going to stand by and let him walk away without so much as a penny towards his son's keep. With the help of her brothers she tracked him down and after some force on their part, Alf agreed to pay a reasonable weekly maintenance. She was only twenty when she bore Arthur but she never divorced. And as far as anyone could see, in all her ninety-two years, she never seriously indulged in male company again. If anyone broached the subject, she would simply say: 'What can a man do for me that I can't do for myself?' No one dared make any suggestions. She seemed to have it all covered.

Arthur never saw his dad again, but the money kept on coming until he was twenty-one by which time, he had married Geraldine and was hoping to become a father himself. Unlike Alf, he was determined to go the full distance.

In the early days Ada, recognising she had to make a living somehow, used the maintenance money to buy stock for a market stall. She bought household items or make-up, whatever was cheap, and sold them at a profit to a population desperate for small luxuries in post-war Birmingham. After a few years, she had enough to buy her first shop, with a flat upstairs for her and little Arthur to live in. She was a good businesswoman. By the time she retired, she had four shops which she swore were not making a profit. She was just getting by, she said. Just keeping them open for the staff. Her estate proved her wrong. Aside from a small annuity put in place for Liza and Will, she left the rest to be shared equally between her son Arthur, and Annette, her only grandchild, under the strict proviso that she should only spend it on herself and not Colin or the children. Ada had always been a very perceptive woman.

The money came at a particular low point in Annette's life. She'd been grief stricken, not only by Ada's death but also by the divorce. The guilt of keeping the money for herself was hard to live with. She just wanted rid of it as quickly as possible. Her dad suggested paying off her second mortgage to take away some of her financial strain. On his counsel, she also kept the details of her inheritance hidden from her family. There was no point in them knowing, he advised, since they couldn't have any of it. Better to let them think that Granny left next to nothing rather than burden them with the resentment of knowing that there was money, but it was out of their reach. So, most of the cash was tied up in the flat. But her family did profit from it, indirectly, because it allowed her to spend more of her salary on them, whenever they asked for it. Now though, it was time to put it to another use. She had a new problem that needed fixing and, this time, there would be no guilt.

She made an appointment with an estate agent for a valuation with a view to selling. She didn't think the value of the flat had gone down. She hoped for a small increase, or at the very least that she would get back what she paid for it. If she could get something less expensive, she would have more money to add to the remainder of Granny's inheritance and her redundancy money.

Next, she turned on the laptop, and went through her outgoings to work out just how much she was contributing to the support of her family. There was the mortgage on the house, which had another ten years left and a monthly allowance for each of the children. She could see now, that was more than generous. Finally, there was the maintenance payment that Colin had proposed was needed to cover everything — bills, food, his car and other expenses. Everything required for the three of them to lead a comfortable, carefree existence.

She compared their lives to those of the foodbank clients

and felt anger. At them and their soft, greedy ways and at herself for providing the spoils of wealth without the necessary social conscience. They were self-indulgent and spoon-fed, and she'd allowed them to become so by constantly succumbing to their demands.

There was worse to come. She added up everything, then did it again to make sure she wasn't mistaken. 'Shit!' She backed away from her findings in alarm. Three quarters of her monthly outlay was going on them. She paced the room, hands running, erratically, through her hair. 'Fuck. Fuck, fuck, fuck, fuck.' She looked at the figures again. It didn't matter how parsimoniously she was living, if she carried on like this she would soon run out of money. What's more, she was giving them enough to keep two, maybe three families going.

She sat back down and rested her head in her hands. What an idiot she was. When Colin had told her how much they needed, she'd just accepted it. Too full of remorse to question it. Too fearful of what he might do next. Besides, he'd been an accountant before giving it all up for his art. He'd always managed their finances. That was how it worked. He told her how much they needed and she went out and earned it. Even after the divorce, when she was forced to manage her own money, he was still dictating the majority of her monthly spend. She'd been on such a good salary she hadn't given it another thought, until now. Now, she realised, this couldn't go on. There was nothing more to it. She had no choice. She rang Colin.

'I was wondering if you were ever going to call me back. I tried you twice this morning.'

'What did you want Colin?'

'It's about Liza. She's really, very upset.'

'And?'

'What do you mean, and? This is your daughter we're talking about.'

'Yes, it is isn't it? And, as her mother I'm telling you that it will do her good to miss out on that trip.'

'How can you say that? You know how much she'll be ostracised by her friends,' he said.

'I doubt that very much, but if she is, then they aren't really friends, are they? Perhaps she should take a long, hard look at them and find herself some proper friends who care about her. Not about how much money she has in her purse.'

'I'm flabbergasted that you can be so callous about it. Just how many kinds of crap are you?'

'I'll tell you what's callous Colin. The elderly eking out the heating in the middle of winter just to make their money last. Families having to exist on a pittance. Parents going hungry because they can't afford to feed themselves and their children. That's callous, Colin. Going on a vastly expensive ski trip when children are going to school with holes in their shoes and empty bellies. That's callous.'

'Oh, here we go,' he said. 'The fucking foodbank. So, you've found another perch to shit on us from, have you? How does it feel up there in the land of the self-righteous? Does it feel as good as knowing that your children can't stand you?'

She gasped. He'd done it again. Made her feel worthless with a few spiteful words. She wanted to be sick again. She stilled herself until she was able to speak. 'Thank you for reminding me how little I mean to you all. It makes the reason I'm actually ringing you so much easier. I've been looking at my financial situation and I've decided that I can't continue to support you to the extent I have done in the past. I'm reducing the maintenance payments and the children's allowances by half.'

'You can't do that. We're already living hand to mouth.'

'If you think that Colin, then you really have no idea. The money you'll be left with is more than adequate to pay for the family's needs and I'll still pay the mortgage. And, if you really are that desperate you could always consider looking for a job.'

'I'm not having this. I'll go to a solicitor.' His voice was getting louder. 'We'll take you through the courts. I'm warning you Annette. You know, I can make things very unpleasant for you.'

She shivered, in anticipation of the frost making its way down the line towards her. He was waiting for her to cave in. She must not buckle. 'That's your prerogative but I'm confident any solicitor will tell you that you've still got a good deal.'

'You cow. You vicious fucking bitch. Just wait 'til I tell —'

'Yes, thank you Colin, and the same to you. Goodbye.'

She let her phone ring out and refused to look at his messages. Since she could imagine what they said, there was no point in reading or listening to them. This was becoming quite an agreeable habit. She checked her hands. Still shaking but this time it felt good. Empowering. She was beginning to regain control of her life at last.

18

BECOMING A DOG LOVER

'You bought this at the right time, Mrs Grey. The area's always been popular but more so now than ever, with all the new restaurants and bars. It's becoming quite a hipster enclave around the High Street. You'll probably get a nice little profit on it.'

The estate agent was very positive but she supposed they always were. It came with the job.

'Nice view from the balcony, that'll add a bit extra on and make it more saleable than the flats in the front of the building.'

Good. Now that she'd made up her mind to do it, she was impatient to sell. 'How soon can you get it on the market?'

'Within the week. I've already got a waiting list for this area. We can start showing people round as soon as we've agreed your asking price and done the paperwork. We don't even need to wait for the photos, if you're in a hurry. It won't take you long to sell. You've got it nice and neutral. Minimalist. People like that. It's easier for them to imagine their furniture in here when the current owner hasn't projected their own personality onto it.'

They took care of everything at a speed that was breathtaking. They had a buyer who agreed to her price before they'd even printed the brochures. Now all she had to do was find somewhere new. She had a long list of flats and houses to look at and went to all of them on her own. Neil and Paula offered to go with her but she said no. Since she was expecting to be living there on her own, she wanted to experience it alone and without distractions. To get a proper feel for it. She'd rushed into buying her current flat and had never really felt at home in it. The last place that ever really felt like home was the student house she'd shared with Claire and Sasha. She wanted that feeling again of being comfortable in her own space. Of being happy to be there. So, she resolved to take a little longer this time. Even if she had to stay somewhere else while she looked. Paula said she could stay with her for as long as she needed.

Each place had its good points but none of them felt right. They were either too dark, too sterile, too poky, or simply just wrong. She tried a number of estate agents but they all had similar results. Her buyer was becoming impatient and she was coming to the conclusion that she'd have to move out early and take up Paula's offer.

She was having a drink with Neil and Chris in their local. Corrine's children were spending the night at their dad's so she came along too. There'd been another unsatisfactory viewing that afternoon and Annette was telling them everything that was wrong with it.

'Mind if I join you?' It was Sean, Neil and Chris's neighbour.

'Hey there,' said Corrine. 'Come and listen to Annette's house hunting problems.'

Annette laughed. 'Yes, please do. The more people I can bring down with my misery the better. I've seen so many places now, I'm getting property viewing fatigue. I just can't find one I want to buy.'

'Huh, that's funny,' said Sean. 'One of my customers is an estate agent and he's got the opposite problem. He's got a house he can't sell.'

'Sean runs an independent record shop in Selly Oak,' said Neil.

Ah yes. She remembered him telling her that at Christmas.

'Yeah,' said Sean. 'This estate agent's a big-time vinyl enthusiast. His office is a few doors up. So, he was telling me about this house he's got on his books. It's cheap enough but he can't get rid of it.'

'Must be something wrong with it,' said Chris.

Sean picked up his pint, 'Dunno. He reckons not. An old woman lived there before. She died and left the house to a relative. Nephew, I think. Lives in Australia. Anyway, he wants to sell it, but the old lady put down some conditions in the will and they're making it hard to find a buyer.'

'What sort of conditions?' said Annette.

'Not sure,' said Sean. 'Something about a dog. We got interrupted. Might be worth a look though, if you're stuck. The area's all right. Not as upmarket as your current place but nice. No trouble. A bit tired I suppose but it's picking up. The guy'll probably say it's up and coming.'

The estate agent said exactly that. 'We're seeing a fair bit of overspill from people who are being priced out of Kings Heath. It's a nice old house. A do-er upper. It's got bags of potential but it needs a bit of attention. Hence the low price. You'd normally be hard pressed to get a four bedroomed house at that price this side of the city but, as I say, it needs a bit of a tidy up.'

'Is it very run down?' She could do a bit of decorating and change a plug, but that was the extent of her DIY skills.

'Not really run down. It's been updated over the years but the late owner, Miss Pinsent, found it hard to keep up with in her later years. It needs a bit of a clearance and a clean. And redecorating, A few odd jobs. That sort of thing.'

'My friend mentioned something about conditions?'

'Ah yes, that'll be the dog. Miss Pinsent stipulated that whoever bought the house also had to take on the care of her dog, and had to agree not to sell it again until after the dog dies. A natural death obviously. No putting the little fella to sleep, or tying it to a post and running over it or anything like that.'

He laughed at his own joke. She'd never been a dog person but she didn't find it funny.

He took the hint from her stony stare. 'Sorry, poor taste. Actually, it's quite a nice little thing. The neighbour's looking after it at the moment, a Mr …' he scanned his papers, 'O'Hare.'

'Okay, I'll take a look. Any chance we could go now?'

'Ah. I've another viewing I'm afraid, and my colleague's off sick. I'll tell you what. Let me give Mr O'Hare a call and see if he's in. He's got a spare set of keys. He might be happy to show you around. If you don't mind that is?'

She told him she didn't mind at all. With any luck the neighbour would tell her a bit more about the area and the house than he could.

'Yes, thank you. Much appreciated Mr O'Hare. Mrs Grey will be coming straight round? Yes, yes. She's nodding

a yes to me. Yes, let's hope so. Yes, it has, hasn't it? Thanks
Mr O'Hare. Thanks. Goodbye, goodbye.' The agent put the
phone down and rubbed his hands. 'We're in luck.'

She decided it was probably his colleague who was the
vinyl enthusiast.

It was a bit further out than she'd thought but she managed
to find the place with the help of the satnav. She seemed to
be winding around street after street which, if nothing else,
gave her a feel for the area. It *was* a bit tired. Faded, you
could say. But there were some sparks of life. Particularly on
the main road where a few interesting shops were sprouting
up. It reminded her of Kings Heath when she was a girl.
Before it became the go-to residence for bohemians who
couldn't afford Moseley.

She'd nearly always lived on the south side of Birmingham, apart from university and a brief flirtation with a
rented flat in Sutton when she and Colin moved here. They
bought their first house in Kings Heath but the lure of
Moseley proved too much for him, once he'd decided his
future lay in art rather than accountancy.

Even after they'd thrown her out, she'd only moved a
few miles away to Harborne which wasn't that far removed
from the same vibe. She'd only picked that because she
thought it would pass his approval criteria. It was okay that
this area was further down on the evolutionary scale in that
respect. She wanted it to be different. She wanted somewhere that she could be different.

She turned into the road and parked outside a large,
shabby detached house not far from the corner. There was
an identical house next door, in a much better state of
health. The road was quite short. There were no more

than a dozen houses, of different sizes and eras, randomly scattered about. One end of it was closed to traffic by concrete bollards. It had probably once been a rat run for commuters but was quiet now, with the lack of cars. It felt slightly remote and out of place in this busy city. Although, if she listened very carefully, she could just about hear the low hum of main road traffic over the birdsong.

On the other side of the house was a passageway which she followed. It led through some bushes to a grassy area behind. Not a park exactly. Not even big enough to be called a recreation field. More, a small stretch of greenery that sat between the back of these houses and those on the next road. The urban equivalent of a village green.

Back at the front garden, she could see there was a drive hidden underneath. It was probably wide enough for the car but she was taking no chances. It was overgrown with a disorderly combination of knee-high grass, weeds and bushes, interspersed with dead and decaying flowers. First impressions were not good.

If the exterior was anything to go by, a lot of work would be needed to make it habitable. And it was much larger than she'd imagined. She should have known it would be when the agent told her there were four bedrooms. It was way too big for her. If she had any sense, she'd get back in the car and drive away without looking back. Still, she was here now, and what if the neighbour was inside, watching? He'd given up his time for her so the least she could do was take a look.

She picked through the tangled vegetation, along a path to the front door and hammered the rusty knocker against it. No one came. She gave it a few minutes and tried again. Still no one. She waited. With any luck he wouldn't turn up and she could forget about it. Another five minutes passed and still no one.

Fidgety from the waiting, she decided she might as well have a poke around. She tried a gate leading to the back of the house. It was stiff but opened with some thrust.

She called out, 'Hello?'

Nothing.

She walked further in, along the side of the house into a large and even wilder back garden. Hmm. She was no gardener either. She cupped her hands to the grimy windows to see what was inside.

There was a rustling behind her. She turned around and saw a movement in the grass. Her first thought was rats. She tensed, then softened when a dog emerged and trotted towards her. It was on the small side of medium. Although dog breeds were not her strongest subject, she was absolutely certain this one had terrier somewhere in its DNA. Its head was square, made slightly curvy by tufty hair protruding from the edges. The colour of its wiry coat was hard to pin down but, if she was pushed, Annette would have called it taupe. Yes, taupe. With the odd splash of white, grey and just a tiny bit of black.

It sat down, leaning slightly to one side, dropped the chewed remains of a tennis ball at her feet and looked straight up at her. Its heavy eyebrows were perched at acute angles over a pair of dark eyes. The effect was an expression of permanent anticipation. As if it were waiting for something, or someone. When it opened its mouth, Annette half expected it to say: 'Is it you then? Are you the one?' It didn't. Obviously. Instead the little dog yawned and shuffled closer. As its mouth closed, it made a noise that could only be described as 'Hrmph.'

Annette's heart melted, just a little bit. She crouched

down to stroke it. 'Hello. I presume you're the sitting tenant?' The dog licked her hand.

'You've met Maud I see?'

Startled, she tried to turn around while still squatting and fell backwards onto her rear end.

'I'm so sorry, I didn't mean to make you jump.' A large hand was held out in front of her. 'Here, let me help you up. I'm Frank O'Hare. I hope you haven't been waiting too long? I didn't realise you'd arrived.'

A large, untidy looking man was smiling down at her. As she took hold of his hand and allowed him to pull her up, she spotted flecks of bright colours on his nails and fingers and noticed that his baggy jeans and wrinkled shirt were speckled with similar marks. When she stood up, she saw that he was well over six foot, broad and a little overweight. He had quite a strong face, framed by a shock of hair that resembled wire wool, and bright blue eyes that were cut in half by a pair of glasses balanced on the end of his nose. He must have been quite a looker in his youth. He was probably in his late fifties now. Hard to tell with such an unkempt appearance. Clearly, looking at his best wasn't his top priority.

She brushed herself off. 'It's quite all right, I should have waited for you at the front.'

'Anxious to have a look around I expect. I'll let you in.'

He unlocked the back door. 'I'm afraid it's a bit of a mess. Edie did her best but she couldn't keep up with it.'

The door opened into the kitchen. It was a big room with cupboards and work surfaces made of solid wood. Against one wall was a Welsh dresser housing an intricately patterned china dinner service. Next to it were numerous cast iron pots and pans arranged on long shelves. All were covered in dust. It reminded her of a farmhouse kitchen, minus the Aga.

In the middle of the room, was a sturdy table that could easily sit eight. It had a place setting for one.

'She was just getting ready for her dinner when she had a stroke,' said Frank O'Hare. 'The meals on wheels people came over to me when she didn't answer. We found her on the floor and got her to the hospital as soon as possible but sadly, she didn't pull through.'

'Oh, so she didn't, I mean it wasn't …'

'Here? No. She passed away a couple of days later. Poor old girl. She was a lovely lady.'

His accent was Irish. From the north, she suspected, but it had been diluted. Presumably from years of living away.

'Look, do you want me to show you around or would you rather just do it on your own? I know it can be a bit awkward when you're being chaperoned. Especially by a man you don't know. If you prefer, I can leave you to it.'

'That would be good. Thank you.'

He shrugged. 'Sometimes, you can only get the feel of a place when you're completely alone in it.'

'Yes, exactly.'

He pointed in the direction of the twin house, 'Just come and let me know when you're done. I'm right next door. There's a gate in the garden that leads into mine, if you can fight your way through to it. Or come to the front. Whichever suits. Are you coming Maudie? No? I think she wants to keep an eye on you, Mrs Grey.'

Maud leaned her warm body against Annette's legs as she took in the big, homely kitchen. When Annette toured the house, she followed her. Each room looked as if it had every expectation of its owner returning within minutes. In the small breakfast room at the side of the kitchen, an open book sat on the table. *Wuthering Heights.* One of Annette's personal favourites. Next to it was an empty cup, stained at the base with dried-out tea, and a small plate that still had crumbs on it. Sunlight streamed through the French windows, despite them being clouded with dirt and framed by silvery cobwebs. 'What a delightful spot to start the day,' she said out loud. She imagined herself breakfasting there, reading the same book, or just closing her eyes and soaking up the sun.

She and Maud moved on to the cluttered lounge. It was the complete opposite of her own functional room in the flat. Minimalist, the agent had called it. Trust an estate agent to put a positive spin on it. Of course she hadn't projected her personality onto it. How could she? She didn't have one.

Here, newspapers lay on the battered leather sofa and a TV remote poked out from between its cushions. Without thinking, she pulled it out, placed it on a nearby coffee table, tidied up the papers and left them next to it. She noticed the dates on them. Last July. A few days before her birthday. Did that mean there was a chance Miss Pinsent died on her birthday? What a strange and sobering thought.

The sunlight shot pretty patterns through the stained-glass windows on and around the front door and sent them dancing about the wide hall. She could have cheerfully sat on the stairs and watched the display but she was conscious of wasting too much time. She crossed over to the other side into a study, lined with dusty bookcases filled to the point of heaving. In the centre sat a grand oak desk, covered with stacks of papers. A higgledy-piggledy walkway ran up to and around the desk cutting through more papers, heaped in precarious bundles. Alongside them were mounds of ageing notebooks, half-piled, half-tumbled against the bookcases and spilling chaotically across the floor.

Upstairs, were three large bedrooms and a smaller one which was still decorated in ancient nursery paper but otherwise, filled with boxes and more books and papers. In contrast, the three bigger bedrooms were reasonably tidy albeit with a curious mix of bulky antique cupboards and cheap, dated MDF wardrobes and divan beds.

Maud ran through her legs as she opened the door to the master bedroom and cocked her head at the old bed, made cosy with eiderdowns and a number of pillows. She leapt up onto it and sniffed a nightdress lying across the bottom. Curling herself up on top of it, she nuzzled into its folds and let out a low moan. Annette sat on the edge of the bed and ran her hands across Maud's bristly coat. Maud whimpered.

'You poor thing. Do you miss her terribly?'

Maud planted her head in Annette's hand and, with that small action, turned Annette Grey into a dog lover who couldn't envisage her new life without a scraggy haired canine at her side.

She took a last look at the house, locked the back door and fought her way through the jungle to an open gate that led into Frank O'Hare's garden. Like the man himself, Frank's garden was big and rangy, generally pleasant looking, and a little rough around the edges. She followed Maud, who seemed to know where she was going.

He was in his equivalent breakfast room, standing over an easel, paint brush in hand.

'You're an artist?' She tried not to show her disappointment.

'Sort of. It's a paying hobby. I teach too. At the local college.'

Well at least he was working. 'Art?'

'No, English.'

'How interesting, my degree was in English. I considered teaching it for a while.'

'And you didn't?'

'No, I ended up in corporate life. You know how it is.' Her hand automatically waved the thought away dismissively.

'Life gets in the way sometimes.'

'Yes, exactly. But it would have been a bad move. I was never really cut out to be a teacher.'

'It can be a trial,' he said. 'I was just about to make a pot of coffee, if you're not in a hurry.'

'Er no. That would be nice. Thank you. I've been rushing around all morning and haven't had a chance to stop for a break.'

'So, what do you think of the house?' he asked over tea and biscuits. They were sitting in his kitchen. It was the same size as the one next door but more modern.

'I like it. It needs some work but it has a homely feel about it that just makes you feel so comfortable.'

She took a sip of coffee. It was the proper stuff made in a filter machine. So much nicer than the instant she kept in her cupboards. She envisaged herself a few months in the future, popping over here for a coffee and a chat. She'd only recently realised that she was a person who liked a chat, and Frank O'Hare seemed like a nice man. He seemed very much like a person who might like a chat too.

'It's always been in Edie's family you know. Her parents bought it from new and she was born there,' he said.

That explained the accumulation of stuff, and the little nursery.

'Maud too. She comes from a long line of Pinsent dogs.' He gave Maud a biscuit.

'She's very sweet,' said Annette. 'How old is she?'

'If memory serves me right, she'd be about three now. A bit of a way to go before we lose her, hopefully. Can you see yourself living there?'

'I can but, if I can be honest, I'm wondering what the catch is. The house is enormous compared to my flat and yet it's little more than half the price. Apparently, my flat is in a very desirable part of town but, still.'

'You're wondering if the place is going to fall down as soon as you move in?' he said. 'Well, I can tell you that Edie's great-nephew had a full survey done before he put the house up for sale and there's nothing wrong with it that a good clean and a bit of redecoration won't fix.'

'Is it the area then?'

'The area?' He offered her another biscuit and took one for himself. 'It's not as smart as some but it's a good place to live. The people are friendly. We never have any trouble, if that's what you're worried about. No, I think it's the conditions.'

'You mean, the conditions around Maud?'

He finished his biscuit. 'Yes, but there are others. You have to clear the place out yourself, personally. You can't get a professional to do it. That's why nothing's been touched in there. And, you have to pass a test.'

'A test?'

'Well it's mostly a questionnaire really. You'll need to provide referees too. Edie was very particular about who it was being passed on to. James, her great-nephew, is very strict about it. He lives in Australia now, but he was very fond of his aunt and he wants to carry out her wishes. He's already turned down eight offers.'

'Oh dear,' said Annette. 'Fingers crossed then. You said it was mostly a questionnaire. Was there another part to it?'

'Yes, but you don't need to worry about that one. You've already passed.'

She was confused.

He nodded to Maud. 'She likes you. That's one of the most important tests.'

He offered Maud another biscuit. She gobbled it down and wagged her tail.

19

MOVING FORWARD

It's fair to say that Frank O'Hare had rather played down the rigour of the tests involved. The questionnaire was extensive, requiring Annette's full background history, and she was asked to provide four referees. She asked the four people she thought might give the best impression of her. She chose Alan, for his spiritual credentials, Malcolm as a high-profile businessman, Chris for both his professional and voluntary work, and Paula because she could give the best references of anyone she knew. At the end of this, she was confident she'd done her best to meet Miss Pinsent's strict requirements, but the last hurdle was the most nerve racking. It was a Skype interview with James Pinsent.

James Pinsent was pleasant but he left her in no doubt that he took the execution of his great-aunt's wishes seriously. He was married to an Australian and they had three children so it was impossible for him to move back to England. His aunt had understood this but she made him promise that whoever he sold the house to, had to meet her exacting specifications.

'It's not about the money,' he said. 'It's about carrying

out Aunt Edie's wishes to the letter. My dad's mum died before I was born so she, kind of, took her place. In spite of the air miles, we were very close. I'm not a religious person, but I like to think she's watching over that house and little Maud, and making sure everything's just right.'

She told him she understood completely.

'Good. Now tell me about yourself. Don't leave anything out. I've got quite a tick list of qualities here to check off.'

He held up a large piece of paper. She did as he asked. It took a good half hour, especially as he kept interrupting with questions.

'Sounds like you've had quite a change in life,' he said when she finished.

'You could say that,' she said. 'I think being made redundant has changed my life completely.'

'For the better I hope?'

'Yes, I believe so but it's still changing so I'll have to wait before I can give a fully qualified answer. This move is the next step. It's a new start. A new adventure.'

'And what do you think of Maud?'

'Well, I've only met her once but she's delightful.'

'If you don't mind me saying so Annette, that answer was a bit anodyne. I need to know what you really think of her. Aunt Edie was very precise about this.'

She paused for a moment. She'd been trying not to get her hopes up too much but, since the day she'd walked into that house she didn't want to live anywhere else. She couldn't explain it. She just felt so at home even though it was nothing like any home she'd ever lived in. It was a mess and she knew she may be out of her depth in taking it on, but she wanted it all the same.

The other thing that worried her was Maud. She was a sweet little thing but Annette had no experience of looking after animals. If her family was the yardstick she went by, she was rubbish at caring for anything, including herself. Truly, looking after Maud was a responsibility, she wasn't sure she was ready to bear. But, if she wanted the house, she had to do it. Besides, the dog was obviously lonely. She'd had enough experience of that to spot it in anyone or anything. What to say to James? She decided honesty was the best way forward.

'I think she's lonely. I'm sure Mr O'Hare is doing an admirable job of taking care of her but I think she misses your aunt terribly. I don't know if I'll be able to fill that gap for her but I'm willing to give it a try.'

'You don't have any pets yourself?'

'No. I'm not going to lie to you, I've no experience of looking after animals at all. Until now, I've never really been that fond of dogs but there is something about Maud. I don't know how to express it really, other than to say, there is something about Maud. Sorry, I'm not making much sense.'

'You're making complete sense,' he said. 'I have to go now. I promised the kids a day at the beach and they're fed up of waiting. I'm going to talk it over with my wife and I'll mail you with my decision later on, if that's okay?'

'Yes, that's fine. Can I just ask a question before you go? I'm interested to know why your great-aunt wanted the new owner to clear the house personally.'

'It is a strange one isn't it? Aunt Edie had her eccentricities so I'm not sure I can tell you exactly why. The best way to explain it, as I understand it, is to do with the kind of person she wanted to take the house on. She didn't have any children so I think she wanted to pass a bit of herself on, through the house. I think she thought if you read her journals and went through her things, a bit of her would become part of you.'

'I see. Yes, I see that now. What a clever idea.'

The next twenty-four hours were unbelievably slow. In spite of a full day at the foodbank and the job club, nothing seemed to take her mind off things. Regardless of the outcome, she was relieved to get his email. She opened it up hesitantly, scanning the first few words and then, when she knew it was safe, taking her time to read the rest:

Hi Annette,

Congratulations!

I'm happy to say you've passed Aunt Edie's tests. I've instructed the agent and solicitor to start the ball rolling. Assuming you're still keen to move in as soon as possible, we should be able to conclude everything in a matter of weeks. Only one more condition. Please keep me updated on Maud and the house. I'd like to keep in touch.

James'

She replied with an excited:

James

Yes, yes, yes. I couldn't be happier. I'll call the agent immediately. Thank you so much.

Annette'

A few weeks later, early one Saturday morning Paula, Corrine, Kelly and George turned up ready to empty out the flat. Neil and Chris followed shortly after in a rented van and, with the help of her friends, Annette moved to her new home.

It didn't take too long to empty the flat. She sent the others on ahead and went out to take one last look from the balcony. She wouldn't miss the flat because it had too many unhappy memories for her, but the view was a different matter. Perhaps when she got the jungle under control, she'd get the same satisfaction looking out from the breakfast room as she had out here.

As she surveyed the scene for the last time, a woman walked across the grass with a large dog. She let it off its lead and it ran towards the water, gambolling and barking. Then, the woman held her arms aloft and called the dog to her. It galloped back and threw itself at her, licking her face ecstatically. Annette was fascinated. She saw her future self and Maud frolicking in a similar park. The idea of it filled her with joy. The woman was laughing now. She picked up a stick and threw it, setting the dog off on another romp. Suddenly, she shifted her concentration from the dog to Annette and smiled up at her. Then, Annette did something she'd never done before. She raised her hand and waved.

When she arrived at the house, the others were already inside. Neil had elected not to park the van on the drive. 'Best we get it cleared before you take the risk of driving onto there,' he said.

She felt a swell of pride when Paula declared that it was a charming old house. Kelly looked doubtful. 'I dunno about that. Sorry Net but I have to say, compared to your last place, it's a bit of a tip. It's like a bloody museum.'

'Kelly, you need some lessons in tactfulness,' said Corrine. 'It's just different that's all. It'll be lovely when we've given it a good clean.'

'We?'

'Yes girl, we. Here, put these on and take that look off your face.' She threw a pair of rubber gloves at her.

Kelly threw the gloves down. 'I don't do cleaning.'

'No surprise there. Time to learn how to do it then. Come on, watch me. Grab a black bag and start by taking the old food out of the cupboards, then we'll wash them so that Annette can put her stuff in there. Check the use by dates before you throw anything away though. Some of it could still be within date. Even if Annette doesn't want it, someone might be able to use it. That's allowed isn't it, Annette? You don't literally have to do everything yourself, do you?'

'I think we're safe getting rid of the old food but let's hold onto anything else for now. I can sort through it bit by bit,' said Annette.

As Corrine and Kelly started on the kitchen at the back of the house, the others were bringing in furniture and boxes through the front. Neil and George carried in Annette's dining table and chairs. 'Where do you want these?'

She directed them to the breakfast room.

'What about this?' Chris was holding one end of her sofa. At the other end, was Frank O'Hare with Maud at his side.

'Let's try to fit it in the lounge, in there,' she said. 'Hello Frank. Nice to see you again. Hello Maud. Everyone, this is Frank my new neighbour and Maud, my new room-mate.'

It took all day to move, shift, clear, and clean and really they'd only scratched the surface. By early evening, they had four rooms sorted. The kitchen, lounge, bathroom and one bedroom. That was enough for one day.

Having closed up his shop, Sean came over with a big bagful of beers and wine. Frank and Chris went to get fish and chips from the local chip shop. They sat in a mismatched array of chairs around the big kitchen table and toasted Annette's new home. Kelly picked up a pot of curry sauce and poured half of it over her meal.

'I used to love that,' said Annette.

'Especially after a night out at a club,' added Sean.

'Oh God yes. Nothing better at four o'clock in the morning after a night of drinking and dancing than filling your face with fish, chips and curry sauce,' said Annette.

'No, sorry Net,' said Kelly. 'I can't imagine you doing anything like that. You're too proper.'

'I'll have you know, young lady, I was a very different person back in the days before I became Annette Grey.'

Kelly snorted. 'Oh yeah? You mean you were Annette Posho McPoshy or something like that?'

'Annette Wilde actually. Although I was Netta to my family and friends. Netta Wilde.'

'Yeah right. Wild by name wild by nature then, was it?' said Kelly, shaking her disbelieving head.

'Hardly wild, but maybe not as tame as I am now,' said Annette.

'I can see you as a clubber.' said Sean. 'Smiths fan, were you?'

'Yes,' said Annette. 'But my favourite band was really the Clash. I had a friend whose big sister was a proper punk and we just soaked all that stuff up. We were really into it, even though punk was pretty much over by the time we found out about it.'

Sean nodded. 'Good call. I'm a big fan myself.'

'A bit before my time,' said Corrine.

'Mine too really,' said Sean. 'But some bands transcend their natural era.'

Corrine laughed. 'Is that so? Maybe I'll have to give them a try.'

Annette could tell she'd impressed Sean. Less so the others. They looked more surprised than impressed. That was understandable. In spite of her recent changes she was still stiff and self-contained, still reluctant to stand out from the crowd. The furthest thing from punk that you could imagine, in fact.

She hadn't always been this way. As a child and right through university she'd been outgoing and liked being different. That was probably why she chose punk over the music of her day. All right, she'd not been in with the popular crowd but that never bothered her because she was her own person and was confident enough to be whoever that was. Somewhere along the line, Netta Wilde slipped away and Annette Grey took her place which was a shame, because being Netta Wilde was a lot more fun.

20

KELLY LOSES A BOYFRIEND AND GAINS A HOME.

In spite of her claim that she didn't do cleaning, Kelly had been around every day since the move, to help shift the layers of dirt in the house. Judging by that single visit to Craig's flat, she hadn't been practising it there but she wasn't as bad at it as she made out.

Right now, they were on their knees, washing the floor in the hall. It was hard work. Annette stopped to stretch out her back and watched Kelly rubbing the floor with her cloth. 'You're very good at this. Anyone would think you did a lot of it.'

'I did most of the cooking and cleaning when my mum got really bad. And after she died. My dad was useless.'

'Oh, I'm sorry, I didn't mean to —'

'Nah, you're all right. I don't mind talking about it to you.'

'So, it must have been extra hard on you when your mum died then?'

Kelly carried on moving the cloth back and forth. 'I suppose so. Never really thought about it. My dad really went to pieces. She was ill for a long time, so you'd think he'd have been ready for it, but he was worse than my brothers. I had to look after him and them. Fucking useless. My nan helped a bit, but she's old. She can't do a lot. She's all right though. I moved in with her when Dad brought Carol home. I couldn't stand it with her around. So I left.'

Kelly sat back on heels and surveyed the floor. 'Shame really. I was doing all right at school. Before the cancer. Mum wanted me to go to university and everything. She was always telling me I could be anything I wanted to be.' She grinned. 'She was full of shit, my mum. On a different planet most of the time. Even before the drugs.'

'It's not too late Kelly. You're only nineteen, and you're a smart girl.'

'Nah,' she said. 'It's not for people like me. Bloody hell, this floor's a different colour now. What did you say it was called?'

'Parquet. I expect it's been here since the house was built.'

'Way old then. Parquet. Nice.'

'Let's go and put our feet up while it dries,' said Annette.

Kelly was opening herself up in small snatches and Annette was trying to give her the space to talk whenever she wanted to, without pushing things too hard. But there was something more pressing that she did want to speak to her about. She had the impression that Kelly was in no rush to leave each night, as if she was avoiding going home. Also, she wasn't her usual self. They hadn't really discussed Kelly's love life since the day of Annette's half-birthday but she'd put money on it not being that great at the moment. As the two of them grew closer, it became easier to mark out the pattern of mood swings that, when traced back, were usually the result of some upset at home.

Since the last big meltdown at the foodbank, Kelly had

moderated her behaviour to a more acceptable level but it was still obvious when things weren't right with her. Annette had gone over that incident in her head numerous times. Each time asking herself the same question. Why did Kelly swallow her pride and come back to the foodbank? It was the concluding realisation that Kelly needed the foodbank as much as she did that made her all the more protective towards her.

'How are things with you and Craig?' The effort of cleaning the floor seemed to have cheered Kelly up so, sitting in the breakfast room with a cup of coffee and a packet of chocolate biscuits seemed as good a time as any to ask.

Kelly shrugged. 'You remember that day I came over to yours and said I was giving him one last chance? Well, he made all these promises. Told me he loved me and stuff, and said he was going to dump Letitia. But I had this feeling that he was still at it so I followed him. To her flat!' She gave Annette a gobsmacked look. Like it had come to a complete surprise.

'Right,' said Annette, slowly.

'Yeah. Right. So, I had it out with him and he says he's got to go there to see his kid. He's got a little boy with her. Fair enough. But I could tell there was more to it. So, I says to him, as long as that's all you're doing. But really though, I knew he was lying. I checked his pockets and found a packet of johnnies. I'm on the pill. So?' She held out her palms and opened her eyes wide.

'Ah,' said Annette, not sure if an answer was actually required.

Kelly carried on regardless. 'Anyway, I have it out with him about the johnnies and he does his nut saying I'm checking up on him and I don't trust him and walks out. That's when I think, he hasn't actually said why he's got johnnies in his pocket. So, I go to Letitia's and he's not there. She's got no idea where he is neither. But she does say he's told her he dumped me at Christmas and they are definitely back together again. And they don't use johnnies either. So, there we are, the two of us, wondering why the fucking hell he needs johnnies.'

Annette could only nod. It was taking all of her concentration to keep up.

'So, she sticks the kid in the buggy and we take him to her mum's. Then, we go round to his mum's to see if he's there. She says she hasn't got a clue where he is but his little sister, who's all right to be fair, runs after us and tells us he's been seeing some woman in Northfield. So, she gives us the address and we go over there. We knock the door, and who the fuck do you think answers it?'

'Craig?' It wasn't a hard guess.

'Spot on. I'm mad as fuck but Letitia. My God. She kicks the shit out of him. The woman comes out and we tell her what's happened, and she joins in. He's there crouching in the doorway while the pair of them are tearing him to pieces. And all he can do is put his hands up — like this — and shout 'keep away from the face'. It was the funniest thing I've ever seen.'

It didn't sound that funny to Annette but secretly she was pleased that Craig had got his comeuppance. 'What happened after that?'

'Me and Letitia went back to his flat, I collected my stuff and we trashed the place. Then, we went to the pub and got pissed.' She threw half a chocolate biscuit in her mouth triumphantly.

'Where are you living now?' said Annette.

'At Letitia's, 'til I sort out somewhere else to stay. Nan's not well so I don't want to go there.'

'Isn't that a bit difficult?'

'At Letitia's? Yeah, a bit. I'm sleeping on her settee. But we do have a lot in common. Mostly wanting to kill Craig.'

So that was it. Well, it was good that she'd finally given Craig the push but sleeping on someone's sofa? And not just any old someone but the mother of Craig's child. Annette made a snap decision. 'Come and live here. I've got plenty of space. We'll sort out one of the bedrooms and you can stay as long as you like.'

Kelly looked dubious. 'You sure? What about your kids?'

'There's room for all of you, if they ever come and stay. They're not exactly falling over themselves to get here.'

'All right, just until I get myself sorted. I don't want to be a pain.'

'You won't be. I like having you around, and you can help me sort out the house.'

'That'll have to be my rent then. I'm broke.'

'I don't want any rent, but how do you get by? Don't you sign on?'

'Nah, I had a big row with them ages ago and never went back.'

'So, what do you do for money?'

'This and that. Whatever I need to do.' She must have realised how that sounded. If not, Annette's alarmed expression must have made it clear. 'Oh nothing like that. I'm not that desperate. No. A mate runs a market stall in town. I help her out sometimes, and Craig's uncle has a taxi firm. I've been doing three nights a week, working the calls and the radio. They're both just cash in hand. But that's the taxi job finished anyway. I can hardly go back there now, can I?'

The old worn-out divans had already been disposed of

and her single beds from the flat had been left in one of the bedrooms. That was the room they chose to clean and make as homely as they could.

'It needs painting really, and the carpets pulling up. All the rooms do. It'll do for now, though.' Annette smirked. 'If you don't mind living in a museum that is?'

Kelly grimaced. 'Sorry, me and my big gob. Actually, it's growing on me. It's got character. Anyway, it's a proper bed with clean sheets. A lot better than what I've got now. It's fine, and I promise I'll behave. Cross my heart and all that shit.'

They collected her things from Letitia's. So little they hardly left a dent in the bedroom storage. So, now Annette had a housemate. Well two, if you counted Maud.

In the following days, the old Kelly began to resurface. The more time she spent with her, the more Annette was reminded of her younger self — much more insecure than her prickly, hard-edged exterior let on. She remembered the first time Colin told her he loved her. She'd been surprised that anyone thought of her as loveable. He wanted her to meet his parents, he said. He wanted them to meet the woman he loved more than anything in the world. It was lovely. A bit over the top, but lovely. Then he spoilt it by suggesting she wore a nice dress and asking her not to swear.

'You do swear quite a lot. I mean, I love it, but they wouldn't understand. They're old fashioned.'

She should have walked away there and then.

Her offer had been on the spur of the moment, and she hadn't really given any thought to the consequences. So, she was pleased to find she was enjoying the experience of living with someone again. Especially someone as lively and funny as Kelly. She knew that in some ways she'd become a sort of replacement mum to her. She found that comforting, since she was increasingly beginning to think of herself as estranged from her own children. The reality was, she'd never been favoured with that kind of relationship with them. They'd been babies when she went back to work. Then, as the demands got greater, it was Colin who picked up the nurturing side of things and she became ever more distant.

She hadn't spoken to them since the night at the Rajdoot. She'd tried ringing them several times but they didn't answer. She'd messaged and voice mailed them, and even left messages with Colin on the landline but they didn't call back. Still, she was convinced this was the best way to play it. Sure, it hurt sometimes but if she was patient, if she just kept at it, she was certain they would come round and see her in a different light. Having Kelly there was a double-edged sword. Sometimes it helped to ease the longing and sometimes it made it harder to wait.

21

DAD COMES TO FIX THINGS AND EDIE COMES TO LIFE.

It didn't take long for Maud and Frank to settle into a routine. Maud spent most of her time at Annette's but on Tuesdays and Fridays she trotted over to Frank's, until Annette and Kelly returned from the foodbank. In the evenings, she would curl up on the old leather sofa on top of Edith Pinsent's nightdress which Annette left there to remind her of her departed friend. As she explained to James in an email: *'It's a comfort blanket. It will be there for as long as she needs it.'*

She was determined to do all the right things for Maud. Although she didn't know much about dogs, she knew they needed exercise. As soon as she moved in, she set herself a task to take Maud for a run every day. She had visions of her and Maud playing ball in the park, just like the woman she'd seen on her last day in the flat. She searched the house for a lead and on finding none, she went out and bought one. But, when she clipped it on to Maud's collar, the dog looked bewildered. When she tried to leave the house, Maud sat down in the hall and refused to budge.

She tried an upbeat, 'Walkies! Walkies, Maud.'

Nothing. Perplexed, she decided to ask Frank for his advice. She unclipped the lead and opened the front door. Maud followed her out. She tried reattaching the lead. Maud sat down again. She took the lead off, and Maud cheerfully scampered alongside her. She looked down at Maud. 'You are a very strange dog, Maud. Do you know that?'

Maud cocked her head to one side. Those comical eyebrows seemed to be even higher and at an even more acute angle than usual, as if to say, 'you think I'm the strange one? Coming here with your shop-bought leads'.

Frank had the answer. 'Edie didn't really take any of her dogs out on a lead. She let them roam around on their own. They did go out with her to the park, if they felt like it. But never on a lead.'

From then on, she let Maud do her own thing.

As far as Frank's routine was concerned, he came over most days. He taught part-time so often popped over to check on them before or after lessons. Invariably, he stayed for a few hours to help with fixing something up, or taking something down.

'You know he fancies you, don't you?' Kelly was sitting under the study window, her lap full of papers. She was sorting Edith's old bills from the other letters and was only half concentrating on the task.

'Don't be silly. He's just being nice.'

'Nah. He so wants to get in your pants.'

'Kelly!'

'Why wouldn't he? He's on his own and he's got this hot woman living next door.'

Annette laughed out loud. She didn't believe a word of it, but it was flattering, and she hadn't been called hot in a long time. Not in that context anyway. A knock on the front door interrupted them.

'Here he comes with his tongue hanging out again,' said Kelly.

'Shut up, you're outrageous. Actually, it can't be Frank. He always comes round the back.'

Kelly stretched up to see who it was. 'It's some old bloke. Looks familiar.'

Annette got up from behind the desk. 'That old bloke is my dad. Something must have happened.' She rushed to let him in. 'Dad! Is everything all right?'

Her father looked startled. 'Hello sweetheart. Everything's fine. I just thought I'd pop over to see how you were getting on in your new house.'

'Mum not with you?'

'No, she's gone to Uncle Phil's for a few days to get a bit of sea air. I was at a loose end so I thought I'd pay you a visit and see if you needed any little jobs doing. Are you going to let me in? It's a big house. Nice floor. Oh my!' His eyes moved rapidly from one area to the next. She could see him making a mental list of jobs that needed doing.

'I'll fetch my toolbox,' he said, list either complete or too full to add anything else.

'You've got a lot in that toolbox,' said Kelly.

Annette's dad was busy planing a sticky door in the lounge.

'I like to think it's my equivalent of the Mary Poppins bag,' he said. Kelly was staring at him nonplussed. 'You've not seen Mary Poppins? Annette, this girl's not seen Mary Poppins. Can you believe it?'

Annette raised her hands in mock amazement. 'No,

really? Oh Kelly. You haven't lived until you've heard Dick
Van Dyke's comedy cockney accent.'

'Hilarious,' said her dad. 'A great family film though.
Any more tea going? This is thirsty work.'

Kelly took his empty cup. 'I'll make it. White with
sugar?'

'No sugar. Sweet enough.'

She threw him a pained look. 'Arthur, that is the oldest
and cheesiest joke ever.'

'Plenty more where that came from young lady.'

They were surprisingly easy in each other's company.

'She's living here then is she, the young madam?' asked her
dad. Kelly was at the shop getting more milk.

'She's got nowhere else to go, Dad.'

'No family?'

'Yes, but she doesn't get on with her step mum. Her own
mum died when she was twelve.'

'Poor kid. Shame. Bit of a rough diamond, but she's a
nice girl.' That was Dad, always seeing the best in people,
until the worst in them slapped him in the face so hard he
couldn't ignore it. 'Seen anything of your two lately?'

'No, not since January. They're not happy with me
because I refused to pay for Liza's skiing trip and told Colin
I was cutting down the maintenance and their allowances.'

Her dad's eyebrows raised to the point where they
couldn't possibly go any higher. 'You did that did you? Well
done my love.'

That was unexpected. She was sure he would try to
persuade her to climb down.

'They're not returning my calls either. Have they been
round to see you and Mum?'

'A couple of times, but only because your mum's created merry hell. She has her uses you know.'

'I can imagine. I expect Colin thought he'd better send them over before she made a nuisance of herself on the doorstep.'

'Well, she's better at making herself heard than you and me, that's for sure. Don't be too hard on your mum love. She really does only want you and the kids to be happy. I know she can be difficult at times, but she does her best. She had a hard start in life you know. A very unhappy childhood.'

'Really?' said Annette. 'She's never mentioned it.'

'She doesn't like to talk about it as a rule, but sometimes it makes her a bit anxious,' said her dad.

'But she had both her parents, and brothers and sister. I would have thought if anyone had a hard childhood it was you.'

He looked at her aghast. 'Whatever makes you think that?'

'Well, with your dad leaving you, and being brought up by a single mum.'

'Not at all love. You've got it all wrong. I had the most wonderful childhood a boy could wish for. I was the only person in my mother's life you see. She made it her sole purpose to make me feel cherished and cared for. As for my dad, I never missed him. I had three smashing uncles who were the best dads I could have had. So, I never needed him and I certainly never wanted him. Whereas your mother? Her dad was a horrible man and her mum was completely downtrodden. He made all their lives a misery. Nobody missed him when he died. Even Nanny Corcoran perked up after then. That's why your mum gets so cross about Colin you see. He may not be as nasty as her dad but, she thinks he's held you back. That because of him you're, what's the word?'

'Repressed?'

'That's a bit strong love, but something along those lines, I suppose. She's always been very proud of you. We both have. Perhaps we should have told you more often.'

'Dad, does Mum know you're here today?' said Annette.

'No. Her nerves are bad at the moment what with the kids acting a bit strange and everything. She just needs a few days peace. I'll tell her when she gets back. And, when we've fixed the house up a bit, I'll bring her over.'

'So, you'll be coming back again to help?'

'If you'll let me. I'm quite taken with the place, and it'll be nice to spend some time with you. I miss my old Netta. Nice to see glimpses of her now and then.'

'I can't think of anything better,' she said, 'Would you do something for me though? Next time you see the kids, tell them I miss them and would love to see them again.'

Her dad stayed for the rest of the day. Later in the afternoon, Frank came over and the two of them helped to rip up the lounge carpet. She was aware that Miss Pinsent had wanted the new owner to clear the place themselves but she couldn't do everything singlehandedly. Some things needed muscle and teamwork. Moving the leather sofa had already proved a challenge for her and Kelly. It was far heavier than it looked. They made furniture sturdy in those days. Bomb proof, probably.

Aside from being threadbare in places, the carpet did the room no favours. It was mainly brown with huge swirls of yellow and orange. It looked much like the one her parents had fitted throughout the downstairs rooms when she was a teenager. Recalling the reaction of her two grandmothers when they first saw it, made her grin. Nanny

Corcoran absolutely loved it whereas Granny Wilde, a woman of discernible taste, seemed to be searching for words that wouldn't offend. Eventually she settled on: 'Isn't that an interesting pattern?'

'Looks like that awful carpet we used to have. Do you remember, Nettie?' said her dad. 'God knows whatever possessed us to buy it. I suppose it was the fashion at the time. I used to shudder every time I opened the front door.'

'Me too,' said Annette.

They chuckled in unison.

'We had something similar,' said Frank. 'It was my mother's pride and joy. Her first carpet. We had lino on the floor until then so I think she thought she'd arrived, ye know? Mind you, for the first couple of years she covered most of it with that plastic carpet protector. Do you remember that?'

'I do. My mother-in-law did the same thing when she got her first carpet,' said her dad.

'Sounds a bit stupid to me,' said Kelly.

'They just wanted to keep it nice. I suppose, for my ma anyway, it was something to take her mind off what was going on outside,' said Frank.

'What was that then?' said Kelly.

Frank's brow wrinkled. 'The Troubles, Kelly.'

'The what?'

'The Troubles. Ah, never mind. Another time. Come on. Let's clear up this mess,' he said.

Since Kelly had moved in, cooking was beginning to become a more pleasurable experience for Annette. Before, she'd existed mostly on ready meals which she now found, to her surprise, were often more expensive than cooking a proper meal. It was nice to cook for someone else, even if it was fairly basic fare. Today, she felt like making more of an effort. She knocked the dust off the only cookery book she possessed and made a beef bourguignon for the four of them to share.

When the day's work was done, they sat down to eat it in the kitchen.

Kelly peered into the casserole dish. 'What's this?' she said.

'It's beef bourguignon,' said Annette. On seeing Kelly's expression hadn't changed, she added: 'It's French. A French casserole. Try it.'

'It looks lovely,' said her dad. 'Nothing like a bit of hard work to make you hungry. You've got quite a bit to do here but it'll be worth it when it's finished.'

Frank took a sip of wine, 'You think this is bad. You should have seen my place when we first bought it. It was really neglected. It took months of work before we could move in.'

We. He'd said, we. Annette wondered who 'we' could be. Frank was on his own now but, clearly, he'd not always been. Kelly must have picked up on it too. She flashed a sideways look at Annette, but said nothing.

'What do you think of the casserole Kelly?' said Annette.

'Yeah, good. I could eat it again, no problem,' she said, smirking.

They carried on talking over a leisurely dinner. The soothing powers of honest labour and the feasibility of stripping the lounge walls and floorboards was discussed. They concluded that the knowledge you had worked hard was indeed comforting, even if your body said the oppo-site, and they would start on the walls tomorrow. And with that, her dad and Frank said their goodbyes and went home.

Kelly curled up on one of the sofas to watch TV. It was one of those reality TV programmes. Not Annette's cup of tea at all. So, she left her to it and went into the study.

Annette picked out one of Edith's journals. Before buying the house, she'd promised James Pinsent she would read them but so far, she hadn't touched them. A few days ago, he'd mailed her to see if she'd made a start on them. She made excuses about being so busy with the move, both to him and herself, and promised she would do it this week. Deep down, she knew the real reason why she hadn't started. It seemed wrong to read somebody else's personal thoughts. Much like her early days at the foodbank when witnessing someone's poverty, it felt intrusive. So, she avoided having to do it. But promises should be kept and anyway, she'd coped at the foodbank. She would cope now.

The first page of the book she'd chosen was dated 14th June 2010. She leafed through it stopping to read at different stages. In some parts there were daily entries, then gaps of days, sometimes weeks before another one. The content was mixed. Some pages were like diary jottings. One, '*made parsnip soup today — too much salt,*' made her smile. There were drawings — doodles and delicate sketches of flowers, fruits and Maud. No, not Maud. Too early. She looked at the name written at the bottom of the page. Betty. Maud's mother? She must ask Frank. Then there were the recipes. Dozens of them. Starting at the back until the two diverse parts met roughly in the middle.

Somewhere near that middle point she came across an entry that left her open mouthed:

'*I sat in the breakfast room this morning and watched the day awaken. As the morning mist began to lift, a fox appeared from the bushes. It stopped halfway through the garden and we locked eyes. I had been so very tired of everything, until that moment. As I watched it return to the bush and beyond, I felt my spirits lift and couldn't help but say to myself, this is life.'*

Poor Edie. She must have been quite lonely. Even though they'd never met, Annette felt a real fondness for this woman that was inexplicable. It had crept up on her through snatches of information about her from James and Frank, and from Edie's personal things still dotted about the house. There was something quite emotive about coming across a trinket or an item of clothing belonging to a person who'd passed away.

Then there was the date of her death. Annette couldn't bring herself to ask Frank if it was the same date as her birthday, the same date her life changed completely, but somehow she knew it was. Now this journal had given her a real sense of who Edith Pinsent was. Edie was talking to her. She was telling her about her life and yet she could just as easily have been talking about Annette's life.

She was suddenly overcome by a great sense of sadness, for Edie and for herself. Yes, for herself. Because hadn't she been tired of everything for so long too? Hadn't she been sleepwalking for years, a blur on the edge of the real world? She put the book down. She wouldn't read any more tonight. It hurt too much.

She went to sleep almost straight away and dreamt of foxes. At a little after four-thirty she woke up and tiptoed downstairs. She peered through the kitchen window, out onto the overgrown garden as she waited for the kettle to boil. With Maud at her heels, she took her tea into the breakfast room and sat at the little table by the French windows, waiting for night to become day.

The silent stillness gradually gave way to birdsong. First

a solitary warble, then a few more until the entire neighbourhood seemed to be filled with the melodious sound of
birds going about their business. The sun began to show
itself among the cloudy gaps above the high trees to the side
of the garden. On the opposite side, a fading moon drifted
downwards behind Frank's trees. There was a haze lingering
above the overgrown mass of greenery like a fine cloud.

On the periphery of her vision she thought she saw a
movement in the tall grass. Maud stood to attention, her
body taut. She pressed her nose against the window. Had
she seen something too? They both watched and waited.
There was another rustle, then calmness. Maud relaxed and
returned to lay down at her feet. There they remained
watching the new day open up, together.

She imagined Edie sitting contentedly in the space
opposite with her tea and toast. *Wuthering Heights* open in
front of her. She sensed a strong and direct connection. Not
just to Edie but to everything around her. She opened her
hand across the table and whispered into the empty space,
'This is life.'

22

FRUIT, FOXES AND OTHER REVELATIONS

They were already hacking away at the grass with a couple of pairs of shears and an ancient scythe when her dad arrived. Annette had left him a message on the door to come around to the back in case they couldn't hear his knock.

Frank wiped his brow with his sleeve, and rested on the handle of the long scythe. When he saw her dad, his face broke into a broad grin. 'Good morning Arthur. Change of plan. Annette wants to clear the garden first. So, here we are.'

'Hello Dad. Yes, I think it's what Edie would have wanted. I think she loved this garden.'

Kelly rolled her eyes. 'She's being taken over by the ghost of Edith Pinsent, Art. We might need to get a priest in if this carries on. Here, have these. I'll go and make us a brew.'

'Take it steady though Dad,' said Annette. 'There could be all sorts of things in this wilderness. There might even be a fox in there.'

'There are foxes around here, it's true. But I don't think

they'll be living in this grass,' said Frank.

'They're certainly going to the toilet in it though. That smell's unmistakeable,' said her dad pointing to a greenish-brown trail leading from the grass towards the kitchen door, each one stamped with the imprint of a trainer. Maud had already picked up the scent.

Annette groaned. 'Oh no. Kelly!'

'Come on Maud,' he said. 'Let's go and break the news to our young friend, shall we?'

Despite the minor setback, they carried on clearing. Kelly called Neil. Partly to enlist his help and partly to tell him the hilarious story of how she managed to walk a ton of fox shit through the house. He came over with some hard-core electric tools, making the job a lot easier.

'Don't go too close to those bushes with those Neil,' said her dad. 'I'm pretty sure they're all fruits. It'd be a shame to cut them down.'

As they went further in, hacking and shearing, the garden began to emerge and the remains of a layout started to take shape. Nearest to the house, were flower beds with straggly daffodils, on their way out now. Making a better show of it were tulips, scarlet by the look of it, about to burst into flower. Peonies were emerging from the earth. Entangled with weeds were roses, looking like they could recover if given the space to breathe. Pretty primulas in bright punches of yellow, red and cream were having no problem surviving, as were clumps of bluebells under the tall trees on one side of the ample garden. Her dad confirmed that the bushes lining the other side, nearest Frank's, were different varieties of fruit. More of them and some fruit trees formed a barrier further down, between the grass and a vegetable patch, the size of two allotments. One side of the patch was completely taken over by dark green foliage bearing little white flowers.

'Strawberries,' said her dad. 'You'll have quite a crop, if we look after them properly. We'll need to put some straw underneath them. I'll bring some next time.'

'I'd forgotten about this,' said Frank. 'Edie was quite a gardener when we first moved here.'

When the grass was cleared, they weeded the flower beds under her dad's guidance. They carried on until late in the afternoon when they tramped back into the house, checking their feet first this time, and flopped down on the sofas. 'I'm so shattered, I can't speak,' said Kelly.

'That makes a pleasant change,' said Neil.

'Very funny. I am starving though.'

'Fish and chips?' said Annette. The suggestion was met with resounding agreement. 'I'll go and get some.'

Neil picked up his phone. 'Hang on, I'll check what Sean's up to. He's only a few doors away from a chippy. Sean mate, you in the shop? Busy? Feel like closing up and joining us at Annette's for fish and chips? Marvellous. Yes please mate. Five cod and chips and whatever you're having. Oh, and you'd better get two pots of curry sauce for the heathens.'

Thirty minutes later, Sean appeared with dinner and drinks. Just as they'd done on that first day in the house, they sat around the kitchen table, eating, drinking and talking. Neil and Sean left, promising to come back at the weekend and. Soon after, Annette waved Frank off.

As she came back into the lounge, Kelly put her finger to her lips and pointed to the armchair where her dad was snoozing. They watched the rise and fall of his chest and listened to his soft snoring.

'Ahh,' said Kelly.

He awoke a few hours later. 'Goodness, I must have dropped off. Have I been out long? Oh dear, it's nearly ten o'clock. I'd better be getting back home.'

'It's too late now Dad,' said Annette, 'I've made up a bed for you. Stay here tonight.'

She got up again at around four-thirty and slipped quietly down into the breakfast room. Maud jumped off the old sofa and joined her. With the grass cut back ready for mowing, the garden took on a different complexion. It looked vast even in the half light. She yawned, still tired. She was just thinking about returning to bed when she saw it. A fox, pushed its head around the open gate from Frank's garden, then disappeared again. A minute later it came loping through the gate, trailed by three cubs. It was a mother. She nosed around the hewn grass while her babies rolled on it, play fighting.

Maud sensed them before she saw them. She shot over to the window noiselessly following their movements. The vixen too, caught the drift of something in the air. She lifted her nose and sniffed, then came towards the French windows and took a few mouthfuls of the leftover fish and chips Annette had optimistically put out for her. Her cubs followed and ate their fill while she watched over them. One of them picked up a deflated ball found in the undergrowth earlier. Another cub leapt on it and they wrestled each other for it. The vixen finished off the food, then coolly moved towards the window and stopped directly outside it. Maud shook with tension but still, she made no sound. The fox locked eyes with her, then shifted her stare to Annette. She held it there for some time then dropped her head, as if acknowledging the gift, and turned towards her cubs.

Annette felt goose bumps rising on her skin. She shivered, 'This is life.'

There was a shuffling behind her. It was her dad, standing in the doorway, dressed in a pair of pyjamas and sweatshirt that Will had left the last time he'd visited the flat. He looked strange dressed in a young man's style. Not like her dad at all. He seemed younger.

'Wonderful,' he whispered. 'Absolutely wonderful. There's something quite magical about them isn't there? Your mum will be sorry to have missed this. She loves foxes.'

Really? She couldn't imagine her mother seeing foxes as anything but dirty creatures. She'd learned quite a bit about her mum in the last two days. It had been something of an eye-opener.

He crept over and sat down next to her. They watched the foxes wordlessly, until the vixen went back to the gate and waited for her cubs to catch up with her. Together they moved, into Frank's garden, towards the fading moon. 'So that's why you wanted to clear the garden,' he said.

'Sorry Dad, I think I wore you out.'

'Nonsense, I like a bit of gardening and I've had a lovely couple of days. Did some work, got to spend some time with my girl, and met some new people. You've got some very interesting friends.'

She thought of the last person to say that to her.

'Interesting, and nice. They seem to care for you very much,' he said.

They watched the day break together then went back to bed. It was Tuesday. Foodbank day. Her dad went home after breakfast. Tomorrow he would go to Uncle Phil's to pick up her mum but he promised to come over at the weekend to help finish off the garden.

. . .

Annette and Kelly gave themselves a few days off the hard labour. They were done in. For the rest of the week, barring foodbank days, they settled down in the study and ploughed through Edie's paperwork and journals.

'I think she liked her cooking. She must have written down hundreds of recipes,' said Kelly. 'This book seems to be all recipes for jams and pickles. Hey, we could make some strawberry jam, when the ones in the garden come out. Your dad said there'd be loads, didn't he? There's a recipe in here for it. Look.'

Annette turned over the pages. She didn't realise there could be so many different types of jams. Before each one was an introduction to explain the recipe's origins. The strawberry jam, it seemed, had been given to her by Hannah, the one-time family cook, and had been in her family for generations. 'I've never made jam before, but if Dad's right about the strawberries, we could give it a try. Let's ask Neil about it. He might help.'

As promised, Neil came over at the weekend, bringing Chris with him. Annette's dad came too and so did Frank. Frank remembered Edie's jams. 'They were very good. Ellen, my late wife, couldn't get enough of them. My daughter liked them too, come to think of it.'

'I had no idea you were a widower,' said Annette. She'd gone over with him to fetch his lawnmower and some more garden tools.

'Oh, didn't I say? Yes, it was a couple of years ago now.'

'Still, you must miss her.'

'She did leave quite a gap.'

'And you have a daughter? Is she like her mother?'

'She looks very much like her, but I suppose she's more like me in temperament. She lives in Edinburgh, but we keep in touch and visit each other when we can. Her name's

Robyn. She's a darling girl. Always worrying about me. You know what daughters are like.'

She wished she could say that she did, but the intricate workings of her own daughter's mind were still a mystery to her and she feared they always would be. One thing she did know though was that she was warming to Frank. She liked the way he spoke about Edie, his affable manner, and the way he took care of Maud. Also, there was something about his appearance that appealed to her. It wasn't a burning desire or anything like that but, if push came to shove, she would have to admit that she found him attractive in a rather scruffy, shambolic way. Clearly though, he wasn't interested in her in that way. He obviously missed his wife very much and, even if he was interested, she was so out of touch in that department she wouldn't have a clue how to respond.

23

NEIL GETS EXCITED ABOUT JAM

Neil's eyes darted across the page at speed, his fingers only loosening their grip to turn over to the next one. 'This is amazing,' he said, as if they'd found buried treasure.

'Dad said the strawberries should be ready in about a month,' said Annette.

'Let's do it then,' he said. 'We'll need to get some jars.'

All sorts of people donated them. Friends, relatives, foodbank volunteers and clients, pupils at Chris's school. By the time the first strawberries were ripe, they were drowning in jars. They sterilised them in batches, until thirty were ready. Neil calculated roughly how many strawberries they'd need for twenty. Not only had Edie provided the recipe, all the equipment necessary could be found in the old kitchen. They were good to go.

Neil was beside himself with joy. 'These pots are brilliant. Genuine antiques. Imagine, we're using the same recipe and the same tools that have been handed down through Edie's family. We're recreating history.'

When the jam was made, they filled twenty-two full-sized jars and one small one. They tested it out on Neil's scones.

'Fucking hell, that's nice jam,' said Kelly.

'Well, I wouldn't have put it quite like that but yes, it is tasty,' agreed Annette's dad.

'Just like Edie's,' said Frank. 'You've made quite a lot. What are you going to do with them all?'

Annette considered the question. 'We'll have a jar each, and we'll do what Neil always does with the remaining ones. Take them to the foodbank.'

They tried a jar out on the volunteers first and everyone liked it but Neil wanted to be sure they weren't just being nice. He had the idea to ask those clients that took a jar to fill in a feedback questionnaire. The next week, nearly all came back with good ratings.

There were still plenty of strawberries. Annette and Kelly went out and picked the ripe ones on a daily basis and put them in the freezer. The fruit trees and bushes were in different stages of growth and were looking in decent shape, considering they'd been left to themselves for years. The first to bear fruit were the gooseberry bushes and a cherry tree. The freezer was getting full and Frank's had to be commandeered into service. Paula suggested they made more jam and tried to sell them at the church's summer fair. Alan, the vicar, was amenable. He had a few stalls selling cakes and crafts, so the jams would be a good addition.

Neil planned the day of the first batch like a military operation. He'd even brought brand new duster coats and hats with him so their hygiene was of a professional standard. It was Saturday morning and they were going to devote the whole weekend to fruit picking and jam making. Chris, Paula and Corrine came along to help, along with Kendrick and Shani who were under instruction from their mum to only pick fruit under Annette's dad's direction and to do exactly as he told them. While they waited for him to arrive, the children took Maud into the garden and threw sticks for her.

'I don't know who's having more fun,' said Corrine. 'The dog or the kids.' Frank strolled through the open gate and stopped to watch them. He turned back and returned shortly after with a ball for them to throw.

'Kendrick keeps asking for a dog but you can't leave a dog at home on its own all day. It wouldn't be fair. Plus, it'll be a long time before I can afford another mouth to feed,' said Corrine.

'They can come and visit Maud anytime they like,' said Annette.

'I might just take you up on that.'

The doorbell rang.

'It's probably Art. I'll get it,' said Kelly.

Annette heard her dad's cheery doorstep greeting and Kelly berating him for being late. 'We got kids going hyper in the garden waiting to start Operation Fruit Pick.'

He said something else which she couldn't make out over the radio. Then the door opened and in he came, with Annette's mother.

'Mum!'

Her mum stood halfway between the kitchen and the hall. Her knuckles were clenched to white around the strap of her handbag. She was not a woman comfortable with new company.

It was Neil, not Annette, who broke the ice. She'd been

too startled to say anything more. 'Hello Geraldine, lovely to see you again. Let me introduce you to everyone. I don't think you've met us all.' He took her hand and led her round the kitchen to say hello to everyone.

'That mad pair are my kids, Kendrick and Shani.' Corrine pointed to the children, squealing with delight as Frank threw the ball and Maud tumbled down the garden after it.

'And that's Frank, my neighbour, and Maud, my sitting tenant.' Annette had regained her composure. 'It's lovely to see you Mum. A really nice surprise.'

'Well, Dad said you might need some help, but it looks like you've already got plenty.' She gave Annette's dad a look that Annette recognised immediately. Her mum was unsettled and flustered, and was probably wishing she hadn't been talked into coming.

'Not at all Mum, Chris, Frank and the kids will be fruit picking with Dad. You'll be a much welcome addition to the cooking party. Come on I'll give you a tour while Kelly gets the kettle on.'

Despite her initial awkwardness, it didn't take too long for Annette's mum to settle in and enjoy herself. She was soon telling the others about when she was a girl and about Nanny Corcoran's jam making. Annette had heard stories about her mum's childhood before but, this time, she listened with greater care for the odd loose word, an intonation here and there that her mother's early years had been less cosy than her demeanour suggested. None were apparent.

It occurred to Annette that she'd always taken for granted the assumption that her mother had been the lucky one, having had two parents. Her father's news that he'd been dealt the better cards was a new concept for her to grapple with. Now she thought about it, her mum had never actually said she'd had a happy childhood, but then, she couldn't remember her saying it had been unhappy either. She'd simply managed the impression and kept the truth locked inside. Not unlike herself.

She wondered if the injustice of it burned within her mother and ate away at her, the way things did with her. Maybe so. Or maybe Annette's dad was her foil. Steadfastly soaking up her rage and reinforcing her fragile confidence, in his usual gentle way, because he knew he'd had the good fortune to be the son of Ada Wilde. In that moment of clarity, the scales fell from her eyes and for the first time in her life, she understood her parents better and, in doing so, became a little more acquainted with herself.

The freezers were emptied and the fruit pickers harvested more gooseberries, cherries and the last of the strawberries. In all, they made over a hundred jars of jam that weekend. On Saturday, they were so worn out that Sean was called on to perform chip shop duties again. It was such a warm evening that they hauled the big kitchen table out into the garden. Frank made up the shortfall in chairs, and they sat around until late.

She saw her mum taking in each of her friends. She didn't bat an eye at Neil's tattoos but the sight of Sean took her a bit longer to come to terms with. In the end, he wooed her with his charm and his knowledge of the Beatles and the early sixties music scene. That, and the fact that he was generously plying her with Prosecco.

On Sunday, Neil and Chris brought with them a barbecue, the size of a small table, along with a portable sound system. They finished up early, enticed by the promise of

jerk chicken and sticky maple pork, and danced in the
garden to the beat of ska and reggae.

Neil put on The Clash's, 'Rock the Casbah.' 'This is for
you Net.'

She and Sean jumped up and began to pogo, much to
the amusement of Kelly and her mother.

'Oh, that brings back memories,' said her mum. 'Arthur,
do you remember when she used to do that in her bedroom
with that friend of hers. What was her name now? We were
scared to death they were going to come through the ceiling.
Do you remember Arthur?'

'Yes love, I do,' he said. 'She was a bit different then. All
black eyes and safety pins.'

Her mum laughed. 'Oh yes, the safety pins. Job lot from
Woolworths, weren't they? The two of them used to put
them all over their clothes. What was her name, Annette?
Your friend. Whatever happened to her?'

'Claire. It was Claire,' said Annette, still bouncing. 'We
lost touch after Manchester. After I got married.'

Her mum shook her head. 'Pity, you were so close.'

By now Kendrick and Shani were jumping too.

Sean egged them on. 'More attitude kids. Come on
Frank, you know you want to.'

Frank got up and threw himself around, waving his
arms in the air. Sean grabbed Corrine and they bumped up
and down together. Neil and Chris joined in and Paula,
declaring she couldn't resist any longer, pulled a reluctant
Kelly up and showed her how it was done.

Annette's parents surveyed the scene with amusement.
Sean said something in Neil's ear. He nodded and went over
to the stereo. The sound of 'Twist and Shout' was too much
for her dad. He pulled her mum up from the chair and, face

to face, they gyrated in a shaky twist like a couple of arthritic teenagers.

'Aren't they sweet?' said Kelly. 'You're so lucky to have such a lovely mum and dad.'

Yes, thought Annette, I am, aren't I? She was only sorry it had taken her this long to realise it.

24

AN UNEXPECTED VISITOR

'Will Frank be there? He said next time we come we could play football.'

Annette looked at Kendrick through the rear-view mirror. He'd even brought his own ball. 'Yes, I think so. I'm sure he'd love to play with you.'

'Can I play with Maudie while they're doing that?' asked Shani.

'Yes of course you can. I'm sure Maud would like that too. But she's her own boss so promise me when she's had enough, you'll leave her until she comes back for more?'

'Remember what Mum said. She's not a doll. You've got to give her some space,' said Kendrick.

'Okay,' said Shani, a beaming smile flashing across her face. 'Can Maudie sleep on my bed?'

'That depends on Maud. If you leave her to choose you never know. You might get lucky.'

'I hope I get lucky.'

'I hope you do too, darling. Here we are.'

The children clambered out of the car with their overnight backpacks. Annette unlocked the door. The house was quiet. She dropped her shopping bags on the kitchen table and read the note left on it:

'*Gone to my dad's. Maud's with Frank. Back later x*'

'Where's Kelly and Maud?' Kendrick stood in the doorway looking disappointed. He was developing a bit of a crush on Kelly.

'Kelly's gone out for a while. She'll be back later. Maud's over at Frank's.'

'Can we go and get her?' Shani was jumping up and down on the spot.

Annette's first instinct was to let her run over to Frank's house but she knew that wasn't Corrine's style and so far, Corrine had managed to produce two well-mannered and thoughtful young people almost entirely on her own. She had no intention of undoing her good work. 'We'll pop over in a short while. First let's take your things upstairs and get you settled in.'

Shani's face fell and Annette shook off a momentary pang of regret.

The children were sleeping in Kelly's room where the two single beds now resided. She'd gone out and bought a new double bed for the other room soon after the barbecue party. Her parents had stayed over that night. Since then, a few of her friends had made use of it too when they'd had a drink too many or were just too tired to leave the house after a hard day's decorating, fruit picking or jam making.

Even though the summer fair had been and gone, they were still making jams. The sales had been reasonable. Mainly thanks to the foodbank clients and volunteers who were dragging passing trade to the stall. Chris's mum brought the aunties, and her parents came along with Auntie Janet and Uncle Trevor. At the end of the day, they had quite a few jars left but they were happy with how they'd done.

After the build-up of the fair and the thrill of the day itself there was the inevitable comedown. It surfaced first in Neil. It was as if he had too many loose ends that needed tying down. Kelly seemed low too, but with her there was more to it. The big jam-making weekend seemed to have triggered something in her. A sort of melancholy. When, one morning, she announced that she was going to visit her family, Annette identified it for what it was. Being back in something akin to a family environment was making her miss her own. When she came back, she seemed brighter. Today was the second visit.

Whether it was Chris's suggestion or whether he'd drawn the conclusion himself she didn't know. Either way, Neil proposed his own solution to her as they painted the lounge walls. They should use the abundant fruit stores in the garden to make more jam and sell them through summer fairs across the city. She agreed to give it a try. If nothing else, it was an excuse to fill the house with the people she liked being with best of all.

There was a bark from the hall.

'It's Maud!' The children scrambled downstairs leaving Annette to make the beds on her own.

She could hear Frank greeting them. He shouted up to her: 'Is that you up there, Annette? You've a visitor. I'll send him up.'

There were footsteps on the stairs. Assuming it was her dad or Neil she popped her head round the door and called out: 'In here.'

There on the landing, was Will. 'Hi Mum.'

Will. He'd come to see her, at last. She wanted to run over to him, throw her arms around him and tell him how much she'd missed him. She stopped herself. She might not know her children that well, but she knew her son well enough to know he would have found that too much. Instead, she held out her hand to him, her expression as open and welcoming as she could make it without looking too artificial. 'Hello Will. You found me then? I'm so glad to see you.'

'Yeah, I thought I'd come over, now the exams have finished. Sorry. I didn't know you had guests. I can go.'

'You will not,' she said, much more emphatically than she'd meant to. 'I'm looking after a friend's children for the night, that's all.'

'I'm not in the way?'

'Not at all, don't be silly. Frank and Maud will keep them entertained for hours yet.' She spread the duvets out on the beds. 'All done. Come on downstairs and tell me what you've been up to since we last saw each other.'

'He's seems a nice guy.' Will gestured towards Frank who was playing football with the children and Maud.

'Yes, he is. He's very good-natured. I think the children like him very much.'

'Do they stay here a lot then, the kids?'

She remembered Liza's accusation on Christmas morning. She didn't want to give the impression she could do without her children by substituting them with other people's. 'Not loads. Occasionally, when their mum needs a night off. They love Maud, and I think the feeling's mutual.'

'Great dog. Liza would love her. I never thought I'd see you with a pet though, Mum.'

'She comes with the house but actually, I'm genuinely fond of her.'

'I think Grandad is too. He mentioned her when we last saw them.'

Good old Dad.

'Grandad's been helping me with the decorating and gardening,' she said.

'Yeah. Nan said they'd been helping you make jam as well.'

'Yes, everyone's been roped in. Friends and family. Even the kids have been fruit picking.'

'Yeah? I thought I might help too.'

She could hardly believe what she was hearing. 'Of course it is. You can come and help anytime you like. You're always welcome.'

'Yeah, thing is, I thought I might stay for a while. If you don't mind?'

She quelled the butterflies in her stomach. 'Yes, no problem. I'd love that. When do you want to come?'

'Would now be too early?'

The pleasure of having Will turn up and ask to stay for the night, and possibly longer, was a wonderful sensation but Annette knew something was wrong. 'Is everything all right? Has something happened at home?'

He looked at the floor.

'Does your dad know you're here?'

He flushed from the neck up. 'No. We had an argument. I don't really want to go back there just now.'

'He didn't do anything to hurt you did he?'

'Dad? No. He's just not my favourite person right now. I'd rather not talk about it. I just need somewhere to stay for a few days.'

'You can stay for as long as you like,' she said. 'But we

should let your dad know where you are and that you're safe. I'm sure he'll be worried about you.'

He snorted. 'Unlikely, but if it makes you happy, I'll message him.'

She was no stranger to those sorts of messages. She knew how it felt to receive them. She could imagine Colin standing behind them, Liza in particular, egging her on to send another vile communication. Part of her was sure he deserved the same treatment but she wasn't like Colin. She wasn't even like her old self. 'You don't think a phone call would be better?' she said.

'No. I really don't want to speak to him.'

She'd never seen him so resolute. So determinedly against Colin. Whatever they'd argued about, it must have upset him very much.

'Why don't I phone him? You go and help Frank with the kids and I'll give him a call.'

'I'm sorry Colin. He doesn't want to speak to you right now. I don't know what it is you argued about but whatever it was, he's clearly upset by it.'

'So, he hasn't confided in you then?' There it was again. That sneer. That implication that she shouldn't get above her station and assume there was a bond between her and her son. That malicious hint that she'd been a last resort.

'He's too upset to talk about it and I don't want to push him. I just thought you'd like a call to let you know he's safe and well. That's all. He hasn't brought any clothes with him so I'll bring him over to collect some tomorrow. He doesn't want to come alone and, given his strength of feeling towards you at the moment, it might be better if you weren't there.'

'I'm not hiding away from him. This is my house. If he wants to come here, he can but I'm not vacating it for him or anyone.'

'Actually Colin, it's my house too, if you recall. We'll be there by ten.' She ended the call, feeling particularly satisfied with her closing remark.

'Yo, I'm back.' Kelly was hardly through the front door before Kendrick and Shani leapt on her. She came into the kitchen with one of them on each hand. She'd become so much chirpier and even-tempered in the last few months. Her shape was changing too. Probably because she was eating regularly. She was still thin but no longer painfully so, and her face was softer, the angles less pronounced. 'I've brought sweets.' She held them aloft just out of reach of the children. 'Can they have them Auntie Net?'

Auntie Net said yes. Kelly gave them the sweets and flopped down on a chair, only then seeming to notice Will at the other end of the table. He'd been helping Kendrick with his reading.

'Hi.' He gulped and gave her a shy smile.

'All right? Surprise visit is it?' There was a hint of animosity in her voice.

'Will's going to stay with us for a while, Kelly. Do you mind sharing a bed with me tonight, while the kids are here?'

'It's okay, I can sleep on the sofa,' said Will.

Kelly gave him an indifferent look. 'Nah, you're all right. I don't mind sleeping with Net, if she don't. We're pretty tight, us two.'

Annette tried to read Kelly's face. She was doing her best to keep it blank but it was obvious that she'd added that last bit deliberately just to show that there was a special bond between them. That he was the interloper here. Whether Will picked that up too, she didn't know. He had other things on his mind. In contrast to Kelly, he was quite easy to see through at this moment. He looked a lot like his dad and right now, his face was very nearly the mirror image of Colin's the first time he saw her at that party when they were both at uni. She was absolutely certain of what he was thinking, and it had nothing to do with Kelly's relationship with her. She hoped Kelly couldn't see it too.

25

THE RAJDOOT RE-REMEMBERED

'I used to share a bed sometimes with my mum, when she was too sick to get up. We used to talk about the day. She always wanted to know what I'd been up to. My little brothers always went in first for a story and when they fell asleep, Dad carried them to bed. Then it was my turn. Towards the end, she was so doped up, she used to drop off before she finished the story. Me or Dad would have to finish it. I'd get in and watch her sleeping. Sometimes she'd wake up while I was about to nod off and say, 'Tell me about your day'. Made me jump out of my fucking skin.'

She and Kelly were lying facing each other in Annette's bed.

'How did it go today?' said Annette.

'All right. Good. Nothing special, but good. Me and my brothers played on the PlayStation. Dad took the three of us out to Nando's. It was nice. I told them about the jam making and stuff. Oh, I took a jar for them. Didn't think you'd mind. When we got back, Carol was there with her two and my little sister. I managed an hour without wanting to strangle them. To be fair, they're not bad kids really. I suppose I just wasn't very tolerant of them when I was younger.'

'And Carol?' said Annette.

Kelly screwed her nose up. 'Hmm, dunno. She makes Dad happy and my brothers like her but, you know, she's not my mum, is she?'

She rolled onto her back, blinking fiercely. It was easy to see the twelve-year-old child, lying with her mum, willing her to hang on to life with all of her dwindling energy. Annette reached out to her and pulled her in close.

Kelly sniffed. 'Sorry, bit emotional. Stupid really.'

'No, it isn't. You miss your mum. That's natural. I would too.'

'So, I expect you're happy to have Will here?'

'Yes, I am. We'll see how long it lasts.'

'Maybe the other one will follow.'

'Maybe, we'll see.'

'I can move out.'

She'd guessed this was coming. To Kelly it must feel like she was being pushed out again. 'No, you won't. I love having you here, and I hope you think of it as your home for as long as you want it to be.'

Kelly smiled shyly. 'Yeah? You're not just saying that?'

'Kelly, I've never been anything other than completely honest with you. You're a breath of fresh air in my life and it wouldn't be the same without you. I don't know how long Will's going to be here but it doesn't matter. The house is big enough for all of us and the time has long passed when I make special accommodation for my children. I'm really glad he's come to stay but he'll have to fit in with my life now. Not the other way around. And you are part of my life.'

'Okay. So, does that mean he'll be helping with the house then?' said Kelly.

'Yes. He might need some instruction though. I don't think he's ever done anything particularly manual. Good job his grandad's coming tomorrow. You'll have to warn Mum and Dad when they get here. I'm taking Will to Colin's first thing to pick up some of his things. We'll only be an hour or so. Assuming we get out of there in one piece.'

Colin was on his own when they got there. He was nowhere near as bullish as he'd been on the phone. Instead he adopted the persona of concerned parent but he went too far, in her opinion. He was so concerned, in fact, that he was bordering on creepy. She wondered if he always behaved like this with them and, if so, whether they found it as over-bearing as she did. It brought to mind the early years of their marriage. His sly criticisms and backhanded compliments. Veiled and dressed up to look well meaning. It brought to mind the claustrophobia. Oppressive and suffo-cating. Of course, that was nothing compared to later. That was him just warming up.

They were in the hall, about to go. He was reassuring Will, yet again, that whatever differences they had, his and Liza's happiness and safety were paramount in his concerns. Annette was just thinking what a strange word to choose, safety, when the front door opened and in walked a giggling Liza with that woman. The one from the Rajdoot. Time seemed to stand still. Annette looked at them and they looked at her. Will looked at them. Colin stopped talking and looked at Will, looking at them.

'You're back early, girls,' he said.

Girls? The woman was fifty-five if she was a day. Not a girl by any stretch of the imagination.

'Class was cancelled,' said Liza still staring at Annette. 'Yoga.'

Annette was fairly sure it was the first time yoga had been used as an offensive weapon. She felt she'd been slapped across the face with it.

'How are you Liza?' she said.

Liza folded her arms. 'I'm still not talking to you.'

'I see. Well, you know where to find me when you are ready to talk. We must be going. We've a busy day ahead.'

'We?' Liza turned to Will. 'You're not going with her, are you?'

The old Annette would have been cut to the quick by that but she was stronger now. She saw the puffed-up triumph spreading across Colin's face, and that made her beyond irritated. She moved a little closer to her daughter and said, quite calmly: 'Liza, I appreciate that you're unhappy with my decisions with regard to my financial support. I've made them for good reasons. Reasons which you probably don't understand. Nonetheless, unhappy or not, that remark was not only rude, it was extremely hurtful and I will not tolerate it. If that's all you have to say to me or about me, then frankly, the fact that you're not speaking to me is a bonus. When you are prepared to talk to me in a civil and more respectful way, you have my new address and you have my phone number. Until then, I do not want to hear from you.'

She marched past them, out into the fresh morning air, her entire body pulsating as if a surge of power had coursed through her.

'I'm staying at Mum's,' said Will as they left the speech-less trio in the hallway. 'Call me.'

Annette took slow, deliberate steps to steady her nerves on her way back to the car. She didn't want him to see how jumpy she was. She fiddled about in the boot, pretending to rearrange his things so that the door would close properly. She could sense Liza and Colin watching her from the lounge window and probably that woman too.

'You're different,' Will said when, at last, she got in.

'Yes, I am, aren't I?' She pulled the car away. As she turned out of the road, something occurred to her. 'Is that a good thing?'

'Yes.'

'Good. That woman. I can't remember her name. Is she with your dad now?'

'Erm, yes. Does it bother you?'

'Not in the slightest,' she said, and she was pleased to find that she meant it. It struck her then that this woman might be the reason behind the fall out. 'Does it bother you?'

'Not much. A bit maybe. She seems okay but, I suppose, she's not you. It's a bit childish I guess but, well … you know.'

She didn't know. Partly because, aside from university, she'd never really had the chance to miss either of her parents and then she'd been too busy trying to get away from them to care. They'd always been there, in the background, judging and annoying her. At least that's what she thought for most of her adult life. Recently she'd come to the opinion that, mostly, they were only doing their job as proper parents. Being honest, supporting her and, in their own way, loving her. Mainly though, she didn't know because she'd assumed her children didn't want her. That it was even possible they didn't actually like her.

That night at the Rajdoot, the night Colin told her they

didn't want her anymore, suddenly flashed before her eyes. She looked at it from a fresh perspective and saw their discomfort as he spelt it out to her. She recalled them both looking back as they walked away from the restaurant, their faces distressed. The thing they were mouthing to her. It was sorry. They were saying sorry. My God, she'd forgotten that. No. That was wrong, she didn't forget. She blocked it out. So consumed had she been with bitterness and resentment. She'd turned inward and thought only of her own suffering. *I didn't see it. I didn't want to. I didn't fight for them. I should have fought for them.*

She patted Will's leg. 'I'm here now, for as long as you want me.'

'I know, Mum.'

26

ROMANCE IN THE AIR

Will looked a bit overwhelmed on their return. She'd warned him there would be a few people there but, she guessed he'd taken her meaning literally. Finding the kitchen full of them must have been a shock. It was a far cry from her desolate little flat. That she had any friends at all was unusual for the mother he knew. Probably, the variety of friends she'd amassed was a bit of a jolt too. He latched onto his grandad and Kendrick as they both showed him the ropes on fruit picking. Kendrick was quite the little gardener now and proudly showed off his skills to Will, his new friend.

Her mum was bubbling with glee. 'One down, one to go,' she whispered to Annette.

'I think Liza may be more of a challenge, Mum.'

'Where Will goes, Liza follows. It might take a while but she'll come round. Besides, you've got a secret weapon. That one.' She pointed to Maud. 'Dad took some pictures of her on his phone. You know how much she loves animals. We showed them to her the last time we saw them. She might not be very happy with you at the moment but she definitely took to Maud. She did her best to hide it, but I could tell.'

'Well Maudie,' said Annette. 'Are you going to win me back my daughter? Extra doggie chocs for you if you do.'

When Corrine turned up with Sean, Neil gave Annette a sly grin. Corrine hadn't actually said who she was going out with and Sean had never crossed her mind. In fact, she couldn't imagine a more mismatched pair but, now she thought of it, they did seem to get on very well.

When she had a chance, she tentatively enquired: 'Tell me if it's none of my business, but are you and Sean seeing each other?'

Corrine continued to spoon jam into a jar. 'Is it that obvious?'

'No, not at all,' said Annette. 'Well, I never noticed it. Although, I'm not really the best benchmark for that kind of thing since I never notice anything. I think Neil's guessed though.'

'Oops. We were keeping it secret for the time being. It's only been a month. It's too early to make it public. For the kids' sake. Looks like we weren't doing as good a job of it as we thought.' She stopped spooning. 'I know he's not the sort of man I normally go for, but I think my taste must be changing. He's so sweet, you know? I'm just waiting for the bubble to burst and to find out he's just the same as all the others. But so far so good. He loves the kids too. We'll see.'

'I think they like him,' Annette gestured towards the garden where Kendrick, was showing Sean how to pick fruit, with Shani interrupting every few minutes.

'Fingers crossed,' said Corrine. 'Talking of not noticing. What about you and Frank? Surely you've noticed he has the hots for you?'

'Er, no. I can't say that I have.'

'Oh please. He's like a lovesick puppy dog. You telling me you really haven't noticed?' She laughed.

Annette held her arms out wide. 'I've been busy. Anyway, I'm sure you're wrong. He's always talking about his late wife. I don't think he's got over losing her yet.'

'What, a man can't miss his dead wife and still fancy the backside off the gorgeous and available woman next door? What do you think Geraldine? You think Frank fancies Annette?'

'Oh definitely. Plain as day,' said her mother as she filled a jam jar.

'She reckons she didn't notice,' said Corrine.

'Really? Well, she's always had difficulty seeing the blindingly obvious, my daughter. I just assumed you weren't interested, love.'

'Why wouldn't I be interested?' said Annette, feeling a touch indignant.

'Well, you know. He looks like he could do with a bit of an iron. After Colin. I mean, say what you like about him, he can dress himself.'

'Yeah, at my expense Mum.'

'True, but Frank's a lovely chap. I'm sure he scrubs up nicely, if you're interested. Are you interested?' Her mum put on that hopeful expression that had last appeared at Christmas when she'd thought Annette and Neil were an item.

'I don't know,' said Annette. 'I've been a bit too wrapped up in other things to think about that sort of thing.'

'Yes, for about fifteen years I'd say,' her mum scoffed.

'Mum!' She sounded like a petulant teenager. Her eyes met her mum's and they broke into raucous laughter, followed by Corrine and Paula.

Kelly came in with a tray of empty jars. 'What's so funny?'

'We were just talking about Frank,' said Corrine.

'Oh yeah,' said Kelly. 'Definitely wants to get into Net's pants.'

She didn't see a lot of Frank over the next two weeks. On the day of the kitchen conversation about him, he told her he wouldn't be over for a while because he had some paintings to finish off for an exhibition. She didn't think he'd overheard them but she wanted to make sure he wasn't avoiding her because of it. If he was, she would have to find a way to put things right. She made him a lasagne. As good an excuse as any to visit. She took it through the gate into his back garden, as casually as possible.

He was in his studio, working on a large canvas fixed on an easel in front of him. The French windows were wide open. His concentration was so intense that he didn't spot her until she was right in front of him. 'Annette! Sorry my head was in the painting. Come in.'

She stepped into the room. It smelled of oils and turpentine. It was a smell she recognised instantly. One she'd liked when Colin first started painting. Later, it had other, more complicated connotations and for years, just a whiff of it made her feel nauseous. For this reason, she stayed out of Colin's studio and had adopted the same approach with Frank. She remembered her vow, that wintry night in

January. She was not going to be vanquished by the past. She was going to conquer it. 'Hi. I was making some lasagne and I thought you might have too much on to make yourself something homemade, so I did you one too. It's veggie I'm afraid, so that Will can eat it. I couldn't be bothered to make two separate lots.'

He put down his brush. 'That's extremely good of you. You're right, I have been existing on snacks and ready meals a lot lately. Believe it or not, I can cook, and Ellen was a vegetarian so I'm quite used to it. As a matter of fact, I often prefer it. We eat too much meat these days. Would you like a coffee? I've a pot on the go. It keeps me going when I have a deadline.'

She looked around the studio while he went off to the kitchen. He really was preparing for an exhibition. There were paintings everywhere. He had three easels crammed into the small room, each one holding canvasses in varying degrees of completion. The style was modern with big, eye-catching brush strokes.

He returned with two mugs. 'I'm a bit behind.'

'Is that because you've been spending too much time with your troublesome neighbours?' she said.

'A little bit, but it's my own fault. I'm not very disciplined about it. I enjoy being over there too much. I like the company.'

Was he trying to tell her he liked her? She couldn't tell. 'Well we miss you, but your work is important so don't let us distract you.'

'Easy to say, but it's such a pleasant distraction.' He left his eyes on her for a moment.

Was he? *Oh Annette, you're useless at this sort of thing.*

'Your paintings are wonderful. The colours are so vivid. When does your exhibition open?'

'A couple of weeks. I have to deliver them to the gallery in a week so that they can be hung. Thank goodness for the summer holidays. These are the last three so I should have them finished in time.'

'Well, if you get tired of ready meals, come over to dinner,' she said.

'When I've finished those three. I promise. Better not before then. I might not come back. When my exhibition's up and running, why don't I treat you to a thank you meal somewhere?'

'That would be nice.' Was he? She still couldn't tell.

When his paintings were finished, Frank came over to dinner with a celebratory bottle of wine. The self-imposed solitude must have left him hungry for company because he seemed happy to while away the evening with them. He talked about growing up in Belfast, coming to university in England and feeling free from the confines of the Troubles.

'There's the Irish history lesson I promised you Kelly,' he said when he'd finished.

'Cheers.' Kelly looked unimpressed. 'Sorry to break this to you Frank, but I do know a bit about Ireland. My mum was three-quarters Irish.'

Frank looked exasperated. Kelly had a way of bringing that out in people.

'Well then why did you act like you'd never heard of the Troubles the last time I mentioned them to you?'

'I was winding you up,' she said. 'You thought I was thick and I didn't want to disappoint you.'

Frank looked appalled. 'I did no such thing.'

She laughed out loud. 'Yeah. Right.'

'You're still winding me up, aren't you?' he said.

'Yep.'

It was time to steer the conversation towards safer ground. Annette asked Will about university. He had a conditional offer from York to study law and economics.

'It's a good solid degree,' said Frank. 'Are you hoping to work in law?'

'Probably. That was the plan.'

'But now you're not so sure?'

'No. Well I am. I mean, I think I am.'

Frank put down his glass and studied him. His students were around the same age as Will, so he was probably experienced in looking for signs of faltering confidence. 'You know, it's quite common to have a few wobbles at this stage and it's fine to be unsure. The main thing is to think it through. Revisit the reasons why it interested you in the first place and see if they still hold true. This is your life. You're the one who's going to be studying for years. You need to be sure you're happy with the choices you've made. Take your time. You still have a few months.'

'Fucking hell, Frank. That was a bit intense wasn't it? No pressure, Wills,' said Kelly.

She and Will had become friends. Will, always quite unassuming, seemed to have gone out of his way not to encroach on her well-established territory and, perhaps realising he wasn't a threat, her aggression dissipated. In its place was a kind of sisterly attachment.

Days after his arrival in the house, Will accompanied them to the foodbank. Annette was too busy in the job club to look after him so Kelly took care of him and showed him the ropes. And he did need taking care of. It was a completely different world for him. Just as it had been for Annette. The contrast between him and Kelly had never been so obvious as that first visit. Not that it stopped him going back. Annette didn't have to ask. He was up early on Tuesdays and Fridays, ready and waiting to go.

'Nice lad,' said George one day. 'He's got a good heart. Takes after his mum.'

27

A VOLCANO RISES

To save two journeys, Annette offered to take some of Frank's paintings to the gallery in the city centre. Surprisingly, given Colin's interest in art, she'd never actually been into a private gallery. He always made them sound like exclusive clubs that only accepted the most commercial of artists so, on principle, he never went in to them just to browse. This one was quite big. A large shop really, on two floors. Frank's show was mostly on the top floor with one or two teasers to be placed, centre stage, in the window downstairs.

When all the canvasses had been unloaded, Frank and the gallery owner went upstairs to discuss what should go where. Unsure whether to leave them to it or wait, Annette idled the time away looking at the artwork on the ground floor, slowly moving sideways with the studious countenance she used to reserve for museum visits. She arrived at an array of paintings on one single wall. Even with her limited knowledge, she could tell they were all by the same artist. In the main they were street scenes. Birmingham given a Parisian café style treatment. There was something about them that rang a bell. She moved in closer to get a better look at the scrawl in the bottom, right-hand corner.

'They're captivating, aren't they?' The assistant had moved in behind her. No doubt hoping for a prospective sale.

'Mmm. I think I might know the artist.'

'Colin? You know Colin Grey?'

So, it was him. She looked at the prices. The cheapest was £2,000. 'Yes, I know him well. I didn't realise he was exhibiting here too.'

'Oh yes, he's a regular contributor. One of our more popular artists actually.'

'So, he sells these does he?'

'Yes, he sells well. Both here and our sister gallery in Solihull. As I said he's very popular.'

'I had no idea. And …' she could barely bring herself to ask this, 'do all of his paintings command such prices?'

'It varies. His very large ones are usually higher, but we do have an excellent finance package if you're interested in purchasing one. Alternatively, if you're looking for something cheaper, Colin would be happy to paint a smaller version for you. He's very accommodating.'

I bet he is. I bet he fucking is, the absolute bastard. She felt a volcano rising inside her. She was going to blow and this time, there would be no holding it in. Not here though. She had to get out. 'Would you tell Frank that I had to leave?' She left the shop without waiting for an answer.

Propelled by some unknown force, she almost ran to the car. The rage fighting to spew forth from her was barely containable. For so long it had been a spark, dampened down by years of control and subjugation, but now it was an inferno, and she was about to unleash it on Colin Grey. He would feel her wrath. She drove like a madwoman, almost missing a red light, until her brakes screeched outside the house that she'd been stupidly paying for, for the last twelve years while Colin Grey had been making himself out to be a penniless artist. All the time raking it in and fleecing her for every penny she had. My God, she despised him.

She flung open the front door, smashing it against a side table and sending the phone crashing to the floor.

Liza, rushed out from the kitchen. 'Mum! What the hell?'

'Where is he?' she roared. 'Where is that conniving shit? Colin, where are you?'

Liza looked panic stricken. She yelled: 'Dad, Mum's gone crazy.'

She heard the bathroom door open. Colin appeared at the top of the stairs, a towel wrapped around his torso, dripping water. 'What's going on?'

She didn't wait for him to descend. She ran through to the kitchen and pushed open the door to his studio. Grabbing two jars of upturned brushes, she threw them to the ground in front of the door. They shattered on impact. She picked up another two and did the same.

By now he'd reached the doorway still wearing his towel. His bare feet stopped him from taking a step further over the shards of glass blocking his entrance. 'What the hell's got into you, you stupid cow?'

She went over to the easel where a painting rested. Another street scene. 'What's this one worth, Colin? Two thousand? Three?'

'What are you talking about? Liza, fetch me some shoes. Quickly.'

She picked up a tube of paint in each hand, squirted them all over the canvas and smeared them with a dirty rag, ignoring his cries. It felt good, but it wasn't enough. She scanned the room and spotted a pile of finished paintings stacked up against the wall. 'What about this one? Four thousand? It's quite a big one isn't it?' She seized a knife from another jar and slashed at it. Oh yes, that definitely felt better.

By now, he was shoving a pair of trainers on his feet. 'You bitch. You fucking madwoman. I always knew you were off your head. Now you've proved me right. Liza, go upstairs, I don't want you to witness your mother finally losing it.' He snatched another painting from her grasp. 'Liza, I said go upstairs.'

But Liza was transfixed. She'd never seen her mother do anything like this before, and was clearly not going to miss a minute of it.

Annette plucked another painting from the stack. 'This one's a bit smaller. One thousand?'

He grabbed the other end of it and they pulled it back and forth, until she let it go just as he was yanking it away. The thrust of it sent him reeling backwards, arse first, onto the glass-splintered floor. His towel fell away as he scrambled up, naked except for his trainer-clad feet. He twisted round to pick it up and reattach, displaying on his back a tattoo of a Clash album, *London Calling*.

'Do you sell the smaller ones at the Solihull gallery, or the one in town?' she said.

The penny dropped, and so did his mouth.

'Thirty years, Colin. Thirty years I've been shackled to you. Thirty years of having to conform to your exacting standards. Of being looked down on and belittled because I was never quite good enough for you. But the one thing I could do was provide you with the money to vomit out this shit that you call art. Poor Colin, the tortured artist who just had to paint, even though he never sold anything. Except that isn't quite true is it? It seems there are people out there who can't get enough of this tat. It seems, you're one of the gallery's most successful artists.'

'I don't know who you've been speaking to —'

'How long?' she roared.

'What?'

'How long have you been taking me to the cleaners?'

'Look, you've got it all wrong, Annette.'

His tone was pacifying now. She recognised the pattern. Any minute now he'd be making out it was all her imagination.

'Someone's been feeding you duff information. I manage to sell a painting here and there, but I'm afraid I'm still a struggling artist.' There it was, that little patronising snigger. 'I know Will and I have had our differences lately, but I can't believe he'd spin such tales. Although I really can't imagine who else would tell you such outright porkies.'

'Try the staff at the gallery. I'd say they're quite reliably informed. Wouldn't you?'

'Oh them.' Another snigger. 'They were probably just exaggerating to try to get you to buy something.'

'Don't, Colin. Don't insult my intelligence. I'm sure if I went back there, I could find out just how many sales you've had. I have no doubt the records would confirm that you've been bleeding me dry for years while secretly amassing your own little fortune.'

He took a step towards her.

She waved the knife in his face, 'Don't come any closer, you despicable fraudster. I've put up with you all this time because I thought it was best for the children but now, I can see that you're poisonous, and I intend to do something about it. I'm stopping all maintenance payments immediately. You have two weeks to set up the mortgage payments before the next one is due because I'm not paying it. And you have one month to either put the house up for sale or start proceedings to buy me out. If nothing's happened by then, I'll put it on the market.'

'Oh come on now. You know you're being unreasonable.' Again, that sanctimonious tone that chilled her to the bone.

'Highly likely but then, it's my turn, isn't it?' She threw the knife on the floor and approached her daughter, still standing agog in the doorway. 'I'm sorry you had to see that Liza but sometimes, a little anger is necessary. You know you'll always be welcome in my home.'

'Don't listen to her Liza. She's trying to turn you against me like she did with Will.'

She eyed the pathetic specimen before her, still clutching his towel around his waist. 'You never even liked The Clash. You just pretended you did, to get me into bed. You didn't even know who Joe Strummer was. Rick Astley was more your style. You really are the shallowest shit I've ever met, Colin.'

28

ESCAPE TO ABERDOVEY

'The thing about Birmingham is, it's close to everything but not close enough. I mean, it's not like the sea's on your doorstep is it? I expect that's why we love it so much. Because it's always such a treat to come here.' Granny Wilde would say that, every summer without fail, on the way to Aberdovey. She was right. When you can't just nip up the road to it, going to the seaside is always special.

Annette didn't know whether it was the anger, or a sudden need to be close to a happier past and memories she held dear, that had compelled her to drive here. But here she was. As soon as she left Colin and Liza she just drove. Away from them. Away from home. Away from everyone and everything. She didn't even know where she was going. It was as if she'd been taken over by autopilot with only one mission in mind. To leave it all behind. Before she knew it, she was in Wales and it all became clear. She needed to head to Aberdovey.

By the time she arrived, the best of the day was over but the sun was still high and strong in the clear, blue sky. If it hadn't been for the pleasant wind coming off the sea it would have been hot, instead of comfortably warm. It must have been a beautiful July day. The beach was full of sunbathers making the most of the last of it.

The first thing she did when she parked up was to find the cottage where they always stayed. It was painted a different colour but she'd know it anywhere. She stood outside while the treasured memories flooded back. Things she hadn't thought about in years. Going to the beach with her bucket and spade, her dad loaded up with windbreaks and deckchairs. Playing hide and seek in the sand dunes with Gran and her mum, or cricket with her dad on the flat sands.

When she left the little house behind, she wandered around the narrow streets with their pretty cottages and along the seafront still lined with colourful Victorian houses. Some of the shops and cafés were a touch more upmarket but really, it had hardly changed at all. It was smaller than she remembered it. Everything seems so much bigger when you're a child.

She bought some fish and chips from a chip shop opposite the beach and found a bench to eat them on.

'Fish always tastes better when you're close to the sea.' That was another of her gran's regular sayings. She was right again. They were delicious.

The late afternoon was just tipping over into evening and families were packing up. She closed her eyes, feeling the heat of the still-warm sun, and breathed in the sea air, lightly dusted with the smell of salt and vinegar.

The last time she'd been here was the summer before she went off to university. She and Claire had chosen Manchester because they couldn't stand the thought of

going to some 'backwater shithole', and they couldn't afford
London. The thought of the two of them, naïve and
pompous made her smile. So young, and so judgemental.
Pity she didn't put that judgement to better use.

After that party, the one she and her friends always referred
to as the accountants' party, she couldn't get rid of Colin.
He was always turning up wherever she went.

'The creep's back again.' That's what Sasha and Claire
called him. Colin the Creep. She did too, at first. They
insulted him to his face but he just kept coming back, until
he wore her down and she agreed to go out with him.

He surprised her on that first date. He was actually quite
sweet and, she felt a bit sorry for him. He gave her some sob
story about family expectations pressurising him to do
accountancy. He told her his heart wasn't really in it and he
was still trying to figure out what he did want to do. He liked
to draw but, they made it clear, he couldn't make a career of
that. He did a sketch of her. It was pretty good. Quite sweet.
A kind of idealised version of her. So she agreed to see him
one more time and then another. Always thinking she would
break it off soon. Before she knew it, they were officially a
couple.

After he took her to meet his parents, they went to the
pub and ridiculed their snobbishness. He said, surely now
she could see what he was up against. He needed someone
strong like her to help him stand up to them. Thinking
about it now, that was what did it for her. The idea that she,
Netta Wilde, was riding in on her white charger to rescue
him. She would be every bit as heroic as Ada. A chip off the
old block. He would be her project. What she hadn't
realised until now was she was his project too. And he was

far more successful at managing his, than she was at managing hers.

As their relationship grew, there were more stories about his suffocated upbringing and the emotional hardship he'd endured. By then she was growing attached to him, so she drank it all in.

When they finished their degrees, she'd intended to try London. She'd ruled out teaching by then and was thrilled to get a job offer at a publishing house. Colin wasn't keen. He said it was too close to his parents, and anyway he kept getting turned down for jobs down there. If they were going to get married, he needed employment and they had to live somewhere with affordable housing. She hadn't considered marriage up till then. They certainly hadn't discussed it. She asked him if that was a proposal.

'If you like,' he said. 'Isn't that what we've been working towards all along?' He made it sound like a business contract. 'I've been offered that job in Birmingham. It'll be ideal when we have children. You can go back to work and your mum will be able to look after them when they're not at school. It will save on childcare costs. She'd like that.'

'I don't think I want children.'

'Really? You've never said that before.'

'It's never come up.'

'Well, you might change your mind when your biological clock starts ticking. If not, that's fine. We'll be all right on our own.'

Of course, it wasn't fine. Colin had his plan and he was going to stick to it, no matter what. The first five years of their marriage were for getting on the property ladder, going out and enjoying themselves. After that, time to start a family.

On their fifth wedding anniversary, he brought the

subject up again. She gave him an emphatic no, but he kept on and on about it, gradually eroding her resistance over the next few years.

His parents were the same. Especially when his sister had a couple of daughters. His mother was obsessed with carrying on the family name, as though the Greys were connected to royalty or some such. Even her parents were beginning to ask if they were going to have grandchildren.

The only voice of reason was Granny Wilde's: 'Don't do it if you don't want to, Netta. You'll only regret it.'

She continued to resist until her early thirties. By then she'd been persuaded by Colin, by everyone else, and by her own fear of unnaturalness, that she'd feel differently when she held the baby in her arms.

She poured every inch of herself into being a devoted mum to Will. She did love him but it didn't take her long to realise that loving him wasn't enough. She kept it to herself, positive there was something abnormal about her.

Liza had been an accident. She'd told Colin no more, despite his persistence, and was never sure whether the diaphragm had been dodgy or sabotaged. If only she'd stayed on the pill. But, at the time, the papers were full of the health risks for women over thirty and he'd made a big thing about her getting thrombosis or worse. So, she gave in again.

When she found out she was having a second child, she dabbled with the idea of an abortion without telling him, but he found the pregnancy test before she had a chance to think seriously about it. He was over the moon and told everyone straight away. There were no options left open to her after that, except to get her head down and crack on with it.

Liza didn't change the way she felt about her children.

She loved them in her way, but she couldn't make them her entire world. She read magazine articles where famous women said that becoming a mother was the best thing that had happened to them. That they felt completed by these perfect little human beings and nothing else came close.

Women at work were the same. Or gave the impression they were. She didn't dare ask whether they were really that besotted with their kids or whether deep down inside, they felt the same as her. Whichever it was, she didn't want to be the first one to break ranks and admit it.

She couldn't tell Colin. Bad enough that he constantly threw back in her face the fact that she hadn't wanted children. Piling it on. Layer upon layer of guilt.

She would have spoken to Claire but the last time she'd seen her, she was shamed by her appalled look when she saw what she'd become.

'Fucking Stepford wife now, are you? What the fuck has he done to you, Netta?'

The only person left to confide in was Granny Wilde. Granny's response took her by surprise. 'Don't tell your dad but he was an accident. I never wanted children. Far too independent. But what could I do? Arthur was there, and it was just me and him. Don't get me wrong, he was my little boy and I wasn't going to let anything happen to him but I couldn't just sit at home and wait for him to shine his light on me. I had to work, out of necessity, but it wasn't just because we needed the money. I wasn't cut out to be a stay-at-home mum, and you're the same Netta. I did my best to make sure he didn't miss out. I made sure he knew I loved him. Even if I wasn't always the best mum, I did for him what I was good at. I worked hard to give him a comfortable, happy home. Do the same. Show them you love them in your own way. Don't let anyone bully you into thinking there's something wrong with you.'

She sighed, the right advice had been there all along, if only she'd listened to it. Of course, she hadn't realised at the time the bully was Colin. She hadn't realised that Granny was telling her, 'You're just like me, you're not a freak.' She was saying you didn't have to be a model mother, and it was all right to be that way. If she had only listened more closely. Perhaps she wouldn't have given Colin the leverage to create the gap between her and her children. The gap that grew into an unbridgeable chasm.

The art started with evening classes. A way of reducing the frustration of a job he hated. She saw no harm in that. Even when he began to take time off to go to the odd day or weekend course, she reasoned it was acceptable to use up his precious holiday quota if it made him more agreeable to live with.

Then came the sick leave. A month off with stress. Naturally, he said it was all her fault. Her behaviour had made him that way. The painting, he said, was helping him to get better. She was no doctor, but he seemed inordinately happy for a man who was suffering from a debilitating mental health issue. She'd seen people at work completely blindsided by it and his symptoms were nothing like theirs. But what could she do? She'd brought it on herself. She didn't have a leg to stand on.

Next came the bombshell, 'I want to give up accountancy and be a professional artist. I can look after the children. You'll have more time to focus on work. You know you prefer that to family life.'

That hurt. Wounded as she was, she made a feeble attempt to reason against it but he was fixed on trying it for a year.

'I mean, it's not like you've ever taken to it is it? You never really wanted to be a mother. If it doesn't work out, I'll go back to work. I've done the sums. With your last promotion, we can get by if we watch what we spend. You owe it to me to try. You owe me that much.'

He never did go back to work. He never really watched the spending either. He wasted money on his equipment and had to have a bigger house with room for a studio, in spite of not selling anything. Well, he led her to believe he hadn't sold anything and she never checked. At some point that changed and he became successful. Her aversion to his studio and his work made sure she would never notice paintings come and go. For all she knew he could have been stockpiling cash for years, planning when to drop her and how to extract as much as possible from her until she was bled dry, in every conceivable way. He always did like his plans.

She was sure they'd had been happy once. Well, Colin had probably always been happy because he held all the cards. Nearly all of them at any rate. But she was sure she'd been happy too, for a couple of years.

She'd been stung by Claire's accusation because she knew there was some truth in it. But she'd changed because she wanted to. Hadn't she? Didn't she want to fit in to please him? *Still you, but better.* That phrase ran over and over in her head. It was the mantra she'd lived by for so long it almost felt like a soundtrack to her life, until even the better her, wasn't good enough. She wanted to be a decent person and a proper mother, but no matter how hard she tried, she just couldn't get it right. Possibly, she tried too hard to lose her deficiencies because, somewhere along the line, everything else got lost too.

At least she'd been good at her job, which was just as

well because the frequent promotions allowed her to keep up with Colin's demands. The more successful she became, the more reason he had not to go back to work. So, she pushed herself harder and harder into being the great provider.

Maybe her nose had been too close to the grindstone to notice the little things. Like the slight remarks that nicked away at her and piled on that guilt. These were the sort of things that built up over time until the pressure of them forced you to close in on yourself and turn away from the ones you needed most. Before she knew it, she'd worked up a divide between her and the rest of her family and she'd turned herself into the kind of person Netta Wilde would have been ashamed of.

Meanwhile, he was there in the background, manipulating them all. Feeding the children stories about their cold, unnatural mother. How utterly contemptuous. Why did she let him get away with it? It was a stupid question. Stupid because she knew the answer, if only she could bring herself to admit it. She let him get away with it because it suited her to throw herself into her career, to come back at night too late to read them a bedtime story and too tired to have to talk to him. It suited her to turn a blind eye while he did his scheming to build his future meal ticket. She'd been conned, but it wasn't just him doing the conning.

She found herself a room for the night at a pub hotel on the front. The only one they had left was expensive because it had a sea view. She took it anyway. She loved the sea and for once, she was thinking only of herself. Today, no one else mattered but her.

She went for a walk on the seemingly endless flat beach,

turning around only when it was beginning to get dark. By the time she got back to her room, the moon was out and the village was lit up like a pretty postcard. Holidaymakers had spilled out of the pubs onto the pavements and there were a couple of beach barbecues going on. She felt like the old Annette. Alone and watching from the side-lines. It was a lonely place to be.

Opening the windows, she took in the salty air and listened to the sound of the waves crashing. She latched on to the in and out flow of the water, thinking only of the sea and the motion, and allowed her breathing pattern to match it.

She emptied the stale thoughts from her mind and imagined her body floating on top of the surf — back and forth, back and forth — until she was becalmed, and all but the more determined late-night revellers were in bed. Only then did she address the calls and messages she'd been ignoring all day. She wouldn't phone them now. She would message them to stop them worrying. It was late and she wanted more time to herself. More time to find out who herself was.

First on her list was Will. She told him she was fine and would call in the morning. Next was Kelly, then her dad, Frank, Neil, Paula and Corrine. Then she switched off her phone to preserve the battery and sat into the early hours drinking in the magic of the small coastal village that had always had a special place in her heart.

In the morning, she borrowed a charger from the hotel to make some calls.

Will answered straight away. 'Mum, is everything okay, are you all right, where are you?' Three questions in one sentence. He must have been worried.

'I'm fine darling. I just needed some time on my own. That's all.'

'Liza called me, Mum. I know what happened.'

'Is she all right? I was pretty angry. I hope I didn't frighten her.'

'No, she's fine. Forget Liza. It's you I'm worried about.'

Her son was worried about her. She was so happy she wanted to cry. 'Don't be. I'm absolutely fine, really. In fact, I feel really good.'

'You're not going to do anything stupid are you, Mum?'

'Good grief no. Well not unless you consider a five-mile beach walk stupid for a woman of my fitness range.'

'Beach? Where are you?'

'I'm in Wales. I'll be back later today.'

'Okay. Kelly's here. She wants to talk to you. I'll put her on.'

'Net, what the fuck?' Darling Kelly, straight to the point.

'Hello Kelly. Are you looking after everything back there?'

'Yeah, holding it all together. We've been up all night. Why didn't you call?'

'Sorry, I … well ... you know.'

'It's okay. You don't have to explain. Will says you're at the seaside.'

'Yes, I'll be back later. Can you do me a favour? Can you let Frank know you've spoken to me? And Neil, Paula and Corrine. I'm just going to phone my dad before heading out for a bit.'

'I'm guessing you're in Aberdovey?' That was the first thing her dad said to her when she called.

'How did you deduce that, Sherlock Holmes?'

He let out a little laugh but she could sense the anxiety in his speech. 'A lucky guess. Will sent me a text to say you were by the sea, in Wales. We've been very worried about you, love. Everyone's been very worried.'

'I know Dad, I'm sorry. I just couldn't face speaking to anyone yesterday. I was so furious. I think I blew myself out but I'm feeling good now. I've been doing a lot of thinking and facing a few home truths. It's as if a cloud has lifted and everything's clearer. I know it sounds silly, but I feel rejuvenated.'

'Well that's good then. As long as you're not going to do anything silly?'

'You're the second person to ask me that this morning. I'm not going to do anything that will endanger my life, if that's what you mean. I'm going for a nice long walk and then I'm coming home.' Long enough to blow the ghost of Annette Grey well and truly away, she thought. 'Can I speak to Mum?'

He passed the phone over.

'Hello Mum,' she said. 'I just wanted to tell you. You were right all along about Colin. I knew it too, but I hid from it. I let him get away with it because it suited me. I didn't have it in me to be a proper mother to the kids and I let the guilt of that drag me down and do some stupid things. I love them, but I never wanted them. It's dogged me for years.'

'I know that Netta,' said her mum. 'Granny Wilde told me years ago. Listen to me. It doesn't matter that you didn't want them because you love them in spite of it. That makes you a bloody good mother in my books. And just because you're not at home baking apple pie doesn't make you a bad person. Don't you ever let me hear you say you're not a proper mum. That's nonsense. You've given those children everything you could. That's more than I ever gave you.'

'Thanks Mum. There's just one more thing I want to say

before I go. I haven't said this in a long time, but I love you both very much.'

'Oh my darling, we love you too. Much more than you'll ever realise. Now you're not going to do anything silly are you?'

29

MAUD SPRINGS A SURPRISE

Will and Kelly were waiting for her when she got back. Kelly wanted to know all the gruesome details but, for Will's sake, Annette said no more than was necessary. His reaction to her return took her by surprise. He threw his arms around her and hugged her so tightly she could hardly catch her breath. The last time he'd done that he was considerably younger and smaller. Frank came over later, pleased to see that she was all in one piece.

The only member of the household who seemed subdued was Maud. She was quite unlike her usual self.

'She's been like it since yesterday. She's not eating. Maybe she's sick,' said Will.

Annette patted Maud's back. She did seem a bit edgy. 'I'll take her to a vet tomorrow and get her checked over, if she's no better. I think I've seen her inoculation certificates in the study. I'll see if I can find which vet Edie used.'

Maud was the same the next day so Annette phoned the vet whose name was on the certificates and booked her in for later that afternoon.

. . .

The vet ran his hands along Maud's sides and placed them on her belly. 'Well, I've got some good news and hopefully, some more good news,' he said. 'She's not ill. In fact, she's in fine fettle. You're doing a good job of looking after her.'

Annette assumed that last piece of information was the second piece of good news. But no.

'If she seems a bit off colour it's because she's pregnant. I'd say she's nearly ready. Due within the week in all likeliness. Young Maud's been a-courting.'

Annette was astonished. How on earth had Maud pulled that one off without anyone noticing? Maud looked up at her, somehow inviting her to be outraged. 'Maud, you minx,' she said.

The vet supplied Annette with instruction pamphlets and the things necessary to help Maud and her puppies when the time came. She returned home still slightly unsure as to how Maud had managed to get herself in this predicament and with absolutely no idea who the father could be. She gathered Will, Frank and Kelly together to give them the news. 'It seems the house will soon be filled with the pitter patter of tiny paws.' Frank got it immediately but Kelly and Will looked confused. 'Maud, is about to have puppies,' she explained.

Kelly put her hands to her mouth. 'Oh my God. That is brilliant. Priceless.'

They went through the vet's instruction booklets several times over, to be certain they knew the signs to look for and what to do when they became apparent. When it began to look as if Maud's time was near, the four of them were thrown into full midwifery duties, taking turns to keep watch over her. She was spending most of her time in the breakfast room now, so they set up her nest in there. Annette borrowed a camp bed from Frank so she could spend the nights with her.

The house was quiet. Maud was restless and couldn't settle. Annette put her hand under the dog's chin. 'Are you frightened Maudie? Don't worry, I'll look after you.'

There was a rustle in the kitchen. Will appeared in the doorway.

'Can't sleep?' she said.

He shook his head. 'Do you think she'll have them tonight?'

'I think she might.'

'I wish Liza was here. She'd be so excited.'

Annette said nothing. Liza hadn't contacted her since she saw her last and she was beginning to doubt they would ever be reconciled. They sat together. Will on a battered armchair they carried in from the lounge and she on the camp bed, waiting for the big moment to happen.

He broke the silence. 'I've been thinking about university. You remember what Frank said about being sure? I don't think I'm ready to go yet. I'm not sure any more about what I want to do. So, I was thinking of taking a gap year. What do you think?'

She remembered the disappointment of not being consulted about his university choices last year and felt a momentary satisfaction that, at last, her son was ready to include her in the conversation. 'I think, if you really aren't sure, then a gap year is a good idea. Have you thought about what you'll do in that year?'

'Yes,' he said. 'I want to do some voluntary work. I'd like to carry on helping at the foodbank but I want to do some other stuff as well. I've been looking at helping out with disadvantaged kids and people who speak English as a second language. Chris knows a lot about it. He gave me some pamphlets. I thought, maybe I could live here with you while I did that?'

'If you're sure that's what you want to do then yes. I'd love you to stay here,' she said, hardly able to conceal her delight.

'I'm sure. I really want to do this, Mum.'

'Okay then. We'll sort it out with the university and pick up the rest of your things from the house.'

He bit his lip. 'There's one thing you should know first. I knew what Dad was up to. I found out a couple of months ago. Arianne's car broke down when he was doing his tax return. He left everything on the table thinking no one would be around but I finished school early and saw everything. I wanted to tell you but, he said I was betraying him. I tried to make him own up to it but he wouldn't. That's why we fell out. I'm sorry, I should have said something sooner.'

So that was why Colin had assumed Will had told her. He even tried to discredit his own son to get himself off the hook. Poor Will. Stuck in the middle and not knowing which way to turn. How many more times had their children been forced to choose between them? She had no idea but she knew that, whether it had been two or two hundred, for the most part they'd chosen him. Whether they wanted to or not.

She gave him a hug. 'Don't feel bad. It's not your fault. You shouldn't have been put in that position. I know in the past I haven't made you or Liza feel comfortable around me, but I want you to know that I love you very much. Sorry. Bit soppy, I know. But I needed to tell you, for me as much as you. And, I'm very proud of you taking this gap year decision. You won't regret it. Volunteering has done so much for me. It's changed my outlook completely and it will do the same for you.'

'Thanks Mum. There's one other thing I need to tell you.' She readied herself. 'I'm not a vegetarian anymore. It was Dad's thing. Well, Arianne's really. We all did it for her. I've tried, but I really miss bacon sandwiches.'

So, Colin had been seeing Arianne for longer than she'd realised. Certainly, as far back as last summer. Maybe even longer. Knowing Colin, he'd have taken his time to introduce her to the kids.

'I was getting quite fond of veggie chilli,' she said.

'Oh, it's fine to make that. Your veg chilli's good. But do you think, one of the days, we could have steak and mushroom pie? I've missed that most of all.'

In her sleep, Annette dreamed she was on the beach at Aberdovey, playing hide and seek with the children in the sand dunes. They were young, and the dunes were deep. She couldn't see them anywhere and was beginning to panic until she saw Granny Wilde holding their hands. All three were smiling at her. To the side, a blurred, shadowy figure stood apart from them. Granny held out her hand to it. Overcome with dread, Annette tried to call out to them to get away from it, but someone was shaking her, whispering something in her ear.

'Mum, wake up. It's started.'

She opened her eyes, forgetting for a minute where she was.

'See,' said Will. 'Here comes the first one.'

They sat together on the camp bed, hand in hand, watching the birth of Maud's babies. Four in all. They hadn't needed to do much. The puppies were healthy and Maud knew instinctively how to care for them.

'She's a natural,' said Annette wistfully.

Dawn broke over the garden. They were so busy marvelling at Maud and her babies they didn't notice the vixen and her cubs trotting across the grass until she was right on top of the window.

Will spotted them first. 'Look,' he whispered.

The vixen and the dog took each other in, Maud, with her blind and helpless pups nestling to her teats, and the mother fox, her cubs almost big enough to be leaving her. Neither made a sound.

As the foxes walked away, Will let out a sigh. 'That was one of the most bewitching moments of my life. I'll always remember it.'

'Me too,' whispered Annette.

'Hey, I've just realised. It's your birthday today. Happy birthday, Mum. I did get you a present but I don't think I can top Maud's.'

Maud became quite a celebrity. Everyone wanted to see her and the puppies. She put up with the attention well.

Kelly swore she was posing for the cameras. 'That's an Instagram face if ever I saw one,' she said.

She sent a photo to her brothers who asked to come and see the pups. Annette's parents came over. For people not usually known for their love of animals, they were completely taken with the little family.

'They're so tiny,' said her mum. 'So adorable. Maud, you're such a clever girl.'

'There's nothing clever about getting yourself pregnant Mum. I still have no idea who the father is.'

'Let's hope it's not a Great Dane,' said Frank.

30

FACING COLIN AND THE GOLEM

'Are you sure you're ready?' Annette sat in the driver's seat, ready to turn on the ignition.

'Absolutely,' said Will.

'Right. Let's get going then.' She pushed the fob in and the engine started up.

He fiddled with the radio as they drove and drummed his fingers against the inside of the door even though she could tell he wasn't really listening to the music. When they pulled up outside the house, she gave him a few minutes to settle himself.

'Shall we go in?' she said.

'Sure. Mum, don't leave me alone with Dad, will you?'

'Okay, I won't. Let's go.'

She let him open the front door with his key. The three of them were waiting in the lounge. She could see Will was finding it difficult to speak so she spoke for him. 'Well, here we are to collect the rest of Will's things.' They stayed where they were, grim faced and silent. 'We'll just go up to his room then. Come on Will.'

As soon as they were in the room, Will started grabbing

random objects and throwing them into the boxes they'd brought with them. She handed him a roll of bin bags. 'Tell you what, why don't you put your clothes and the soft things in the bags and I'll fill the boxes?'

'Okay, sure.' He left her to pack the books and fragile items.

Colin came into the room with Arianne behind him, wearing that T-shirt. Jesus, did she ever take that thing off? He glared at Annette, 'Can I have a word with my son?'

'Yes, of course you can. Fire away,' she said.

'Alone.'

Will looked panic stricken.

She stopped her packing. 'No, I don't think so.'

'No? You're telling me I can't speak to my son. Who the hell do you think you are?'

'I know who I am, Colin. I'm not denying you a chance to speak to him. I'm simply saying you can't be alone with him.'

Arianne stuck her head out from behind his back. 'Haven't you done enough damage to this family? Get out before we throw you out.'

Annette moved forward until she was right in front of them. She stood at her full height, with her hands on her hips. 'I don't know who you are and I don't care, but if you take a look at the mortgage statements, you'll see my name on there. This is my house. Everything you see in this house? I paid for. I probably paid for that T-shirt you're wearing. Which, by the way, is not only exactly the same as the one I was wearing when he first met me, but is also ridiculously too small for you. So, do not tell me to get out of my own house. And do not suppose that you know anything about my family and the damage that I, or anyone else has caused. If you want to hang around with this fraud that's up to you.

If you've got any sense, which you probably haven't, you'll get out now before he takes every ounce of confidence you have and destroys it. Now, if you'll excuse us, my son and I have packing to do. So, unless you're going to help, kindly fuck off and leave us to it.'

'How dare you talk to me like that? You're just jealous,' hissed Arianne.

'Oh, believe me, I really am not jealous.'

Arianne rested her arms on her ample chest and moved her head from side to side. 'You're jealous because Liza likes me and not you.'

Oof! That was below the belt. But she could take it now. Just about. 'How old are you, sixteen? For fuck's sake, I'm a grown woman. Liza and I might not be on the best of terms, but jealousy? Get over yourself and grow up.'

Colin cut in. 'Go downstairs Arianne. This isn't helping.'

Arianne left in a sulk.

He held out his arms to Will. 'I can't believe you're really doing this, mate. I mean look at her. Look at the depths she's prepared to go to. She'll do anything to get one over on me. That's what this is all about you know. She didn't want you. She never wanted you. She just dumped you on me and went off to work.'

Another body blow. But she'd expected it and had already made a pre-emptive strike.

Will cleared his throat. 'That's not quite true is it Dad? I know Mum didn't want children. She told me herself. But that doesn't mean she doesn't love us. We both know staying at home was your choice, and that's cool if that was your thing. But it's not cool to keep blaming Mum for everything. And it's not cool to pretend you have no money when really you have plenty. I've seen your bank statements. I know.'

Colin's mouth opened into a large O. Then it closed and

there was an uncomfortable quiet in the room until he found some words to fill it. 'Whatever I did, I did it for you and Liza. Sooner or later she was going to stop making the payments. I couldn't trust her. You'll find out mate, you just can't trust her. You should never, ever trust her.'

'No Dad, you didn't. You did it for yourself and no one else. Bad enough that you've been lying to Mum all these years, don't make it worse by lying to me as well.'

She could see Will coming apart. Colin too. Whatever his motives, those few words from Will had drained him. She'd been worried about what he would come out with next, desperate as he was to claw back the upper hand. But now, he was deflated. Completely sapped of energy. She had to step in and rescue the situation. She touched his shoulder. 'Colin, perhaps it's best if you wait downstairs while we finish off.'

He nodded agreement and left them to it. They finished the job quickly and almost wordlessly.

She picked up the last of the bags and handed one to Will. 'Time to go.'

'Yeah,' he said and took the stairs without looking back. They closed the front door behind them and trudged down the path.

As they reached the car, Liza came running after them with a book in her hand. 'Will, you forgot this.'

'I don't want it Lize. You have it.'

'But it was a present from Arianne. You haven't even looked at it,' she said.

He shook his head. 'I don't want it.'

She frowned. 'Will you come back to visit?'

'I don't think so, but we can hang out somewhere else. You can come and see me at the house. Come over and see the puppies. You'd love them.'

She wrinkled her nose. 'Yeah? They looked a bit gross in the photos. Like worms.'

Will smiled. 'That's because they were less than an hour old, you dunce. They're more like puppies now. Aren't they Mum?'

'Yes. They're getting bigger and more normal-looking every day,' said Annette.

'Yeah, and really comical,' he said.

Liza looked back at the lounge window where Colin and Arianne stood watching. 'Maybe. I don't know.'

'Come if you want to, darling,' said Annette. 'We'd both love to see you. Time to go, Will.'

He tossed the last bag onto the back seat, glanced at the lounge window, and got in. 'See ya, Lize. Come and visit.'

They drove off leaving her on the kerb, clutching the book to her chest. They watched her until she was a dot in the rear-view mirror.

'Do you think she'll be all right?' said Will.

'I hope so,' she said.

31

COLONEL STEPS FORWARD

Customers weren't exactly beating down the doors to buy their jams but over the summer their sales ticked over steadily enough to make a small profit. As the garden's fruit stocks dwindled, they turned to Frank, who had a few fruit bushes and a damson tree in his garden and they went blackberrying, until eventually, they ran out.

They'd all come to Annette's to make jam but, halfway through the morning, the fruit was gone. They were in their usual places at the kitchen table. Outside, the sun was peeking through the clouds, after three days of rain. The atmosphere was still damp and lacklustre. It felt like the end of a great adventure.

Annette was the first to speak. 'I suppose we'll have more time to do the things we've been putting off. I, for one, can get on with sorting out the study. Still, I'm going to miss it.'

Neil cleared his throat. 'We don't have to stop. We could carry on. We've got some money in the kitty to buy some fruit. If we can get it at a decent price and the sales carry on at the same rate, we should be able to keep going for a while longer. There are some smaller markets and fairs further out that allow casual day traders.'

'Yeah?' said Kelly. 'I'm in. Net?'

Neil and Kelly were looking at her, waiting for her to say something. Their expressions were non-committal but she guessed that was just an act. They wanted, maybe needed, it to carry on. She wanted it too but the problem was, the jam making wasn't bringing in the money. She still had her reserves from the sale of the flat and the remainder of her redundancy and inheritance. And her outgoings had been drastically reduced since she'd stopped paying out to Colin but, like the fruit, they wouldn't last forever. In the last few weeks, she'd seriously been considering getting a job. Still, she could go on for another month. Another month wouldn't do any harm.

'Okay, if we can keep it going without being out of pocket,' she said.

'It's been fun helping out,' said Paula. 'But I think I could do with a rest. I'll still come and give you a hand when you're stuck though.'

Annette's dad looked at her mum. 'I think you three are the hub really, but we'd be happy to help when we can. Wouldn't we, love?'

'Yes,' said her mum. 'We enjoy it.' The others said they would help when they could too.

'We need to find a supplier,' said Neil. 'Anyone got any ideas?'

'There's the wholesale market. That's where most people buy large quantities from,' said her dad. 'Or you could go to one of those fruit farms on the outskirts of town. Or, if you want to keep it small, I suppose you could try the local allotments.'

'I like the sound of using the allotments,' said Annette,

'We could keep it local then. How do we find out more about them?'

'We could ask Clyde,' said her dad.

'Who?' said Annette.

'Clyde. He lives somewhere around the corner. Stops and chats to me now and then when I'm working in the front garden. Nice chap. He's got a couple of allotments nearby.'

'I really need to get to know my neighbours better,' said Annette.

'Yes, you do,' he said. 'I think I know where he lives. I'll go and knock on his door.'

On his return from Clyde's, Annette's dad had two pieces of news. The first was that Clyde thought he could help and would be down shortly to talk to them. The second was that Clyde would be bringing his dog, Colonel, who was a great friend of Maud's apparently, and was pining for her as she hadn't been to visit for a while.

When Clyde rang the doorbell, hardly a glance was given to the well-turned-out elderly man with a Caribbean accent. All eyes were on the big, scruffy, bundle of hair at his side. A combination of black and steel grey with light and dark streaks. A giant Brillo pad on legs.

The man pushed back his straw trilby and rolled his eyes. 'I know, dogs are supposed to look like their owners, right? But he sure doesn't look like me. He was my daughter's dog, so I inherited him. He's got a nice temperament and he keeps me company. It's pretty quiet in the house since my wife died. I never realised what a noisy woman she was, until she was gone.'

Colonel paid no heed to the uncalled-for attention. He

sniffed the air and lolloped past them, straight into the breakfast room whereupon he nudged Maud's nose, nuzzled the puppies, surprisingly softly, and flopped his large frame down on the floor beside them.

'I think we need look no further for the culprit,' said Annette's mum.

'Oh, my goodness,' exclaimed Clyde. 'I don't know what to say. Colonel, you rascal. What have you been up to?' Colonel gave Clyde a doleful look, and dropped his broad, unkempt head onto his paws. Clyde tutted. 'He knows he's done wrong. That's his guilty look.'

'Yeah but look at them,' said Kelly. 'They're like a happy couple. How can you call that wrong?'

'More like the odd couple,' said Frank. 'Are you sure it's even physically possible for him to be the father?'

'Well two of the pups have the same colouring. We'll have to wait and see how big they are when they've grown a bit,' said Annette's mum. 'Anyway, he thinks he is. That's all that counts at the end of the day.'

The discussion of the paternity of the puppies concluded for the time being, talk turned to the potential opportunity for the nearby allotment growers to provide them with fruit.

Clyde said he would talk to his fellow members. 'We're not allowed to turn the allotments into a business but we can sell our surplus. There are quite a few of us growing different fruits. More than we can eat. The chance to make a bit of money on the side might appeal. I'm going down there as soon as I get into my allotment clothes, so I'll start making enquiries straight away. It's the least I can do, under the circumstances. Come on Colonel. Colonel, come on.'

Colonel sunk his head even further and let out a low whine that said he had no intention of moving. Will gave his substantial body a pat. 'Couldn't he stay here until you come back? I'm sure he'll be no trouble.'

Clyde turned to Annette. 'I don't mind. It's up to you.'

Annette stroked Colonel's back. 'Let him stay. I'd hate to break up the happy family.'

Clyde returned in the early evening with news that several of his allotment friends were interested. Some already had fruit picked and frozen that they would be willing to sell for a reasonable price. 'Come down with me tomorrow and we can talk money,' he said. 'Now Colonel, it's time to go home. I have to cook dinner and you've been here long enough.'

'Why don't you stay for dinner with us?' Annette indicated towards the garden. 'We're about to have a barbecue. There's plenty to go around and it's about time I got to know my neighbours better.'

'Well, if you put it like that, why not? It's been a few years since I was in that garden. It'll be nice to get back in there again. I used to help Edith years ago, before it got too much for her. She was a very nice woman. You remind me of her.'

The next day, she met Clyde's allotment friends. They agreed to supply them with all their surplus produce, as well as some already stashed in their freezers for a good price. So the jam making was back on.

'If we're going to branch out, we need to be a bit more professional,' said Neil. 'I'll check out the rules and regulations. We should order some proper jam jars and labels too.' As if reading her mind, he added, 'Don't worry they don't cost very much. What do you think we should call our product? For the labels.'

She thought for a minute. 'How about Edie's Jams?'

32

THE DATE THAT WASN'T

'Is it, like, a date then?' Kelly was doing the asking but they'd obviously been talking about it between them. They had her cornered in the breakfast room, their chairs arranged so that she'd have to climb over them to get out. She was already regretting telling them. She should have left it to the last minute and sprung it on them. Like a fool, she'd mentioned that they'd have to sort their own dinner out on Saturday and she'd been under interrogation ever since.

'I don't know. I didn't ask. Are you supposed to ask? I'm a bit out of practice,' she said.

Kelly shrugged. 'Well he should have made it clear. Did he make it clear?'

'No, not really. He just promised me a meal when he finished his exhibition and, that's what this is.'

'Yeah but, as friends or you know, future lovers?' Kelly looked over at Will. She was clearly trying not to smirk, and he was no better.

'Future lovers? Oh please. What rubbish have you two been watching? We're two middle-aged people who just happen to be going for a meal together, that's all.'

'We don't mind if it's more than that, Mum,' said Will. 'We just wanted you to know that.'

'Yeah,' said Kelly. 'I mean he's got a touch of the nutty professor about him but, to be fair, he's a nice old geezer.'

She couldn't help but find them funny. What a conspiratorial pair they were now. They could be brother and sister. When he'd first moved in, she'd been worried Will's attraction to Kelly would spoil things and make it difficult for them all to live under one roof. She needn't have been. If he had entertained more romantic, or even lustful, notions at some point, they never really surfaced. As far as she knew at any rate. Instead, he and Kelly had settled into a different kind of intimacy. A sort of sibling cosiness.

She wasn't sure how or why it happened. They had some things in common, she supposed. They had both, in their own way, been forced to come to terms with absent mothers. Although Will was lucky enough to get a second chance with his. She wondered if that had been the basis from which their relationship grew and whether they ever talked about it when they were alone. She couldn't be sure. All she knew was they'd become a family and it was nice.

'Thank you both so much for your considerate comments. I'm touched. However, I'm sure me and the old geezer will be able to sort things out on our own. No need for you to trouble yourselves any further.'

'Ooh Wills, I think that was a telling off, don't you?' said Kelly.

'Definitely. That was definitely telling us to mind our own business,' he said.

'Talking of minding your own business, haven't you got things to do? I'm sure there must be a wall that needs painting or something.' She shooed them away.

She had to concede, they had a point. She really didn't

know whether this was a date or just dinner between friends. A thank you for all the meals he'd shared at her table. At first, he'd seemed quite casual about asking. Then she caught a hint of self-consciousness. The restaurant too was an expensive one. The sort you dressed up for. It seemed more the kind of place you took someone to that you were trying to impress, rather than a friend. She was probably reading too much into it. Still, she would splash out and buy a new dress, just in case. Aside from the jeans and T-shirts she'd bought in January, she really didn't like any of the clothes in her wardrobe. They were what was left of her corporate life. The clothes she'd kept back for emergencies after donating the rest to the job club, and her old weekend uniform. She'd planned to treat herself to something for her birthday but, with everything that went on around that time, it came and went. She was still practically living in the same six items of clothing she'd been wearing since her half-birthday.

The image consultant she'd seen when still at Masons had told her which colours brought out the best in her and which styles most suited her frame. Back then she'd had short, dark hair. She hadn't been to a hairdresser in a year, so it was getting quite long now and the greys were more obvious. Her skin type was still the same though. Cool and clear. That was the term the consultant used. So was her shape. A neat hourglass, apparently. She'd liked the idea of being neat at the time. It gave the impression of not standing out. Fitting into things without too much trouble.

At the end of the consultation, she'd been given a wallet of colours she should wear. The overriding advice was, wear bright, clear colours. Being the sort of person that she was back then, aside from the one bright pink shirt she'd been cajoled into buying, she'd ignored that part of the recommendation and stuck with the more muted end of the wallet's colour palette. Black, brown, grey and white.

She dug out the wallet from the bottom of her underwear drawer and went shopping. The places she used to go to were avoided. So were the colours that had once been her staples. Today she would buy for Netta Wilde, not Annette Grey. It took her hours to find something. Mostly because she had to stop herself from straying towards the unadventurous conservatism that had ruled her choices for the best part of her adult life.

Eventually, she found an emerald green tea dress in a small independent shop, tucked away in the back streets of town. It was as far from her old Annette style as she could imagine and she loved it. Pleased with herself, she went on to buy a midnight blue day dress, a mint-green summer skirt that sat just above the knee, two brightly coloured tops, and two jumpers. One crimson and one purple. She felt the ghost of Annette Grey receding further into the background. Hopefully soon, she'd be gone altogether.

When the big night came, Frank called for her. As she descended, with the three of them waiting at the bottom of the stairs, she felt bizarrely like a prom queen in one of those American movies. Kelly and Will, the proud parents. She half expected Frank to whip out a corsage for her to pin on her dress.

'Wow,' said Will.

'You look amazing,' said Kelly. 'Really amazing.'

The kids lingered on the step to wave them off.

'You do look lovely. New dress?' he said, as the taxi drove them away.

'Thank you. Yes, it is. I thought I'd better make an

effort. It didn't seem like the kind of place to wear my usual scruffy jeans to.'

'You never look scruffy. I hope you haven't gone to too much expense?'

'Not at all. It was cheaper than it looks.' She cast an eye over him. His jacket and trousers were top quality and he'd pressed his shirt. He might even have had a haircut. Her mum was right, he scrubbed up nicely and the result was not entirely displeasing. 'You look good too,' she said. 'I don't think I've seen you in that suit before, have I?'

'No. I don't wear it much. I've had it for a while though. Ellen got it made for me. She was sick of seeing me looking like a tramp.'

The restaurant was as plush as she'd expected. High-end French. She was glad she'd bought the dress.

'This is delightful,' she said. 'Have you been here before?'

He nodded. 'Yes. I used to come here with Ellen. It was her favourite.'

So, he'd brought her to his wife's favourite restaurant, wearing the suit she'd bought him. This was not a good start.

'She liked French cooking then?'

'Oh yes. All things French actually. She spent some time in France. Lived there for a while.'

'Before the two of you met?'

'Er, yes, and once or twice after then. Ah, here's the wine.'

Had she touched a nerve? It sounded as if it was still hard for him to talk about her. She moved the subject on to a less delicate topic. 'So, Maud's puppies are growing. We'll have to find them homes soon. Any suggestions?'

He seemed preoccupied. 'Not really. I'll ask around.'

'How's your exhibition coming along? Have you sold much?'

'It's going well. One or two sales so far, and a couple in the pipeline. Not bad.'

'I'm sure you'll get more. Your work is wonderful. Have you always painted?'

'I played about with it as a child and a student but I didn't do it in earnest until about eight years ago. I stopped for a while before Ellen ...' He threw back a mouthful of wine. 'Afterwards, I needed something to distract me, so I started it again. If she's looking down on me now, she'll probably be shaking her head in dismay. She was very cultured. My efforts weren't exactly to her taste.'

They were back to Ellen again. After that, he went quiet. Something was happening to Frank. He was no longer the easy-going man who sat across her kitchen table telling funny stories and dispensing unassuming words of wisdom. He was uncomfortable, reticent and, above all, absorbed. Most likely, in the memory of Ellen.

She tried alternative lines of conversation. His teaching, his life in Belfast, his daughter, Edie. None of them lifted him. She was working so hard it was wearing her out. If the night was to be salvaged at all, they had to put their cards on the table. 'Frank, can I ask you something? Why did you invite me here tonight?'

He blushed. 'I owed you a meal. I wanted to thank you and...I, er...I thought you might like this place.'

'So that's it, two friends sharing a meal?'

'Yes. Well, not quite. I do like you Annette. It's just that ...' he seemed to be searching for the right words.

She offered some to him, 'You're not quite ready for anything more than friends, are you?'

'I'm not sure. I thought I was. Then coming here. It was a mistake.'

'Yes, it was. Why don't we skip dessert and go somewhere else? Somewhere you'd go with a friend. Somewhere you'd never consider taking Ellen to.'

'There is one place. It's an old favourite, but it's a bit scruffy. I only took her once and she vowed never to set foot in there again.'

'Great, let's go there then.'

Annette pushed the door open, and scanned the room for Frank. Anxious to get out of the restaurant, she'd ignored her full bladder. So, as soon as they'd reached the pub, she left him to get the drinks and headed straight for the toilet.

Yes, it really was as grubby as the bathroom suggested it would be. Gentrification was creeping ever closer but, so far, the Hope and Anchor was doing a good job of keeping it at bay. The Victorian stained-glass windows looked reasonably clean, but the nicotine yellow walls had surely not been painted since before the smoking ban. The floor had that sticky sheen that took years of spilt beer to develop. The kind that made it difficult to move on, if you stood in one place for too long.

The pub was close enough to the college and university to be a popular student haunt, but there were also plenty of people in their thirties and forties who had probably been regulars since they were students. All of these social groups seemed to be happily co-existing on a square of lino, the size of a box room, at one end of the lounge. On the edge of it a DJ was pumping out the Stone Roses' 'I Wanna Be Adored.'

Frank was at the bar in conversation with the barman, a big man with a big face, red blotchy skin and very little hair. She approached them from the side, neither noticing her at first.

The big man was talking: 'Chilled rosé? You've gone a bit upmarket haven't you, Frank? Christ, you'll be asking for olive-flavoured crisps next.'

'Just give me the bloody wine will you, Adrian?' said Frank.

'Glass or bottle?'

'Bottle,' said Frank defiantly. 'And two glasses.'

'Funny what a woman can do to you,' said Adrian. 'One minute you're wearing an egg-stained jumper and drinking Bishop's Farewell and the next, you're buying bottles of chilled rosé and running an iron over your shirts. I hope she's worth it, Frank.'

She stepped up into their line of vision to save him the necessity of replying. Adrian gave her a blank smile. He probably hadn't realised she was with Frank. He looked as if he was about to direct her to the nearest cocktail bar.

'I thought we'd have a bottle,' said Frank sounding every bit like a man who drank pink wine as a matter of course. 'Adrian, this is my friend, Annette.'

Adrian held out a hand. 'Very pleased to meet you Annette. One bottle of chilled rosé coming up.' He gave Frank an exaggerated wink. 'I'll put another couple in the fridge for later but don't get too hooked on it, Frank, or I may have to alert the darts club.'

'I was amazed you actually stocked one bottle of wine but you're telling me you have three? I had no idea I was in such a sophisticated establishment,' said Frank.

'Oh yes, we can do sophistication here at the Hope and Anchor. I've got some Kraft slices out the back if you want to make it a cheese and wine party. Just say the word mate. I'll be out there like a shot.'

Annette laughed. 'I can see why you like it here.'

Frank grimaced, 'Sorry about Adrian. He just doesn't know when to shut up.'

'Don't be. He's very funny.'

'And another thing,' called Adrian as they moved to a table. 'Don't try too hard matey. It makes you look like a dick.'

'Thanks for the advice. Please don't be offended if I don't take it.' Frank called back.

Annette took a chair. 'I like this place. It reminds me of the old pubs I used to go to when I was younger.'

He handed her a glass of wine. He was relaxed now. Back to the Frank she knew. 'I know it's a hole but I've been coming here for so long I'm practically part of the furniture. It's always been a bit of a sanctuary for me.'

'From what?'

'Oh, you know. Life and the bad things that happen in it.'

'I suppose we all need a place like that,' she said.

'And where's yours?'

That was a good question. Where was her sanctuary? 'It didn't used to be a physical place. Before I was made redundant, my head was my sanctuary. I lost myself in it when things got too hard. I don't do that anymore. I'm not sure where it is now. Except Aberdovey. Mind you, that's a bit of a drive for a quick spiritual detox isn't it? I'll have to find somewhere a bit closer.'

He looked surprised. 'I wouldn't have had you down for

the kind of person that turns inwards. You seem to be more of a confident, outgoing sort.'

'Do I? It's a bluff. I was, when I was younger but that eroded over time. I stopped being me, I suppose. Things happen and you change, don't you? My ex and his family would say for the better.'

She gave a wry smile as she thought of Colin's well used catchphrase in the early days. *Still you, but better.* 'That dress is still you Annette, but better. That haircut's great. Still you, but better. If only you could tone down the anger, you'd still be you, but better.' It wasn't true. She wasn't better and she wasn't still herself. Toning down the anger didn't make it go away. It just made it less visible to the naked eye.

'For a long time, I let myself believe they were right, but you know, being Mrs Annette Grey was a real drag. I'm steadily working my way back to being more like Netta Wilde. She was much more entertaining.'

She'd never talked to anyone like this before, not even Neil who she had a natural affinity with. Then again, he often sensed what she was thinking anyway so there was no need to talk. She enjoyed getting it out in the open with Frank. Perhaps being friends was the safest option. She hadn't had that many men in her life but, one way or another, they'd been disastrous. Colin was a rebound from Doogie and look how badly that turned out. The few she'd had before them were all of a similar type. Arrogant bastards who thought they were doing her a favour going out with her. And Doogie? She pushed thoughts of him aside. It never did any good to think about Doogie when she'd had a couple of drinks.

Yes, she certainly had a history of choosing hopelessly inappropriate men. The odds were stacked against Frank being any different, although, she did actually like him.

That was more than she could say about most of the others. No. Stick to safe for now. That way she'd always have someone to talk to.

Without notice, she blurted out: 'Yes I think it's best all round if we just keep it platonic.' She realised at once she'd caught him unawares. It seemed she was still getting herself lost in that cobweb strewn brain of hers.

'Yes, I suppose you're right. We get on very well as friends. No need to rock the boat.'

No need to rock the boat. Why did he have to go and say that? That was such an Annette thing to say. The last thing she wanted to do was to steer a steady ship. Sadly, she knew she had to. Neither of them was ready for anything more.

Her attention was caught by a change in the music from eighties indie to eighties pop, and in particular, the song presently playing. It was 'Never Gonna Give You Up.' She screwed up her nose, making him smile.

'I know. It's terrible, isn't it? I hated it then and I hate it now. It's retro night, I think. The kids seem to love it though.' He gestured to the dancefloor where the young people were moving, as lightly as they could on the sticky floor.

'Me too, but Colin loved it. This was his type of music down to a tee. Especially this guy.'

'I thought he was a Clash fan?'

'Not really. At least not when I first met him. Although he did pretend to like them to get into my good books. He was firmly in the mainstream camp. Right up until he rein-vented himself as an artist. It was as if he'd written himself a to-do list for the day after he stopped being an accountant. Overnight, he changed the way he dressed, the books he read and the music he listened to.'

She emptied her glass and watched the wine slosh in as Frank filled it up again. He sat back, seemingly happy for her to continue. She took another swig. It helped loosen the tongue. 'Quite spooky really. Especially since all the things he took up were the ones I'd always liked. Even weirder, it was as if he'd made up his mind only one of us could be that way, and it should be him. He constantly criticised me for being the way I was and, at the same time, appropriated all the things about me that apparently made me a bad person.'

She took another mouthful. 'Mind you, I still occasionally caught him listening to this sort of stuff, if I came home unexpectedly early. No matter how hard he tried, he couldn't let go of the cheese. I think it was his reward to himself for the suffering he put himself through. I used to imagine him in his studio, forcing himself to listen to 'White Riot,' teeth gritted, telling himself it was the music artists listen to. That they really liked this stuff so he would too. He was such a fake.'

Frank smiled. 'I suppose we all are in a way.'

'Do you think so? Are you Frank?'

'Maybe, sometimes. I'll get us another bottle.'

She viewed the empty one with alarm. Finished already? She vaguely remembered sipping it as they talked. For a light drinker she was consuming an awful lot of booze lately. 'Here let me.' She grabbed her purse. It was odd not having to pay for everything. It would take a while to get out of that particular habit.

'Oh no. I owe you lots more than a meal and a few bottles of wine, the number of times you've fed me. Back in a minute.'

It took him longer than that to return. There was a queue and, when his turn came along, Adrian seemed keen to talk. She watched the young people on the dancefloor trying to look ironic while moving to the formulaic rhythms of Stock, Aitken and Waterman. It was way too Colin for her to enjoy.

Just when she thought she couldn't stand anymore, the DJ put on the Happy Mondays, '24 Hour Party People' and the square filled up. It could have been the wine, or even the desire not to be safe anymore. Something drew her over there. The DJ was on a roll now. Next came the Smiths and then the Jesus and Mary Chain. She was twenty again. Cutting loose with Sasha and Claire. Not caring what she did or who was watching. Not worrying about tomorrow and definitely not giving a toss about yesterday.

Frank came up and danced alongside her. His eyes were closed and his face was the image of unadulterated joy. She held her arms aloft and whooped. He opened his eyes and did the same. The others caught on and everyone on the small patch of sticky lino began whooping and cheering and jumping with them. She remembered how good it felt to be one of a pack. Touched by the music and the warmth of belonging to something. In love with the feeling of being alive, and in the moment.

33

THE MORNING AFTER THE DATE THAT
WASN'T

Somehow, they managed to get a taxi back home in one piece. They'd downed the second bottle of wine, and possibly a third, so it was all a bit of a blur. She remembered persuading the DJ to put on some Siouxsie and the Banshees, Sex Pistols and The Clash. She remembered Adrian shaking his head and muttering something about them being sorry in the morning as they left the pub, hot and sweaty. She remembered both those things but, the next morning, she couldn't remember why she'd thought it was a good idea to go into Frank's house rather than go home to bed.

They practically fell out of the taxi into his house.

'Coffee,' he said.

'Yes,' she replied, even though it hadn't been a question.

She was in his kitchen, watching him make it and talking endlessly. She didn't seem to be able to stop herself. Half of it didn't even make sense. She was rambling on about Maud, Edie, her younger self, her life with Colin, the divorce, her time of desolation, her desperation to change, and on it went. Out of the blue he kissed her, quite tenderly, on the lips. It was just one kiss but it stunned her into silence. Perhaps that had been the objective. He looked troubled. Probably worried he'd done something he shouldn't have.

Without any kind of forethought, she took his head in her hands and kissed him back. First on his mouth. Then, all over his face. Then, their lips met again and locked. He wrapped his arms around her and pulled her in to him. She didn't fight it. She wanted it, so much it almost hurt. Like that stab of pain when you suddenly realise how much you've missed something. She began to pull off his clothes, her mouth still on his, her breath heavy and loud. He unzipped her dress and it fell to the floor. They stood together in their underwear, trembling. She put her hand into his pants. He was ready for her. He groaned, as soft as a whisper, as she touched him. They slipped off the underwear and kissed each other's bodies. The sound of their lips smacked audibly against bare skin. She pulled him over to the kitchen table and leant against it. 'Fuck me.' She put his hand in between her legs. She wanted him inside her. She couldn't stop now. She had to have him.

The second time was gentler. They'd gone up to his bed, but they were something close to high and couldn't sleep. They talked about music, and the artists and bands they loved most. Then they talked about writers, books and poetry. In the early hours, it seemed right. Slower and more softly this time. Then, at last, they slept.

He must have woken up first because when she awoke, she was alone. There was a cup of tea on the bedside table next to her. She reached out for it and took a sip. It was warmish. Just about drinkable. The curtains were still closed, giving the room a shadowy appearance. There was just enough light to see it was crammed with furniture. How hadn't she noticed it last night? Too busy being consumed with passion. Passion? That was new. Well, maybe not new but certainly a distant memory.

She slid out of the bed and sat up on the edge and only then did she feel the banging in her head. She had an urge to throw up and was unsure whether to run for the bathroom, or wait for it to subside. Opting for the latter, she sat on the bed until the feeling was gone. One of the disappointing things she'd noticed about her new self was a tendency to drink too much. It wasn't like she did it all the time, but when she did, she really didn't seem to be able to control herself. That was something her old self still found rather repellent. She found her clothes draped across a chair. She was sure she'd left them in the kitchen. He must have put them there for her.

When she was dressed, she opened the curtains and as light filled the room she saw the full extent of the surrounding clutter. Facing the bed was a large gilt-framed mirror resting against the wall, sitting on an antique lacquered dressing table. Both were covered with a thick layer of dust. Directly in front of the mirror was a vintage, art deco glass tray holding pots of creams, perfumes and assorted toiletries. Two trinket jars, one half full with balls of cotton wool and the other holding hair grips and clips, sat next to the tray. Judging by the powdery coating on every piece, none of them had been touched for some time. They were like a very poorly maintained shrine. They had to be Ellen's.

She sensed an emptiness in the house and listened carefully for sounds of movement. There were none so she turned her attention to the rest of the room. A large armoire wardrobe dominated one wall. She peered inside. Aside from a few pieces of women's clothing, it mostly contained Frank's clothes. Her eye was drawn to an exquisitely embroidered, turquoise silk dressing gown next to an equally dazzling burgundy satin dress.

The other dominant piece of furniture was an elegant duck-egg-blue screen in the chinoiserie style. Stacked behind it were several old leather trunks. She opened the top one. It was full of magazines and photos. The photos were mostly of a beautiful flame haired woman in different poses. There were some of her and Frank. As she suspected, he had been a very attractive man in his younger years. There were also some of the woman with a child. A little girl with the same red hair.

Ellen. It had to be. Frank had said a lot about her, but he'd never mentioned what she looked like and there were no photographs downstairs. She flicked through one of the magazines, dated March 1985. A corner had been turned on the fashion pages and she opened it up. There she was, in all her glory. She read the text: '*Ellen wears …*'

She thought she heard a noise downstairs and quickly put everything away. Out on the landing, she listened again. She must have been mistaken. She called out his name but there was no answer. She tried the other bedrooms. One of them clearly belonged to Frank's daughter, Robyn. The other two were full of antique furniture, boxes and wardrobes full of women's clothes. The bathroom was the one room that was must have been his domain. It was clean, tidy, and sparse.

A walk downstairs confirmed her suspicion that Frank wasn't at home. She guessed he'd been too embarrassed to face her this morning and had made himself scarce. That was fine. It would give her the chance to save face too. She checked the time. Eight-thirty. Neither Will or Kelly were early risers. If she hurried, she'd be home before they woke up. She tracked down the rest of her things and left.

34

A HEARTY NOSE FLICK

Annette was sure Frank was avoiding her and, although she wasn't consciously trying to, she thought she was probably avoiding him too. It had been over two weeks since their night out and she'd only seen him in passing, when the others were about. Neither of them had made any effort to catch the other alone. She didn't know how she felt about that. She wanted to see him. Without him around, there was a blank space that she couldn't fill, and everything felt slightly wonky. But that night had frightened her. Or, to put it more plainly, she'd frightened herself. She'd examined the details of her behaviour as they emerged through the fog of her hangover and was shocked by its intensity. Not since Doogie had she been so rampant, so unchecked, and so raw.

Doogie had been both right and wrong about her. She did miss him. She missed the way he egged her on to be spikier and spunkier. He absolutely loved her attitude. Said he had a permanent hard-on whenever she was around him. If she'd looked down far enough at that party, when she was telling him to go fuck himself, she would have probably seen a humungous bulge in his pants. The more she swore at him, the more badly she treated him, the more he was turned on. When they split up, she missed the sex with him. God, did she miss the sex with him. They did it all the time, wherever and whenever they felt like it.

Once, they got caught up in a fight. A group of wankers who didn't like their look, jumped on them. They probably thought a bunch of students would be soft but they were wrong. Doogie and his crowd were more than a match for them. She'd joined in, along with Claire and Sasha. At the sound of police sirens, they scattered in different directions. He grabbed her and they ran off together.

They stopped to let the air back into their lungs by some derelict houses. A thin stream of blood was trickling down from his temple onto his T-shirt. She had this tremendous desire to slide her tongue all the way along his face and lick it off. To savour its metallic tanginess mixed with his salty taste. She'd never been more attracted to him than at that moment. She was so aroused, she pulled him into an entry and they did it there and then against the piss-stained wall. They rutted like animals and she couldn't get enough of it.

Yes, she missed all of that, but she was happy to do without the other things. The way other girls threw themselves at him, even when she was with him. The countless times he stood her up and the nights she spent alone, wondering if he was fucking someone else. She didn't regret leaving that behind. And, in spite of the sex being the best she'd ever experienced, it was getting out of control. Sometimes bordering on violent. So, he was right. She did miss him. Miss it. But she didn't regret leaving either of them behind. Not at first.

She never had it with Colin. That's partly why she took up with him, she supposed. The fear of what it did to her was too great and she chose the safer path. Poor Colin, how it would kill him to know that he was the safe option, even after his artistic rebirth.

Had he already known that? Was that what drove him to his transformation from steady, boring accountant to less steady but still boring, pretentious artist? If so, he'd missed the point. What he didn't realise was that his job had nothing to do with it. It was his mind. They just didn't connect, and never would.

Did he finally get it? Was that when everything changed? Is that why he embarked on a course to systematically grind her down, just to exact his revenge? Surely, even Colin wasn't spiteful enough to be that Machiavellian? No, he wasn't. He needed more than that to tip him over the edge.

She'd been mulling these thoughts over and over since that night with Frank and, in particular, one question had been preoccupying her. Had she been the author of her own downfall? True, Colin had spent years making her feel inadequate but hadn't she struck the first blows? From the moment they met she made it clear he didn't meet her exacting mark. That kind of thing gnaws away at you. It changes you. Whether you want it to or not.

And again, if she hadn't succumbed to the fear of herself. If she'd not chosen to marry Colin, would she have had a better life? Would she have been the person she was when she was Netta Wilde? She wouldn't have had the children but she'd never been a fan of that argument that people, mostly women, put forward about it being all worth it for the kids. *'Wouldn't be without them.'* As if thinking, for a minute, that they might never have existed was a despicable crime that couldn't be contemplated. She dared to think it. Yes, she may have had a better life without him. She may even have met someone more in tune with her. Someone like Frank perhaps. Then again, now that Frank had caught a glimpse of the real her, maybe he'd been put off. Maybe they weren't quite so in tune as she'd assumed.

Thinking about Colin made her realise that the deadline she'd given him had passed and she'd heard nothing from him. There was no way she was going to let him get away with it. Besides, the money would come in very handy. It was time to crack on with it.

She arranged a valuation appointment with the same estate agent she'd used for the flat, then messaged Colin:

'*Haven't heard from you so am assuming you've done nothing re: the house. Estate agent meeting me there tomorrow at 12.00. Be there if you want to.*'

He didn't reply but he'd read it. The little ticks at the side of the message had turned blue. That was enough for her. He didn't need to be there. In fact, she'd rather he wasn't.

Will was in the breakfast room, taking photos on his phone of the puppies. 'Just sending the latest update to Liza. She likes to hear about them.'

Liza hadn't been in touch either. Hopefully, she wouldn't be there tomorrow. It could be quite upsetting for her.

'Will, I'm meeting an estate agent at the house tomorrow. He's going to value it and put it on the market.'

'Okay, cool. Then you'll have a bit more money so you don't have to worry about going back to work yet, right?'

'Yes that's right. Does it bother you. Selling the house, I mean?'

'No. Liza warned me it was going to happen, so I was

prepared for it. It was never really the same after you left anyway.'

His words came as a surprise. 'Oh, I didn't realise my leaving had been so hard for you.' Inside her head, she could see an image of herself, or rather the person she'd like to be, rolling her eyes. Of course she knew, but she'd chosen to ignore it. Once again, she remembered that time at the Rajdoot and them looking back, trying to tell her they were sorry.

'Mum! Really? Honestly, sometimes.' He shook his head, as if he couldn't believe her stupidity.

'Sometimes, I'm rubbish at noticing things. Is that what you meant to say? Was it the same for Liza?'

'What do you think?' He gave her that same look again.

'I don't know Will, I really don't. Like I said, I'm rubbish.'

'No, you're not. You just don't see yourself as other people see you. That's all. Do you want me to come with you tomorrow?'

She knew it was wrong to take comfort in them missing her but she couldn't help it. For a moment, he was her dear little boy again and she wanted to give him a cuddle or pat his head. She was certain he didn't want to go back to the house. Even if she had to face Colin, she didn't really need anyone to provide support. She was strong enough now. But she would ask someone to set his mind at rest. 'No, you don't need to come. It's a good idea though. I'll ask one of my friends to go with me.'

With perfect timing, Frank strode through the gate towards the house. Annette and Will exchanged looks. Considering their eagerness at the time of the date, he and Kelly had been noticeably quiet about it since. They were still in bed when she had crept back into the house that morning. Their questions about how the night went had been very superficial, almost to the point of disinterest. Yet, she was sure she'd caught them secretly discussing it once or twice. And their sly glances when Frank walked by didn't go unnoticed.

'Why not ask Frank? He'd be a good choice,' said Will.

So, she asked him. More to placate Will than anything, but also because it was time for them to have a talk, and the car was as good a place as any to have it.

It seemed Frank had the same idea. As soon as they were up the road, he started talking, 'Sorry I wasn't there that morning, when you woke up. I thought you might want some time to think things over what happened. I suppose, if I'm honest, it took me completely by surprise and I needed to do some thinking as well.'

'It came as a bit of a shock to me too. A nice one though. Sorry if I got a bit forceful. It's been a long time, and the wine. Well, I think it all got the better of me.'

'No, no. It was good, really. You weren't forceful at all. You were great. Fantastic, actually.'

'But I think you're still grieving for Ellen, and anything more than friendship might be too much for you.'

'Is that still what you want? Friendship?' he said.

She sighed. 'I don't know what I want. Except that I don't want to lose someone who's rapidly becoming one of my best friends. I've missed you these last weeks.'

'Oh God, I've missed you too,' he said. 'I think I have feelings for you, Net. Feelings I can't put my finger on yet. Everything's a bit mixed up for me too but if you think friendship is best for us right now, then I'll take that.'

'That sounds good. Why don't we take things slowly and

see where it leads us to?'

'That's a capital idea.'

'And please come back over for dinner. I'm making far too much food for three.'

'Okay.' He turned his attention to the passing traffic. 'About Ellen. It was complicated. She was complicated. It has made it hard to move on. Robyn's been going on at me for ages to sort through her mum's things. She's coming home for a long weekend. I've asked her to take a few days off to help me clear them all out. I expect she'll want some of Ellen's furniture and clothes. All that antique stuff was hers. She had great taste, unlike me. I'm a bit of a duffer when it comes to that sort of stuff.'

'That's good. If you're ready for it, that is,' said Annette.

'I think I am, and I'd like you to meet Robyn. She's a great girl.'

The estate agent had already tried the doorbell and was waiting for them when they arrived. Annette let them in. There was no reply when she called out to see if anyone was there. She took the agent around the house herself. Arianne's things were scattered about the main bedroom. It looked like she'd taken up permanent residency.

Frank waited downstairs. He found his way to the studio. After they'd finished touring the rest of the house, they joined him in there.

'Nice studio,' he said.

'We had it converted from the old garage especially for Colin,' said Annette. The fact that she'd paid for it irked her even more, now that she knew what Colin had done.

'Well, it's Moseley. We do have a lot of artistic people around here,' said the agent. 'It's light and airy and the view of the garden is nice. It would make a good garden room or playroom. I think we should market it as both. Top trumps, Mrs Grey. This is a very desirable house. Even more so than your apartment.'

They went back into the hall. The agent was still talking. 'You'll have no trouble selling it at the price we've agreed. I'll get the ball rolling, shall I?'

The front door opened and in walked Colin, unshaven and greasy-haired. He was normally so meticulous about his appearance that it came as a shock.

'Colin. Great timing,' said Annette. 'I was about to tell Mr Locke to put the house on the market. You'll be pleased to hear, it's worth a lot more than when we bought it.'

He grimaced. 'I've made arrangements to buy you out so, there'll be no need to put the house up for sale. Sorry to have wasted your time, mate.'

'I was just saying, you'll get a buyer. No problem,' said the agent.

'We're not selling,' said Colin.

'Right. Well, if you change your mind.' The man wasn't giving up without a fight.

Colin held the door open for him. 'I won't be changing my mind.'

'Well that rather depends,' said Annette.

Colin shot her an icy stare. 'No it doesn't.'

'It depends on what you're prepared to offer me,' said Annette. She shook the agent's hand. 'Thanks for coming Mr Locke. Could you send me your valuation over as soon as? I'll be in touch.'

Colin closed the door on the agent. 'I'll want a second valuation, naturally. I'll arrange it.'

'And I want proof that you've been arranging to buy me out,' she said.

He loomed over her. 'Are *you* calling *me* a liar?'

From the corner of her eye she could see Frank edging towards her. Bless him. He was preparing to protect her. She pushed her shoulders back. 'I'm saying I want proof.'

He muttered something under his breath and pulled a piece of paper from his back pocket. He shook it open and slapped the back of it with his hand, 'This do for you?'

She cast her eyes over it. It appeared to be a letter from his solicitor confirming that he'd instructed them to act on his behalf. 'It's a start.' She took a photograph of it on her phone. 'You have two weeks to get another valuation. You can mail it to me and I'll send you Mr Locke's. Then we can get this thing moving.'

'Don't worry, it'll be done. As usual, I'll do your dirty work and mop up the chaos you've left behind. Poor Liza, she's —'

'No Colin. Don't even try to drag me into your guilt trip. I know, and so do the kids, that you wouldn't think twice about using them if you needed to. So, don't tell me they're your main concern because, if you do, I may be driven to no other recourse than punching you in the face.'

He sneered at Frank. 'So, now we see the real Annette coming out. Just as psycho as the day I met her. I tried to help you grow into a decent human being, but you just can't help reverting back to type, can you? You'd better watch it mate. She'll fuck you over before you know it. And just when you think she can't push your face in the dirt any more, she'll put her foot down on you and shove it in further.'

She took a step closer to him, so close she could feel his short, panicky breath blowing into her eyes. There was a film of sweat above his top lip and a smell coming off him like stale whisky. She lifted her hand and flicked his nose with her forefinger. He jerked back with a surprised start.

'Fuck off Colin.'

Whether it was the last defiant flick, or the whole scene that had amused Frank, she wasn't sure but he'd definitely been tickled. He spent the entire return journey chuckling to himself.

'I seem to have given you cause for amusement, Mr O'Hare,' she said, trying to keep a straight face.

'I'm sorry but it was hilarious. Especially that last bit. I hadn't realised you were such a tough woman. If ever I need defending with a hearty nose flick, I shall know where to come.'

They were so taken over by hysterics that she had to stop the car. Water was streaming down her cheeks and her nose was running. It was comical, no doubt about it, but it was also exhilarating. So positive. All these positive things that were happening to her these days. They were making her so light. So very much lighter. Almost featherweight.

He handed her a handkerchief. She wiped her eyes and blew her nose. 'It may have been entertaining, but I can't tell you how brilliant it felt.'

'You don't need to. I can see that. Seriously though. That man is terrified of you.'

'Colin? No. He towers over me.'

'Height's got nothing to do with it. I saw the fear in his eyes. I'm absolutely sure he's afraid of you.'

Could that be? Surely not. Frank must have misread the signals. Anyway, it didn't matter now. She'd stood up to Colin and he'd done nothing to come back at her. All those years worrying about that very moment and when it happened? Nothing. She got away with it.

She kissed Frank. 'Thank you for being there. It was nice to have you as my wing man.'

'Even if you didn't need one?'

'Even if I didn't need one.' She held out the soggy hand-kerchief, then changed her mind. 'I might just give this a wash first.'

'Probably for the best. What was all that nonsense about shoving his face in the dirt by the way? What on earth did you do to the man?'

They pulled up outside the house. Her dad was tidying the front garden and gave them a wave. The moment was gone.

35

THE DAUGHTER AND THE DAUGHTER
FROM ANOTHER MOTHER.

'Everything go all right?' Her dad sounded apprehensive.

'Yep. He says he's going to buy me out. I've given him two weeks to set it in motion.'

'Good girl.' He gestured towards the house, 'We brought someone with us.'

'Who?'

'Go in and see,' he said. 'Come and have a look at this rose bush Frank. I think it's got mildew.'

If her dad wasn't telling, it could only mean one person. She left Frank to examine the rose bush and went in the house, down the hall towards the kitchen, doing her best to maintain a casual air. *Don't walk too fast. Don't look too excited.* All the same, her heart was racing and that speedy, pulsating thump, thump, thump was vibrating throughout her body. She was aware of voices as she approached the kitchen but the thumping had filled her ears too, and everything else was white noise.

From the doorway, she scanned the room. No one new in there. Just the usual faces. They stopped talking and looked up at her. Neil came over and took her hands. 'Slow down. Breathe,' he whispered.

She acknowledged him with a blink, then slowly took in the air until the inner noise subsided.

He kissed her cheek. 'In the breakfast room.'

They didn't hear her tiptoeing in. She stood for a minute, hardly believing what was in front of her. Her daughter. Her darling girl, had come to see her at last. Just when she'd given up hope. Tears of joy were pricking at her eyes but she forced them back down. She didn't want to ruin everything with her silliness.

Her mother was cooing over the puppies in the armchair. 'That one's my favourite. I call her Minnie, because she reminded me of a little mouse when she was tiny. She looks more like her father now.'

Liza was sitting on the floor with Minnie in her arms. 'She's so cute. They're all beautiful.'

Annette perched on the arm of her mother's chair. 'They are, aren't they? I don't know how I'm going to part with them. Hello darling. It's so nice to see you.'

'Liza's staying with us for a few days while her dad sorts a few things out,' said her mum. 'We thought she might like to see the puppies, as we were coming over to help out.'

'Yeah, well it was either come here or be on my own all day,' said Liza.

Her mum stroked Liza's hair. 'That is true. I did say, we tend to spend all day here when it's a big jam-making session. Now you've seen them, I'm sure you're glad you came.'

'Well I'm certainly glad you did,' said Annette. 'Where's Will? Does he know you're here?'

Her mum stood up. 'Not yet. He's gone with Kelly and Chris to meet someone. Malcolm was it? He's lending them a van to pick up the fruit. There's quite a lot apparently. Good job we've brought an extra hand today. Right, I'll go and get stuck in.' She gave Annette a sly wink. 'Five more minutes, young lady and then it's time to earn your keep.'

Liza pulled a face and went back to stroking Minnie. Annette mouthed a silent thank you and slid into the armchair. She scratched Maud behind the ear. The dog gave a contented groan and leaned in for more. 'How have you been, darling?'

'All right. Back to school next week though. Boring.'

'Have you seen much of your friends over the summer?'

'Some of them. The real ones. Being a pauper sorts out the ones that don't really care about you.'

Annette forced back a sudden pang of guilt. 'You know you're not really a pauper, don't you?'

Liza snuggled the puppy in her lap. 'I know. There's no need to get all Mother Teresa on me. It's just a point of view. I'm not trying to get the sympathy vote or anything. I know there are people starving in Africa.'

'Liza, there are people starving in Britain. I see them every week.'

'Yeah. Will told me. He's really into that stuff now. It's like he's found his thing. I suppose that makes you happy?'

'Yes, it does. And, you make me happy too. I'm really happy to see you. Even if Nanny did drag you here.'

'She didn't have to drag very hard. I wanted to come. I wanted to see the puppies and Maud. And Will. She paused. And you. I've got to say though, this place is a bit of a hovel.'

'Oi Princess, watch yer fucking mouth. Some of us call

this hovel a home.' Kelly was behind them, arms folded, nostrils flaring.

Will stood next to her, a big grin on his face.

'Oh my God,' said Liza. 'I'm so sorry, I didn't mean it to come out like that.'

Will hugged his sister. 'Take no notice of Kelly. She's not really as fierce as she pretends to be. You came Lize. Brilliant.'

'I suppose we have let the sorting out go a bit, in the rest of the house, and the place is full of jam and jars,' said Annette. 'We've just been too busy. All our cleaning time is spent on the kitchen and storage areas to keep up with hygiene regulations. No time for anything else.'

'More important things to worry about Mum. Malcolm's here and we've got a shitload of fruit to bring in.'

A shitload? That was new. He was definitely spending too much time with Kelly.

'Clyde's brought some friends to help,' he added. 'Oh, and Colonel's here for his daily visit.'

Colonel romped into the room. He rubbed noses with Maud, inspected his children and dropped down next to them.

Liza's eyes opened wide. 'Is that the —?' Annette, Kelly and Will nodded their heads in unison. 'How?'

'Latest theory,' said Will, 'is that she stood on a chair.'

They worked without a break for the rest of the afternoon. By the time they'd finished, half of the fruit was used up. The rest would be gone by tomorrow evening. Chris had the barbecue already fired up and the music was playing. They carried the big kitchen table outside and sat around it to make the most of the late summer evening.

Malcolm flopped down onto a chair. He and Frank had been playing football with Kendrick and Shani. The kids were still bouncing around but the two men looked done in.

Annette sat down next to him. There was something she'd been meaning to say to him for a while. 'How are you doing Malcolm?'

He blew air out of his mouth. 'I've just realised how unfit I am but other than that, I'm great. And you. How are you doing Annette?'

'I'm doing great too. Actually Malcolm, I wanted to thank you.'

'Oh, it's nothing. You know we hardly ever use the vans at the weekend.'

'No, not for that,' she said. 'Although, thank you for picking up the fruit. No. I wanted to thank you for making me redundant. And for asking Paula to look after me.'

'Well, that's a first,' he said. 'I don't think I've ever had someone thank me for giving them the push before. You know I never wanted to let you go, don't you?'

'Yes. I realise that now but actually, it was the best thing you could have done for me. Without it I wouldn't have had all of this.'

He grinned at her. 'Well thank you for the thank you. While we're on the subject, I should say the same to you. I'd been kicking the dust around, pretty much doing nothing with my life, since my divorce. It was all very amicable so I wasn't expecting it to, but it hit me hard. And I don't see so much of my boys now that they're grown up and have their own lives. I guess you could say I was struggling to cope with life alone. The foodbank and the job club. They've really helped. So, thank you.'

She vaguely remembered Malcolm's divorce when she was still at Masons. She had no inkling that he was having problems dealing with it. He never said. More to the point, she never asked. 'I had no idea Malcolm. I'm so sorry I should have picked up on that.'

'Not at all,' he said. 'I did all I could to hide it. Got to man up, and all that. Anyway, it's all behind me now. Not only has that place given me something to focus on, it's also given me a new relationship. Do you remember Melanie?'

'The Christmas kisser?'

He nodded his head, 'The Christmas kisser. Such a lovely lady. Fingers crossed.'

'Fingers crossed,' she said, and she meant it.

Knowing how these barbecues usually went, her parents came prepared and brought an overnight bag with them. Liza didn't look too convinced at first but when Will suggested she shared his room, it won her round. She must have been missing him.

The next morning, they all breakfasted together in the kitchen. Annette still couldn't quite believe it was happening. All her family were together, including Kelly who was currently making her status quite plain to Liza.

'Yeah, I'm like Net's daughter from another mother.'

Once again, Annette remembered the telephone conversation at Christmas and Liza accusing her of taking no time to find someone to replace them. She held her breath and waited for the backlash. Liza stuffed toast into her mouth and said nothing.

'What's that supposed to mean?' asked Annette's mum.

'It's just another way of saying they're really close,' said Will. 'So close they could be mother and daughter.'

'I see. And that's all right with you two is it?' said her mum.

'Yeah,' said Will. 'No problem for me. Pretty accurate, I'd say.'

Kelly gave him a peck. 'Aw Wills. I'm touched. I might even cry.'

'Oh, please don't, or I might have to reassess,' he said.

She punched him in the arm.

'Oh, now I'm definitely going to have to reassess.'

All eyes turned to Liza, still chewing on her toast. It was hard to tell which way this was going to go. Will eyebrows rose upwards and his head gave a slight nod at his sister.

She mirrored his gesture and coughed down the last of her mouthful. 'Yeah, it's cool, Nan. Really. Mum, I don't know what happened to you, and I can't believe I'm saying this by the way, but you got really cool.'

'Er, correction. She's always been cool,' said Kelly.

Liza and Will exchanged looks again. 'Nah.'

36

CONFUSION AND FORGIVENESS

Robyn was almost a carbon copy of her mother. At least, that was Annette's impression from the stolen glimpses of Frank's hidden photographs. The most noticeable thing about her was not her hair, the colour of burnt copper. Or her fair skin, decorated with a myriad of pale freckles. It was her arresting grey eyes, sprinkled with flecks of gold, that seemed to change colour when the patchy sun hit them, so that it was hard to pin down an actual shade. There seemed to be nothing of Frank in her appearance, except her height. Annette imagined how he must have felt when he first met Ellen. No wonder he couldn't let her go.

'Annette, it's so great to meet you. Dad's told me loads about you. Come in, please.'

Robyn took her into the lounge. It was normally reasonably tidy compared to her own. Today it was overflowing with boxes, books and objects, none of which she could recall seeing before.

Robyn waved her arms at her mother's memorabilia. 'Ignore the mess. We brought some stuff downstairs so we could sort through them in comfort. Our backs were aching up there. There's no room to do anything other than crouch in between the junk. There's just so much of it. My mum and Edie had a lot in common. I hear you've been working your way through her stuff.'

'Still a good way to go. Too many other things to distract me,' said Annette.

'Yes, Dad told me all about the jam making, and the foodbank. And the barbecues.' So much information. What else had Frank had told her? 'He's just gone to the charity shop. He'll be back soon.'

'Don't be afraid to ask if you need any help. Your dad's been so kind to me. It's the least I can do.'

'I'll give you a shout if it we do, but I think we're good,' said Robyn. 'I hope you don't mind me saying so Annette, but meeting you has been really good for Dad. It's great to see him so upbeat. He's been down for so long. I'd almost forgotten what he was like, happy.'

'I suppose it's to be expected though. He seems to have found it very hard to come to terms with the loss of your mum. I think he still misses her very much.'

Robyn's smile shifted. 'Does he? Are you sure?'

Annette shifted uncomfortably on her feet. 'Well, yes. Well, that's what I thought. You don't seem to think so, and you know him much better than me. Have I misunderstood?'

'Does he talk much about her then?'

'Quite a lot. She never seems far away from his thoughts. And then there's all her things. He seems to have really struggled to let go. But then, I imagine, it's not that easy to move on when you lose someone you care so deeply for.'

Robyn frowned. 'Things are not always as they seem. Talk to Dad. No wait. I'll talk to Dad.' She looked hesitant, then smiled. 'You really are good for him Annette. I'm so glad he found you.'

How could she respond to that? She made it sound like a big romance. A life-saver even. What had Frank told her? She settled on: 'He's been a great friend to me too,' realising by Robyn's expression that it had failed to meet her expectations. 'I mean, we're taking things slowly. Very slowly. We don't want to ruin a great friendship.' She was rambling now. Digging herself a large hole. 'I'm holding you up. I just came over to invite you both for dinner tonight, if you don't have other plans. Nothing fancy. Just a big pot of pasta. There'll be a few of us there.'

Just a big pot of pasta. A few of us there. She marvelled at the ease with which these phrases rolled off her tongue nowadays. It was as if she'd said them all her life.

Back in her own house, operations were running like a well-oiled machine. Kelly, Will and Neil were in the process of sticking the new labels on jars in different bedrooms. Using a separate room for each of the more plentiful fruits was the best way they had of avoiding confusion. The three main bedrooms had been renamed by the flavour of the jam stored in it. Plum, strawberry and blackcurrant. Downstairs, the study was now the rhubarb room. The lounge was the cherry room and the kitchen, just gooseberry. The larder had smaller stacks of less abundant produce and 'mixes' like apple and blackberry, rhubarb and ginger, plum and lemon verbena. They kept going until every jar was professionally and legitimately labelled, stacked and packed.

They had another two fairs to go to over the weekend. It was Thursday. Tomorrow they would all be too busy at the foodbank so everything had to be ready to grab and go, early on Saturday and Sunday morning.

Thanks to Neil, they were so much more professional

than when they'd first started out. They were now the proud owners of a food hygiene certificate and had taken out insurance. Since they'd decided to stick to church and small craft fairs, neither were really compulsory but they'd agreed to dip their toes in, to test the waters of going fully pro. They were even considering applying for a trader's licence so that they could apply for pitches in farmers' markets. One step at a time though. For now, they were happy to carry on for the rest of the summer, doing what they were doing and just breaking even.

It was also Liza's first day back at school. Annette tapped out a quick message to see how it went. She'd sent another, the night before, to wish her good luck. It was a bit over the top but she wanted to make sure the lines of communication remained open and she liked the feel of having her daughter with her. If not physically, then on the end of a line and talking to her.

A message came straight back. It had gone well. New form teacher was nice. New friend would like to see the puppies, if that was okay?

She tapped in a reply to say that was fine.

While she may not have looked like Frank, there was definitely something of his personality in Robyn. She had the same effortless charm and warmth. They came to dinner for the next two nights and on Saturday and Sunday, when they arrived back tired and worn out, she and Frank had dinner waiting for them. Everyone fell just a little bit in love with Robyn, including Kelly who was quite awestruck in her company. Having never shown the remotest interest in fashion before, Kelly developed a liking for vintage clothing overnight, thanks to Robyn. Between them they decided it would be a great idea to go through Edie's and Ellen's wardrobes on Monday afternoon. If Annette didn't mind.

'I think Edie would have been thrilled if you managed to find something worth wearing in there,' she said, 'She must have kept all those clothes for some reason. I'm pretty sure some of them pre-date her. Let me tell Liza though. She might like a rummage in there too. I'll see if she wants to come over after school.'

She had no idea if Liza liked vintage clothes. She'd never seen her wearing any, but it was a good excuse to call her. 'Just wanted to let you know that Kelly and Robyn are going through Edie's and Ellen's wardrobes tomorrow afternoon. They think there might be some nice vintage pieces in there. Did you know Robyn's mum was a model? I thought you might want to come along.'

'Yeah, okay. Sounds good. Can I bring Jade, my new friend?' said Liza.

'Yes, of course you can. I'll pick you up from school and drop you both back home after dinner, if you want?'

'Cool. I'll call her now and see if she can make it. Either way, I'll come. See you tomorrow.'

To her relief, Jade was a nice girl. Sure, some of Liza's other friends were nice enough but they had an expectation about them. An expectation that you would like them because they were pretty and well dressed. An expectation that they would have whatever they asked for. Jade seemed different. She was polite and self-confident without being arrogant. Liza was different with her too. There was a notable absence of the tension that was quite often present when she was with her wealthier friends. The girls were lying on their fronts on the floor, inches away from Maud's sleeping babies, running their fingers along the puppies' backs.

'Oh my God, they are so sweet,' said Jade. 'Liza, you're so lucky. Is it all right if I show them to my mum when she comes to pick me up, Mrs Grey?'

'Yes sure, but I really don't mind dropping you off,' said Annette. 'It's no trouble.'

'Oh, I know but I only live up the road. Mum said she'd pick me up on the way back from Pilates, as she's passing the door. There's just me and her and she doesn't like me to be at home on my own.'

When Jade's mum Jackie arrived, the girls brought her through to see the pups.

'They're adorable,' she said. 'Bit of a handful I expect?'

'It's not so bad now they're getting bigger,' said Annette. 'I've got Will and Kelly here to lighten the load. They've started to house train them now which will be much better, when they get the hang of it. I think one of them will stay with us. I'm under pressure to keep one. I expect it will be a lot bigger than Maud though, given the size of Colonel. That's the father.'

'Colonel? Isn't that Clyde Wilson's dog?' said Jackie.

'Yes, do you know Clyde?'

'Yes, very well. I was at school with one of his daughters, Sharon. We're still good friends. I grew up just around the corner. My mum still lives there. We moved back here from Coventry to be closer to her. Small world eh? Actually Annette, I've got a confession to make. When Jade told me where you lived, I just had to come back and take a look.'

'Come back? You've been here before then?'

'Sharon and me used to come here all the time when we were kids. Edie was such a nice lady. Her parents were alive then and they liked to have us all round. Every year they'd

have a big Christmas party for all the kids in the neighbourhood. Old Mr Pinsent used to dress up as Father Christmas
and hand out little presents. They were so lovely. It's nice to
be back here again.'

When Jade left, she took with her a bag of old clothes
and jewellery. Then it was time to take Liza home. It was
just the two of them in the car. Liza was cradling her take-
home bundle.

'Did you enjoy yourself?' said Annette.

'Yeah, it was great. Robyn is so beautiful. She could
easily be a model but she's not interested. She said she'd
much rather be doing something with her brain. She's really
cool,' said Liza.

'Yes, she is. I didn't realise Jade lived so close to me.
She's nice. I like her.'

'Yeah, she is. I didn't realise either. She just moved here
in the summer holidays so she doesn't have any other
friends. She seemed a bit alone on our first day back so I,
kind of, took her under my wing. We just clicked, straight
away. Actually, I was thinking I could come and stay at yours
sometimes. So I can hang out with her a bit more.'

'Absolutely. Anytime you want, darling. Anytime.'
Annette whispered a silent thank you to Jade.

They pulled up outside the house. She could see
shadows in the lounge window. Annette switched off the
engine and took a deep breath. She'd been building herself
up to this moment and she didn't want to ruin it with her
nervousness. 'Liza, before you go, there's something I
wanted to say. I think you've been angry with me for some
time and, I wanted to say, that I understand and that it's all
right. I wanted to say I'm sorry for not always being the
easiest mum to be with. I'm sorry for only giving you money
when what you really wanted was my love, and attention.

And I'm sorry it's taken me this long to say it. And that it's taken me this long to tell you that I've always loved you very much.'

Liza fiddled with the ruby-red ring sitting on her finger. Part of her afternoon's haul.

'It's a gorgeous ring,' said Annette.

'Yeah,' said Liza, in a small breathy voice.

Annette took hold of her hand and kissed it.

Liza looked out towards the lounge window. 'I'm not angry anymore.' She reached over and kissed Annette's cheek, then got out of the car.

Annette touched the soft part of her face where her daughter had placed her lips. How long since she'd kissed her like that, unprompted? Two years? Three? Longer. She watched Liza walking slowly towards the front door, willing her to look back. After what seemed like an age, Liza found her key and rewarded her with a quick wave. The relief came out as a long sigh. She waved back as the door closed. The curtains twitched and the shadows moved away from the window.

37

FRANK TELLS THE TRUTH

The last bit of sunshine was sending its rays directly down to her. Well, that's what it felt like anyway. As her eyes were closed, she couldn't actually see if it was doing the same to the rest of the garden. Her back ached and her feet were on fire. She eased the feet out of the shoes that had been rubbing her all day and put them up on the chair in front of her. There wasn't much she could do about the back-ache except plump up the cushions and settle herself into them.

It had been another busy day at the foodbank. In the last three weeks, every day had been busy. Neil told her it was the back-to-school effect, 'It's an expensive time.'

She got that, but she didn't see why people had to be so hostile about it. Not just to her but to others in the same situation. Today, they'd had to break up a fight over a box of Rice Krispies, for God's sake. Today was the kind of day that made her question whether she was cut out for the foodbank. Whether she shouldn't just get another job and be done with it. If Colin didn't hurry up with that money, she'd have to get one anyway so why not just do it? Because she still couldn't face it. That was the truth of it. And because, in spite of the odd bad day at the foodbank, it gave her a completeness that nothing else could. Not even her old job.

As always, Paula gave some sense to her thoughts, 'It's okay to get fed up with it sometimes. It shows you've moved on. It's easy when you first get into this to think of them all as martyrs but they're just ordinary people, like us, who happen to be worse off financially. Like us, some customers are pleasant and others are real pains in the arse.'

The sound of ice clinking against glass made her open one eye and then the other. Frank was sauntering through the gate with a jug of Pimm's and two glasses. 'I thought you might like a nice cold drink to revive you,' he said.

'You have no idea,' she said. 'Are we celebrating something?'

'Well, since I've just dropped Robyn off at the airport, it was intended as more of a pick-me-up but, come to think of it, it is a bit of a celebration too. I think I'm moving on, at last.'

That phrase made her smile. It took her back to her half-birthday. She made a bet with herself that Frank would be the sort of man who wouldn't care if she had croissant pastry stuck to her face. She was sure of it. She would have to test him out sometime. They sat, side by side, watching the sun descending behind his house.

'Ellen was a difficult woman to live with,' he said after a long silence. 'For years, I just thought it was her upbringing that made her that way. Her parents were moneyed. Very posh. Very cold. And she was used to getting her own way. Incredibly spoilt.'

She put down her glass. She didn't want to interrupt him but she wanted to show he had her full attention.

'It was very hard on our marriage. We argued such a lot. We were at the point of calling it a day when she fell pregnant with Robyn. So, we agreed to give it another go. We thought having a child would change everything for the better, but it didn't. We tried to make it work but she just got increasingly irritable and spiteful. Mostly with me but sometimes with Robyn. Her moods were all over the place. I was in denial about the state of her mental health for years but eventually it dawned on me that she was probably sick. I begged her to go to the doctor so many times but she flat out refused.'

He poured himself another drink. Instead of drinking it, he ran his fingers around the edge of the glass. 'One day, she walked out. I came back from work and she was gone. She sent us one letter saying she'd moved to France and didn't want us to contact her. We didn't hear from her for nearly five years after that which, to be honest was a relief for both of us. Once we got used to the idea she wasn't coming back. Then, out of the blue, she turned up with her suitcases, announcing that she'd come home. She still had her door key. She just walked in and sat down, as if she'd only popped out to the shop half an hour ago. It was the most bizarre thing. I was so stunned, I didn't know what to say, or do.'

So, that was what Robyn was hinting at. That was why she seemed so surprised by Annette's assumptions. Sensing there was more to come, she said nothing and waited for him to continue.

'Rob was at uni by then. I called her and she was mad as hell. She came straight home and had the most furious row with Ellen. I just stood by like some dumbstruck idiot still trying to comprehend what was happening. That's when it came out. She said she'd gone to a doctor in France. She'd been diagnosed as bipolar but was stable, thanks to the medication. I always thought she left me for someone else but she said she went away because she was afraid that she might harm Robyn.'

Annette whistled through her teeth. 'That was quite a sacrifice. Not many people could do that.'

He took a mouthful of Pimm's. 'After that announcement, what else could I do? I had to let her stay. I got it into my head that she needed someone to take care of her, and I wanted to do it. I felt I should have done more to help her in the first place. It was my way of making it up to her. She was here for nearly a year. Long enough for she and Robyn to reach something of a reconciliation, and long enough for me to be reminded of the girl I fell in love with.'

'But I thought. I mean, you said she was here for nearly a year?' said Annette.

'Yeah. One day she was gone again. Just like that. She went back to France. That's where she killed herself. A couple of days after we got the news, we had a letter from her. She said she'd always loved us and asked for forgiveness. We had the funeral over there. When I went over to arrange everything, I found she'd been living with someone all the time she was there and she went back to him when she left us. The poor guy was distraught. In a terrible state. Not only did he find her, but she never told him about me and Rob. He knew nothing about her mental health problems either. She kept us all in the dark.'

He went to take another drink, then stopped himself. 'I still don't know to this day if she really was bipolar but I'm absolutely certain there was something wrong with her. As I said before, she was complicated.'

'Frank, that's such a tragic story. I thought you'd always been happy together. I completely misunderstood,' she said.

'Not your fault. It's all me. I just wanted to remember the best of her. It was a kind of coping mechanism, I guess. Over time, the dark side of her merged into the background. As Robyn put it when she gave me a bollocking, I'd overwritten the reality of living with Ellen and made everything out to be rosy.'

'Very sensible girl, your daughter. What else did she say?'

'That you were under the impression I was too in love with Ellen to make a go of things with you. And, if I didn't start telling the truth I was in danger of losing you. And if that happened, I'd only have myself to blame for being such a delusional old eejit. Or words to that effect.'

Annette laughed. 'Kids eh? So bloody clever.'

He screwed up his face. 'I didn't mean to lie to you. I was actually planning to tell you the truth that night we went out but I just couldn't find the right moment. Then, I was going to tell you the next morning. I went off for a walk to build myself up to it, but when I got back you were gone. If ever there'd been a need to leave a note, that was the perfect example. I am a first-class fool. But you know now. We have no secrets.'

'No secrets,' she repeated, taking a mouthful of cold Pimm's.

The sun had all but gone. Its very tip slid behind the rooftop and it disappeared completely taking with it the heat. She felt the goose pimples rising to the surface of her limbs and shivered.

38

THE GOLEM'S REVENGE

It was an early start the next morning. They had an autumn fair to go to at a church near Moseley Village. Why it was called that when it quite clearly hadn't been a village for a very long time was a thing that puzzled Annette, even as a child.

'I expect it's because it makes it feel homelier,' said Granny Wilde when she'd questioned it way back then.

When she was a teenager, it had a crusty underbelly that felt quite subversive. Home, but never homely. It was only when she moved into Moseley, close to the actual 'village,' that she felt as far away from home as it was possible to be. In truth though, that wasn't really Moseley's fault. Standing behind their stall and talking to the good people of the area who were buying their jams, she realised now, she'd given Moseley Village a bad rap. It was actually quite nice. It *was* actually quite homely, in a gentrified, big-city-bohemian kind of way.

It seemed Moseley quite liked them too or rather, their jams. They were going down well enough to make them worry that they hadn't brought enough stock with them which was a first. Some of the customers looked familiar.

'That last women said she'd bought some off us at one of the summer fairs,' said Neil. 'We must be getting some returners.'

'That's great,' said Annette. 'They must think they're good.'

'Yeah,' said Kelly. 'Look, keep an eye on this bloke coming over. He's already been here twice and tried every sample. He's taking the piss if he comes back for more and don't buy nothing.'

'Maybe he's hungry,' said Neil.

Kelly huffed. 'Fucks sake Neil. Does he look like he can't afford a decent breakfast?'

They watched the man come back and try each sample again. Kelly bristled. Annette and Neil each put a calming hand on her.

'Any you like in particular?' said Neil.

The man gave him a startled look, as if it was the first time he'd noticed the three of them. He cast his eyes across the full gamut of jars on the stall, 'They're all pretty decent. You been doing this long?'

'Not long. It's a new venture,' said Annette.

'Shops? You selling in any shops?'

'No. We're just a small outfit,' said Neil.

'Just the three of you is it?'

They nodded. Well, Neil and Annette nodded. Kelly continued to scowl.

'Interested in selling in any shops?' he said.

'Er, possibly,' said Neil. 'We haven't given it much thought. We've been trying to grow organically.'

The man rummaged in his pocket and pulled out a card,

'I've got a couple of little shops. Delis really. I'm always on the lookout for independents with a good, quality product. Give me a call.'

'Trying to grow organically? What the fuck was that about?' said Kelly when the man had gone.

They all laughed.

'I couldn't think what else to say,' said Neil. He read the card. 'What do you think? Should we go and see him?'

She knew what he was asking. This was more than just making a few extra jars when they felt like it. This was a commitment, 'It wouldn't hurt to talk to him, I suppose. If you're ready for it?'

'I think I am,' he said. 'Are you?'

'I think so.'

'In case anyone's interested, so am I. Thanks for asking,' said Kelly.

When they packed up, there were only a few jars left. It was the best they'd ever done. What with that, and the prospect of new business, things were looking quite rosy. Annette left Neil to make the call and arrange the visit. She asked him to talk it over with Chris first, before making a decision. 'Whatever you decide is fine with me,' she told him. She wanted him to be in control of it so that it didn't overwhelm him. She didn't say that, as such, but he understood.

The three of them parted ways. Kelly had managed to get a few hours work with a taxi firm, rivals of Craig's uncle, and she was heading straight there. Annette had promised to pick Liza up in a couple of hours. Hardly any point in going home. It was a dry day. Still warm for September. She decided to take a walk around her old neighbourhood.

Normally she went out of her way to avoid it in case she bumped into Colin, or some of their old so-called friends but the morning had gone so well, nothing could dampen her spirits now.

She browsed the shops and restaurants, stopped for a coffee and poked her nose around the door of the Fighting Cocks, the first pub she and Claire blagged their way into at sixteen. It was a bit less spit and sawdust these days but it was still the same old Fighting Cocks. She ambled along the streets, recalling the good times with Claire. She was in a happy place.

She reached the corner of her old road. She hadn't purposefully meant to come here but then again, she was here, of her own free will. That had to count for something and, fun as it was, there was only so much time you could spend wandering around the streets. She might as well knock on the door and see if Liza was there and ready to go.

It took a while for someone to stir, first at the lounge window, then in the hallway.

Arianne opened the door, 'Yes?' She was encased in lycra. Black leggings and a Day-Glo vest, cocooning that substantial bosom of hers. Her hair was bundled into a knot on the top of her head. Her eye makeup was smudged on account, no doubt, of the sweat leaking from her brow.

'Is Liza at home?' said Annette.

'No.'

'Do you know when she'll be back?'

'No.'

'Do you know where she is?'

'No.'

'Well then is Colin in?'

'No.'

She was really beginning to piss Annette off. 'Look, you seem to have a problem—'

'Oh fuck off.' Arianne slammed the door but Annette was too quick. She shoved her foot in the way before it closed. Arianne kept on pushing, ramming it up against her toes. The pain was becoming quite unbearable.

'Will you just stop,' shouted Annette. With both hands, she gave the door a shove forcing Arianne back into the hall. She stepped in and shut the door.

'I'll call the police. I'm calling Colin,' said Arianne, running into the lounge.

Annette followed her. There was a small trampoline in the middle of the room. Arianne placed herself behind it and grabbed her mobile. She stabbed at the phone with her forefinger then put it to her ear while holding up her free arm, palm facing Annette, as if it were a shield. The house was quiet, except for the sound of Colin's answerphone message. 'Colin, I'm being attacked by your ex-wife. Come home now!' she hissed.

Annette laughed. 'Are you mad? I'm not attacking you. I just wanted to talk to you. I just don't understand why you have such a problem with me. I mean, it's not as if we're rivals is it? Colin and I were over when you two met. Even if we were still living in the same house at the time there was nothing between us. In fact, he did me a favour by divorcing me.'

Arianne's mouth fell open. 'Is that so? Why am I not surprised? Did you a favour? Well, isn't that just typical? I thought Colin was exaggerating but, my bad. If anything, he was underplaying it.'

My bad? Jesus Christ. Not even the kids said that. No. She would let that one slide. 'I'm sorry?'

'You broke his heart and all you can say is he did you a favour? You are such a cow.'

'What are you talking about?' said Annette.

Arianne sniffed. 'You know full well what I'm talking about. You and whatshisname. He was a broken man after that. And those poor kids. You don't deserve to be a mother.'

Annette's entire body jolted. For a minute all she could fixate on was the trampoline and the thought of Arianne bouncing up and down on it, her breasts flailing and out of control. Then she landed back in the present. She knew. There was only one question to ask.

'How long?'

'Oh, he told me years ago. We've always been close. That's what happens when people are in love. I don't suppose you'd know about that, would you?' Arianne's phone went off. 'It's Colin,' she said.

'It's all right, she's leaving now.'

She could hear Arianne as she left the house. Hear her gloating. The bitch. The bastard. The bitch and the bastard. A match made in hell. Feeding off each other. Feeding off her.

He told her. Years ago, she said. *Always been close.* He'd given away her secret, years ago, and let her go on thinking it was safe. Her throat ached. Her body ached. She was an open wound again.

She stumbled back towards the village, her eyes on the ground. Her mind flitted from one thing to another until, crash! She walked into someone and fell to her knees.

'Mum? What's the matter? What's happened?'

Had he told her too? *You don't deserve to be a mother.*

Everything had gone to shit again and she couldn't pretend anymore.

39

THE RETURN OF WHATSHISNAME

It had been strange being back in Manchester. It was all quite different to when she was there before. In the eighties it had been run down and dirty but she'd been surprised on her return, in 2003, by its shininess. A new city for the new millennium.

She was different too. A wife, mother and a career woman. There was hardly any trace of the girl that had lived there before. She'd been lobotomised by mediocrity Everything she did when she lived there had been lost to her. There were no more pub afternoons, club nights or weekend-long parties. No more friends to talk to or to have a laugh with. Just day after day of working at Mason and Partners, and coming home to Colin with his non-stop whining about his hard life, and his constant need to be in her face, pointing out her faults. God, it was tiring.

Naturally, he'd been arsey about her going there. But he wanted her to get on so he had to put up with it. And hadn't he been the one pushing her to work for Masons rather than go for something creative? Hadn't he pushed her to go for this promotion and all the others before that?

As boring as the new job was, she looked forward to her weekly trips to the Manchester office. Three days of being put up in a hotel. Eating and drinking what she liked and doing what she wanted with her evenings. Not that she did anything particularly bad. Most of the time she stayed in the hotel, or walked around looking for her old haunts. Occasionally she went out for a drink with some of the Manchester team. They were quite fond of one particular pub close to the office. It was always crowded with nowhere to sit, but it did a happy hour that seemed to stretch out all night. It reminded her of her student days and made her want to slip into old ways. It was a dangerous place to go.

They dragged her along one evening to celebrate someone's birthday. She'd intended to stay just for one. Two if you counted the freebie. But Colin had been so bloody annoying on the phone, trying to make her feel bad about having a night out when the children were missing her so much, that she decided to stay for another.

She'd just finished her drink when someone planted another two down on the table for her. She turned to thank them, hoping it wasn't Malcolm Jefferson, her new manager. He was going to be transferring down to Birmingham with the department and she really didn't like him.

'Netta Wilde. I thought it was you. You look fucking incredible.' Straight to the point, as ever. No sense in pretending he wanted anything other than sex.

'Doogie?'

'Netta Wilde.' He said it as if he was rolling it around his tongue, getting used to the taste and feel of it again.

She could have told him she was Annette Grey now, but she knew she'd always be Netta Wilde to Doogie. She'd liked the idea of that. She'd never really got the hang of being Annette Grey.

'I heard you moved back to Birmingham. Work trip is it?'

'Yeah. How you doing?'

He grinned at her with those succulent, luscious lips. 'I'm fucking brilliant, me. Doing all right. You still married to that accountant wanker?'

'Yeah. You?' she said.

'Married? Nah. I was with someone long-term but we split up.'

'Sick of you playing away, was she?'

He sucked his teeth. Old habits die hard it seemed. 'You haven't changed, have you? No actually, I'm a lot better behaved than I used to be but she wants kids and I don't. It was a case of irreconcilable differences. We parted amicably though. We're still mates. You?'

'Kids? Yeah, I've got two.'

'Two? You're looking good on it. Happily married then?'

She'd really wanted to say yes and give him the finger but instead she shrugged. 'Well, you know.'

He leapt on it. 'Ah ha. Bit of a boring bastard, is he?'

Fucking Doogie. Always on the mark. She fucking hated him.

They did it in his flat. She hadn't wanted to take the chance of being spotted by any of the other Masons people staying in the hotel. They started on each other in the lift. By the time they closed his front door, he'd already undone her shirt and was unzipping her skirt. She pulled his pants down and was trying to climb onto him but he stopped her.

'I have to see you naked first. You always had the most amazing body.'

'Stop messing about Doogie, I've had two kids. I'm

hardly likely to look incredible, am I? Just fuck me before I explode.'

'Oh no. Come on. Let me see.'

She took her clothes off, laughing. 'You're such a pig. Such a shithead.'

'Oh yes, yes, yes,' he shouted. 'That's my Netta. I have so missed those insults. Give me more. Oh, you beautiful, beautiful woman. Look at you. You are so fucking gorgeous.'

He carried her to his bed and went down on her, and she thought she really would explode. She'd forgotten about the nice side of Doogie. The side that made her feel like she was the most extraordinary woman in the solar system. He probably said those things to all of his conquests but, for some reason, she'd believed him. Maybe it was the way he said them, with such conviction, that made him seem genuine. Unlike Colin, who always sounded like he'd memorised them from a 'how to' manual.

From then on, she told Colin she was sharing with someone from the office and whenever she was in Manchester, she stayed at Doogie's. They copulated like rabbits. They did it everywhere and anywhere. They had no shame. It was just like before. Except, this time he swore he wasn't fucking anyone else. It was the truth, as far as she could tell. She wouldn't have cared if he was. She wasn't emotionally invested in him. She just wanted the sex and the illicit buzz that came with it. That's what she told herself, anyway.

As with all good things, her time in Manchester came to an end. There was no more excuse for her to go there. He told her she'd been his first love and he never really got over her. That had to be a lie. The way he'd treated her back then.

But he was adamant. He wanted to carry on meeting up but she refused. There was no point: he'd soon tire of her. Especially when she began to show.

She couldn't pin it down to a specific date. She'd always left the diaphragm at home, fearing Colin would notice if it was gone. She suspected him of searching through her things while she was away. They'd used condoms but there had been occasional reckless moments when they'd run out. What did it matter how? She was pregnant again. All good things come to an end.

She wasn't one of those women that flourished in pregnancy. It made her ill. Back in Birmingham, she'd changed her routine to hide the morning sickness from Colin. Leaving for work earlier and going without breakfast. She'd still been sick, but that was the least of her worries. This time she had to seriously consider whether to have an abortion. It had been months since she and Colin had been intimate. Too many to pretend it was his. In any case, the colour of the baby's skin would have made it obvious. It didn't matter whose baby it was though. It was another child, and she could hardly be a mother to the first two. How would she cope if she was left alone with three?

At the same time, she'd been stupefied with fear, of what Colin would do if he found out. What if he took them away? She may be a bad mother, but she loved her kids. She had to make a decision quickly but she couldn't. She needed to talk to someone about it. She'd been on the verge of confiding in her parents or her grandmother once or twice. The shame of abandoning her family, for nothing more than pure lust, held her back. She missed Doogie much more than she'd expected and, once or twice, had to talk herself out of calling him. She was lonely and confused, and time was running out. If she carried on doing nothing it would be too late. Then it would all be out in the open. Everyone would know.

The anxiety of it took her over. She hardly ate and what she did eat, she struggled to keep down. She was dog-tired. From the sickness. From the lack of food and sleep. And from worry.

Working late at the office one night, she felt a sudden movement inside. Then a dampness in her pants. She ran for the toilet but it was on the next floor and in the rush she tripped on the stairs and saw herself tumbling down, then lying in a heap at the bottom before the lights went out.

The first thing she became aware of when she woke up in the hospital was the empty space inside of her. The next, was the thick pad between her legs. Then there was Colin, leaning against a wall on the other side of the room staring at her, his mouth shut tight. There was a menace coming off him that she could almost taste. She shuddered as he pushed himself off the wall and moved slowly towards her, as if it were a great effort for him. She felt the fear rising as he stood over her, his fists crunched into tight balls.

'The doctor said you'll be all right,' he said. 'They couldn't save the baby though.' He let it hang in the air for a while. Deliberately, no doubt. 'Whose was it? I know it couldn't be mine, so whose was it? I'm not angry Annette. I just need to know. You'll do me that kindness, surely?'

Of course he was angry. Every pore on his body oozed anger, hatred and venom.

'Doogie's,' was all she could manage.

He flinched. If it had been anyone, Doogie had to be the worst of all possible scenarios. Even though he didn't really know him, he'd always hated him. Hated the fact that Doogie was everything he was not. 'Are you still seeing him?'

'No.'

He'd seemed satisfied at that. 'I'm going home now, to take care of our children. Before I can decide what to do, I'll need to know more. We'll talk about it when you're better.'

He left. She rested her hand on the place where a baby used to be and wept.

40

SOUND ADVICE FROM EDIE

She was home. Home among her own things and among Edie's things. Sometimes it was hard to remember which of her things had once been Edie's. She'd been in bed for three days. Kelly and Will were at the foodbank. Frank would be popping in later to check on her and she had Edie's journals for company. She found them comforting.

Poor Liza, having to deal with her mother in that state. Luckily, she'd had the presence of mind to call Will. He and Frank drove straight over to pick them up. Afterwards, when she'd become more sensible, she found out she'd been jabbering incoherently and doing that shaking thing again. Just like that time in Malcolm's office. The doctor said her body had gone into shock. Again. It pained her to think that they'd seen her like that. Especially as they now insisted on treating her like an invalid. And it pained her to think that the only way she had of handling shocks was for her body to go into complete meltdown.

She opened Edie's journal at a bookmarked page. The entry was 19th March 2017. Edie had written:

'*Lately, I have come to realise that the fear of being found out is worse than the finding out.*'

That sentence had been snuggled in between a description of Maud's bowel movements — she'd eaten something off apparently — and a reminder to buy herself some new walking shoes. There was no indication as to why she'd written it. Annette had gone through the book four times to find a link but none could be found. It was as if Edie had put it there, specifically for her which was, of course, nonsense. Still, it was very apt.

After the miscarriage, when they discharged her from the hospital, Colin made her test for AIDS and all the sexually transmitted diseases to make sure she wasn't infected. It was his way of humiliating her further. His way of telling her she was unclean.

He wanted to know all the details about her and Doogie. How they reconnected, what they did and how she felt about him. Then, he made her talk through every time she and Doogie had had sex. How and where they did it. Did it make her come? Was that *really* the sort of thing she liked? He called her a disgusting pervert, and she believed it. Now that she thought about it. If she was the pervert, how come he was the one who wanted to know every single thing? How come he was the one so obviously getting off on what she told him? That was Colin all over, always taking the moral high ground while secretly wanking off at the thought of another man taking his wife from behind, in some dodgy restaurant toilet.

When he'd pumped her dry of information, he said he would need some time to consider whether their marriage was worth saving. If she'd been her usual self, she would have probably told him it wasn't, but that person was gone. Flushed away with that little half-baby. What was left was a coward who couldn't stand to lose any more of her children. She'd taken a long, hard look at herself and despised what she saw. She was selfish and a liar. Worse, she was a killer. She had as good as murdered her child. Her and Doogie's child. She was rotten to the core, and she deserved everything she got.

He strung it out for weeks before telling her he was prepared to forgive her, but only for Liza and Will's sake. Another lie. He never forgave her. He spelt out the new terms of engagement so there could be no confusion. She would need to prove to him that she was worthy of their love. She was vulgar, repugnant and immoral. What's more, she was an unfit mother. Unnatural. He'd always thought it but this unfortunate matter had confirmed it. She would have to change. From now on the children's well-being would be his sole driver. She would need to work hard to show that she was good enough to be part of this family. If he thought they were suffering because of her, he'd have no choice but to divorce her and take them away. She took it all. She wanted the pain. She needed something to fill the hollowness in her belly.

After three days thinking of nothing else, she could see perfectly clearly now. Hindsight was a remarkable thing. Losing the baby had been the tipping point. The moment everything turned on its head. He'd been working by stealth on remodelling her for years but she'd put up some resistance until then. Her affair with Doogie and the pregnancy gave him a reason to legitimise it. It gave him a reason to obliterate Netta Wilde and she was too weak to do anything about it. Only now could she see that was the point at which he began to exact his revenge. And he was so good at it. So very good at it.

He told her they would never speak of it to anyone. It would break her parents' hearts to know what kind of a daughter they had. It would destroy her grandmother and, if the children knew what she'd done, with that man and to that baby, they'd hate her. It would be their secret. The deeper it became buried, the more she believed him, but that didn't stop him using it to flog her. Every time she needed to be pushed back down into place. Every day she lived with the fear of him wielding it like a knife and cutting through her. Every day she lived in fear of him telling the people she cared about and them, turning away from her with disgust and repulsion. Every day he forced her deeper and deeper into the shadows. She endured all of that because he promised never to tell anyone. He let her go on thinking it was their secret to be kept forever when all the time he'd given it away to Arianne. She should have known he couldn't be trusted.

Part of her, the old part of her, imagined the two of them discussing it. Plotting against her and she hated them for it. She recoiled from those thoughts. She refused to be that person. It was the old Annette who'd lurched out of that house, panic stricken and imploding. She could not, would not, allow her to retake control. She was different. She had her friends and family now. She had Frank. She had a life that felt like it was worth something. She'd gone through so much in the last year to find them and to find herself, Netta, that she was prepared to fight Annette Grey with everything she had. Edie was right. The fear of being found out had ruled her for the last fifteen years. The time had come to break its hold.

There was a knock on the bedroom door. Frank opened it and looked in. 'You're awake. Good. How are you feeling?'

'Fine. I'm absolutely fine,' she said. 'Would you come and sit down with me? I have something I want to tell you.'

'So now you know everything about me,' she said.

'Everything?' he said. 'No stone left unturned. No secrets whatsoever?'

She'd let it all spill out, unconstrained. The affair with Doogie. The baby. The fact that she never wanted children, and the way Colin had used all of those things to crush her. She even told him about the night he took them all to the Rajdoot to tell her he wanted a divorce. There was nothing left that she could think of but you never know, do you? 'Well, I'm sure there must be a few lurking somewhere at the back of my mind,' she said.

'Thank goodness for that. Otherwise we could be in for some very quiet months ahead and winter's coming.' She slapped him on the leg. He kissed her. 'Seriously though, I can't even imagine how you got through all of that. With no help at all from Colin, or a professional, from the sound of it.'

She shook her head. 'I was too ashamed to ask for help. I thought the miscarriage was my fault and I'd caused the baby to die. It tore me to pieces, and he took advantage of it. I suppose it damaged him a little too. He was never the same after that, although he wasn't exactly perfect before. The weight of all that guilt dragging me down. Him always implying that I wasn't like other women, that I was disgusting and a substandard mother. Little jibes. Carefully inserted remarks to remind me, and everyone else, that I wasn't normal. That I wasn't good enough. It ate away at me.'

She sighed. 'I'd go to work and wonder what he was saying to the kids about me. I'd come home and look for signs of them turning against me. I felt like they all despised me. That awful night when he told me they didn't want me anymore, I hated them. Can you imagine that? I hated my own children. I was so full of loathing that I couldn't see what was in front of me. The truth was they didn't detest me. They loved me. They were just confused and hurt, and were being forced to take sides.'

She paused to catch her breath and swallow down the pain in her throat. It was good to get it all out but it didn't come easily. 'What we've done to those children between us should be unforgivable, but they have forgiven us. Or me at least. Now, I have to forgive myself for all the wrongs I've done to them and to myself. It wasn't my fault that I lost the baby, I've finally realised that. And I realise that it's okay if I didn't want children. It's okay that I couldn't be an ideal mother. I've made up for it in other ways. Anyway, what the fuck is an ideal mother?'

Next, she told her parents. They took the news of the affair well enough. Their dislike of Colin probably helped and she was beginning to suspect that they lived much closer to the real world than she'd ever given them credit for. It was when she told them about the miscarriage that they lost their composure. Her dad went out to the kitchen on the pretence of making a fresh pot of tea. He switched on the radio, but they still heard him sobbing. She wanted to go and comfort him but her mum told her to leave him.

'He'll be all right, love. Let him have some privacy. You

should plant something in the garden. Something nice that will come into bloom about the time the baby would have been born. It'll help you to find some closure.'

'Yes, I think I'd like that. Will you and Dad help me to pick something?'

'Yes, of course. We always favoured a nice rose,' she said, looking straight into her daughter's eyes without blinking.

Annette's mouth opened and filled with a short intake of air. So, just when you thought there was nothing new to learn about your parents, it turned out you knew nothing about them at all.

When she told the children, Will simply said that losing the baby must have been so hard for her and he didn't blame her at all, for anything.

Liza had more questions. 'Were you in love with him?'

'Doogie? Yes, I think I must have been. Although I didn't realise it at the time.'

'What was he like?' she said.

She could have told her that he was the most beautiful man she'd ever laid eyes on. That the sight of him was enough to send the most exquisite shivers down her spine. But that wasn't the thing that had made her love Doogie. 'He was funny, and he made me feel good about myself.'

Liza laughed. 'Nothing like Dad then?'

Annette laughed too. 'No. Nothing like Dad.'

The next question hit her like a bullet. 'Was it a boy or a girl?'

She cleared her throat. 'It was a girl.'

'Did you give her a name?'

'No. But I think, if she'd lived, I would have liked to have called her Ada.'

It was the first time she'd given the baby an identity and

it brought the loss flooding back. Dear, darling, bloody Liza. Always hitting her where it hurt. Even when she didn't mean to.

'I would have loved a little sister. Do you think she would have looked like me?' she said.

'I expect so. But her skin and hair would probably have been more like Jade's.'

'Oh God, I love Jade's hair. I would have been so jealous. I know it was horrible for you Mum, but you've still got us. We're still with you.'

After that it had been time to tell her friends. She knew them well enough by now to be sure it wouldn't change their regard for her. Kelly said she was amazed she'd only had one affair. If she'd been married all that time to a shithead like Colin, she'd have had hundreds. When she told Neil, he held her until she cried herself out. Until, at long last, she felt she had let it all go.

The night after she told Neil, she dreamed again of Aberdovey beach, Granny Wilde, and the children in the sand dunes. This time the hazy shadow from the last dream, the shell of a child, had been filled in and she could see little Ada standing with them. She had her eyes, Doogie's cheekbones and mouth, and dark hair that formed tight ringlets around her nape. The four of them were waiting for her. She walked towards them, across the long stretch of white sand. The waves gently lapped behind her. The sun was hot and brilliant but a warm breeze made it feel just perfect. It was so serene. So peaceful. If there was a heaven, then she was in it now.

41

BYE NETTA WILDE

There could be no doubt that the study smelt of must. Every time someone walked in, they told her, just before they went straight back out again. It had been a bit whiffy when she moved in but was more so now that they'd emptied and decorated the old nursery for Liza. Everything that had been decaying and crumbling in there was now in here, waiting for her to sort through them and give more meaning to Edie's life. The strange thing was, Annette hardly noticed the smell herself. She must be getting used to it.

Maud stood in the doorway sniffing the air. Even she was reluctant to come any further. Little Betty was less discriminating. After sidling up to her mother she plucked up the courage to enter the mouldy lair. She weaved in and out of the gaps between the boxes, the stacks of books and the yellowing papers. Occasionally, she knocked something over or got stuck in a blind alley, as if it were some kind of maze built specially to trap an inquisitive young pup.

Betty was the only one left now. Annette's parents had taken Minnie. She was their new baby. Annette wondered if

Minnie would help to make up for all their lost babies, just as she probably had when she was small. She didn't know how many there had been and it felt wrong to ask. They had quite a few rose bushes in the garden. Surely not all of them had been planted for that reason?

Neil and Chris decided they'd start their family with Buster, the biggest of the pups. It might not have been what Chris's mum had been envisaging but they seemed happy with it. Finally, there was Fred, the youngest of the litter. He'd kind of adopted Frank and now that Frank had let go of Ellen's things, he felt the need to fill the empty spaces. So, Fred moved in.

Of course, Betty was staying. She was the latest addition to Annette's own family. Two dogs, and two and a half young people. So much had changed in her life in the last eighteen months. She could hardly believe the difference. And all because she'd been made redundant.

She replied to a message from Neil about the next step in their business venture. He'd been to look at a small commercial kitchen and thought it might be suitable. They had a regular order now with the man they met at the Moseley fair to supply his shops. A couple of similar businesses had also registered their interest. Things were looking up.

Through the window she saw the car pull up in front of the garden. Was it that time already? She ushered Betty out of the study and closed the door behind them, the hint of decay just catching the back of her throat as she did. Hmm, she really must get on with sorting out Edie's things. She owed her that much at least. She ran upstairs and sprayed perfume all over herself in case the odour had seeped into her. God knows why. It was, after all, only Colin and Liza. Mind you, if anyone was going to point out she smelt like a festering old manuscript, it would be Liza.

They sat in the car for a while, talking. Actually, it looked like more like Liza doing the talking. What a wonderful thing her daughter was. It was amazing to her that she'd never seen it before. Strange that this girl who'd always seemed so self-centred, selfish even, had been the one to reconcile them. Where she and Will had turned their backs on him, Liza had told her father that his behaviour had to change if he wanted her to carry on loving him. Not that Annette had given her daughter all the details. In fact, she'd said next to nothing about Colin's hold over her, but she hadn't needed to spell it out. Liza worked it out for herself.

Apparently, Arianne had been elated after Annette's breakdown. By Liza's reckoning, that was bad enough. But it was when she told Colin that she knew about the baby and he made a nasty remark about Annette and Doogie that she finally lost it.

'I just flipped,' she'd told Annette. 'How could he be such a bastard? It's not as if he's been blameless in all of this.'

So, she told him that she knew what he'd been up to. She told him he'd been a pretty crap husband and dad and if he really cared about her and Will, he'd do the decent thing and start treating their mother with some respect.

Shortly after that, Annette received an email telling her the money for the house was on its way and he was sorry for the delay. Not exactly the apology she'd been looking for but it was a start.

Last week he sent another mail:

'Hi

Hope you're well. I've been offered a six-week teaching residency in Spain from the end of November. The artist who was going to do it had to drop out which is why I haven't had much notice. I've spoken to Liza about it and she's happy for me to do it, if she can stay with you. Would you mind? I'd really appreciate it if she could. It's a great opportunity for me.'

She'd mailed him back straight away to say yes and she was very pleased for him. They would never be friends but at last, they were becoming the parents they should have been.

Now he was outside being lectured by their daughter. Liza was staying for the weekend and had asked if Colin could come in as he had something for her. She'd said yes, of course. She could hardly have said no. That wouldn't have been in the spirit of things as they were now. It wasn't just Colin that needed to pull his socks up.

When Liza finally let him get out, he took two boxes out of the boot. Not more boxes. She was drowning in the things. Liza waved to her as she came along the path and she waved back. Colin gave her a shy smile.

'Hey Mum,' said Liza. 'Dad's been having a sort out.'

'I found some of your old stuff,' he said, hovering on the doorstep. 'Mostly from uni days, I think. I thought you might want them.'

'Oh, I thought they'd been thrown out years ago,' she said. 'Come in. I was just about to make a coffee, if you'd like one?'

Liza gave her an approving nod. 'That'd be nice, wouldn't it, Dad?'

'Er yeah. That would be nice,' he said, the strain showing on his face.

They went into the lounge.

'Can I have a look in this one?' said Liza. 'Dad wouldn't let me.'

'Let's have a look together,' said Annette. Colin shifted in his seat, as if he was struggling to get comfortable.

There were a lot of old photos in there, in those packets that you used to get them back in from the chemists. Most of them were of her, Claire and Sasha acting like idiots but there were some of her and Colin too. They did look like an odd couple. Doogie was in some of them with his arm around her. The two of them looking explosive. Like they were capable of setting each other on fire with just one kiss. Ironic then that he wasn't the one that brought her down. She pushed them back into the packets before they could see what she was looking at.

Liza held up a beret covered in badges — bands, CND, Che Guevara – the usual stuff.

'Badges were a thing back then,' Annette explained.

'Cool,' said Liza. She took something out of a plastic bag and examined it. 'Dad, you made a mistake. This isn't Mum's.'

Annette recognised it immediately. 'No actually, it is mine. It used to be my favourite T-shirt.'

Liza frowned. 'But that's … I mean, it's The Clash, right?'

'That's right. Well spotted,' said Colin. His face contorted into something that was probably supposed to be a grin but looked more like a wince.

'Yeah,' said Liza at a pace that suggested she was still working through what this meant. 'Isn't it …?' She turned to Colin and frowned.

'I'll make that coffee,' said Annette.

She could still hear Liza from the kitchen, even though she'd lowered her voice. 'Seriously though, Dad. This is totally fucked up. You have to let it go.'

Annette coughed before she re-entered the room. Liza's

smile was forced. The kind that said she was trying too hard to pretend everything was normal. 'Can I try them on?'

'If you want to.'

With Liza upstairs, the room fell silent. Annette continued to look through the photos. It was less awkward than the two of them staring at the ceiling.

'No Will?' he said finally.

'No. He works on Saturdays now, in a friend's record shop.'

'Will, working? Never thought I'd see the day.'

'You'd be surprised,' she said. 'What's in the other box?'

'Vinyl albums and tapes. I thought it was about time I gave them back to you.'

She opened it up. All of her old Clash albums were in there, the Sex Pistols, X-Ray Spex. All the music she used to love. All the things that used to be dear to her. She picked up a single and read the writing on its sleeve:

'Netta
Our first dance together.
Love you always,
Colin xxxx'

"Close to Me.' Do you remember me buying you that?' he said.

'Yes, it was just before you took me to meet your parents. I remember the dance too. I think calling it our first dance together was a bit of an overstatement.'

He laughed. 'I suppose so. I guess I was a bit of a romantic back then.'

Liza walked in and saved her the need to reply. 'What do you think?' she said.

'You look great,' said Annette. 'Keep them if you want.'

Colin stood up. 'I'd better get back.'

Annette followed him out. 'I'll walk you to the car.'

. . .

They stood by the car, a few feet apart from each other. He nodded to the lounge window where Liza stood watching them. No doubt making sure they were on their best behaviour.

'She looks just like you did, in that outfit.'

'A bit. My hair was shorter, and she's far better looking than I was.'

'No. You were just as lovely.'

She raised her eyebrows. 'By the way, I'm changing my name back to Netta Wilde. So, if you and Arianne get married, she needn't worry about there being two Mrs Greys.'

He wrinkled his nose and she remembered how she used to find that particular habit of his quite attractive. 'What happened to us?'

She shrugged. 'I suppose, when broken bones aren't allowed to heal properly, they grow back twisted.'

He smiled at her. More a half smile really. 'Is that supposed to mean me or you?'

'I meant us both. I think we broke each other.'

'Hmm.' He opened the car door. 'I'm not planning to marry again anytime soon, by the way. I'm not ready to move on yet. Bye, Netta Wilde.'

She watched him turn the car around and drive away.

'Bye, Colin Grey.'

A long chapter had closed. Time to start a new one.

A WORD FROM THE AUTHOR

Hello

I hope you enjoyed reading Netta's story. If you did, would you mind leaving a review?

Your reviews are important. They help me to reach more readers and they help other readers to decide whether this book is for them.

You can leave a review at your local Amazon store .

To find out more about other stories written by me, read on…

READ NETTA'S COMPANION STORY, BEING DOOGIE CHAMBERS

If this book leaves you wanting to know more about the world of Netta Wilde and her friends, you can join Hazel's **Readers' Club** and get **Being Doogie Chambers,** a free book available exclusively to members of the club.

https://hazelwardauthor.com/readers-club/

MORE BOOKS IN THE NETTA WILDE SERIES.

FINDING EDITH PINSENT

Two women. Two timelines. One heart-wrenching story.

★★★★★ 'Outstanding!! Wow. Just wow.'
★★★★★ 'A rollercoaster ride and feelgood heart-warming experience.'
★★★★★ 'Edie is so realistic, you will fall in love with her.'

SAVING GERALDINE CORCORAN

One shameful secret. One hidden letter. Two unlikely guardian angels.

★★★★★ 'A truly powerful story told brilliantly.'
★★★★★ 'Sadness, love, humour, surprise. You name it I felt it.'
★★★★★ 'Superbly written and well worth reading, but be prepared to cry and laugh and cry again!'

EDUCATING KELLY PAYNE

How to learn about love ... the hard way.

★★★★★ 'The writing is phenomenal, the characters so real you can really see into their soul.'
★★★★★ 'I loved it! I'm wiping my eyes as I write.'
★★★★★ 'Kelly's journey is a cracker.'

MEETING ANNETTE GREY

Two strangers. One Park Bench. One life changing conversation.

Netta Wilde feels as if she's always known Edith Pinsent, even thought they never met. At least that's what she's always believed. A Netta Wilde mini novel.

CALLING FRANK O'HARE

It's nearly time to hear Frank's story.

Keep an eye on his Amazon page for more details on the next book in the Netta Wilde series.

You can **pre-order** it now — out no later than 1st April 2024.

BEING DOOGIE CHAMBERS

A free novella, exclusive to members of Hazel Ward's Readers' Club.

Doogie Chambers is in love with Netta Wilde. He thinks she's Debbie Harry crossed with Siouxsie Sioux. She thinks he's Heathcliff.

Be the first to know about Hazel's latest news and the general goings on in her life. You can follow her in all the usual places or join her **Readers' Club** and get regular monthly newsletters, a free novella and the occasional free story.

https://hazelwardauthor.com

Printed in Great Britain
by Amazon